JED

JED

a novel by

JIM WETTON

ATLAS PUBLISHING • SOLANA BEACH, CALIFORNIA

Jed

Written by Jim Wetton.

Published by Atlas Publishing LLC, Solana Beach, CA
www.atlaspublishing.biz

Cover art and design by Colin C. Moyer, with final layout, design, and copy revisions by Atlas Publishing LLC.

Chapter-ending interior illustrations and Independence and Fredericksburg town maps by Gary D. Bratton.

Part I map adapted from American Military History, United States Army Center of Military History, 1989.

Part II map adapted from Geological Survey, 1970, US Dept. of the Interior.

Part III map created by user:Golbez (own work) [GFDL (http://www.gnu.org/copyleft/fdl.html) and used under CC BY 2.5 (http://creativecommons.org/licenses/by/2.5)] via Wikimedia Commons.

Part IV map adapted from US Bureau of the Census.

Chapter 29 Battle of Fredericksburg map created by Hal Jespersen.

The primary fonts used in this book are Billy Argel Major Guilty, IM Fell French Canon and French Canon SC, and Monotype Photina MT.

The Fell Types are digitally reproduced by Igino Marini: www.iginomarini.com. All fonts listed are used under the terms of their respective licenses.

ISBN 13: 978-0-9969679-5-2

First edition. Manufactured in the United States of America

To *my* Alma

—JW

Contents

Part I Untamed Youth

Part II Bittersweet

Contents (cont.)

Part III Turbulence

Part IV Peace

I

Untamed Youth
1831–1837

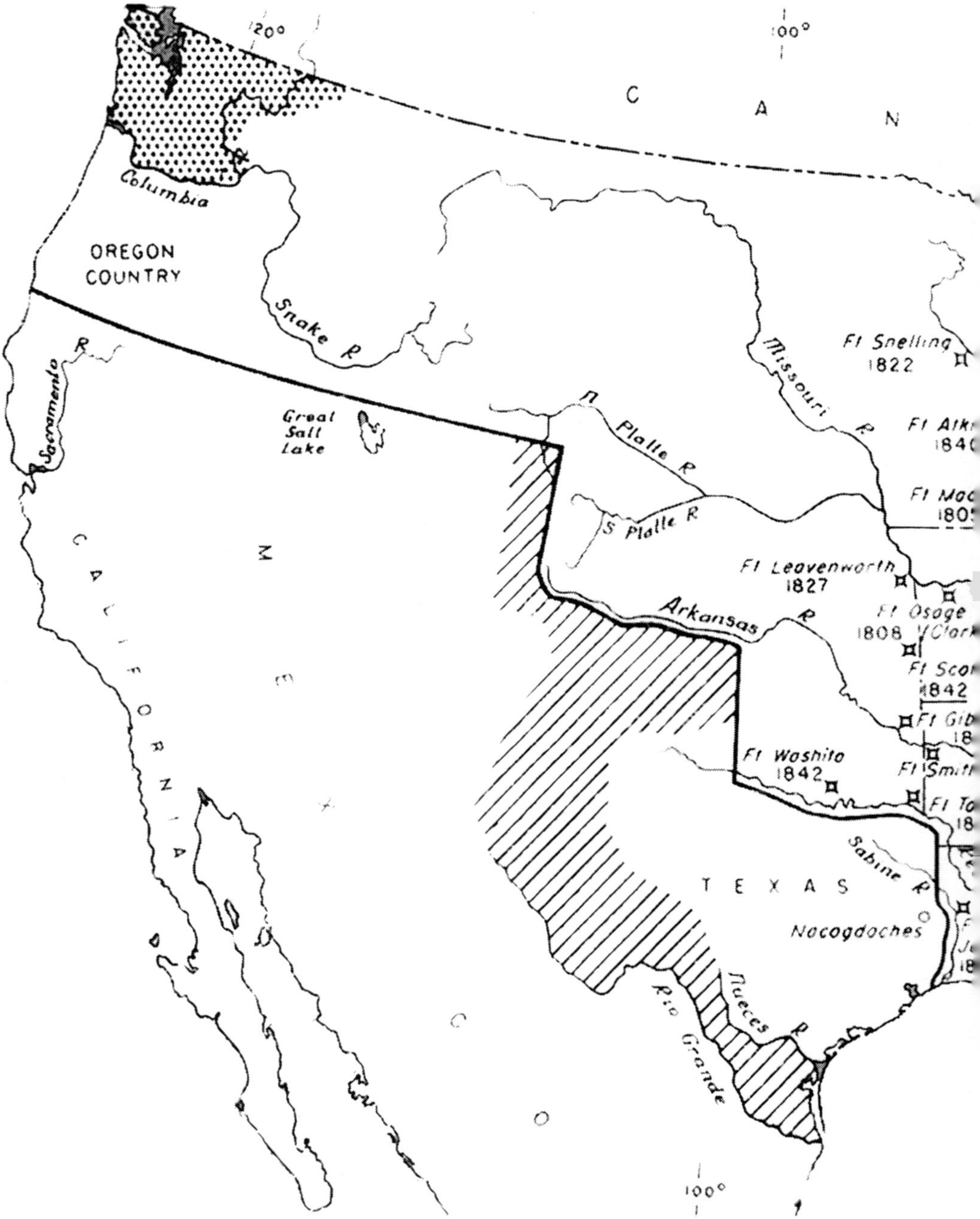

120°
100°
C A N
OREGON COUNTRY
Columbia
Snake R
Sacramento R.
Great Salt Lake
Missouri R
Platte R
S Platte R
Arkansas R
Ft Snelling 1822
Ft Leavenworth 1827
Ft Osage 1808
Ft Washita 1842
C A L I F O R N I A
M E X I C O
T E X A S
Sabine R
Nacogdoches
Nueces R
Rio Grande
100°

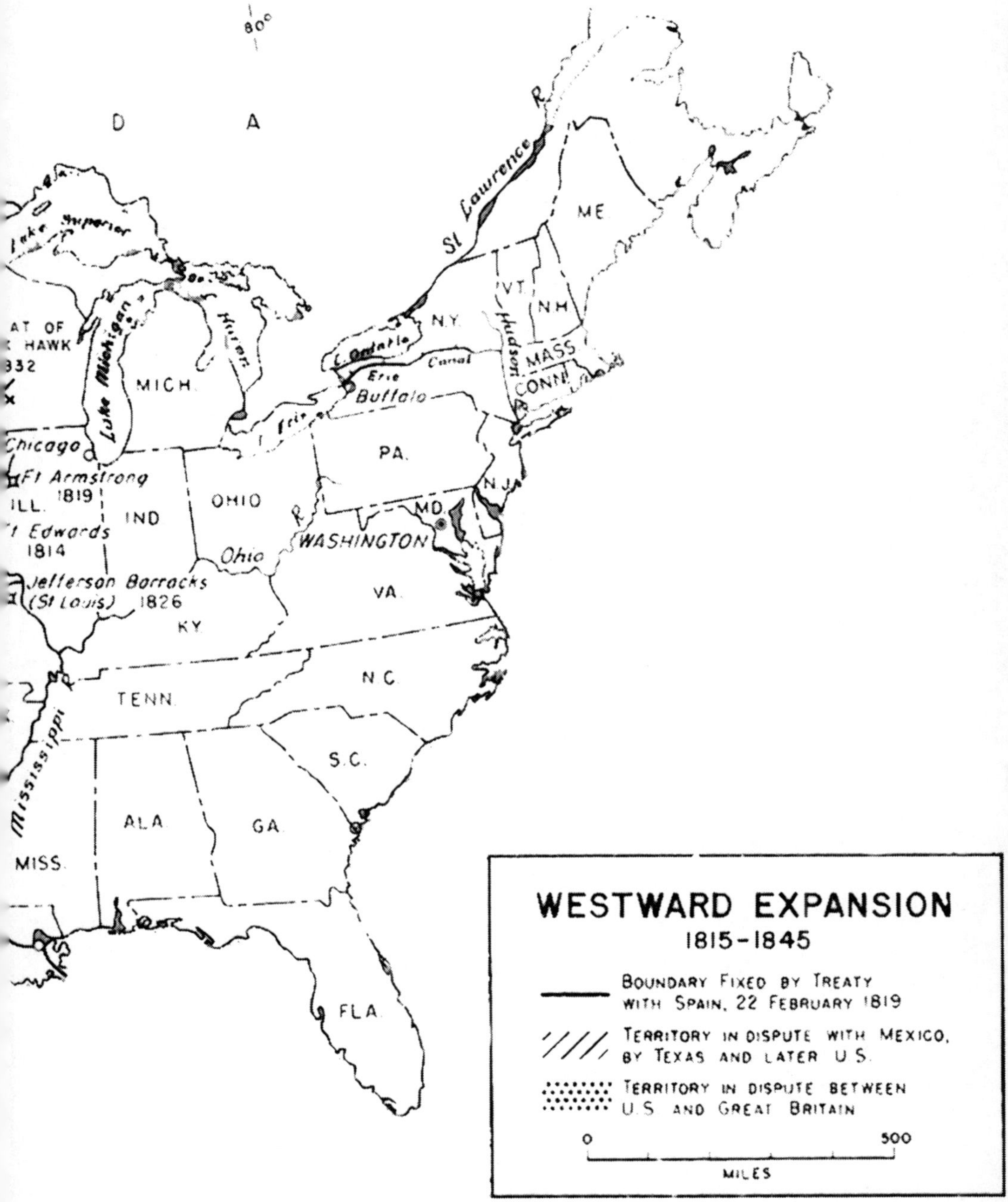

80°
D
A
Lake Superior
Lake Michigan
Huron
MICH.
St Lawrence R.
ME
VT.
N.H.
N.Y.
Hudson
MASS
CONN.
L. Ontario
Erie
Canal
Buffalo
L. Erie
PA.
N.J.
MD.
WASHINGTON
OHIO
Ohio R.
IND
ILL.
Chicago
Ft Armstrong 1819
Ft Edwards 1814
Jefferson Barracks (St Louis) 1826
AT OF
HAWK
332
KY.
VA.
N.C.
TENN.
S.C.
Mississippi
MISS.
ALA.
GA.
FLA.
WESTWARD EXPANSION
1815-1845
Boundary Fixed by Treaty with Spain, 22 February 1819
Territory in dispute with Mexico, by Texas and later U.S.
Territory in dispute between U.S. and Great Britain
0
500
MILES

Chapter One

A Boy No More
1831

The ground was damp and smelled of mold. The closed-in area under the porch was dark, though some light filtered through the wooden slats above. It was his secret, his little hideaway from the world. Jedidiah peered toward the circle of dirt that was sunlit from a tiny hole on the far side of the crawl space. He wanted to know if the mother chipmunk had returned for the bread crumbs he'd left. He stared up at the porch floor, weatherworn from above but silky smooth from his viewpoint. Here he often dreamed of the places he would go, people he would meet, and adventures he would have. But on this particular morning, he was hoping that some of those dreams would soon come true.

"Jedidiah!" His mother's voice competed with the stomping of her shoes on the porch. "Jedidiah Monroe, where *are* you?" she called, her voice trailing off to the other side of the porch but then becoming louder and more demanding. "We need to get going, Son—your father will be done soon!"

Jedidiah crawled quickly through the broken siding on the far side of the house, then ran around to the front, yelling, "I'm ready, Momma!"

He hastily wiped his pants, desperate to conceal where he'd been. He looked up in time to catch the flutter of his mother's dress as she began the short walk to the church. He grabbed his hat and hurried along the trail to catch up with her.

He was happy that he hadn't stayed for his father's sermon and instead had come home to help his mother. Now that church was over, it was time to go back and set out the refreshments she had spent all morning baking—this was their weekly routine. Hustling back to the church, he wondered, *Will this be the last time I ever have to do this?*

Jedidiah looked up at the church that he knew was meant to be his someday. The stark whiteness of the wood siding was bright under the sun, while the majestic obelisk-shaped steeple soared high in the morning sky like a welcoming hand. He gazed at his favorite part of it, the bell tower halfway up the steeple. The bells rang loudly as the clapper struck the brass, pealing and reverberating across the valley. The resounding clang always ignited something deep within him.

He saw his father on the steps of the church, tall and confident as he greeted the parishioners. So many friendly faces, most those of people he'd known since he was a small child. He noticed that as they exited the church, each Bible-carrying member of the congregation seemed magnetically drawn to his father. They seemed to linger as long as possible while eyeing him with varying degrees of reverence, respect, and admiration. Jedidiah smiled as he compared himself to the man he looked up to. They shared the same olive skin and long wavy brown hair; Jedidiah wondered when his would be sprinkled with gray like his father's.

Jedidiah finally broke his gaze to again scan the clanging bells above. The church was everything to his father, and the congregation was his extended family. Jedidiah reflected on the enormous responsibility this entailed and how so many had come to rely upon his father. Pastor Zachary Monroe made it clear that no matter what was happening in his life, nothing mattered more than the people of his church did.

Will that be me someday? pondered Jedidiah, feeling what seemed to be a cold breeze stir as a shudder raced from the nape of his neck to his tattered boots.

The air was crisp without a cloud in the sky, and the trees gave just enough shade to offset the sun's effect on the baked treats that his mother, Martha, had placed on the tables. The crowds would soon gather around, indulging in lemon drops, oat cookies, and lemonade.

As Jed watched his father on this particular Sunday, he could see that the man had more on his mind than the sermon he'd just preached on the second coming. No, on this peaceful and quiet morning, his father was not himself. He was acting differently, preoccupied.

Reverend Henry Spaulding and Pastor Andrew Higgin, two of his father's longtime friends, were visiting Wheeling for a short time while organizing a trip west with their group, the Missionary Society. Perhaps delivering the service in front of them had rattled his father. But Jedidiah knew that public speaking had never been stressful for his father.

Then Jedidiah remembered the conversation he'd had with his father earlier in the day about his desire to journey west. He was fairly certain that this was why his father looked so anguished. Nevertheless, he hoped that his request would be discussed further at the dinner table that evening. The evening's meal had been planned for more than a week, and Jedidiah's father had mentioned several times how much he was looking forward to seeing his old friends.

Jedidiah was filled with excitement and anticipation, hoping that his father had finally relented to his request to travel west and would approach the two pastors for their support. During Jed's earlier conversation, or rather argument, with his father, he had shared his deepest desires while pleading his case as best he could.

Even so, the conversation had not gone quite as he had hoped.

That morning as his father was preparing to leave for church, Jedidiah had asked, "Are you going to ask them today, Father, or are you going to wait until supper tonight?"

After a brief pause, impatient with not receiving an immediate answer, Jedidiah added, "I'm not a little kid anymore, Father! I know this would be the best thing for me."

Father and son had quarreled frequently on the issue of his desire to explore the world. Jedidiah tried his best to persuade his father, but his approach was sometimes too strong for addressing a man who was usually contemplative, careful, and certain when making decisions, especially those concerning his only child.

Jedidiah had tried to be convincing about his motives. He didn't know if his pleas had fallen on deaf ears or if his real reasons had shown through. He'd admitted to himself long before that the thrill of the West was the real allure, but he knew he couldn't reveal that to his father. He was tired of baked goods and lemonade. He wanted to see the rivers and mountains that he had only read about, to see for himself if the tales of the West were real or just fables.

"Just think of it this way," Jedidiah had argued, "I can get all of my . . . what did you call it? . . . jittery energy out of my system out West and then come back and take over for you."

Jedidiah examined the look on his father's face, then added as solemnly as he could muster, "I mean, isn't that what you want?"

"We'll see, Son." Jedidiah could still hear his father's loud sigh. "Let's see how the day goes, and when they're all here for supper tonight, I'll decide what's best."

Jedidiah's dark brown eyes narrowed. In response, his father sternly added, "And not before that, Son, and only if I think it's the right thing to do. You hear me?"

"Alright," Jedidiah said, as his eyes darkened and his head dropped ever so slightly. Then he quickly interjected, his voice rising as he hoped to push his father to a decision, "But you know I'm ready!"

The frown and deep sigh that followed caused Jedidiah to realize that their discussion had come to an end.

* * * * *

Jedidiah was taller than the average fifteen-year-old, and his skinny frame had yet to fill in the way he privately hoped it would. His voice still cracked at times, especially when he was nervous, and like most young men his age, this caused him to blush with embarrassment. Jedidiah trusted his father's reassurance that his voice would someday be baritone, smooth, and deep, and that his blemished skin would eventually change for the better as well. But nobody could come up with an explanation for the uncontrollable twitch in Jedidiah's right index finger, and the frenzied tapping drove his parents crazy.

"I can't help it!" Jedidiah had told them. "I don't even know when I'm doing it, but it seems like it gets worse the jumpier I get."

He remembered being scolded about his thumping finger that morning as his father opened the front door to leave for church. Jedidiah put his hand over his finger in a noble attempt to stop it from twitching before making one last feeble attempt to state his case. This was somewhat successful, giving him the confidence to approach his father once more despite all the signs that should have told him that this was indeed a terrible idea.

"Father . . ."

The fire burning in his father's eyes was the first and only thing Jedidiah saw as Zachary Monroe turned to him, his voice booming, "Jedidiah, I told you . . . *I will decide*!"

Jedidiah's eyes widened. His father took a deep breath, then in a softer tone said, "Now, you go get yourself ready, Son, and help your momma with the baked goods. I'll see you after church."

They momentarily locked eyes. His father nodded his head toward the kitchen and waved his hand as he admonished, "Go on, Jedidiah, get a move on!"

* * * * *

On his walk to the church, Zachary prayed for God's guidance in making the right decision for his son. As he walked, the air seemed serene, but had an eeriness to it as well. It was as if the answer to his many prayers was being wistfully placed in his heart. Yet, why was he still so uneasy? He barely heard his footsteps in the dusty gravel, yet he heard the frogs and crickets singing what sounded like their own special hymn. It made it easier for him to absorb the fact that this decision was going to be one of the hardest he'd ever had to make, and he was reassured by the presence of God, despite his lingering apprehension.

He knew his two colleagues would take great care of his son. *It actually would be a great experience for him.* He set his eyes to the sky to pray, and noticed a large eagle perched high above, looking down at him from the end of a limb, absolutely still as its eyes pierced his own. *Yea, I know . . . there's no other way to settle him down, but . . . he's just a boy.* He looked back toward the end of the road, still thinking of the eagle's penetrating eyes. *Was he trying to tell me something, or have I already decided?*

He stopped at the base of the steps leading into his church. *Oh Lord,* he prayed silently as he walked up the final steps to the chapel door, *give me the courage and wisdom to make the right decision for Jedidiah.* It had been his lifelong hope to pass the church on to his son, but he wondered now if this was the right way to do it.

He chuckled a bit as he thought of another prayer he needed to make. *And Lord . . . please give me the wisdom and the words to explain it to Martha, too.*

Closing the thick door behind him, Zachary walked with heavy steps down the middle aisle of the church. He sat down in the front pew before looking up at the wall and the soft eyes of Jesus with His outstretched arms. Zachary felt a sudden need to be embraced by those loving arms, and unexpected warmth swept over him as he thought about the question that he planned to ask his friends that night.

Yes, that's how I'll approach it, he thought. *Jedidiah would be a great help to Andrew and Sara, and in turn they could teach him what it takes to be a pastor.*

Zachary scanned the inside of the chapel. He looked at the walls, beveled windows, and old wooden pews. He gazed at his pulpit and let out a sigh of accession. *And then I can give him all of this to take care of.*

He looked up again at the soft eyes of Jesus and nodded his head slowly. *Please watch over my little man.*

* * * * *

When evening finally came, Jedidiah was nervous with anticipation. He barely touched his plate, even after several sharp looks from his mother.

"Supper was delicious, Martha," Reverend Spaulding said with a contented smile.

"It surely was," added Pastor Higgin. "But best I can recall, I've never had a meal of yours that wasn't splendid."

Martha chuckled humbly and started gathering up dishes.

"Let me help you with the cleanup," offered Sara. "You know these men are just champing at the bit to get out on your porch to smoke their awful-smelling cigars. Right, *gentlemen?*"

The women swished their kitchen towels at the men, shooing them to the front porch and closing the door behind them.

"Now that's better," Sara said with a grin.

The three pastors made themselves comfortable on the front porch of the Monroes' modest home as they enjoyed after-dinner cigars. The two guests suspected nothing, though both had noted the odd look on Zachary's face that evening.

The Monroe home was a simple two-story house made of wooden slats and packed clay and painted an off-colored green. Church members rebuilt the wooden staircase just after Jedidiah was born—the first room at the top was Jedediah's, followed by a small hallway leading to Zachary and Martha's room. Each room had a window that overlooked the grounds below; Jedidiah's looked out over the area in front of the house, while Zachary and Martha's gave way to the back garden below. The main level had a living room, a dining area, and what Martha Monroe called a "suitable" kitchen. The Monroes spent countless hours outside on their porch, at ease with its wooden planks and a termite-infested railing that wrapped around two sides of the house.

After supper, Jedidiah slipped back into his secret hideaway—it was the perfect spot for eavesdropping. He was so focused on the men above that he paid little attention to the mother chipmunk, who was eyeing him in hope of more bread crumbs.

"You know, Henry," his father began, "it would be a great chance for any young man to gain experience in fulfilling the Lord's work, traveling with the Missionary Society. Don't you agree?"

Young man? Jedidiah held his breath. *Is he doing it, is he really going to ask?* There was a long pause, and Jedidiah's blood went cold. *Oh no! Why did they stop talking? No, no, please don't end it just like that.*

"I assume you're speaking of Jedidiah?" Pastor Higgin answered.

Jedidiah blew out a long sigh of relief, not even thinking to catch himself, while the mother chipmunk, for her part, turned and gave him a stern glare. *Come on, Father . . . don't back down . . . not now.* His finger, which had been twitching since dinnertime, was now doing so in sympathy with his racing pulse.

"Yes, actually I was," his father continued. "I think it would be a great opportunity for him to follow the Lord's plan and learn about himself as a man at the same time."

"You know, gentlemen," his father added, "I would love to join you, but my health hasn't been the best lately. Taking a trip as grand as this just wouldn't be advisable for me."

His father stopped talking as a faint thumping sound came from under the porch floor. Jedidiah quickly put his left hand over his twitching finger. Unable to identify the source of the sound, Jedidiah's father continued. "You see, gentlemen, I really think I've heard my prayers answered, and the Lord has told me that it would be better for Jedidiah to make this trip on his own, and to learn from someone other than his own father."

Jedidiah could barely keep quiet, still crouched in forced silence under the porch. He didn't care about the stale air mixed with raw dampness, and fought off the urge to stretch out the cramps that were beginning to form in his legs from crouching for so long.

It's perfect, Father . . . you did it, thought Jedidiah.

Jedidiah tried his best to stay calm, but the excitement was too much for his fifteen-year-old mind to control. Once he heard the words of agreement from both Reverend Spaulding and Pastor Higgin, all restraint was lost.

Sounds like those of a wild animal came from under the porch and startled the three men. They jolted from their rocking chairs and perched over the porch railing in time to see Jedidiah crawling out from under the porch, dirt and leaves covering his face and hair. His smile and the light in his eyes were outward manifestations of the joy and elation that filled his body.

Stuttering like a baby lamb, he blasted out, "F . . . Father? . . . R . . . Rev erend Spaulding? . . . P . . . Pastor Higgin . . . I . . . I . . . can? . . . is it? . . . will I? Oh my gosh!"

Caught up in excitement, Jedidiah ran into the house to tell his mother the great news . . . the news that he was really going west.

"Momma! Momma!" he shouted, completely unaware that his father had yet to discuss any of this with her.

Chapter Two

I Promise, Momma

1831

The Spauldings and the Higgins bid their good-nights, and their buggies were soon out of sight. The sound of their horses clomping down the road faded into an eerie stillness that fell over the Monroe household. The quiet was a little unsettling, especially for Zachary, who knew he had some fast talking to do. Jedidiah had been excused to his room while Zachary and Martha reclined in rocking chairs on the front porch.

Zachary stared into the darkness of the night, sneaking occasional peeks at his wife as he attempted to measure her emotional state. Crickets and bullfrogs sang their evening serenades, and fireflies danced happily on the black velvet beyond the porch. But this evening the stage's most important player was a tense and scared mother.

"Zachary, is this the right thing to do?" Martha cried softly. "He's just a boy . . . and Zachary . . . he's my only child!" The tears grew larger and the sobs louder as they sat outside under the new moon. Jedidiah sat close to the open window in his upstairs room, trying his best to eavesdrop on his parents over the crickets chirping in the distance and the bullfrogs croaking down by the creek.

Jedidiah poked his head out of his bedroom window, anxious not only to hear, but also to glimpse his parents as they talked. He wanted to hear every word and see every expression that had to do with what was going to happen to him. He didn't know whether to pray, hope, or just wish real hard. Once the crickets and frogs simmered down, he could hear their words, and felt an urge to jump out his window to state his case.

Zachary tried to come up with the words that would ease his wife's concern. "He's about to come of age as a man, Martha," Zachary said.

"He needs to gain the experience that I can't give him here. I look back and remember what it meant for me when my father sent me out West. At the time I thought he was protecting me from the war with England, but now I know it was a chance for me to grow up, plant my roots, and start my own life."

The silence filling the air was broken only by intermittent sniffles and the wiping of eyes. A slight breeze ruffled the leaves in the trees, and darkness loomed around them—only the star-filled sky cast any light on an otherwise gloomy moment.

After a few minutes that to Jedidiah seemed like an eternity, Martha said, "Let me make sure I'm hearing this right, Zachary Monroe. You're sending *my* only son away from me to fulfill *your* idea of giving him a chance to set up roots and build *his* own dream?"

As Martha looked up at the endless expanse of the twinkling heavens, Jedidiah believed he could see tears shining on her cheeks. "*If* this idea of yours happens," Martha said, her voice breaking, "and *if he never comes back*, I will never be able to forgive you. You understand that, Zachary Monroe?"

"Momma, I'll come home again." Jedidiah's voice was barely audible from his open bedroom window. Upon hearing those soft words from her son, Martha began to weep and as she covered her face with her hands.

The chairs on the porch creaked as both of Jedidiah's parents turned their heads up toward him. "Y . . . you . . . better!" Martha yelled out as she got up from her rocking chair and walked down the dark gravel pathway, looking as if she badly needed to be alone. Jedidiah's heart ached as he watched her from his bedroom window, and he began to have second thoughts.

* * * * *

Ever since that fateful night when his father made the decision to allow Jedidiah to go with the Missionary Society, laughter had been conspicuously absent from the usually boisterous and jovial Monroe home. Each day closer to Jedidiah's departure brought an array of emotions from the entire family. Jedidiah watched his mother closely during those few days and could tell that she was the one most affected by his plans. His heart ached knowing that he would have to say farewell to each of his parents. It was his farewell to his mother that he was dreading most. *Tomorrow morning is going to be hard,* he thought as he hopped into his bed, maybe for the last time in his parents' home.

* * * * *

Jedidiah was the first to notice the Higgins' buggy turning off the main street and approaching the house. The morning was damp and cool from the night's dew. The smell of breakfast still lingered, and a heavy and apprehensive emptiness filled the house. *It's really happening,* he thought as he stood up from the rocking chair on the porch, *I'm really going west. I just can't believe it's really happening.* He turned to go inside to gather his luggage while his father went out to greet the Higgins.

Jedidiah took a glance up toward his bedroom and noticed his mother gazing out the window. She wore a whole different kind of emotion, one that sent shivers of guilt down his spine. Instead of her usual cheerful disposition, her face showed only sorrow and emptiness as she glanced at the Higgins' buggy and then at the beauty of her newly planted gardenias. His mother had always had a beautiful face filled with joy, but today she looked suddenly sad, as if life had . . .

Jedidiah turned away, guilt swelling his heart. He walked into the house to take one last look around. Inside the family room, he took mental notes and promised himself that he would never forget anything he saw—the furniture, the portrait of Grandpa Jacob mounted above the mantel, the dining table where so many meals had been shared, and finally the family Bible that the family had read together every night after supper. He closed his eyes and spent a moment to forge a memory of his boyhood home into his mind. *I'm coming back, so it's not like I'm never going to see any of this again.* Even as he had the thought, Jedidiah shook his head to try to ease his melancholia.

"Jedidiah, come out here please," Jedidiah heard his father say as the Higgins climbed down from their buggy. As he approached his father and the Higgins, Jedidiah reached out his hand and said, "It's so nice to see you both again. I couldn't sleep a wink last night. How about you two? I bet you're just as excited as I am. Right?"

"Yes, well, we slept very well, Jedidiah," the Pastor answered kindly. "But at our age sleep comes easily and excitement is a bit tempered."

"Jedidiah, now I want you to help out Pastor Higgin and Mrs. Higgin," his father said, "just as if you were here helping out your mother and me. You hear me, Son?"

Pastor Andrew Higgin was a portly man with graying thin hair, and dark eyes that showed both conviction and compassion. He spoke with clarity and in a simple manner that any young man could warm up to. He was a kind man in spite of thick bushy eyebrows that made him look like he was frowning all the time; no amount of teasing from his wife would make him trim them.

"We're so looking forward to having you with us, Jedidiah," added Sara. "You know, we're going to need a strong upstanding young man to assist us with our work. And to be honest, we've wanted to get a pack mule to help us haul our supplies, but I'm sure you will do just fine," she added with a grin. At that, everyone laughed.

Sara Higgin was a simple and caring woman. Not able to bear children, she involved herself in the welfare of others, especially nonbelievers and the young. She had a kindhearted look, with a warm smile that put those around her at ease. She had just a hint of gray in her dark brown hair, which she always kept up in a tight bun, most of the time covered with a bandana. Her deep blue eyes made her face glow when she smiled, which was most of the time. She was short and round and a magnet of kindness to anyone in need.

"You see, Jedidiah, we're not as young anymore, so we'll be relying on you to help us with a lot of the chores, and at the same time, hopefully I can teach you the art of setting up your own church just like your father here," Pastor Higgin said.

"Anything you need, Mr. Higgin, I'm there for you. And you too, Mrs. Higgin," Jedidiah said.

"Please, Jedidiah, just call me Pastor Higgin, or if it's easier, just good ol' Pastor will do."

"And Jedidiah?" added Sara Higgin, "we'll be spending a great deal of time together over the next several months, so I would like you to feel free to call me 'Sara.' It just seems too formal, that 'Mrs. Higgin' gibberish and all."

"Yes, sir, and yes, ma'am. That all sounds real nice, and if it's all the same to you, please call me Jed." Jedidiah ignored his father's frown. *I think it's time I started to use the name I want to go by. Sorry, Father.* He knew the name Jedidiah had been carefully selected from the Bible. *I know he's probably fuming right now.*

Jedidiah looked at the wooden swing tied to a limb of the tree, and memories of his mother and himself swinging and laughing uncontrollably engulfed him. He remembered that his mother had hoped to swing her grandchildren on that same swing someday, but now . . . *no, it will still happen—you just knock it off, Jedidiah.* He looked up and noticed his mother looking down at him. *Is she having nostalgic thoughts similar to my own?*

Jed looked up at his bedroom window again. He found that his mother was still standing in his bedroom, intently gazing down at him. He imagined he could see tears welling in her eyes, and saw her hand move up to her chest as if she were touching her heart. With one final nod, she turned from the window and was gone. No last words were spoken; none were needed.

Earlier that morning, Jed and his mother had sat on the bed for an hour talking and reminiscing about the past, their conversation interspersed with laughs and tears as they said good-bye.

"Momma, you know that I'll write to you every single day, and before you know it you'll see me coming around that corner over there." Jed pointed to the corner of the church building. "I'll even have a bouquet of flowers and some nice chocolate just for you. I know how much you like chocolate. Right, Momma?" he said gently.

He looked into her eyes and they were glazed over with a blank stare that seemed to be looking out over the yard, though Jed could not be certain. "Remember when I used to run around and chase all those ducks and rabbits?" Her mind was somewhere else—Jed didn't know where.

"Yes, I do, and you want to know something?" she said softly.

"What is it, Momma?" Jed asked.

"I want that little four-year-old back in my arms again and not going far, far away from me," she said while wiping her cheek with the back of her hand.

"I *will* write, and I *will* come back home, Momma," Jed repeated.

With a quick gesture, Jed shot up from where he sat and ran out of the room. His quick footsteps stomped down the wooden stairs like a herd of buffalo.

Would she ever hear the beautiful sounds of those stomping feet ever again? Thinking he had left her, her heart stopped momentarily until the stomping returned, back up the stairs and into his room. His smile lit up the room, and the flowers in his hand erased the sadness in her heart, for the moment anyway.

He leaned over, put the fresh red roses in her hand, and kissed her cheek softly. She didn't care that the "bouquet" in her hand was more dirt than roses, or that he had picked them from her own rose garden.

He knew that she loved her roses, and also that no words were needed to show the love he had for her. He could see how much this meant to her. He sat down beside her and his tears came without shame. They locked eyes and sat that way for what seemed like hours, neither wanting to be the first to look away.

Slowly he got up, turned, and walked to the doorway. Pausing but not looking back, he said, "I promise, Momma."

* * * * *

Even now, hours later, Jed was still sensitive from the emotional farewell with his mother. He knew he couldn't bear to turn and look back up at his window. Instead, he imagined her curled up on his bed holding the roses he had given her, dirt spilling onto the quilt and tears rolling down her face. He knew that she thought he was gone for good, but he was going to prove her wrong. He paused and looked one more time at the empty wooden swing. *I'll be back Momma, I will be back!*

Jed's luggage was loaded into the buggy, consisting entirely of one trunk with a broken handle, and a hand-me-down valise. The pastor and his wife climbed up on the buggy and sat quietly as they awaited their young traveling companion. Together the three of them would make the long wagon ride to the Ohio River loading dock.

Jed tried to focus his remaining time on saying good-bye to his father.

Jed and his father stood together in silence at the bottom of the porch steps. They heard a woodpecker doing his best to chop a tree down with his bare beak. Zachary broke the silence and with a crack in his voice said, "That pesky bird's going to get the best of me, you know?" His eyes met Jed's. "Who am I going to get to help me trap it once my best trapper has left me?"

An uneasy hush fell over them, becoming more awkward as the seconds clicked slowly by. *What am I supposed to say to him at a time like this?* Jed pondered the idea, and thought it probably would've been easier to say their good-byes as he and his mother had, inside the home and in private. Then again, that had been no easy task either.

The silence between them broke when Jed's father turned and said, "You go with the Lord, Son, and make your mother and me proud. You hear?"

Zachary put out his hand to offer a gentleman's handshake. Jed looked down at the soft skin of a man who turned the pages of a Bible for a living, and knew that he would have nothing to do with the formality of a handshake. He grabbed his father around his shoulders, hugged him tight, and held on, burying his face in his shoulder and never wanting to let go.

"I will, Father, and I will come through with my promise to Momma . . . I will be back, and I will take over your church for you . . . you just wait and see!"

The tears of both men flowed freely, and with one more tight and loving hug, Jed turned and jumped up onto the back of the Higgins' wagon.

Jed looked around at all the familiar landmarks. His heart ached and he wanted to wail like a baby, but he stayed strong, trying to build up the fortitude he would need in the days to come.

As Jed sat, he heard his father speaking to his new traveling companions.

"You take good care of him, all right?" Zachary said.

"Don't fret, Zachary," Higgin assured him, "he'll be just fine, and always remember, the good Lord will be with us all the way."

The horses were nudged ahead, and the wagon wheels creaked. Jed lifted his head slowly and held it for his father, and their eyes said it all as they met in unspoken understanding. He knew his father was proud of him, and he too was proud to do well in his father's eyes.

Jed glanced up one last time to his bedroom window and there she was again, standing with tears streaming, her right hand lovingly over her heart, and the other clutching blood-red roses.

He couldn't say a word.

He could only feel.

I love you, Momma.

I love you, Papa.

And . . . I will be back.

Chapter Three

Hear the Whistle A-Blowin'

1831

The uneven road leading west from Wheeling and then north to the Ohio River landing was lined with dense timberland. The trip from the Monroe house to the landing was just about a day's ride barring complications. There'd been talk of putting a landing in at Wheeling, but was still likely a few years away.

The sky was morning blue with a touch of clouds that lingered over the northern mountain range. Jed watched a scurrying jackrabbit hop along and then disappear into a hollow log. The smell of wild grass drifted in the air to the steady cadence of plodding horse hoofs, wagon wheels, and jostling boxes of household goods.

Fidgeting at his perch on the back of the wagon, Jed could not refrain from peppering the Higgins with a plethora of questions. Pastor Higgin and Sara chuckled as they tried their best to answer each one, but the queries came so rapidly that they wondered if Jed even took a breath before each one. *He's definitely excited about this trip,* Pastor Higgin thought. He glanced at his wife, raising an eyebrow as he gave her a familiar grin—*how am I ever going to tame this youngster?*

Jed asked another question, but Pastor Higgin was too deep in thought to hear him. *Can I ever do what Zachary has asked of me?* He was overwhelmed by what he had agreed to do. *What happens if I fail?* He snapped the reins sharply, not only to get his horse moving, but more so to clear his mind. *I've got to try . . . I promised Zachary.*

He cracked the whip above the right ear of his lead horse, which caught Sara's attention. "Everything all right, Andrew?"

Pastor Higgin didn't answer. *Yes, he's got raw excitement, I'll give him that. Let's just let him grow up a little first and then we'll see.* He looked to the sky as if asking it a question. *I hope that's all right, Zachary . . . we'll just let him grow up first and then we'll see—how's that?*

Sara watched her husband intently. His knotted expression belied the weak grin that he sent her way. Sara turned her gaze forward to the rugged road ahead, placing her hand on her husband's without speaking a word. His hand went slack, the tightness and frustration receding at least for the moment.

After they stopped the wagon so the animals could rest, Jed jumped down to stretch his legs. He looked around at the open meadow full of yellow and orange wildflowers. He jerked his head toward the sound of hoofs pounding across water, and spotted a family of deer frolicking in a pond just below the trail's embankment. He stared at the wild animals in wonder.

"When do ya think we're gonna see some of them Injuns or fur trappers you-all have been talkin' about?" Jed yelled, not taking his eyes off the deer.

Pastor Higgin grinned at Sara as he tied the reins to the brake lever. He climbed down slowly while contemplating an answer for his neophyte companion.

"Well, son, we'll be on this trail for a bit until we meet up with the rest of the missionary group at the Ohio River landing. We are unlikely to see such folks as those until we are farther west. It's still a ways, Jed—plus as you've seen, the road isn't in the best condition with the rocks and cracks left from winter."

Pastor Higgin was accustomed to traveling, but kept the pace leisurely and free of unnecessary risks. The year previous, he had been a day's ride east of Wheeling when his wagon lost an axle. He was returning from a Bible conference and had to leave a full load of Bibles behind and walk the rest of the way home. The look on Sara's face when he hobbled through the front door at half-past midnight told him enough to know that he'd never do that again.

Pastor Higgin walked to the back of the wagon and pulled a handful of oats from a dark wooden barrel. After giving a half-dozen handfuls to the spare horse still tied to the back of the wagon, he filled a small woven bag with oats and walked up to the lead horse. After positioning the feed bag beneath the horse's mouth and placing the strap over its head, he turned to Jed, who had come closer to the wagon and was watching curiously.

"Plus, Jed, by taking it slow to make sure we get there in one piece, we're making sure we don't break any of Sara's valuable cargo." Sara's head whiplashed in response to her husband's comment, and she squinted her eyes while shaking her head slowly. Pastor Higgin added in a comical tone, "You've got to understand, Jed, I'd never hear the end of it if any of Sara's belongings were broken. She's pretty particular when it comes to her valuables."

"And you both better remember that if you know what's best for you," Sara replied as she climbed down from her seat. The Higgins' china set was an heirloom passed down from Sara's great-grandmother, and Pastor Higgin's comments notwithstanding, it was the most valuable thing they owned.

Taking a moment to catch her breath, Sara grabbed the water buckets, handed them to Jed, and asked him to go with her to fill them with water from the pond. They walked down the side of the trail and forged through the tall grass surrounding the pond.

They returned with Jed carrying both buckets filled to the top with cold clear water and Sara giggling behind. Swarms of gnats were circling in front of his face and irritating his nose, but with both hands full, he was unable to swat them. Pastor Higgin was still chuckling when he took the buckets from Jed and poured their contents into the wooden barrel strapped to the side of the wagon. When he was finished, Sara grabbed the water ladle hooked to the side of the barrel and took sip of the cool water.

Looking pleased by the taste, she handed the ladle to Jed, and while he dipped it into the refreshing water she said. "You know, Jed, you're going to see many exciting things as we move farther west, but keep in mind that the main reason that we're going west is to share the word of God."

Jed looked at her after wiping his mouth with his sleeve, and forced an agreeing nod. "Oh, I know, it's just that—"

"And it will be God who shows us the ones who need saving," Sara interjected.

Jed put the ladle back onto the side of the barrel, conceding to simply listen.

"It might be an Indian or an orphan boy, or it could even be a smelly ol' trapper."

"Smelly ol' trapper?" Jed bellowed out with a loud laugh.

Looking to her husband, and then acknowledging the frown and raised eyebrow as she received no shelter, Sara defended herself firmly. "You two can work on the nonbelieving heathen savages—me, I'm going to clean up the animal-carving, skin-scalping, dirty, no-good fur traders if it's the last thing I do! They're just a disgrace to good Christian people!"

"Now, Mother, don't be giving Jed here any wrong impression of what lies ahead." Pastor Higgin's endearing reference to Sara as "Mother" brought a knowing smile to Sara's face.

Since the time when Sara and Pastor Higgin realized that they wouldn't have children, he often referred to her as "Mother" to reconfirm his unconditional love for her. She in turn often called him "Father," making their inability to raise a family a bit more bearable.

"You see, young man," Pastor Higgin addressed Jed, "my wife, whom I do love dearly, has an outpouring heart that she will freely give to any poor soul who comes to her in need. She's just had some bad experiences with the, uh, what would you call it . . . ?"

"The smelly, foulmouthed, impolite nature of the typical fur trapper?" Sara yelled out with a laugh.

"Now don't get me wrong, Jed," Sara continued as she grabbed onto the side of the wagon to pull herself up to her seat. "Those fur traders and supply traders also have a need of cleansing, that's for sure, and that's just what we're going to do. But it's the fur traders that have been known to bring liquor to the Indians, and by doing that, all kinds of bad things seem to happen."

With a sympathetic glance at his distraught wife, Pastor Higgin directed Jed back onto the wagon. "We'd best be moving along Jed. We'll have plenty of time for this discussion when we get on the riverboat."

"The what?" Jed asked excitingly. "Is that what we're gonna be going on, a real riverboat?"

"Whoa there, youngster, slow down a bit, you're even starting to get the horses anxious." *Boy, if I could just bottle up some of this youngster's energy, we'd all be set for life,* Pastor Higgin thought as he shook his head in amazement.

"Sorry, I'm just so excited about all of this and my words get on ahead of me sometimes."

Pastor Higgin leaned over to pull the reins off the brake. He turned one last time and looked back at Jed. "It's quite all right that you're so excited, son—you're going to see a lot on this trip—but what's best is that the learning you're going to get will not be the schoolbook type you were used to back in Wheeling."

Jed scrunched up his nose and tilted his head to the side, not knowing exactly what the Pastor meant. Pastor Higgin turned to face the trail, and chuckled at Jed's expression. He gave out a couple loud clucks to the lead horse, and the wagon lurched forward and creaked its way down the dusty trail.

After they were moving steadily, Pastor Higgin yelled back to Jed over the rattling and clunking of the wagon. "It's sure going to be fun to watch what God has in store for you Jed, and I know your father has great plans for you too, right?" Jed remained silent in obvious thought, a nice reprieve for the Higgins after the first several hours of lengthy questions.

He held tight to the splintered wood siding of the wagon and stared at the ground below. The crates of dishes and kitchenware clanked behind him, and although tied down, their wardrobe chests and valises continued to shift and bounce, making Jed nervous with fear that they would fall out. "Well? I didn't hear you, Son" Pastor Higgin interjected. "It is something you want, right? I mean, I know how important it is for your father. He told me he can't wait to see you learning the ways of being a pastor and someday taking over for him at the church."

There was no response, and the only thing Pastor Higgin could hear was the noise of the wagon. "Is that what you want too, Jed?" he yelled out again.

"Oh yeah, well . . . I mean, of course, that's the plan," Jed stammered back loudly. "But I'm thinking, uh, I, you see, I've got a whole heap of learning to do, and I don't think it's just about being a pastor."

Pastor Higgin and Sara glanced at each other with knowing looks.

"I mean, I do want to make him proud, and I do want to be a pastor someday," Jed said as he tried to make sense of all the mixed-up thoughts in his mind. "I'd never do anything that would hurt or disappoint my momma and papa, and that goes for the two of you as well. I mean, you two are going out of your way by taking me along, and I surely do appreciate it."

Jed sat quietly on the end of the wagon, pondering just what he was getting himself into and what it could mean. For the next few hours he endured the bumps and jolting caused by the uneven trail as the wagon made it over hills and through valleys. At one point he watched a coyote as it made a feeble attempt to intercept them. Jed watched in wonder as it stopped in its tracks, obviously finding easier prey to stalk.

It seemed to Jed that he'd been sitting on the back of the wagon forever. His legs were beginning to cramp, and his hindquarters were getting raw from all the bouncing. He thought a lot about what the Pastor had asked him and what his father wanted for him. He pulled himself to one side, and though his muscles were sore from holding on so tightly, he was able to turn around to face the Pastor and Sara.

"I'm truly thankful for all that you two are doing and all the possibilities I have ahead of me. Heck, I'm just so excited to be riding in this here wagon, even though my hind end is getting a bit sore." At that, they all laughed.

Before taking his seat again, Jed took one last look forward. His mouth opened wide as the wagon made its way around another bend and crested one last hill.

In the far distance, he could see it.

The river was in plain view with its winding curves snaking through the valley below. The sun caused a reflection of the water's glistening deep brownish-blue onto the hillside that they now descended in the wagon. Though Jed knew it was moving swiftly, the river looked quite calm, and Jed felt an urge to feel its coolness.

Jed tried to keep his eyes on the riverboat as the wagon approached the landing. He could see the boat's chimneys spewing out puffs of white smoke that swirled and jetted into the deep blue sky. The closer they got, the bigger the boat grew and the more excited Jed became. He had never seen the smoking stacks before, yet he'd read about them. He was mesmerized by their size, and wondered how the boat stayed upright. The whiteness of the riverboat was blinding in the sunlight, with its multitude of decks leading to the wheelhouse up top.

Jed sat speechless the last few hundred yards of the trip. He was fixated on the massive boat in front of him, and tried to count the stairs leading to each deck. He envisioned himself sitting on the end of the long ramp jetting out from the front of the boat. He imagined his feet dangling above the swiftly moving river below, and could feel the wind in his face.

The boat's name was now in plain view, boldly painted in black just above the mammoth paddlewheel that rotated slowly aft . . . *Nebraska*. Jed couldn't wait for the chance to explore every inch of it.

Pastor Higgin pulled up alongside the other wagons from the Missionary Society. They formed a line on the dock to which the *Nebraska* was secured with ropes and lines. There were three long wooden ramps with rope railings leading from the landing to the riverboat.

Jed was fascinated by the commotion that surrounded him. It was a mass of delightful chaos, with wagons, horses, crates, and cargo taking up every available space on the landing. He heard people screaming orders, families yelling out their plans and directions, and the ordered steps of men in uniform as they went back and forth across the wooden ramps. The uniformed men worked hastily to place passenger cargo in a huge holding area beneath the first deck. The whole scene before him was in complete contrast to what he had experienced just a few hours before on the quiet little trail from Wheeling.

Jed daydreamed that he was at the helm of his own wheelhouse, yelling orders to his crew down below, telling them to get moving with all the supplies littering the loading ramp. He was lost in his fantasy world, and the excitement overtook his senses and blocked out any voices around him.

"Jed!—Jed!—Jedidiah Monroe!" Pastor Higgin yelled above the whistles of the boat, breaking Jed out of his trance as the next "riverboat captain." "Come on, Jed! You need to get off that wagon and start moving the supplies down that ramp and onto the lower deck. There are no porters to help, so you're it, son. You'll have plenty of time to get acquainted with riding on a riverboat later, but right now I need you to help us along. Let's get going, young man!"

Jed jumped into action, and the excitement of the riverboat made the chore of hauling supplies from the wagon into the storage bins on the lower level of the boat an easy task.

His first trip across the loading ramp caught him off guard. The ramp wobbled and swayed as he walked across it, so he had to learn to walk in the center where it was more stable. Any closer to the edge, and the whole ramp tilted to that side, making it even more difficult to navigate the ramp when others were using it at the same time. It was surprising that more people hadn't fallen over, and more cargo hadn't been lost, as a result of the unstable design.

Sara instructed Jed to wait until his last trip before moving her crate of fine china. "And be careful with it, Jed!" Her words sent a shiver of panic down his spine. *Can't someone else take it over?* he thought of asking, but couldn't bring himself to it.

Jed reassured her that he had made several trips so far and had figured out the best way to cross. Nevertheless, her worried look remained as he made a show of feigning confidence.

On his last trip across the boat ramp, Jed held tightly to Sara's treasured crate of delicate china. He planted his feet securely down the center of the ramp. He was relieved to see that he was the only one on the ramp as he took one slow step at a time. The crate was heavy but well balanced in his long arms. He made the mistake of glancing down at the water below, but quickly corrected himself and diverted his eyes forward, scolding himself as he did so.

He was over the halfway mark, and in a matter of seconds, Sara's prized possessions would be placed securely in the cargo hold—*just a few more steps*—his confidence was strong and relief was only moments away.

The loud riverboat whistle jolted Jed from his concentration, breaking his balance and causing him to stumble and lose his grip on the crate. His heart erupted in panic as Sara's crate of china slipped from his hands and bounced off the rope railing into the dark brownish-blue water of the Ohio River.

He didn't know what felt worse, the sound of the splash or the shriek from Sara. Jed watched as the crate teetered back and forth on the surface of the river until it slowly slipped farther under, to be consumed in one big plunge as it disappeared into the river's depths. He contemplated jumping in after it, but soon thought better of it.

He looked at Sara—the look she returned was worse than any his scary schoolteacher Miss Plumber had given him back home. "Jedidiah Monroe!!!" screamed Sara. Suddenly, all eyes were on Jed.

"I . . . I am so, so, sorry, I...I was startled by that dang whistle or horn or whatever it was.... Why did they have to do that anyway? Now look what they caused!"

"You will be paying me back for that crate of china, young man, and you will also watch what comes out of your mouth, you hear me?!" Sara scolded. She turned and rushed off in a heat of anger.

Jed stood in dismay, looking for some way to make up for his mishap. He hated how everyone was looking at him. He'd been embarrassed before, but nothing as big as this, and now everyone was talking about him. He wanted to go home.

"Come on, Jed, don't you fret none." He heard the comforting voice of Pastor Higgin. "Accidents happen, son; she'll get over it. Let's go on and get our supplies tied down tight in the lower deck, all right?"

Jed felt a bit of the guilt lift off him as he shrugged his shoulders and plodded behind Pastor Higgin to the lower deck.

Once all the supplies were on board and wagons and horses were safely secured at the stern, the Missionary Society gathered at the bow. This was the time for a last-minute meeting, warm greetings, and prayer before departing down the Ohio River. Jed looked at the members of the society as they mingled about. He was pleased to be greeted warmly without comment on his earlier mishap. He noticed that most of the society were couples in their thirties or early forties.

He didn't see many children, and he felt special to be part of this adventure at such a young age. He noticed that there were a dozen or so men of the cloth, or so he presumed by their clothing. As he scanned the group, he saw Reverend Spaulding, who tilted his hat at him, and Pastor Higgin, who was talking with an elderly man who by Jed's guess must be pushing a hundred or so. To Jed's disappointment, though, he couldn't find Sara anywhere, and his guilt began to surface again.

A gray-bearded man stood on a crate and called everyone closer to him. After leading the group in prayer, he proceeded to tell them what course they would be taking over the next several days. Jed couldn't hold back his excitement, and though still deeply sorry for losing Sara's china, he marveled at the thought of seven days riding on this magnificent riverboat.

Steam began to shoot from the stacks above, and the giant paddle wheel began to rotate faster. The landing docks were filled with well-wishers who were all waving and cheering the departure of the *Nebraska*. The sounds of water and swishing paddles could be heard, and the excitement of the trip filled everyone's souls.

Jed rested his arms on the starboard railing to watch as the boat broke from the landing and the distance between boat and land grew wider. He watched the water below swirl in a circular motion and crash against the sides of the distancing boat dock. Jed blocked out the noise from the excited voyagers, though he could still see the mass of people celebrating around him. He moved to the corner of the railing and was transfixed on the motion of the boat and the stillness of the movement; the only sounds in his head were the swishing of the paddlewheel and the steam whistling out of the boat's stacks.

He thought of home. It had been a full day since leaving, and it had gone by so quickly. The letters—the promised letters—he hadn't even had time to think of them on the wagon ride.

Yes, I will get better at that, he thought, but the sincerity and conviction of his promise were quickly fading. As he looked at the river ahead and behind, he realized that he was not home anymore, and the question of returning was not as clear as it had been on the front porch in Wheeling. *I'll write once we get settled in Independence,* thought Jed as he tried to convince himself. *Momma'll understand.*

He walked down to the main deck, feeling as if he had suddenly become much more mature. He knew he was turning sixteen the next day, and yet he felt much older. He thought of his mother and father, and wondered if they were going to celebrate his birthday at home.

He stopped at the railing again and looked at the river splashing against the sides of the riverboat. He followed the path of a flock of birds flying high above in perfect formation. He stretched his neck to get a better look ahead to where the boat was taking him. The breeze off the river gently blew through his brown hair, and a peculiar feeling came over him. It was the feeling of approaching Independence, but this independence was no longer just a town.

Chapter Four

Getting There Is Half the Fun

1831

"Dear Momma, the riverboat has . . ." Jed attempted, and then crumpled up another piece of paper to throw over the edge.

Why is it so hard? Just tell her the fun you're having. But it was hard, and the words just wouldn't come. Once again the paper and quill were put down and stored away in his satchel, but he was determined to write again when they landed at the next town.

"All ashore for those disembarking for the great city of Cincinnati!" shouted a man with a long black beard and an oversized blue bugle hat. Jed made his way out of his berth, attempting to gain his bearings. He was glad to get out of his tight living space and stretch his legs for a bit. His berth was a quarter the size of his room back home and had no window, which didn't help to alleviate the stale scent that filled the air. He used a candle to see at night, but the flickering light gave him a headache that made writing a letter home nearly impossible. His bed was too short and his door wouldn't shut all the way, which made him nervous at night.

Jed leaned over the railing, trying to see what this new town was like compared with the small ones he'd seen so far. Once his eyes focused, he froze in amazement, staring with his mouth wide open.

The pastor joined him on the deck and stood next to him at the railing. "What's gotten into you, boy, haven't you ever seen a big city before?"

The sights Jed now saw were wonders to his raw eyes—the north side of the river was filled with large store buildings, streets busy with horses, wagons, and pedestrians intertwining as they tried to gain the upper hand on the right-of-way. From the deck he could see a cannery, several mercantile shops, a few busy saloons, and one very large red brick building that seemed to have the most activity.

He noticed several Negro families being escorted into the building by a few white folks, but saw with interest that very few leaving. He thought it odd, but didn't think much of it, as his attention was drawn to all the other things in town that made him realize he wasn't in Wheeling anymore. The air was still, with a scent of cinnamon, which made him look to see if there was a bakery nearby.

"Can we get off and explore, Pastor Higgin?" Jed asked.

"You know, Jed, I think that's a great idea. But keep in mind that we're only going to be here for a while, so you go ahead and stretch your legs a bit, but you better be back on board when that whistle blows, you hear?"

Jed didn't respond—he bolted for the ramp and then sprinted down the dock. It felt so good to be on land, and he was going to get the most out of it, no matter how little time he had. He raced up one street and then over a couple of blocks to another. He'd been cramped in his berth so long that the running was invigorating for him.

He allowed his legs to feel the freedom of the open space—he sprinted as fast as he could until he could run no farther. He found himself back at the river's edge, and he leaned over the railing of the landing to catch his breath, feeling the wind as it cooled the back of his neck. His gaze spanned the vast river with its sparkling current swirling past. He watched a lone duck wobbling not far from him, eagerly searching for any bits of help from human bystanders. He stared at the duck and wondered how any feathered animal could possibly survive without the help of all the crumbs thrown to him. He moved his attention to the other side of the river. He overheard the crowds of people shuffling past him, talking of daily events: tea parties, dinners, and something about comparing the river to the Jordan with a railroad under it. *Don't know much about that,* he thought, *never seen the Jordan.*

He looked hard at the other side of the river and playfully wondered if he could throw a rock across it and hit land. He'd heard that the land in front of him was the state of Kentucky, and he was amazed with its nearness.

Wow, just think of it, Momma, I'm standing in one state and lookin' over at another! Just wait for that letter to come, Momma.

Reluctantly, Jed made his way back across the ramp and on board the *Nebraska* minutes before the steam whistle blew, indicating that it was time to shove off. He propped himself next to the railing and watched as the riverboat inched away from the docks below. The boat's steam shot skyward from the smoking stacks, leaving clouds of whiteness in the air behind them. The small wheelhouse's whistle screamed again, causing Jed to put his hands to his ears and squint in pain. *Gettin' a little tired of that thing.* His grimace turned into a grin as the giant paddle wheel turned faster and faster.

He watched the small wharf he'd stood on moments before growing smaller and smaller. He still wondered if he could have thrown a stone clear across to the other side. To his disappointment, the river looked wider from his new viewpoint on the riverboat, so he didn't think it would have made it. *I should have tried though.*

As the *Nebraska* made a sharp snakelike turn, Jed focused on the dark red brick building standing tall in the town, watching as it slowly disappeared. He walked toward the front of the main deck and looked up the river, trying to see what might be next.

Who'd have ever guessed I'd be living this kind of life? He felt like pinching himself.

Jed found a fun game to play by himself. He continued walking around the main deck, following the railing as much as he could without taking his hand off the wood rail. He lost count at twenty-five times around, but it helped him keep busy. He didn't want to go back to his berth and take the chance of missing something exciting.

* * * * *

The riverboat veered to the left at Louisville, Kentucky, and entered the Louisville and Portland Canal, the rocky sides barely far enough from the boat's hull to keep from crushing its sides. Jed's eyes popped out upon seeing the proximity of the walls.

As the boat traveled through the canal, the air was filled with the stench of oil and burnt metal from all the factories that were building new riverboats. Jed felt his throat tighten, and he had a hard time breathing. The sounds of hammers on metal were heard from each factory they passed, so loud the passengers could hardly hear one another speak. Jed put his handkerchief up to his face to filter the smell, and hoped they'd be past soon.

Jed, still holding his handkerchief close, watched the activities at the factories as they passed by. For a moment, he pondered the impact that all those workers were having on this river, and in a way, the entire country. He had never been involved in anything like that before, and as he went through the canal, the reality of his journey began to gain a whole new meaning. A real purpose and responsibility was developing in his young mind, and he came to realize that he was part of something special that was yet to be unraveled farther west.

Every night, Jed and Pastor Higgin spent time talking. Jed enjoyed their talks and the way the pastor never tired of answering his numerous questions. Pastor Higgin was beginning to take a real liking to Jed as well, and felt a paternal fondness for the young man. Jed began to feel at ease around the pastor and Sara, and the bond between the three was bolstered.

* * * * *

On the third morning after traveling through the Louisville canal, Jed suddenly awakened when he sensed the riverboat turning sharply. He dressed quickly and raced to the front of the boat, leaning out over the railing to get a better look.

"Morning Jed, how'd you sleep last night?" asked Sara.

"Very well, thank you, ma'am," answered Jed as he peered over the railing and looked down at the river below.

Jed looked ahead. He could see another river coming into view from the left side of the boat. It had a much deeper brown color to it, and at first Jed thought it was just the runoff of mud from an earlier storm. He quickly discarded that idea when he saw how wide it was and how swiftly it was moving. Jed looked intently at the mouth of the river and noticed all sorts of vegetation, but the color was what intrigued him the most.

"Are we turning or staying on the Ohio?" Jed asked, still staring at the mouth of the river.

They moved up the railing to get a better look as the *Nebraska* veered north and passed a sign reading, "CAPE GIRARDEAU, MISSOURI."

"Isn't Independence in Missouri?" asked Jed.

"Well, yes it is, Jed," answered Sara. "But keep in mind that we still have two more days before we're there—though I do believe that we're about to move off the Ohio and onto the Mississippi."

"The Mississippi?" Jed said loudly. "I've always wanted to see the Mississippi River, Sara! I'm a bit surprised though at the color, wonder if it's always been that color?"

Sara didn't give an answer, nor was Jed looking for one. They watched intently as the riverboat moved closer to the joining river. "I hope we're gonna be on this river as long as we were on the last one. I sure love riverboating, don't you, Sara? I just don't know what's more fun, being on the river or getting to jump off and explore at every stop along the way. What's your favorite, Sara?"

Jed abruptly excused himself before Sara had a chance to answer. He ran off to move closer to the front of the boat and gain a better vantage point, leaving Sara chuckling.

Jed watched as the boat traveled up the new river, periodically looking behind at the Ohio as it faded in the distance. He gazed at foliage on the banks, at twigs and branches as they floated by. He daydreamed seemingly for hours, until he noticed a site far down the river.

"Hear ye, hear ye! All passengers hear ye!" yelled the bearded man with the oversized bugle hat. "All passengers may NOT disembark at the next stop!"

Jed raced down the deck and up to the man, his face flushed. He grabbed at the man's arm and demanded, "Hey, why can't we get off, mister?"

"Whoa there, young man!" yelled the porter defensively. "First, you get your little paws off my jacket!"

Jed realized his childish behavior was a mistake when he saw the scowling looks from the other passengers who were standing nearby.

"Listen here!" The porter said gruffly as he pulled Jed by his shirt-sleeve over to the railing. "You've got no right spouting off like that, you hear me?"

Jed's head remained low, and he stared at the wooden deck at his feet. He could feel the large man towering over him, and sensed all the other passengers' eyes glued to him.

"It's no business of yours what we do or why we do it!" the porter continued loudly.

The burly man took his hat off and wiped his brow. He took his hand off Jed's arm and then looked around at the faces staring at them.

"Look, you seem like a nice kid," he said more softly as he began to relax. "I can see you really want to get off the boat, but we just don't have time to let anyone off at this stop. We're only picking up one passenger and bringing on a small supply of goods. There'd just be no time to do anything anyways, you understand?"

The man gave Jed a light pat on his back before disappearing into the wheelhouse. Jed, feeling flushed, dug his hands into his pockets, lowered his head, and tried to vanish by quickly walking in the opposite direction from the other passengers.

He stopped abruptly at the sight of the most beautiful girl he'd ever seen. She was walking across the boarding ramp holding a small brownish satchel, followed by a porter carrying a large wooden trunk with stickers all around it.

Jed was instantly mesmerized at her beauty. She was dressed in a long, light blue dress with a white bow tied in the back, and she carried a blue and white parasol. Her light brown hair was pulled back with a yellow ribbon. She had fair skin and bright blue eyes and a tiny nose, and when she smiled, her face lit up. She seemed to be about his age, and when she got closer he could see a few freckles sprinkled on her cheeks and nose.

Jed froze and stared with his mouth gaping, unable to say a word as she walked by him. *Did she see me?* he wondered. *She had to have seen me!*

How great it would be if I were able to talk with her, finally someone I could really talk to. To this point, Pastor Higgin and Sara had been his only sources of conversation. Even though Reverend Spaulding and the others had been cordial, they were reluctant to really engage him in good conversation.

While Jed was deep in thought, his mystery girl disappeared from view as she descended to the lower deck. Jed vowed to find a way to run into her again and somehow introduce himself.

The *Nebraska* resumed its journey, moving from the Mississippi to the Missouri River and onward toward Independence. Jed continued taking as many glances at his new love interest as he could get away with. She seemed to always be at a distance, either standing on the far end of the deck or on the opposite side of the dining room. Jed was determined, though, and continued taking peeks whenever he could. He came to the conclusion that she was definitely elusive. *I've got to talk to her,* he thought. *At least find out what her name is.*

Much to his disappointment, however, bad weather was approaching and would find a way to disrupt his plan.

As he lay in his bunk, he thought of the girl. *If he I could only go out and find her,* he thought. But that was impossible with the storm hitting hard. He could hear the sheets of rain hitting the top of the main deck along with the wind whistling an eerie howling sound. He tried to close his eyes, but couldn't relax with the crashing of the deck chairs being whipped around outside. He felt like praying, but didn't know if he should pray for the storm to let up or for help in finding the girl.

The porters were told to keep the passengers in their rooms for safety, and that meant that Jed would be confined to his bunk with just his book and a stack of writing papers to occupy his time. All the sheets of paper were blank except one, and that one had only a few short words: "*Dear Momma, I . . .*"

He was awakened, like most mornings, by the blast of that goshforsaken whistle. *I really think it is time to get off this boat. That whistle is driving me mad and with all this rain . . .* He frantically shook his head, disgusted with his surroundings. *I've got to get out of here.* He intently made up his bunk, gathered all his gear, and headed to the upper deck.

This new day was the one they'd all been waiting for. Excitement filled the air, and thoughts of numerous potential adventures ahead occupied Jed's mind. Despite the disappointment of not meeting that beautiful girl, Jed was preoccupied with the news that they were finally in Independence. *I sure did want to talk with her, guess it wasn't meant to be,* he conceded.

Jed looked over the deck railing at the river port and the town scattered up the bluff behind it. He thought of his parents and wished they were there to see what he was seeing. He knew they would have thoroughly enjoyed the voyage, except for the past few days when the storm had blown in.

He chuckled when he thought of his mother's obsession with keeping her hair dry. *She would've been a mess with all that rain against her tight clasped hair,* he thought.

With a laugh, he remembered the time when his father had to hold his coat over her head for the entire walk back from church just so she wouldn't get one strand of hair wet. Boy, did he miss them so.

"Let's get moving Jed, we've got a lot of work to do!" The sound of Pastor Higgin's instructions startled Jed. "I want to start with the large crates first, and then we can come back for the smaller valises." Jed nodded absently, his brain still fuzzy from its world of memories.

"Our little house is just under a half a mile from the docks, right next to the town's church," Pastor Higgin added. "You'll be all right getting the crates this time, right Jed?"

Jed nodded, still deep in thought. He violently shook his head to clear it, and began to make his way down to the bulkhead to retrieve the Higgins' supplies. Memories of the lost china crate sent shivers down his spine.

His arms and lungs burned from making numerous trips between the cargo bulkhead and the dock. He had to admit that hauling the supplies was much easier this time, though he still became extremely tired. He was relieved when he saw that the ramp at the dock in Independence was solid, with metal railings, compared with the wobbly one at the dock where they had started their journey.

Once finished, he sat on the back of the wagon, wiped his brow with his sleeve, and waited for the Higgins to join him. He looked around and watched the sea of people scurrying about, all with their own agendas about to unfold. He observed the burly porter with the bugle hat yelling out orders from the top deck, and couldn't help overhearing a man and woman yelling at each other about some lost luggage.

He was glad to finally make it to Independence, and looked forward to getting settled in the Higgins' home. With all the commotion and eager anticipation of adventures to come, the memories of his endless effort to find the anonymous girl ceased.

Sudden movement from the front of the wagon startled Jed from his thoughts, and he held on tight as Pastor Higgin grabbed the reins and headed down the road; Jed tried to envision what his new home might look like.

* * * * *

The small two-bedroom house made of log and clay was adjacent to the town's church, whose members provided the house to their pastor and his family. It was simple but beautifully constructed from the wood of local maple trees. A thin porch railing led to two steps, one of which needed repair. The filtered sun shone bright on the corner of the porch where the wood had faded over the years. Four framed black willow chairs were placed around the deck, with a potted black cherry blossom tree placed on an upside down barrel where it would be the most fragrant.

The breeze came from the river and blew through the side, cooling the house when the windows and doors were propped open. They all agreed that the breeze was nice and much needed, as the house had been closed up for so long that musty odors practically overwhelmed them when they first walked in.

Sara was overjoyed to see that a garden had already been planted in the side yard. She immediately set plans to add her favorite daffodils and mums. "This is exactly what I wanted, my very own garden!" she cheerfully declared. "I'm going to brighten up everyone's morning and fill this house with so many flowers that neither one of you will ever have a bad day, you hear?"

"Yes, Mother, you just do that," Pastor Higgin said, enjoying his wife's tone.

The kitchen was small, with a wood-burning stove next to the back door and a mahogany table with four wooden chairs sitting in the center. The kitchen cabinets were built above a ceramic washbasin and painted white. Each cupboard was filled with all the plates, cups, and glassware the three of them would ever need. Above the stove, various sizes of pots and pans hung from metal hooks fastened into to the kitchen's ceiling beam. Sara eyed them questioningly to see if she might need a stool to reach them.

There were two bedrooms, a master room upstairs and a guest room downstairs. Jed had been assigned the guest room, and to his liking, it came with its own fireplace. He rubbed his hand across the top of the mantle and thought of the picture of his Grandpa Monroe that hung above his fireplace at home.

The main living area was quaint, with a fireplace of its own, a sitting bench, two rocking chairs, and a small desk to be used when the Pastor worked on his weekly sermons. Jed felt very blessed to be welcomed into the home of the Higgin family, and made an oath not to take it for granted. He told himself that he would do his part in keeping this house a home to all.

While Sara got the house in order, Jed and Pastor Higgin wandered next door to look at the church. Jed observed the elation on the Pastor's face as they went from room to room, especially when they entered the main sanctuary; it was completely whitewashed, including the four pillars that supported the high ceiling. There were two sections of ten white wooden pews, and from the smell of the room, they'd been freshly painted. Two small steps at the front of the sanctuary led to a wooden pulpit with a large wooden cross mounted on its front.

Behind the pulpit, a large replica of Jesus hanging on the cross was mounted on the wall so that all who were seated could see it while listening to the pastor's sermons. The statue of Jesus reminded Jed of a similar likeness that was behind his father's pulpit back home.

"Hey, Jed, you want to hear my first sermon right now?" Pastor Higgin teased.

"Uh, no thanks, Pastor," Jed teased back. "But would ya mind very much if I go outside and sit for a bit? There's a heap of commotion in town from the boat and all, and I'd kind of like to watch what's going on, if you don't mind."

"Not at all, son" Pastor Higgin agreed. "In fact, I think I'll join you after I go get us some lemonade. That's if Sara's made any yet, but knowing my wife, it's already on the table, and I'd be surprised if she hasn't finished decorating the house already."

They laughed. Then Jed made his way outside to the front of the church, and the Pastor went through a side wooden gate to the back door of their new home.

Arriving back with two glasses of lemonade, Jed and Pastor Higgin sat on the benches outside the church doors and watched the scene in front of them.

"Thanks for the lemonade, Pastor," Jed said, gulping down the last drop. "If it's all the same to you, I'd like to walk around town and see what's out there. Is there anything you need me to do before I take off?"

"No, you go on and have some fun, but be back before dark, you hear? Supper will be on at five, and you know, the missus doesn't like her dinner to get cold," the Pastor warned.

"Alright, I promise, plus I want to talk about what our plans are gonna be now that we're finally here." Jed barely finished the last part of his sentence as he was getting up from his chair; he then rushed down the wooden walkway and hopped onto Main Street while several horses and buggies passed him by.

I hope he remembers to be back by dark, thought the Pastor as he turned back toward the front doors of "his church." *She's a great cook, but she can be a pistol if her meal is ruined by getting cold.*

Chapter Five

The Town, the Dream
1831

Independence was just as Reverend Spaulding and Pastor Higgin had described it. The first thing Jed noticed, though, was that the sign for the town read not **Independence**, but rather **Wayne City**. He was confused by this, but figured he'd just trust the Pastor and ask him about it later.

The town, consisting mostly of worn brick buildings, was bustling with crowds of people. Its three main streets ran from the waterfront up a gradual bluff that seemed to peak about a mile or so inland. The river and a trio of boat docks were adjacent to Front Street, a hard dirt-packed street that followed the river from one end of town to the other, running east to west. Three streets veered off Front Street and ran south away from the river; Main Street, Jed knew, was the one that led to his new home.

Located on the south side of Front Street, the blacksmith shop was run by an enormous man who offered potential customers a nasty look as he pounded horseshoes with a heavy hammer. Jed watched the man's face with shock as streams of sweat ran into the man's eyes, causing him to react violently with each swing. Jed could smell the sweat of the large man blended with the acidic odor of the heated metal, and it made him gag. He backed away in fear as the large man tossed shoes viciously out of the fire pit and into a large barrel of water, bringing clouds of steam into the room. Jed stared at the boiling water, then slowly looked up at the burly man. When their eyes made contact, Jed instinctively backed out of the shop and on to more pleasing sites. *I'd never want to meet up with that man in a dark alley, that's for sure; he looks like he eats bears for breakfast*, Jed thought, and quickened his pace to get away from the shop. He stopped a half-block down, and turned around quickly to see the name on the blacksmith's storefront—*Braxton's Blacksmith—got to remember that name.*

There were three mercantile shops spread from one end of Front Street to the other. The biggest was at the corner of Main and Front Streets. He watched the bustle of activity going in and out. Jed cocked his head to the side at the scene in front of him. Supplies from the wagons were going into the mercantile store but not coming out. He wondered if it was open for business or just getting set up. Four wagons were spread out, two on Main and two on Front, and all of them were stacked high with supplies. He watched men haul crates, barrels, and large sacks filled with all sorts of staples inside, before coming back to get more. One workman in particular amused Jed. Several sacks of flour had fallen off the back of the wagon, and the driver was frantically trying to scoop the spilled flour off the dirty and dusty road. *Hope that flour doesn't get sold to the town's bakery with all that dirt mixed in*, Jed thought with a chuckle.

He decided to come back later, even though his curiosity was begging him to find out more now. He wanted to see more of the town, but was on a time restriction with Sara's supper. He made it a point to look at his pocket watch frequently and to keep moving. *Don't want to get her mad at me again, that's for sure.*

Jed walked toward the livery stable connected to the wagon repair shop. He greeted the owner and found out that he owned both operations. *Henry Mare, got to remember the name. Think Mare and the four-legged animal*, Jed schooled himself before looking around further.

Henry Mare's livery and wagon shop were located on the west side of town on Washington Street; fortunately, the wind blew to the west most of the time, making the smell of horse manure a bit less offensive to those who lived in the homes on Main Street. Jed noticed four horses out front that were trying their best to drink water from the trough while shaking their heads frantically to fight off flies.

The leather-skinned owner was a husky gentleman with a long salt-and-pepper beard and rough callused hands that had seen their days of handling wood, metal, and livestock. Jed waved a friendly good-bye, and the man put out his hand to wish him well. The smell of whisky on his breath and a foul body odor made Jed's eyes water. Jed politely excused himself and moved on, thinking that the man either needed to stop drinking, take a bath, or both.

The sheriff's office was next to the large mercantile store, and the sheriff was leaning back in his chair out on the boardwalk and watching the comings and goings of the townsfolk. He and Jed nodded their heads to each other; the sheriff then tilted his hat up with a finger to get a better look at Jed as he walked by. He seemed to be in his early fifties and had no problem with his appetite, judging from the size of his belly. He had a thick black moustache, and his beady eyes bore down on Jed to the point of making him feel guilty. Jed's finger began to twitch as he picked up his pace and moved on from the sheriff's office.

There were two boardinghouses; a German family, the Waldorfs, managed one of them. It was next to the smallest mercantile store at the easternmost end of Front Street, which was nice because it was on the opposite side of town from the livery stables. The second boardinghouse was called Stevens's Diner; it was much larger and nestled next to the town's church up on Main Street. Jed was surprised to see a boardinghouse named after a diner, but once he saw it, he understood. The large building was split between living quarters and a dining area that had a large patio extending from it. It was a short walk from Front Street, but it had the benefit of being the only place in town to have a meal.

Jed noticed that most of the guests were enjoying their meals outside, which made sense with the sun out, a light breeze blowing gently, and the smell of baked bread in the air. The scent from the diner carried all the way across the street, to where Jed was leaning on an oak. The delicious aroma made him realize that it had been a while since he had eaten.

He walked across Main Street and looked inside the diner. The room was filled with tables set with silver tableware and glasses turned upside down, but was otherwise empty. Above the fireplace was a large painting of an old man standing by a sparkling lake, and Jed wondered why the old man carried such a scowl. Everything seemed to be set to host hungry guests, but it seemed strangely quiet and rarely used. *Wonder if anyone ever eats in here?* Jed thought.

He walked back out to the porch and thought of the time. *I've got some time; I'll just sit a spell,* he thought, knowing very well that he'd better not eat anything or he'd hear about it from Sara.

The server appeared to be in her midforties, and was wearing a long brown dress with a heavily stained apron. She seemed to be the one in charge judging by the way she carried herself. "Sit anywhere you like, son. I'll be right with you."

After serving an elderly man, the server returned and studied Jed inquisitively. "You're new around these parts, aren't you?"

"Yes, ma'am, just arrived with a missionary group on the riverboat *Nebraska*. I'm staying with the Higgins down the street. Their house is next to the church."

She viewed him skeptically. "You look a bit on the young side to be traveling with any missionary group. Are your folks here with you?"

"No, I'm here by myself, but the Higgins are looking after me," Jed said defensively. "My name is Jed Monroe."

"*Well, now*" the server said, more impressed as she looked at Jed, "it's very nice to meet you, *Mr. Monroe*. I'm Mrs. Stevens, but you can call me Patricia, and I'd like to be the first to welcome you to Independence, and to my boardinghouse and diner. It's not much, but in my humble opinion, it's the best. You'll always get a heap of food and always hot, and young man, when you do start to drink coffee, I'm known to serve up the best pot of coffee this side of the Missouri."

Jed looked up at her, and with a quirky smile said, "Well, Mrs. Stevens—I mean Patricia—I think I'm gonna have one of your famous cups of coffee now if I do say so myself. But I'm gonna have to pass on your heapin' hot food for now, even though it smells awful good." The two laughed as she turned to get a fresh pot of coffee for her new friend.

After filling himself up with four cups of coffee, Jed realized that his finger was twitching wildly. He thanked Patricia and calculated that he had just over an hour until supper would be ready. He decided to walk some more to work off the skittish restlessness brought on by the coffee. *Shouldn't have had so many cups; can't get this finger to stop.*

Jed bid farewell and continued back into the center of town. He found a small hotel that looked like it was about to fall down, with rotten wood sidings, a broken railing, and three broken windows in front. He noticed that the hotel was between a caretaker's office and a saloon. He looked around to get his bearings, and found that he was on the corner of Washington and Front Streets.

The saloon caught Jed's attention, with its piano music blaring, the sounds of women laughing, and the scent of tobacco filling the air. He stopped just outside the double doors and rested next to a hitching post. As he stood outside, he tried to peek inside through the crack of the swinging doors. With a mischievous grin, he wondered, *what would the folks back home say if they saw me going into this here saloon?* He chuckled and thought about going in to explore, until a drunken man suddenly came barreling through the door, knocking Jed off his post and into the dirt street.

Jed, shaken and hoping that no one had seen him, quickly brushed himself off, and without looking around, he ran as fast as he could down the street and back toward the large mercantile shop.

Still unsettled over the incident outside the saloon, he slowly crossed the street, rubbing the back of his neck to see if it was still connected. As he got closer to the mercantile store, he heard the sounds of a loud commotion coming from outside its doors. Jed approached the dozen or so men who were crowded on the small boardwalk, listening to the loud bellowing of a man standing on a tree stump.

The large man was dressed in what appeared to be a large thick bearskin coat that at first glance seemed more alive than dead. He had a full thick beard peppered with gray and shoulder-length hair that hung loosely from a skunk-colored coonskin hat with a black-and-brown tail that hung to his lower back. Jed, feeling curious, decided to join the group and listen.

"Yes, gentlemen," the burly man said, "I stand here before you, and in God's honest truth, it's exactly how I just described it. I've seen mountains taller than the sky, and birds bigger than that saloon over yonder. I've seen rivers flowing into seas of salt, and I've killed bears the size of wagons, and I stand here before you stating it all to be true, and you heard it right from this fella's mouth."

With an exchange of enthusiastic voices from his audience, he continued. "Now, I could go on and on, but to tell you the truth, I'm a bit tuckered from my last trip up the trail to Santa Fe, so it's time for me to get some early slumber, but come around here again tomorrow, and I'll have a lot more tales to tell. Just ask for me when you come around; I'm Jim Bridger."

Jed glanced up at the building, so he could remember the spot when he returned tomorrow to hear more from this Jim Bridger fella. Jed looked for a name on the building. *Wright Mercantile* was freshly painted on the side in bold slanted letters. He would definitely be back tomorrow to hear more of the big man's wild stories.

He still had a little time, so he slid his thin-framed body past the trail of men delivering supplies. The room was filled with boxes and unopened crates, and so much dust had been stirred into the air that he immediately sneezed as he made it inside. He wiped his nose on his sleeve and then curled it upward at the musty smell. *Hmm, I was right, they haven't got it opened up yet, can tell just by the smell of it,* Jed thought as he walked toward a man opening boxes of supplies.

As the older man turned around, Jed could see that he was dressed in a white shirt and dark brown pants held by black suspenders. Jed noticed that his shirt was wrinkled and in need of a good soaking, probably as a result of handling so many boxes. He had a kind face, but it was worn from what Jed figured was years of hard work. Jed instantly took a liking to the older man, thinking, *he reminds me of Papa.*

The elder man looked curiously at Jed, "Boy, do I know you?"

"No, sir, I don't think so. I just arrived here from Wheeling, Virginia on the *Nebraska*, and I'm just getting to know the town a bit."

"Well, that's a coincidence," the man replied. "We, I mean my daughter, was on that exact same boat, but she only came from St. Louis, not nearly as far as you traveled. As you can see, we're not quite open yet. I've been here in Independence for over a month trying to get this darn place opened up, but when it's just me it takes a while, if you know my meaning."

He slowly looked up and down at Jed's features, as if measuring him up for something. Jed hadn't seen the HELP WANTED sign posted in the window when he entered, and therefore didn't understand why the shopkeeper was looking at him so oddly.

"Ya here for the job?"

Jed, puzzled by the question, replied, "Uh, actually mister, I was interested in coming back to hear more stories from the gentleman who was outside your mercantile store, the one with the bearskin coat and coonskin hat."

"Oh, Jim! I'm not so sure he's a gentleman, but he seems to attract large groups anywhere he can find a soapbox to stand on. Heard he was quite the mountain man in his day. Don't know much about that, but by the way he talks, he sure seems to have seen a lot. Who knows if there's any truth in that tale of killing bears with his own hands? For me, I'm way too busy right now to be spending time standing around listening to a bunch of wild tales."

Jed snickered at the thought of the burly man and his bearskin and said, "Yea. Still though, I'd sure like to hear more tales. But I'll tell you what." Jed's tone caught the shopkeeper's attention. "I'd like to take the job. I'll come by tomorrow to help you get set up so you can open up this place, if that's alright with you?"

"Boy, you must have been reading my mind. I've been looking you over, and you'd be perfect for the job. Can't pay much to start, but once we get it going, I just know it's gonna boom. You see, it's just me and my daughter, and she's busy setting up our home, so she's had no time to help me here."

The two shook hands. Jed turned to leave, but stopped abruptly and then turned sharply. "By the way, mister, I'm Jedidiah Monroe, but you can call me Jed."

"It's nice to meet you, Jed. I'm Fester Wright, but you can just call me Fez."

Jed made his way out the door and sprinted up Main Street to the Higgins' house. It was getting dark, and he didn't want to upset Sara, especially since the memory of losing her crate of china was still lingering.

I've got a feeling they'll be surprised when I tell them that I already landed a job, Jed thought, already forgetting the main purpose of his trip west.

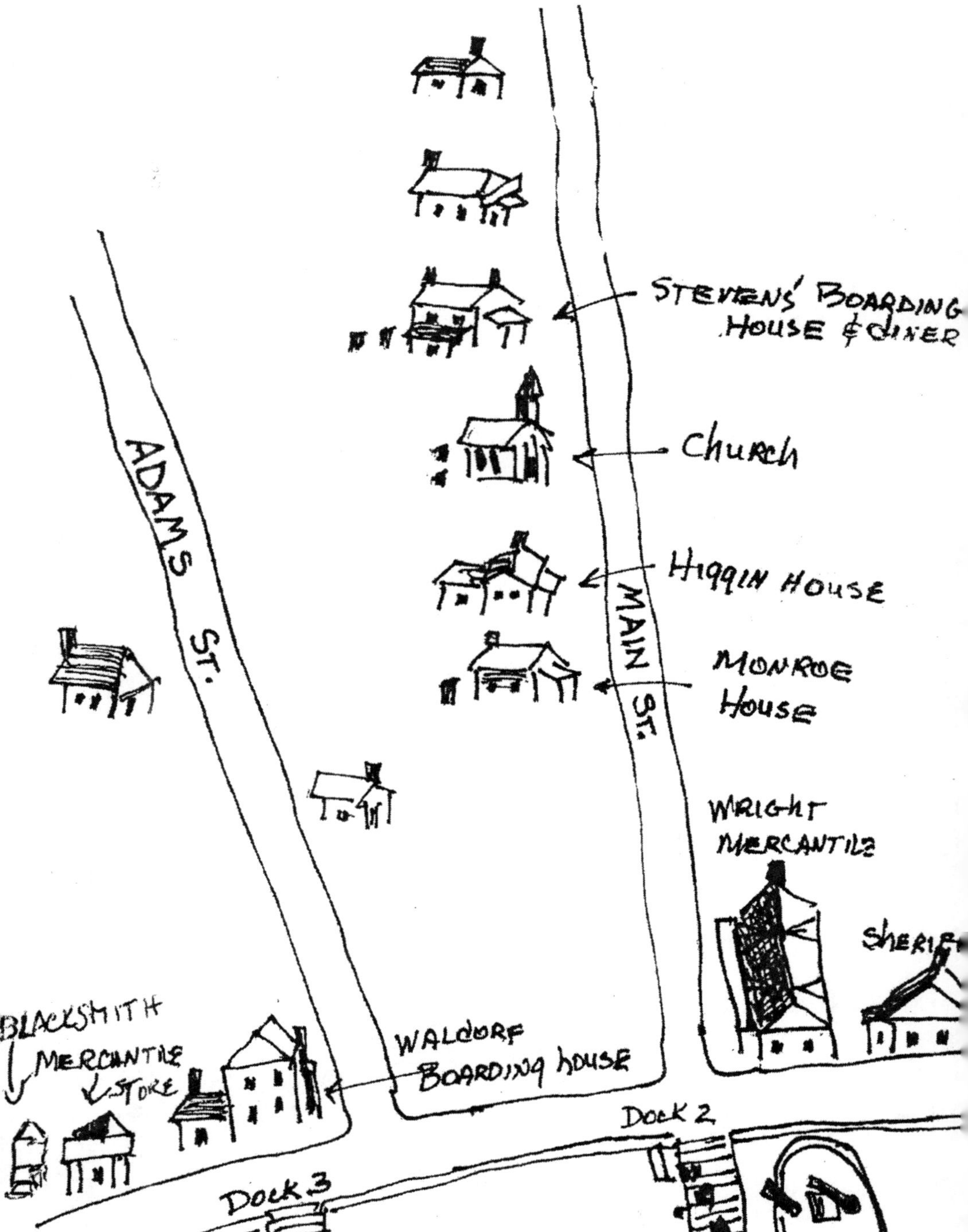

STEVENS' BOARDING HOUSE & DINER
Church
HIGGIN HOUSE
MONROE HOUSE
ADAMS ST.
MAIN ST.
WRIGHT MERCANTILE
SHERIFF
BLACKSMITH
MERCANTILE STORE
WALDORF BOARDING HOUSE
Dock 2
Dock 3

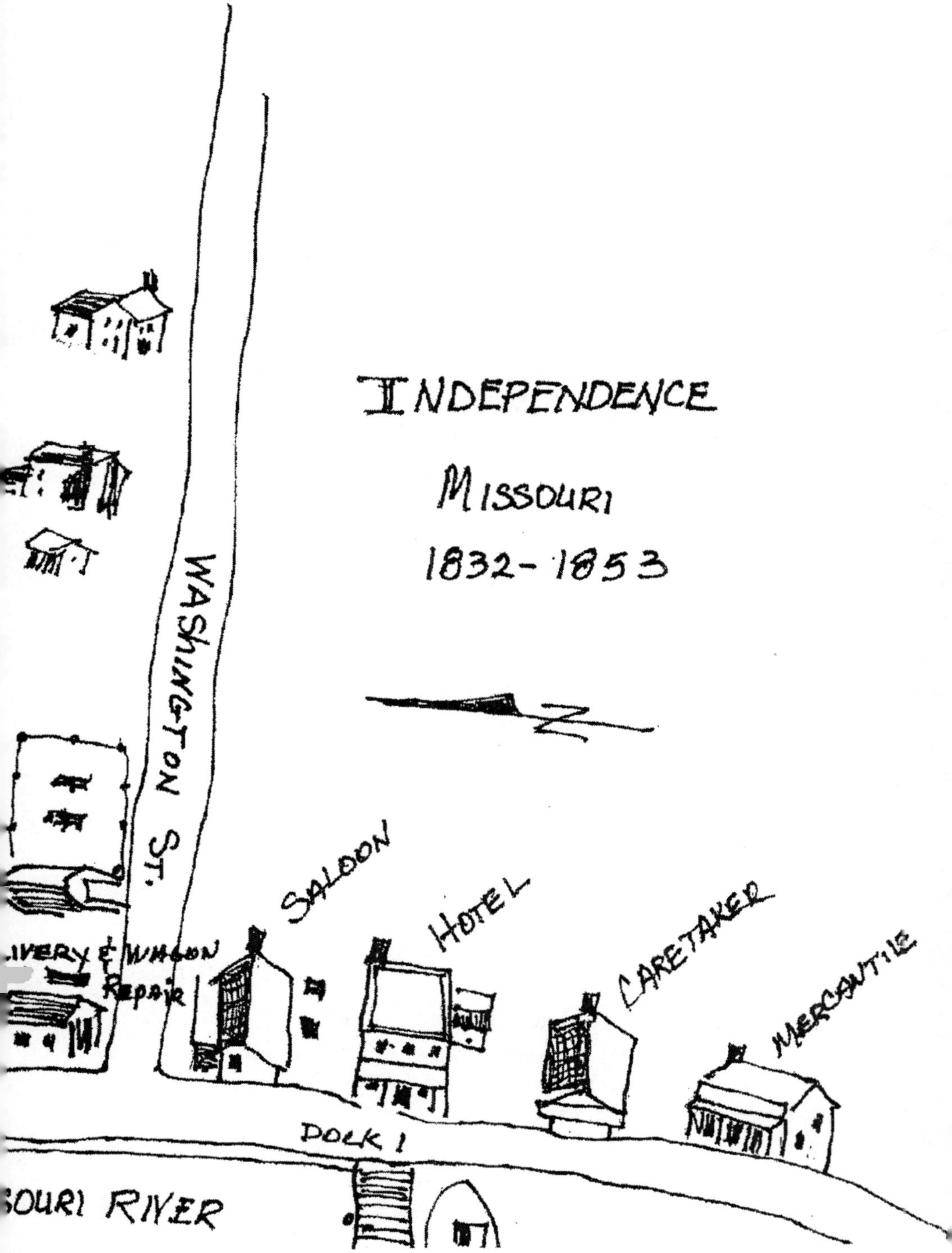
INDEPENDENCE
MISSOURI
1832-1853
N
WASHINGTON ST.
SALOON
HOTEL
CARETAKER
MERCANTILE
IVERY & WAGON Repair
DOCK 1
SOURI RIVER

Chapter Six

Restless Youth

1831

It was awkward when Jed brought up the subject of his new job during supper, and although Sara was pleased that he hadn't been late, she became very quiet upon hearing his news. The Higgins were concerned that Jed would spend all his time at the Mercantile and forget his obligation to the church. In turn, he argued that he could allocate his time between both places. He was unable to sway them to his point of view or assuage their disappointment, however, and felt that he'd let them down. *I know I can do both*, he told himself.

He also had to remind himself that he was out West to fulfill his father's wishes in addition to seeking out adventure. He had agreed to assist Pastor Higgin with the church and the Missionary Society's work, but a kind of restlessness had begun inside him, and he wasn't quite sure what to make of it. The thought of venturing beyond Independence was tugging hard and making him restless. He'd felt it back in Wheeling, but now that he'd made it this far, the pull was stronger than ever. *I don't know what to do*, Jed thought. *I'll ask Pastor Higgin about it after supper—that is, if he'll talk to me about it*—Jed decided, still feeling guilty about his job at the Mercantile.

* * * * *

Several weeks passed, and Jed's job at the Mercantile turned out to be a blessing in disguise—Jed helped Fez get his shop open and was able to set up a mercantile account for the church. He also retrieved a few supplies that the Higgins needed in order to open the church. Sara and the Pastor became comfortable with Jed working there part-time, their approval helped along considerably by how convenient it was to fill their supply needs with him there. "I guess we have our own in-house courier now that he's employed there," Sara said to her husband at supper one evening. Jed was relieved by the tone of her voice and eager to help her with any list she needed to have filled.

Meanwhile, Jed still hadn't found the nerve to bring up the subject of his restlessness with Pastor Higgin. The church had been set up, and the Missionary Society was ready to make its first visit to the Osage and Kansa Indians. Jed helped load the wagons with the extra Bibles needed to open up conversations with local tribes. *So many Bibles,* he thought. *There's really that many Injuns out here?* He had an urge to go with the missionaries to see for himself, but Sara had asked him to stay behind and fill her supply order at the Mercantile.

Jed watched as the wagon of Bibles headed up Main Street before disappearing out of town. He put Sara's list in his pocket and headed down to Wright's. While daydreaming of wild Indians holding Bibles he started to cross Main Street, but suddenly found himself caught off guard by a pounding of hoofs that deafened his ears and made his heart violently skip a beat.

He turned away hastily, but not before a man on horseback whisked by him, so close that Jed could have reached out and grabbed the horse's tail. Jed tried to get a look at the man's face, but all he could see were his riding flaps, a dark leather coat, and a hat tied to his neck that flapped in the wind and against his back.

Jed turned back toward Main Street in time to see a caravan of wagons approaching. The first wagon was empty and being pulled by a bright white mare with a long full mane that billowed around her neck in the breeze. Jed was impressed by how it strutted tall and straight as if it were trying to impress the folks in town. The driver was seated and held tightly to the reins, clucking his teeth loudly to keep the horse trotting.

The next four wagons were enclosed in dirty white canvases that were draped over metal arches. Jed could see household goods stacked in each one as it passed. He saw dressers, mirrors, and in one wagon he thought he had actually seen a full-size piano. He shook his head in wonder as the final three wagons began to pass. They too had canvases, but to Jed's amazement, these wagons were filled with people.

He dashed down to the Mercantile to see what this was all about. He had to pick up supplies for Sara, but first wanted to find out more about the wagon train and where in the world it was headed.

He ran through the open front doors of the Mercantile, keeping a keen eye on the activity around him. Excited over the wagon train, but trying not to make a scene, Jed went through the motions of filling

Sara's list. He noticed an elderly man at the counter and heard him discussing the extremely large supply order for the wagon train that Jed had just seen. Jed's eyes were glued to the man as he described the order. Jed paid little attention to the girl behind the counter, figuring that Fez had asked a neighbor girl to help him out for the day. As he listened to the details of the order, Jed knew that because of its size, Fez was going to need his help.

Jed put Sara's list back in his pocket and walked to the counter. "Good day, sir, I'm Jed Monroe, and I couldn't help but overhear the size of your supply order. I'd be more than happy to help gather all the supplies and load them into your wagons for you. It looks like you've got your hands full."

"Well, boy, uh, well sure, that'll be most helpful, and I can see from her glances that this pretty young lady would appreciate your help as well." The man put out his hand to Jed and introduced himself as Mr. William Becknew.

While Jed was holding his hand out, his eyes moved from Becknew to the girl behind the counter—immediately, his eyes bulged wide in disbelief. "Uh . . . oh uh . . . oh yes, it's very nice to meet you," he stammered as he struggled to regain his composure.

Jed continued to stare at the girl behind the counter. *It's her! I can't believe it's her!*

Dizziness consumed him, and his face flushed. He tried in vain to regain his sanity so that he could help with the wagon master's needs. He could feel his throat becoming dry, his stomach knotting, and his finger twitching madly.

Once all the supplies were loaded into the Becknew wagons, though Jed was anxious to get back inside to find out more about the mysterious girl, he took time to ask Becknew a question he had been harboring. "Just out of curiosity, sir, where are you-all headed with all these supplies, anyway?"

Becknew pondered the question for a moment, grinning at Jed's intense curiosity. "Oh, it's just another trip down the Santa Fe—why, you want to join us?"

Jed felt temptation tugging hard. "Maybe I'll hitch a ride with you someday, sir, but right now I've got to get back inside." Wild adventures, roaming buffalo, and herds of cattle flashed in front of him as he tried to clear his mind. He slowly made his way back inside to see if he could spot that . . . that girl again. *Could it really be her?*

Jed walked directly over to Fez and inquired about the identity of the new helper behind the counter.

"Your daughter?" Jed asked in disbelief. "Fez, I saw her getting onto the *Nebraska* at St. Louis, and then I never saw her again because of the storm. *His daughter . . . his daughter was right here under my nose this whole time.* Jed sighed and shook his head in wonder.

"I . . . I guess I've been so busy helping you and Pastor Higgin that I never even realized there was a girl around," Jed admitted.

"Well, she wasn't really around, Jed," Fez corrected. "Remember, she's been at my home getting it settled most of the time. I needed her there to put, you know, her 'womanly touch' into it, since I have no clue how to do it.

"I see. So today was the first time she's been here in the Mercantile, and I'm not crazy for not noticing her before, right?" Jed replied.

"No, she's been here several times, just not the same times as you, that's all. But what's the big deal about it all anyway? It's just my daughter, ya know?"

Jed tried to compose himself and control his young infatuation with the daughter of the man who had employed him for several weeks. *How do I tell him that I think I fell in love with his daughter the day I first saw her?* "Well, uh, could you tell me her name? You know, so I can properly introduce myself the next time she comes in?"

"Her name is Abigail, Jed," Fez said, still not understanding what the fuss was all about.

Jed excused himself for a much-needed walk and to clear his head. He was confused about his restlessness. He had a relentless drive to go West, but knew he was supposed to be learning how to be a Pastor like his father. If that wasn't enough to have swirling around his mind, he also had found the girl he thought was gone for good. *Is this a sign from God? Is God telling me to settle here, raise a family, and follow in my father's footsteps? Or am I still supposed to sow my wild oats before He has me do all that?*

* * * * *

"I know, I know what my father wanted of me!" Jed was trying not to be argumentative. "But right now, I look west from here and see opportunities that will slip from my fingertips unless I act quickly."

He and Pastor Higgin sat outside the church, which overlooked the street and passing wagons heading out on the trail going west. It was usually a comfortable spot for him to sit and talk with his mentor. But this time, he wasn't sure exactly what was bothering him, which was making the conversation awkward and confrontational. Though Jed was growing up, he was indeed puzzled at this particular juncture.

"What about your mother, Jed?" Pastor Higgin asked. "What about your promise to her—will you make good on that promise?"

"Yes, I will, but I just know that if they saw what we're seeing, they'd tell me to go and discover all that I can out in the world, and they'd give me their blessings, too."

Pastor Higgin gave Jed a skeptical look, knowing that the younger man's argument was a stretch at best. He was also afraid, because he could see that Jed was beginning to believe that what he was saying was true.

The two found themselves at odds, one eager to travel but troubled by a promise from son to father, the other concerned about an oath he had made to keep another man's son safe.

"Okay, how about this?" the Pastor said. "Stay here for a few years—help me out at the church and work for Mr. Wright down at the Mercantile. You'll learn more about what it takes to travel west from him and from others heading that way. And that would give me more time to show you what I do. Then after that, I think you'll have a better understanding of what you really want, and what God wants for you as well."

Jed stared straight ahead. He heard the Pastor's words, but his mind had drifted once again. He imagined himself with Jim Bridger in wild country, catching wild cougars, skinning them, and trading with Kansa Indians. The idea of everything West, territory after territory, was overwhelming. In his mind, West is where he should go, had to go. But he realized, reluctantly, that the Pastor was right.

"Pastor Higgin . . . ," Jed started hesitantly, "I think you can tell that I've got an awful itch to get on yonder trail—"

Before Jed could continue, he was drowned out by the sound of pounding hoofs, and paused as a trio of riders went by. He cleared his throat. When he looked at Pastor Higgin again, he could see the look of disappointment and disapproval in his eyes.

"But as much as I'm wantin' to see all that I've been hearing about out West, I understand what you are saying, and what matters most to me is making sure that whatever I do, I don't disappoint you and Sara. That's why I know that I can only go out West with your full blessing. That's why I'm going to stick it out here a bit longer."

Pastor Higgin beamed with paternal pride upon hearing his young student's decision. But there was one more matter that he wanted to address.

"And what of your parents?" Pastor Higgin added. "Do you ever think of them anymore? Have you written them, at least?"

"Oh, uh, of course I do . . . it's just that I've been so busy and occupied with the church and the Mercantile and all. I haven't had the time to send either of them a letter," Jed responded.

"How many letters has your mother sent you so far, Jed?" Pastor Higgin asked with a tone of disappointment.

"I don't know. I guess, probably t . . . ten," Jed reluctantly answered. "The thing is, she's never scolded me about not writing or anything, Pastor. It's like she's alright with the way it's all turning out, you know?"

Jed tried to dart around the Pastor's cool stare, but knew he'd stretched the truth about his mother's letters. He felt the awkward silence once again, and not even the sounds from Sara's kitchen broke through the icy feeling in the air. He knew he'd broken his promise to his mother, and the way that Pastor Higgin just sat there made him feel even worse.

The dark night was now upon them, and the crisp air buzzed with the sounds of crickets and lit up from the playful flickering of fireflies. Sensing that there would be no further discussion until he acknowledged what the Pastor had said by doing something about it, Jed stood slowly, excusing himself and acknowledging a gentle nod from the Pastor, and asked if they could talk again in the morning. They bid each other a good-night, and then Jed made his way to his room . . . to retrieve his paper and quill.

Dearest Momma,

I know it's been a while since I've sent you a letter, but you wouldn't believe all that I've seen so far. While on the Nebraska, we journeyed up and over three separate rivers, and now have landed here in Independence. Momma, it's a great town here with so much going on, with all the wagons and people planning their trips West and all. The excitement is in the air,

Momma, and the folks traveling West are so passionate about their trips, I just feel like jumping on with them!

Hope Papa is doing well, and tell him I'm trying hard to make him proud. Pastor Higgin said I am learning the church ways real nicely, and he thinks I too will have my own church one day. I know I promised to take over Papa's church when I return, and I'm getting great schooling here to be able to do just that. I also know that I promised to write you every day, and I'm so very sorry to disappoint you by not doing so, but just so you know, I'm fine and healthy and have met so many wonderful people. You should meet this mountain man who says he fights and kills bears, cougars, and snakes, and then trades them for goods from the Indians. Momma, do you still have my rose? I think of you and Papa all the time, and I know you both would be very proud of me. I don't know when I'll be able to write again 'cause I'm so busy and all, but I just wanted you to know that I love you.

Regards,

Jedidiah

P.S. And Momma, I met a real nice girl, too! I'll tell you all about her next time I write.

He set the quill aside and then stared blankly into the darkness of the night through his curtain-draped window. He scrunched up his nose, shook his head slowly, and thought, *They're gonna hate what I wrote. It's probably better they don't hear anything from me than reading a bunch of rambling that will just cause them to worry. Sure don't want them to fret over me . . . but I did promise to write . . . every day, too.*

Jed sniffed hard and put his chin against his chest, disgusted with his failure. *Alright, get a hold of yourself! I'm gonna write when it's time to write, when I have something to write about. Plus, why fret?—they aren't going anywhere.*

He paused and chuckled when he realized that he was thinking out loud to a room empty except for a tiny brown stuffed bear that Sara had put in the corner. He became homesick as he thought of the way Sara sometimes treated him like a little boy. Though he would never admit it, he actually enjoyed that. He thought hard about his next move. He rested his head on the palms of his hands while staring at the blazing fire above the rock hearth.

Momma . . . Papa . . . I am gonna make you proud, you'll see.

He sat motionless, his hand on the finished letter; time seemed to stand still. The fire that had been blazing earlier had now died down to just golden-yellow and orange coals. Outside, a pack of coyotes howled in the distance to let the world know of its latest catch. The smell of Sara's pot roast still lingered in the house hours after they had finished supper. He felt alone. It was just he and his letter staring back at him under the candlelight. His finger twitched over the word: *Momma.*

He tightened up his fist. He walked over to the fireplace. With one last thought of home, he unrolled his fingers with a single smooth motion. The letter that had been crumpled inside his fist floated onto the coals.

He shook his head up and down with confidence, telling himself he was doing the right thing and promising that he would write home again, but only when he had made something of himself. *Gotta remember,* he reassured himself, *I have plenty of time . . . they're not going anywhere.*

Chapter Seven

Courtship on the Missouri
1836–1837

"Sounds like another riverboat docking, Jed," Fez hollered from deep in the back room of the Mercantile. "I'm hearing whistles or horns or something down there, and if it is another boat, we're gonna be getting some folks in here right quick. Peek your head out and see if I'm a-right, will ya?"

Each time a new riverboat came into town or a wagon train left, Jed felt the tug to sow his wild oats. Jed thoroughly enjoyed helping Fez at the Mercantile, and also did his best to spend time with Pastor Higgin at the church.

He had to be honest with himself; the extra time spent in Independence had allowed him the luxury of learning more about blazing trails, but more importantly had permitted him more time to get to know Abigail.

The two had been formally introduced soon after Jed found out that his "lost girl" from the *Nebraska* was in fact Fez's daughter. She kept herself busy by helping out her father at the Mercantile and maintaining the household they shared. Jed, on the other hand, shyly stole glances at her more times than he would admit.

Casual conversations about the mercantile business, events in town, or stories about Western travelers had been the extent of their relationship. Jed tried his best to show that he was interested in her, but at his age he had little experience when it came to courting young ladies.

Abigail's interest had been even subtler. Though she had feelings for Jed, she thought it unladylike to make them known. She went about her business as if Jed meant very little to her, while at the same time she would tease him with her own style of flirting.

Fez saw right through the masquerade and knew that the chemistry between the two could not be denied. For months, Fez had repeatedly nudged Jed to become more assertive, but still Jed failed to act.

One day while the three of them were in the back room of the Mercantile, with dust in the air and the smell of moldy floor boards, Jed and Abigail were at it again, teasing each other while stocking inventory, but as far as Fez was concerned, they were getting nowhere fast.

Fez had finally had it. "Okay, you two, enough is enough!" he laughed and then grinned a sly smile. "We're done playing this cat-and-mouse game. It's about time you two broke the ice and got on with it."

Jed and Abigail stopped in their tracks and jerked their heads toward Fez. They looked at each other with "What, us?" expressions, then back to Fez. He found it funny that their unconvincing expressions of feigned confusion matched exactly as they stared with their mouths gaped open but not uttering a word. As if on cue, their faces turned crimson and they bashfully slumped their heads in silence. In the now-hushed room, a dropped pin would have sounded like a brick as it hit the floor. The faint sound of a dog barking in the distance could be heard as Fez cleared his throat deeply before boring his eyes into the two procrastinators. Still, he said nothing, waiting instead for Jed and Abigail to follow through with the initiative he believed was lacking.

After what felt like forever, Abigail, blushed face and all, turned to her father. "Papa, I don't know *what* you're *talking* about—"

Fez put his palm up. "Now, Daughter, don't go getting all smart with me. I can see what's going on around here, and it's about time you two quit beating around the bush and start getting to know each other better. You both want that, right?"

The young couple turned to each other shyly, and Jed was the first to speak. "He's . . . ah . . . he's right, you know?" Abigail looked at him, her face flushed red, but her eyes filled with anticipation as she hoped he would say more. "I've been thinking of you ever since the day I first saw you. I just . . . I just couldn't find the nerve to take the first step . . . I mean . . . I mean you're so . . . you're so beautiful, and I—"

"Yep, she's the spittin' image of her Momma, if I do say so myself," Fez interrupted cheerfully. "She wouldn't admit to any resemblance to her papa even if you tried to convince her, but she and my Mary, rest her soul, are each one of a kind, Jed."

"Papa!" Abigail jerked her attention to her father. "I'm sure Jedidiah has no interest in our family lineage or your idea of similarities."

"Actually," Jed cut in, "I think . . . I mean, I've always thought . . . I mean I . . . uh . . . ever since I saw you on the riverboat, I've wanted to get to know you better, and thanks to your father here, maybe . . . I mean if you want to . . . we could kind of . . . you know . . . start to—"

"Oh come on, Jed, just say it!" Fez bellowed out while enjoying a good laugh. "You want to get to know my daughter better! Now just say it, 'cause I know my daughter well enough to know that she's feelin' the same way!"

"Papa!" Abigail stammered, this time her face fiercely red with embarrassment.

Seeing that he'd done all that was needed, Fez decided it was time to leave the two lovebirds alone to work out their feelings for themselves. He turned and with a teasing twinkle in his eyes said, "I think I'm gonna to see what sort of riverboats are docked out there, and maybe mosey around by the riverside for a spell, and . . . uh . . . are you two kids going to be all right until I get back?"

"Papa—go!" Abigail yelled with a laugh.

Fez's deep belting laughter could be heard all the way to the docks after he left Jed and Abigail alone to begin what he hoped would become something special.

* * * * *

During the six months that followed, Jed spent more time at the Mercantile than at the church, and most of the townsfolk began to talk in their inner circles; it was easy to deduce why.

The courtship had finally started and the two were inseparable, but it wasn't until a fateful day near the end of 1836 that their bond gained new meaning and a lasting foundation.

Jed was walking back to the Higgins' home from Abigail's house. He had a glow about him despite the grueling wind and pounding rain. He'd just given Abigail a necklace for Christmas, and she had hugged him tighter than he'd ever remembered. His mind was on her as he walked slowly home until—

The sound of earth crushing and crashing broke him from his solitude, and he jerked around violently. Barely able to see through the pelting rain, he thought he could make out a small group of people rushing toward the riverbank. Somebody yelled, "Help!" He sprinted. He arrived at the riverbank with little time left to act.

"Jed! Jed! Get the line—grab the line, Jed!" It was the eldest Waldorf yelling—he couldn't see him through the rain, but he saw the line and instinctively knew what to do.

The stranded father and his children were trapped on a wooden platform that had broken from the ramp. The storm was fierce, with a blasting wind and cold rain that had turned to marble-sized hail that whipped sideways into their faces. The river had risen twenty feet and was flooding Front Street. Fez and the other shopkeepers had woken from their slumbers and were frantically trying to secure their properties, unaware of the accident at the dock.

The stranded family had been rushing up the ramp and attempting to get to solid land when the lightning struck. The ramp was like a piece of cedar snapped in half, and its entire length had been shredded. The father was desperately hanging on to his children while clinging to a splintered piece of wood from the ramp, and the raging river was rolling mercilessly over the top of them.

The mother, who'd made it safely to Front Street, was frantically screaming, but barely audible given the pounding thunder. Jed raced down the dock, threw the father a line, and tried his best to secure it to the landing. The dock was slick from the rain, and Jed slipped, hit his head, and had to let go of the rope. For a few nerve-rattling moments, the broken piece of wood bobbled and toppled amongst the waves of the tortuous river as the rope continued to slither from Jed's hands. He was the only one on the landing, and the only one who could save them. Despite being barely able to see through the blood that had welled in his eyes, and hampered by a harsh pounding in his head, Jed finally managed to grab the line and secure it to the landing, after which he immediately fell unconscious, half on the landing and half in the river.

* * * * *

Jed woke with no recollection of time or his surroundings, and was unaware that the Waldorfs were safe and recovering at the church. He could feel the cold cloth on his forehead and the warmth of the wool blanket, but didn't know who was comforting him. He tried to focus, but everything was a blur. The image in front of him grew increasingly clearer as he began to see Abigail's beautiful blue eyes—filled with concern. He lay still, trying to comprehend exactly what had happened, while the touch of Abigail's hand on his face brought back memories of the past few years. He began to remember bits and pieces of recent events, but more importantly, he began to remember the kindness of the woman who was displaying so much love for him. There was a sharp pain in his head. Jed closed his eyes and his mind drifted into the blackness once again.

"Jed . . . Jed, can you hear me? It's me . . . it's Abigail . . . it's Abigail, Jed . . . please . . . open up your eyes."

"Let him rest, dear," Fez gently said, softly touching his daughter's hand. "He'll be fine, he just needs some rest."

Fez and Abigail quietly closed the door and moved into the living room, where the fire was warming up nicely. Abigail, exhausted and scared, sat down and began to cry.

Fez, with the sheriff's help, had carried Jed to their home. Pastor Higgin and Sara were busy setting up the church as a haven for displaced folks on Front Street. Sara knew that Jed was in good hands at the Wrights' home.

"Now, now, Sugar, don't you fret none, he's a strong young man and he'll pull through just fine, plus . . . he has you to wake up to!" Fez consoled his daughter, keeping his hand tightly around hers.

"Papa . . . ," she attempted through a choked heart, as she still feared the worst. "Papa, he has to be all right, I . . . I need him to be all right . . . I need to tell him . . . I need to tell him that I love him, Papa." She turned to Fez. "I love him more than anything in the world, Papa, and I need him to be all right!"

Fez looked at his daughter with a warm heart, and thoughts of his Mary flashed in his mind. What he would give to be able to say those words to Mary again.

Yellow fever had taken his wife back in 1829, and that's when he decided to pack up, move out West, and try as best he could to begin a new life with Abigail. It'd only been the two of them for the past seven years, but he now looked at his daughter and saw his beautiful wife, remembered how they had felt about each other, and gained a sense of her presence with them that day.

"Yes, sweetheart, I know exactly what you're going through. Trust me—you'll have all the time in the world to tell him just that."

Fez took his hand from Abigail's, stood, and walked over to his favorite chair. He picked up the picture of his wife, sat down, and with his fingers gently caressing the edges of the glass frame, whispered, "I sure do miss you."

After a short pause, he looked at Abigail, her eyes glued to the fire. He looked back into the eyes of the woman in the picture and whispered, "She'll be just fine, Mary, I promise," and he slowly placed the frame back on the table and wiped the tears from his eyes.

* * * * *

Six months passed, and even with Jed fully recovered from his concussion, the town still talked of that eventful night. He had received a letter of commendation from the mayor of Independence, and one of tremendous thanks from Mr. Waldorf. Each of these Sara had set in a frame and hung in his room.

He had just turned twenty-one, and a restless calling from the Western trails nudged him daily. He knew now that it wasn't so much the need to convince Pastor Higgin to let him leave as it was a matter of talking Abigail into it.

Fez had sensed Jed's restlessness for some time. On a clear and still afternoon, he decided it was time to have a good talk with the man he expected to be his son-in-law someday. He asked Jed to help him with some roof repairs; he couldn't think of a better spot for an uninterrupted conversation.

They hauled their tools up a rickety wooden ladder and were sitting atop the peak of the rooftop when Fez looked up over his half-rimmed glasses and said, "You've been thinking about an awful lot lately, Son. If it helps any, you can always take over the Mercantile once you two get married. That is, if'n that's what you want."

"I don't know, Fez. I know I want to settle down and all, but there's still so much I want to do and see—I just don't know if I can do both."

Fez laid his hammer down and found a spot on the cusp of the roof on which to sit, "You know, Jed, I was a lot like you in many ways when I was your age. I had an itchin' to wander, too. And when I met Abigail's mother, I had a hard time hiding it from her. But to tell ya the truth, she knew it was in me without me even talking about it. So, just give Abigail the chance to show you that she sees it in you, too."

"Yea, I know. I really do need to talk to her about it. I'm just hoping that she understands and all."

"Trust me, Son" Fez said. "She already sees it, and she's probably already come to grips with it. Ya see, Jed, she loves you and your adventurous spirit. It's all a part of you, and she knows that just as her mother knew it about me."

"Did you ever venture off, or did you stay put?"

"Both. I got it out of my system, and then I got myself married and settled down," Fez answered with a smile of remembrance. "But you've got to talk to her, Son."

The roof work finished, Jed decided to ask Pastor Higgin if he could borrow his buggy. The next day, Jed and Abigail found themselves seated in the buggy on a dirt road leading out of town. Jed couldn't have asked for a better day. The temperature was mild, though Abigail had brought along a light shawl in case it got chilly later on. The wildflowers were blooming, and there was a fresh scent of wild garlic in the air. After passing the farm owned by Herman and Rachael Simpson, they turned right toward the river. The Simpsons were loyal worshipers at Pastor Higgin's church, and Rachael sang in the choir.

The spot Jed had picked out was only a few short miles away, but would take them away from the sights and sounds of the town. Jed needed to talk with Abigail away from the womenfolk in town staring at them and whispering. They came to a stop and Jed looked around—he wanted the setting to be just right for what he needed to say.

"Whoa, there!" Jed eased the mare and brought the buggy to a stop, scattering a flock of pheasants. They sat in momentary silence and listened to the soft buzzes of honeybees hovering above the tree on the opposite side of the road. Abigail could smell the sweet scent coming from the jasmine nearby, and it reminded her of her childhood.

"You should go already," Abigail said, breaking the silence. "I mean, if that's what you really need to do, Jed." She shifted in her seat deliberately. "I don't want us to build a life together if you're always going to want to wander off to find a different dream. I want to be that dream of yours, but I won't be until you are through with your itch to travel."

Abigail fought off the tears that were welling up in her eyes and tried to swallow down the lump in her throat, but was confident that she was making the right decision in letting him go. She knew that in order to keep him, she would need to release him.

"We could get married right when I get back, you know?" Jed said, trying to relieve his guilt.

"Sure we could Jed, but . . . Jed . . . you haven't even asked me yet."

He pondered this fact for a moment and then with a soft chuckle replied, "I guess I might need to remedy that someday, huh?" Her friendly shove in response almost knocked him off the seat of the buggy, causing the horse to kick up her legs until Jed quickly managed to grab the reins.

They continued talking, enjoying their time together, and in some ways, making plans. The picnic was perfect. They had found a shady spot along the river, under an oak that was gnarled and twisted from years of growth. Abigail had prepared slices of beef and bread, corn, and to Jed's surprise had even brought cherry pie. After the meal, they relaxed on the blanket, ignoring the snorts and chewing noises coming from the mare.

Jed was lying on his back, chewing on a long weed while looking up into the branches of the shady oak. The feel of Abigail lying next to him made him feel secure and complete. The last thing he wanted to do was break her heart. "I would only be gone a year or so, you know?" The sound of wild beetles clicking in the tall wild grass and the breeze softly rustling the leaves of the oak were all that was heard until he said, "I've got to find out what's out there, Abigail." She still made no sound. "I promise I'll be back."

He remembered that he'd made that very same promise to his mother back in 1831. *Yea, and how'd you come through on that one, Jed?* A bright purple-and-yellow butterfly drifted just above their heads. They followed its pattern as it flitted around and around with no apparent path or purpose.

The silence was broken when Abigail spoke just above a whisper. "I'll be right here whenever you come back, Jedidiah Monroe." They watched as the butterfly flew upward and out of sight. A tear fell from Abigail's cheek.

* * * * *

Another few months went by with little talk of Jed's possible travel and even less talk of wedding plans. Abigail noticed that Jim Bridger was back in town, and a knot developed in her stomach. She knew that the subject would be coming up sooner than she'd hoped, and it wasn't going to be about a wedding.

"Jed, this here is a good pal of mine who I met on my last trek down to Santa Fe," Bridger yelled out. "His name is John C. Fremont, and he's setting up our next wagon train going West.

Bridger and Fremont first met on the Santa Fe Trail a few years before when they traveled with William Becknew on one of his many Western expeditions from Independence to Santa Fe, Mexico. The two had become good friends, and now traveled together frequently, mainly on the Santa Fe Trail. Of late, the two had been discussing the chances of going northwest someday, instead of southwest as they usually did.

"When are the two of you heading out again?" Jed asked.

"Well, we usually need a couple weeks to get our supplies in order, rest our hinds a bit, and put more in our belly other than the beans and jerky from the wagon train," Fremont explained. "No disrespect, Jim, but your cook has a ways to go in his line of work, in my opinion. A nice steak and fixings at the Stevens's Diner is what I'm talking about, and after that, a nice bath. Give me that kind of living for a couple of weeks, and I'll be good as new and ready to tackle the trail again—and of course, your cook as well." The three laughed as they walked up Main Street toward the diner for a much-needed meal.

"So, what'd you have in mind, Jed?" asked Fremont as they sat down, enjoying the aroma of freshly baked apple pie as it filled the air. "How far south did you want to go? All the way to Santa Fe, or did you want to go with another expedition toward Oregon Country? That trail likely won't be truly open until a few years from now, but it's still accessible, just a bit more rugged and less tamed than the Santa Fe."

"Actually, I've heard so much about the Santa Fe that I feel like I already know it. I'd kind of like to see what's up Oregon way," Jed replied, as plates of steak, potatoes, and corn bread were placed in front of them.

"Well listen, Jed, I think I've got a great idea, and Jim, see if you agree," Fremont added as he began to cut up his steak. "We're getting fit for a shorter trip up to Fort Laramie in a few weeks, and that would give you a little taste of what we do. It's not as far as the trip to the Oregon Country and back, but it'll give you an idea. Plus, the Fort Laramie trip would take less time and you'd be back here before Christmas."

With a full mouth and barely able to speak, Bridger added, "And I do reckon that would please your little lady as well; you know what I mean?" He resumed engulfing his half-pound steak as he belted out a hefty chuckle.

"Alright boys, where do I sign up?" Jed asked, unable to hide his excitement.

"Whoa there, young man," Bridger interjected, wiping his beard with a cloth napkin. "We don't just rush into these trips, son. First, you'll need to talk it over with your little woman. If it's one thing that's always kept me out of trouble, it's insisting that all the men on my expeditions get the go-ahead from the womenfolk they're leavin' behind. It just makes leavin', and better yet comin' back home, a whole lot better for all of us, if you know what I mean?"

"Yea, well, Abigail and I already talked about this a ways back," Jed said. "She's even insisting that I go, says I need to get it out of my system or something like that."

"Be careful with that one," Fremont warned, soaking up the rest of his steak juice with corn bread. "Trailblazing can crawl into your hide to the point that you find yourself always wanting more. So be careful when you tell her it's just this one trip, 'cause if you're like me, it won't be."

When Jed met Abigail the next day, the wind was light and coming off the river, and carried with it the sweet scent of honeysuckle from plants nestled along the riverbank. As they strolled, not far from the riverboat landing, they could smell wild sassafras in the air.

"You do know that I love you, don't you?" asked Jed anxiously, holding hands with Abigail as they strolled along the river. "And this trip will only be for four months, not the year I told you before. Plus, when I come back, we can go ahead and get ourselves married and all." *You got to ask her first, Jed,* he scolded himself.

The light from the setting sun was in front of them, and the glare reflecting off the river made it hard to see. Jed stopped and turned to Abigail, holding her close. "You know you'll be with me the whole time, don't you?" He took her right hand and placed it on his heart. "You'll be right here day and night, and when I return we can be together again forever." He pulled her lowered head up to face him as tears flowed down her cheeks.

"Why the tears?" he asked softly, feeling a twinge of guilt.

"They're not tears; it's just the glare from the sun off the river making my eyes water." She put her head back on his chest. "Don't ever pull me away from this heart of yours, you hear me, Jedidiah Monroe?" They held each other, and neither one wanted to let go.

* * * * *

"When's the date?" asked Fez, as he was sitting at his kitchen table the following morning and watching Abigail prepare breakfast.

"He plans on leaving in two weeks."

"No, not that date, when's the date of your wedding, silly?" Fez grinned as he leaned back in his chair.

"Papa, he hasn't even asked me yet, how can I give you a date?" Abigail answered angrily.

The large wrought iron kettle dropped to the floor, and water splashed all over the wooden floorboard. Abigail dropped to her knees to clean up the mess, crying as she crawled around on the wet floor. Fez rushed out of his chair, gently pulled her back up by an elbow, and held her in his paternal arms.

"I just hope, Papa, that when he does return, he'll still want me, still love me, still . . . "

"He'd be crazy not to, Sugar," Fez whispered angrily.

"I'm trying to be strong, Papa, I'm really trying." Her words were barely audible above her crying.

The mood was still glum the following day, along with the weather. It had turned icy cold—dark clouds loomed above, sustaining the darkness felt inside the Mercantile. Fez was in the storage room taking inventory of canned goods. Jed was restocking wares on the opposite side of the Mercantile, his thoughts shifting from Abigail to his upcoming trip and back again. Fez looked out from the back room and watched the younger man intently. He could see by Jed's expressions that the young man needed someone to talk with. Putting his inventory folder aside, Fez swallowed his anger and walked down the aisle. He propped himself against a pickle barrel.

Jed turned and tilted his head warily. "What gives, Fez?"

"You know, I was just thinking about a time way back. I remember how awkward I felt when I first asked Abigail's mother to be my wife," Fez began. "I stayed up all night long trying to memorize this grand speech that I was going to give her. But you know what made it much easier?"

Jed stopped stocking the dry goods, put the box down, and took a seat on a wooden crate. "What made it easier?"

"The day that I was going to do it, Mary's father stopped by my shop and surprised me by telling me that he couldn't have been more proud of the fact that I was going to be a part of his family. With his approval, I was in heaven. Ya see, I didn't even think the man liked me. So from then on I knew that I was going to pull it off. And you know that speech I spent all night preparing?"

Jed nodded.

"Well, I tossed it in our pot-belly stove and watched it burn."

Jed frowned and tilted his head, trying to understand the meaning.

"You see Jed, I just spoke from the heart. Son, I know you've been trying to find the right words, but I'm telling you, it's not about the words you say, but how you say 'em. Now I know you haven't actually asked my Abigail yet, but I want you to know that I couldn't be happier for you and for her. I was the happiest man alive when I had my beloved Mary with me, and I see so much in the two of you that I saw in the two of us. I know you'll make her happy, Jed, and I know she's gonna make you happy too."

Fez gazed at the ground, and he thought about his late wife. "Do me a favor, Son, don't wait until you get back from Fort Laramie—do it now, and I mean right now. Get a buggy, take her somewhere and ask her, and when she says yes, you tell her that Papa couldn't be happier."

Jed leaped up and gave Fez a warm hug. "You were right, I just didn't know how, and you just showed me!"

* * * * *

The cold afternoon caused Abigail to pull her jacket tight around her neck. She tucked her gloved hands under her thighs, and lowered her head to fight off the chill of the breeze that was hitting her face. She was still curious why Jed had insisted on taking a buggy ride, but she learned quickly that he wasn't taking "no" for an answer, so she reluctantly gave in and bundled up.

The secluded place by the river just past the Simpson farm had become their special place. Even though the honeycomb was missing this time of year, the smell of honeysuckle still filled the air, and a sense of belonging filled their hearts. Jed pulled the buggy to a stop just above the slow-moving waters of the river. He could see that Abigail was shivering, so he took his jacket off and wrapped it around her before turning to face her. She looked at him suspiciously, but her eyes lit up with hopeful anticipation.

"Abigail?" Jed gently put his hand on her cheek to turn her head toward his. "I knew the first time I laid my eyes on you on the *Nebraska* that I had to have you, but then I thought I had lost you. You reappeared to me at the Mercantile like a dream come true. You were the one who woke me from the blow to my head during that storm last year. You have always been there for me, and I want to always be there for you. You're the love of my life and the reason for my existence. I can't live without you, and I promise that I will provide for you and take care of you until the day I die."

She was looking into his eyes, which were wet with tears of joy that matched her own as happiness overwhelmed them. He took her soft gloved hands and held them tight in his strong rugged ones. "Abigail Wright, will you do me the honor of becoming my wife and my soul mate from now and forevermore?"

"Yes!" she screamed, and flung her arms around Jed's neck.

Each was deep in thought while they rode back from their special place by the river. The crisp air felt invigorating to Abigail, who was still reeling from the question Jed had asked and the answer she'd given.

They tied the buggy up in front of the Mercantile and rushed inside. The store was packed with many of the townsfolk, who were collecting supplies for an anticipated storm. Jed and Abigail playfully ran by Bridger, Fremont, the Higgins, and the Simpsons, all of whom stared at their odd behavior.

They rushed to Fez at the sales counter. He looked up mischievously and asked, "Is everything all right?"

"We're getting married!"

They turned to the rest of the patrons and once again yelled, "We're getting married!"

Cheers erupted from the crowd in the Mercantile, and soon all were congratulating the engaged couple.

Fez couldn't have been happier for the couple, yet the feeling was bittersweet. He excused himself and went into the back storage area to be alone. *Look it there, Mary, your baby girl is getting married. I told you I'd watch over her . . . boy, I sure wish you were here to see it for yourself.*

He came back out front and was the last one to congratulate the happy couple, doing so with much pride and sincerity.

As the crowd was thinning, Fremont slapped Jed's back, and not-so-quietly whispered in his ear, "Hey Jed, ya still going to Fort Laramie?"

"You bet," Jed spoke loudly for all to hear. "You bet I'm going!"

Abigail lowered her eyes, and an uneasy shiver went down her spine, but no one noticed except her father, who draped an arm around her shoulders.

WYOMING
FT. LARAMIE
NORTH PLATTE R.
SCOTTS BLUFF
NEBRAS
CHIMNEY ROCK
COLORADO
KANSAS
ARKANSAS
SANTA FE
OKL
NEW MEXICO
TEXAS
N
JED'S JOURNEY: INDEP
SCALE: 0 100 200

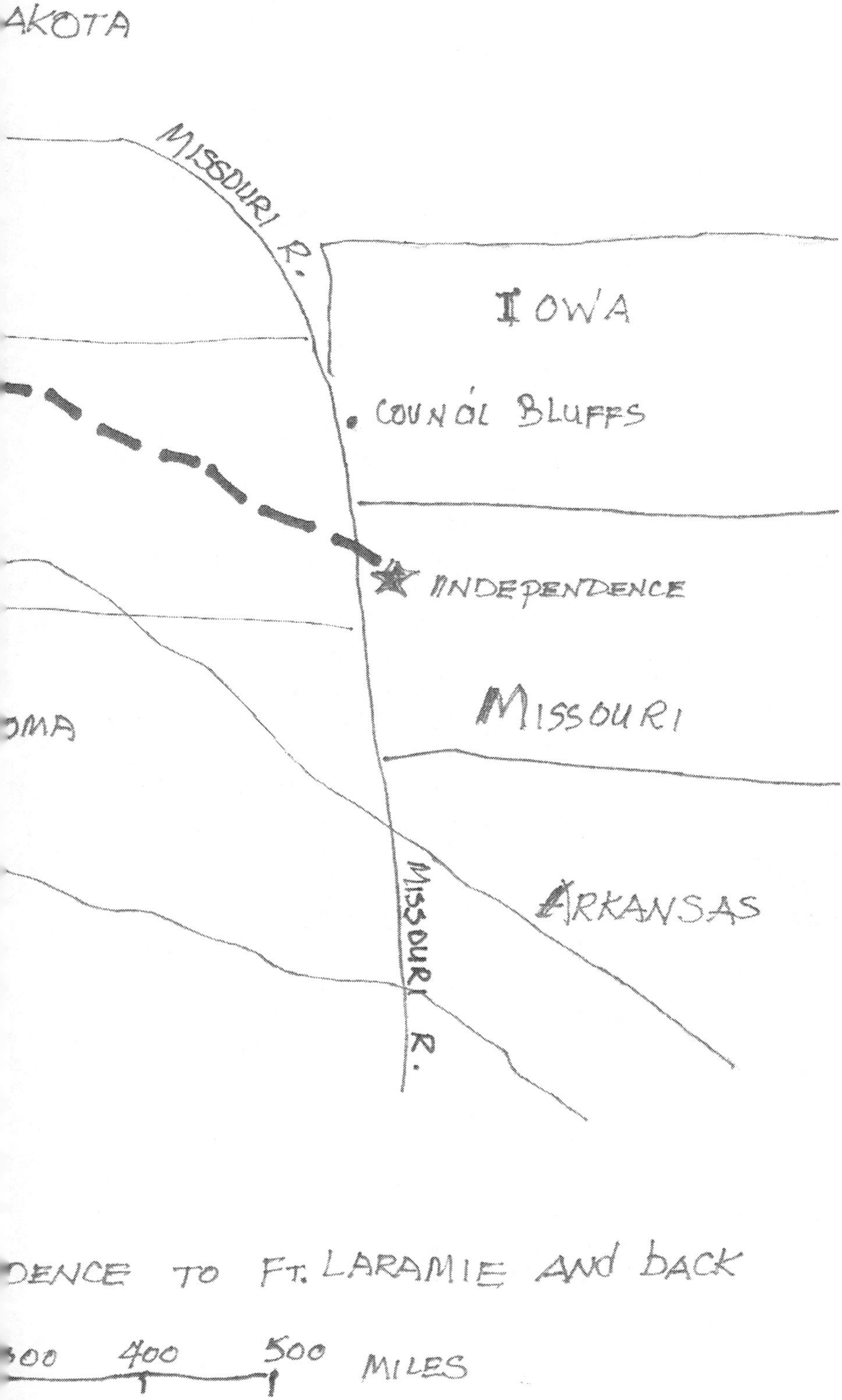
AKOTA
MISSOURI R.
IOWA
COUNCIL BLUFFS
INDEPENDENCE
MISSOURI
OMA
ARKANSAS
MISSOURI R.
DENCE TO FT. LARAMIE AND BACK
300 400 500 MILES

Chapter Eight

Fort Laramie Is Not Home

1837

"I just love the smell of spring," Sara said as she placed the tray of coffee on the warped wooden table. Her focus quickly turned to the family of quail crossing beneath the porch. She hushed her husband with a wave of her hand. He stopped clanking his spoon against his coffee cup and squinted back at her in comical defiance. Jed watched and laughed quietly from the opposite side of the porch while enjoying the aroma of coffee and Sara's freshly baked biscuits.

Sara sat in the corner chair that she had claimed next to the faded railing. It was her favorite spot to capture the morning sun as it filtered through the hickory trees on the east side of the house. Watching the quail family, Pastor Higgin noticed how many hickory nuts had fallen and wondered if they were going to have problems with squirrels again.

It was a peaceful morning. Pastor Higgin relaxed while he wrote his upcoming Sunday sermon and Jed enjoyed a morning off from the Mercantile.

"So, Jed, it sounds like you're set on going?" Pastor Higgin asked, still fixated on the hickory nuts.

Jed frowned, not knowing what the Pastor was looking at so curiously, opened his mouth in an attempt to answer.

"And what about Abigail?" Pastor Higgin blurted out while turning his attention from the hickory nuts to the family of quail.

Sara made a coughing sound and then turned her eyes in the same direction of her husband's. She'd already told Jed all that she thought about his travel idea, so she left any additional discussion to her husband.

Jed felt left out with the Higgins' backs turned to him. He grabbed a biscuit, shoved it in his mouth, and bellowed out with his mouth full of food, "Okay you two, I've already told you—she's really alright with the whole idea, you see?"

Sara and the Pastor gave each other knowing looks, sat back in their seats, and pulled their attention back to Jed as he continued. "In fact, we agreed that it'd be a good chance for me to see what's out there, while giving Abigail time to plan the wedding."

Pastor Higgin frowned skeptically. Sara exhaled a disappointed sigh as she got up to make more coffee.

"Pastor Higgin, I really think this expedition will be like a trial for me to see where God wants me." He looked at his mentor for some sign of agreement. "I hope you and Sara know how much I appreciate all you've done for me, but I hope you both understand that I need to do this for myself." Jed looked into the Pastor's dark unblinking eyes while he shifted in his seat to let Sara by so she could sit back down. "Please, you do understand that, don't you?"

"All I can see is that you're setting yourself up to be mixed up with filthy fur trappers—those heathens—and what about the suffering Indian families, how are you going to help them?" Sara discovered that she couldn't resist giving more of her opinion to Jed after all.

"Now, now, Mother, we don't know that, and we're here to spread our Lord's love to all, and that includes fur trappers," countered the Pastor. "This actually might work out best for all parties."

"I'm sure that'll be easy since I'll be seeing both of them out there," Jed responded. "I'll make sure that I spread the 'good news' to all the—*heathens* I run into." Jed and Pastor Higgin hid their amusement from Sara as she left in a huff to get the fresh pot of coffee from the stove.

"Have you given any more thought to reaching out to your folks, Jedidiah?" Jed always knew when Pastor was bringing up a sensitive subject, because he used Jed's proper name. He could see through the porch window that Sara was trying her best to listen to the conversation.

"Yes, I have," answered Jed, his right finger tapping wildly. "I just don't have the time right now to sit down, collect my thoughts, and put them all in a letter. But I promise, I'll do it right when I get back."

Jed shifted in his chair to allow Sara to scoot by again. She brought out a tray with a loaf of her special pumpkin bread. The smell of baked pumpkin filled the porch. She placed the tray down, then frowned when she noticed that the family of quail had disappeared into the bushes.

"Do they even know that you're engaged?" asked Sara. "I thought I heard from Fez that the date was set for December. If so, that would give your parents the necessary time to travel here from Wheeling."

"No, you're right," Jed said with little conviction. "It's just that I don't want to think of all of that right now; besides, the wedding and all the plans are being handled by Abigail anyway. In fact, she probably has them all set as we speak."

"Now, don't underestimate the importance of that event, Jed. It means more than you might think to Abigail, and it means even more to God," the Pastor counseled Jed while putting his hand on top of Sara's. Her face lit up as she remembered their special day, and she once again peeked over the railing to see if her little quail family had reappeared.

Jed's talk of wedding plans had always been awkward, and it was something he had left up to Abigail. He excused himself and headed toward Stevens's Diner, taking the back route through the bushes, which caught Sara's attention when the family of quail reappeared, their mother leading the way through the Higgins' yard.

* * * * *

"Hey, Jim," Jed yelled as he approached the crowded patio of Stevens's Diner. Jed pulled up the last chair available, sat down across from his good friend, and looked at the burly man's plate of bacon and eggs, and a dish he still couldn't quite acquire a taste for, grits.

"I need your help, Jim," Jed started. "I have no idea what I'm supposed to pack for this trip we're all taking to Fort Laramie. I'm a little embarrassed even to ask, but I thought if I could ask anyone to help me out, it definitely would be you. So, Jim . . . can you . . . I mean will you . . . but only if it's . . ."

"Whoa there, boy!" Bridger choked out as he tried to slow his friend down. "Sure I'll help you out. But you've got to promise me, son, that you'll let me get in a bite or two—I'm starving, you know what I mean?"

* * * * *

Bridger took a last bite and wiped his plate clean with a biscuit. Over the past hour or so, he'd told Jed nearly everything he could think of that could help him on their upcoming trip. But what Bridger saw in his young friend worried him. They were going to rough country where only a few had gone before, and he knew that at best, Jed was as inexperienced as the next.

Turning his attention back to Jed, Bridger said, "Now keep in mind that you'll need to carry some sort of rifle, gunpowder, and lead balls, not to mention rods for setting the ball, but you know all about that stuff, right?"

Bridger looked intently at Jed, whose reply was only a mute stare. What he saw in the young man's face answered his question. Considering this, he pushed his empty plate away before stretching his arms over his head and looking beyond the diner and the town. He saw the blue mountain range looming above a line of trees in the distance. He marveled at the puffy whiteness of the clouds that hovered over the highest peak and saw how the wind currents quickly moved them from the blue mountain range to the next one west. It was those mountains that he would travel through with his untested young friend, and that worried him.

"Now, you've got to listen and pay careful attention, son!" Bridger pulled his chair up close to Jed's. "You never know what you might run into out there on the trail, so you'd better be prepared. Sometimes it means the difference between surviving and not surviving, and if you ask me, I'd much rather be the fella who comes back, if you know what I mean." Bridger noticed the slightly worried expression that crossed Jed's face, but ignored it and continued. "Keep in mind, Jed, that you'll be doing more walking than riding, so you'll need some strong sturdy boots." Bridger raised his eyebrows when he looked down at Jed's worn-out leather boots, which included a large hole above his left big toe.

Disregarding this early warning sign, Bridger continued. "We'll have a team of oxen do the pulling for all the wagons and other than taking turns driving the rigs, you'll be doing the hoofing on the ground." Bridger took one last look at Jed's worn boots, and when he looked up, it appeared that Jed was getting his message about getting some new ones.

"What about a horse, Jim?"

"Yea, you'll have your own horse," Bridger answered. "But you'll need to use him sparingly so you don't wear him out. Brushing him down and giving him a good feeding nightly will make him your best friend, but override him and you'll lose him before we pass Courthouse Rock."

They were finishing their coffee when Bridger turned to Jed and said, "I think that about does it, my friend. You sure you're ready?"

"Absolutely!" Jed lied. "Heck, Jim, if you said we were heading out tomorrow, I'd be ready." The two stared at each other, Bridger still unsure of Jed and Jed still trying to convince Bridger otherwise.

As they were walking down Main Street, planning to meet Fez at the Mercantile, Bridger stopped Jed in full stride, hopped up on the boardwalk, and spun him around by a shirtsleeve, nearly knocking him down. He looked Jed straight in the eyes.

"Listen now, Jed!" Bridger said firmly. "It's real life out there, boy! Once you get out five or so miles, all you're used to will be gone, and there's no turning back!"

"I got it, Jim!" Jed said arrogantly. "I'm telling you, I'll be ready! Quit your worrying, will you?"

"I'm serious, Jed!" Bridger replied with no softness in his voice. "I'm not going to be the one who has to come back here to tell your pretty girl that some bear ate you up or something like that, so you better be tellin' me straight!"

"Don't worry, Jim!" Jed reaffirmed. He paused and waited for more of Bridger's unwanted advice. Hearing none, he continued. "Now that we have all that out of the way, I've got some supplies to pick up here at the Mercantile."

Bridger paused in silence, bearing down on Jed with a piercing glare. Several seconds passed, during which Bridger began staring at Jed's boots.

"And yes, I am going to buy myself a new pair of boots, just to make you happy, my friend," Jed said as he grinned sheepishly.

Just as quickly the tension between the two dissipated, and their calm expressions returned. Jed went into the Mercantile while Bridger headed to the local watering hole for a much-needed drink.

* * * * *

Sunday was a brisk morning with dew still heavy on the ground. The air was filled with sounds of metal scraping metal, clasps connecting, and eager oxen stomping in readiness to hit the trail. Smells of the morning's breakfast of bacon and hot coffee still lingered long after the last plate was cleaned. The wagon train leaders and their families finalized the preparation of their gear while keeping eyes on their rambunctious children, who were eager to discover what adventures awaited them.

"Now you listen good, Jedidiah Monroe," Abigail schooled her fiancé. "You have a date back here in four months, and I'm expecting you to be there as I walk down that aisle, you hear me?"

"You just wait for me to come around that bend over yonder," Jed said, pointing to the small hill at the end of Front Street. "Besides, you're gonna be so busy with the wedding plans and all that you won't even have time to miss me. In fact, you probably won't even remember that I'm not around here anymore."

Abigail didn't care for that last comment. She knitted her brows and pursed her lips as she looked away from Jed in order to stifle her anger. When she looked at Jed again, the fear showed full on her face. "You come back to me, Mister, and yes, I do plan on being Mrs. Jedidiah Monroe. But I need you back here to do it, you got that?"

A loud whistle could be heard from one end of the wagon train to the other, and oxen snorting, wheels creaking, and whips cracking broke the silence created during the moments of tense good-byes.

After one last, long stretch down from his horse, Jed pulled Abigail to him, kissed her hard on the lips, and quietly said, "I love you, Abigail *Monroe.*"

Time stood still as Abigail watched the last of the wagon train round the bend and fade from sight. The lingering sounds of wheels and oxen hoofs could be heard, and then there was complete silence.

Abigail turned into the open arms of Fez. "Papa" is all she said, as he wrapped his arms around her and let her cry.

* * * * *

The first several hours on the trail went by with Jed reflecting on what lay ahead and what he had just left behind. "You doing all right, Jed?" asked Fremont as he rode his brown mare and came alongside Jed.

"Doing just fine, John," answered Jed as he walked along with his horse in tow.

"It's good that you're letting your horse take a breather from time to time. It'll help him make the trip. The last thing you need is to lose that ride of yours, so the more hoofing you do, the better he will be."

"Yea, that's exactly what Jim told me back in Independence."

Jed returned to his thoughts. He hadn't been too sure about his mount at first. He had thought the horse was too young and wild, and would jump at the first sign of any critter crossing his path. As it turned out, Jed was the jumpier of the two, and his strong smart steed seemed to be looking out for him rather than the other way around. His horse had a thick reddish-brown mane and dark glassy eyes that watched Jed everywhere he went.

Jed chuckled when he thought of his tough young stud of a horse and then of whoever named him. *Scooter? What kind of name is Scooter?* he thought, shaking his head. Looking into Scooter's eyes, Jed told him, "You and I are becoming good friends—right, big guy?" *Scooter—oh my gosh, Scooter—who'd have done such a thing as calling their horse Scooter?*

Jed couldn't hold back his bellowing laugh, and realized that it felt good to actually laugh again. He hadn't realized how tense he'd become since leaving Independence.

Fremont was in charge of monitoring the wagons and keeping them all together while Bridger scouted on ahead. "Just let me know if you need anything from me, John," offered Jed.

"No problem. I'll probably take you up on that once we pass 'the rocks,' " Fremont replied. "That will give you a few weeks to get used to the trail and what you can expect out here. We'll see, but I might get you out front to lead while I finalize the mapping of the area and transcribe it all down on paper. The government keeps hollering at me to map out everything I see and send it back to them, so this might be a good chance for me to get caught up."

"Anything you need, John," Jed said. "It's my first trip, as you know, but I'm a fast learner."

Jed watched as his friend turned his horse toward the front of the wagon. He yelled out, "You know, John, I could also help you out back here, watching the tail of the train. I could let you know if we have any problems. That way, you don't always have to keep riding back here to see how we're doing."

Fremont pulled his horse to a stop. "That sounds like a great idea, Jed. I'll take you up on that, but don't hesitate to tell me if you decide you want to learn how to lead the train as well. Just give me a whistle if you see or hear anything back there that might cause alarm, ya hear?"

Jed agreed, and was excited about his new "duties." He watched Fremont turn his horse with one knee to the ribs, and off he went to the front to continue leading the train.

The terrain was gentle, with smooth rolling hills and hard-packed dirt that made it easy for the wagons to cross over it. The weather had been clear and seasonably cool, but very pleasant, which allowed the travelers to enjoy the first leg of the trip. All on the train knew that the hardest trek would be after Fort Laramie, so they were basking in the temporary ease of their travel thus far.

Fremont had informed Jed that they had left at the perfect time of year, with enough grass left on the prairie to feed the livestock. There also wasn't any risk of snow at this time of year, which could trap them if it came down heavy.

Jed was taking it all in and dreaming of what lay ahead. He spent a lot of time thinking of his future with Abigail. He reflected on the fact that he was going to be married soon, and then after that . . . *children.*

Children? he thought, and noticed that his finger was twitching. *I wonder how many Abigail will want. I wonder how many I will want. Three? Five? Seven? Whoa there, boy, slow down a bit, let's stay focused on the trail and not worry about the "Monroe Family" quite yet.* He began to chuckle at the thought of himself as the head of his own "herd" of children, and the vision of Abigail that came to mind brought a smile to his lips.

After two weeks on the trail, spirits were still high. There was an old gent on the second wagon who played a fiddle after supper every night, and many folks danced around the campfire and sang their favorite songs. This reminded Jed of Wheeling, where the townsfolk would come by the church every other Sunday evening, bringing their choice dishes, singing songs, and listening to Jed's father as he played his fiddle. Jed sat on a fallen tree, and the memories engulfed him as he watched the folks from the wagon trail laugh, dance, and sing without a care in the world. *Just like home, right Jed?* he thought with a bit of lonesomeness and guilt.

Fort Kearney was a welcome sight for all. The wagon train had traveled over two hundred miles since leaving Independence, and the animals, though well cared for, showed signs of wear. It would be a time for the pioneers to resupply their wagons and post letters to loved ones back home.

Jed stared at the fort's postal box for a long while. He paused a moment without looking away, then turned with a sigh and went back to his horse. He slipped the saddle off Scooter's wet hide and hung it on the rail beside the fort's corral. After brushing his mount down, Jed led him into the corral. His bedroll under his arm, Jed left Scooter and prepared himself for a guilt-ridden night, as he knew there would be no letter going out that evening.

* * * * *

The Platte River guided the wagon train over the next four hundred fifty miles. It was a broad brown river that was too muddy for drinking or bathing. The prairie grass quickly changed from over six feet high before Fort Kearney to a short six inches on this part of the journey. Jed was told that this was a potential problem for the animals. He noticed that folks from the wagon train had purchased grain at Fort Kearney to help them make the journey. There were fewer trees along this stretch of the trail, so the settlers had to use buffalo dung to fuel their fires. That was something new to Jed. *Wait until I tell ol' Fez about this one,* he thought as he laughed.

It seemed to Jed that no matter the obstacle, the pioneers tackled it and moved on. He rarely noticed anyone being out of place or causing problems. Each family had a routine that it followed from daybreak to sundown, and Jed enjoyed watching them in their own little worlds. Each one seemed excited about starting a new life, some at Fort Laramie and others farther west toward Oregon Country.

Jed continued to wonder what kind of family he would have with Abigail. *Will I be a good father, a good husband? How will I provide for them? I can't provide for them out here on a trail—where's the pay and security in this?* He continued pondering these questions, and the thoughts racing through his mind made him uneasy.

Cut it out, Jed, he scolded himself. *You'll be a great father and a great husband, and if there's one thing you should always remember from Papa, it's that the good Lord will always provide, so knock off the second-guessing.* He shook his head, trying to clear it of doubts.

"We are ahead of schedule, folks," Bridger explained as all of the settlers gathered around the meeting wagon. "We can thank the great weather, and a good supply of grain and water, for helping us make such good time getting to this point. Now, we'll be heading out again tomorrow morning, and by the next day we should be able to see Fort Laramie in the far distance."

Cheers rose from the assembled crowd. "I need to warn you, though," Bridger interrupted as he raised his hands in the air. "There are camps of Osage Indians in various areas between here and the fort. Rest assured that they are harmless, and I spoke to a few of them on my last trip this way to let them know that we'd be comin' through. The Indians actually have made peace with Fort Laramie, and they use it for supplies just like the white folks. I just wanted yins to be prepared and not startled when you first see their camps."

* * * * *

Fort Laramie was much larger than Fort Kearney, and had much more activity surrounding it on all sides. Indians, trappers, settlers, and soldiers were all busy with the daily routine of buying and selling supplies. Furs were draped over rail posts that lined the area around the corral. The fresh smell of raw leather lingered from still-drying animal hides. Beads, dried cornhusks with brightly colored corncobs, and clear glass bottles of oil ointments were spread out for all to gaze on. A thick flat wooden plank was propped up against the corral railing with words burnt into it: EVERYTHING FOR SALE OR TRADE.

Jed noticed that very little dialogue was shared amongst buyers and sellers, but somehow everyone knew the other's meaning. Trading was strong and amicable, and the only unpleasantness to the fort was the smell of animal dung lingering in the still air. The fort's tall wooden structure, completely surrounding the post, was meant for security and did not allow any breeze to flow through. Several settlers who were part of Jed's wagon train were getting ready to head farther west, while others were making Fort Laramie their new home.

While Jed walked his horse to the stables, his mind began to swirl again. He took the horse's saddle off, brushed his mane, and set up a good supply of grain for the hungry and tired animal.

"Good job there, Scooter," Jed said as he looked into the big black eyes of his newest friend. "It seems like we've become good friends over the past few months, haven't we? Question is, my friend, are you gonna take me back home, or are you planning to haul me farther west with the others?"

He was overheard by Fremont, who was brushing his horse two stalls down. "Having second thoughts about continuing on there, Jed?"

"Well, kind of," Jed began as he finished tucking his four-legged friend in for the night. "Just having a conversation with my good ol' buddy Scooter."

Jed waited for Fremont to finish grooming his horse, and then the two began to walk to the post's café for some much-needed "real food."

"You know, John, this whole experience has been great and all, but I've come to realize that my real place is back in Independence with Abigail."

"I figured you were going to come to that conclusion, could see it in your eyes. But my friend, I also knew that you had to make that decision on your own, and not even Abigail could've helped you out with that one."

They were almost to the railing that lined the outside of the fort's café when Fremont slowed his stride and stopped. Jed turned toward Fremont and tilted his head quizzically. Fremont picked up a rock and casually threw it before speaking. "Jed, these trails will always be here, and you can always come out with us when you have an inkling to stretch your legs and all. You see, there's nothing wrong with any man wanting to get out once in a while to see this here country from time to time. You just figured out where your roots are gonna be, not your chains." Fremont gave Jed the most serious look he could concoct. "You have a good thing, so try not to ruin it."

Fremont suddenly grinned and patted Jed on the back with such force that it took the wind out of him, and they soon they were both laughing. "Come on, my trailblazing friend, let's go celebrate your upcoming wedding—I'll even buy the first round!"

"Beer or sarsaparilla?" Jed asked, a questioning look on his face as he tried to read Fremont's reaction.

"Oh boy, what am I going to do with you?" Fremont answered, slapping Jed once again on the back as they made their way to the café.

* * * * *

Roughly seven hundred miles east, a young woman paced the floor of her home. "It's been almost four months, Papa!" Abigail yelled. "I haven't heard a word from him. He's been through two forts . . . with mailing posts . . . and one of those forts twice!"

"Now, now, Abigail, you're not going to want to have that kind of attitude when he does come around that bend, now will ya? You want him to see your beautiful face and your warm smile. Don't let him know you've been frettin' or walking around in a hissy fit."

* * * * *

Shouting and whistling could be heard from the landing. "What in the world?" yelled Fez. "What's with all the ruckus down yonder?"

"Wagons are a-coming!" yelled a young man as he ran to tell Sheriff Daniels.

"Papa . . . could it be?" Abigail asked hopefully. She quickly put her dusting broom away, and took off her apron and threw it on the counter.

"Now, don't get yourself all in an uproar, Abigail. You don't know that it's 'his' wagon train coming back. Plus, why would he be with a wagon train anyway? Weren't they all staying out there or moving farther west?"

"It's one wagon, three horses, and two men riding their own mounts!" yelled another excited man as he ran by the Mercantile.

"Papa, I know it's him, I can just feel it!" Abigail yelled out as she began to run down to the landing. Fez began closing and locking the Mercantile doors so that he could go down to the landing himself.

Just as Jed had said he would, he came around the bend next to the river. When Abigail arrived at the landing, she saw him, and immediately relief swept through her. Though he had been careful with good ol' Scooter for the entire trip, Jed gave him a friendly jab in the ribs, to which he responded with a full gallop toward Abigail. Not but twenty yards from the landing, Jed pulled Scooter to a halt, jumped off his loyal companion, and ran the rest of the way into the open arms of his soon-to-be bride.

By the time Fez had finally made it down to the landing, the sole wagon had also arrived with supplies from Fort Kearney and three new horses that Jed had traded for. Fez came to a stop a few yards from the couple, who were still in a warm embrace. He looked at them with the fondness of a father and the melancholy of a husband who had lost his dear wife.

Once he regained his composure, Fez walked up to Jed, patted him on the back, and said, "Welcome home, Son!"

Yes, he was home, but Fez wondered—*for how long?*

II

Bittersweet
1838–1854

UNITED STATES AN

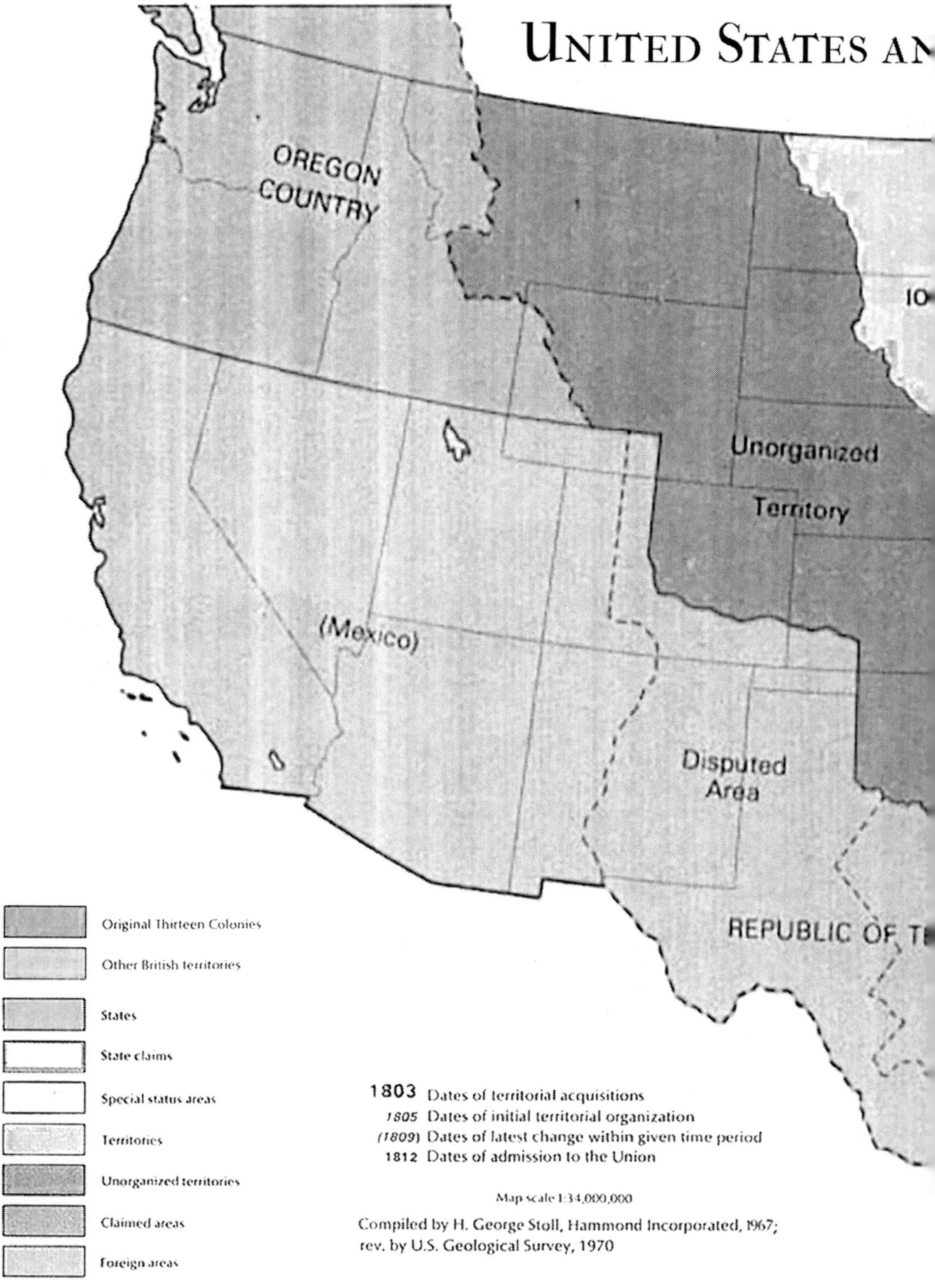

1803 Dates of territorial acquisitions
1805 Dates of initial territorial organization
(1809) Dates of latest change within given time period
1812 Dates of admission to the Union

Map scale 1:34,000,000

Compiled by H. George Stoll, Hammond Incorporated, 1967; rev. by U.S. Geological Survey, 1970

ERRITORIES, 1840

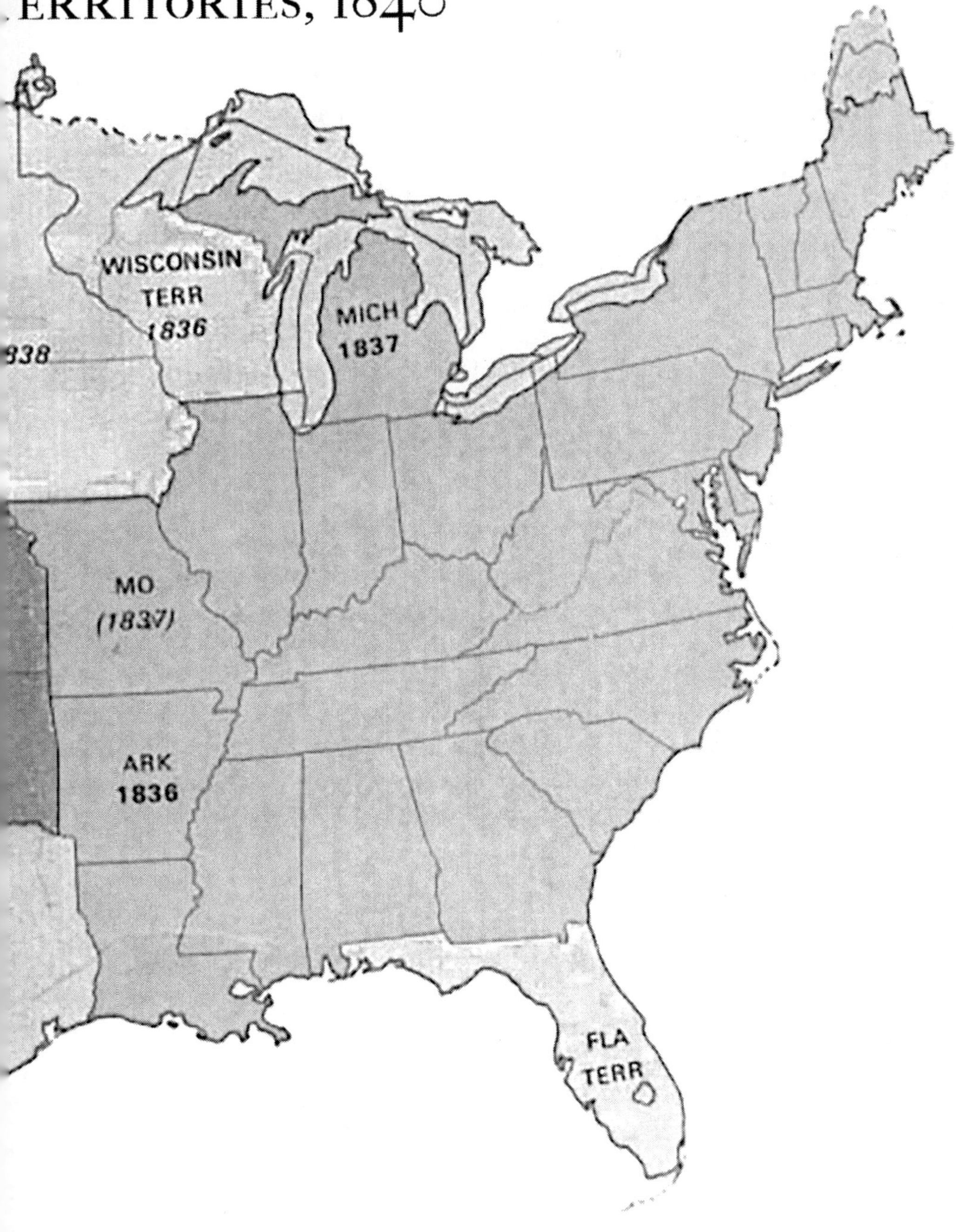

Chapter Nine

Wedding Bells: A Cure for Tragedy

1838

It floated down in a swirling motion. Time stood still until the letter came to rest on the Higgins' parlor floor next to Jed's knees, which had hit the floor just before. Jed's dazed stare was to nowhere, and he was barely coherent. Abigail moved closer to him in bewilderment, trying to read the reason for his cold blank expression

"Wh . . . what is it?" she quietly asked, but there was no answer. She knelt down and picked the paper up from the floor. The letter that had first brought excitement to Jed's demeanor had turned him into a lost soul reaching out to the other side of heaven to try to make sense of it all. She turned the letter over as she rested against the hearth, doing her best to thaw the chill racing down her spine.

"Dead? . . . Dead? . . . Who? . . . No . . . it can't be . . . oh, Jed . . . it can't be!" She spoke softly but in shock, the trembling words tumbling from her. She went to him and put her hands on his cheeks, moving closer on bended knees to look deep into his eyes, but he wasn't there. "Oh, Jed . . . I'm so sorry," was all she could manage to say through the pounding ache in her chest.

No response—just a blank stare of emptiness as Jed knelt in silence.

The crime was sudden, based on the letter from the family lawyer in Wheeling. His parents were apparently sound asleep when the intruder entered through the kitchen door.

"Who would ever want to hurt them, Jed?" Abigail said quietly, still holding the letter.

Jed gave no answer while staring blankly through the side windowpane.

"They didn't deserve this . . . no one deserves a thing like this, Jed!" Abigail's voice cracked and her chest felt crushed by the heaviness of the moment. She wanted to take the pain from Jed, to erase the words in the letter, but felt helpless. She lowered herself back down to look Jed in the eyes. "Oh, Jed . . . I . . . don't know what to . . . oh, God . . . why?" Her tears now flowed freely as she put her arms around Jed's neck and held him tightly.

His eyes were still empty, but began to fill with tears as he struggled to receive her compassion. She put her head on his shoulder and held his twitching hands in hers while listening to his quiet cries of grief.

The horrific news spread quickly to Wright Mercantile, then to Stevens's Diner, and then through the rest of town. Sara walked up to the door of Jed's room after leaving Abigail, who she'd let rest in the living room downstairs. She knocked softly, and the answer came as a faint whisper. "It's open."

Jed was sitting in his rocking chair and staring into the fire, his eyes dull, swollen, and red. Sara crossed the room and knelt next to him. She took his hand in hers.

"Jed?" She spoke softly and gently, as the mother she never was, but had always seen herself as someday becoming. "Jed, my dear, your parents would have been so proud of you and so happy for you and Abigail. Their passing, though it stings like the fiercest bite, can't take what they stood for away from you. Their love for each other, and for you, must continue to shine on through the life that you and Abigail are about to start. It's what they would have said if they were here sitting next to you now, as I am. You must . . . you must fight on, Jed."

Despite Sara's strength, her voice had begun to crack and her eyes to well. She quickly turned away, and seeing a chair a few feet away, she pulled it beside Jed, gulping and blinking hard before sitting down and facing Jed once again. Now she noticed the finger twitching and the loneliness in his face. She saw the frown lines deeply embedded into his forehead and the rattled tension in every one of his muscles.

"You have a wonderful woman who is ready to spend her entire life with you, Jed. She needs you, dear—she needs your strength. Your folks need your strength. They need you to carry on in their name. Keep the memories, Jed. Keep the lessons they taught you alive. I knew them well, and I know that they would want you to always remember the love they had for the Lord and the plans they had for you. Jed, they will always be right here in your heart."

She placed her hand to his heart, her eyes locked on his. "Stay strong, Jed, stay strong in the Lord, and He will get you through this."

After a few moments of silence, he turned to her and said in a crackling voice, barely audible, "I should have written, Sara, but I didn't. I should have written . . . that's all she wanted from me, and now it's too late."

The emotions he had suppressed finally broke through. His strength to hold them back failed as gut-wrenching cries burst forth. Sara held him tight as a mother would her son. Her maternal warmth soothed him, and he gave in to her kindness and compassion. Watching silently from the doorway, Abigail's tears flowed down her cheeks, and her heart cried out to her husband-to-be.

It took a few days to make the arrangements, but with Sara's and Abigail's help, the memorial service and Pastor Higgin's message were beautiful and heartfelt. Most of the townsfolk attended and expressed their condolences. His parents had been laid to rest a few weeks before, so he didn't feel the need to go back to Wheeling, though there were some legal matters—most notably the house and church that had been left in his name—he would need to take care of, but not right away. The lawyer had wired him that the house would be cleaned and then boarded up until he made his way back to Wheeling.

His father's church would be ministered by the assistant pastor, Chester Albright. Jed knew Albright and was confident that the church would be in good hands. Pastor Albright had been the assistant pastor for a few years and had become close friends with Jed's father. Jed knew him as he was growing up and remembered how close he and his father had been. That sudden bittersweet memory hit Jed hard despite his sense of confidence in the man who would now fill in and secure the foundation that his father had laid years before.

He'll do you proud, Papa, I know he will, but . . .

Jed thought of the scenario while standing at the church door. He shook the hand of the last guest and watched him walk toward the back of the churchyard. His chest felt heavy, and enormous guilt fell over him. *I was supposed to take over the church for Papa, and now I'm here and Pastor Albright is there. Oh, forgive me, Papa!* His throat caught as he held off the urge to cry. *I swear . . . I'll fulfill your wishes . . . someday . . . and I will make you proud of me . . . I promise!* He shook his head slowly, disgusted with himself over his last thought. *I promise? Will this promise be any different from all the others, Jed?*

He turned, walked back inside the church, and sat alone on the second pew. He vowed, to the statue of the crucified Christ hanging on the wall, that he would make his parents proud.

He thought of Abigail. He thought of the wedding. *Oh, yea, the wedding.* It didn't seem to mean the same to him anymore.

Tears fell on his pant leg as he raised his head and looked again at the life-size statue of Christ that looked back from the west end of the chapel. *But it meant means the world to Abigail,* he thought, knowing that it would have meant the world to his parents, too.

That's where I'll start . . . the wedding. Feelings of faithfulness and purpose began to come back to him. He knew that in order to ease his feelings of loss, he would have to recapture the feelings of hope.

Jed heard a door creaking, followed by slow methodical footsteps down the middle aisle of the chapel, each step growing louder. When they ended, he could feel someone's presence next to him. Abigail's hand touched his shoulder, and he reacted immediately by placing one of his hands over hers. She gently caressed his hair and stroked one of his cheeks with her free hand.

Jed looked up slowly, and when their moist eyes met she said, "I'm right here, Jed—I'll always be right here."

He had the urge to break down again. The tightness in his throat made him want to surrender and release all emotional control to her. Jed swallowed hard and pushed down the urge. He looked up into her eyes again, searching and longing for strength.

They stared into each other's eyes for several minutes, ignoring the chatter and commotion coming from the side yard. In that moment they bonded as one soul, and Jed realized that their life together must go on, and that he had to do his part to make Abigail's dream wedding a reality.

Jed turned to her. He took her hands in his. His all-too-familiar grin reappeared, to Abigail's delight. Then with a wide smile, a wink, and a whisper he said, "Hey, fiancé . . . I do believe we have a wedding to get on with, so what do you have to say about that?"

Abigail smiled widely as she pulled Jed to his feet, embraced him warmly, and said, "Yes, we do!"

They held hands as they walked down the center aisle of the chapel. They continued out the back door to congregate with friends and family.

A few weeks after the memorial for Jed's parents, Jed and Abigail prepared themselves for their big day. It was the special day that

Abigail had dreamed about her entire life and the one that, Jed had to admit, terrified him.

Jed awoke on their wedding day not knowing what to expect. He envisioned Abigail, beautiful and excited. He tried not to think of his parents, who would not be in attendance. The snow outside the chapel windows glistened in pure whiteness, and the frost on the windows reminded everyone that the blustery winter was upon them. The plans for this glorious day had all come together, even though Jed at times had doubted whether he would ever recover from the loss of his parents.

Jed dismissed the concern shown for him by many of his friends. His display of calmness and composure was meant to let everyone know that he was fine—he even joked that Abigail was the nervous one. Most could tell that he was forcing it, though.

When he and his groomsmen came out from the side room, Jed looked at the packed room of friends and felt the warmth of love surrounding him. He temporarily lost that feeling when his eyes darted to the front pew on the groom's side of the church, and all he saw was emptiness. He felt a dagger of sorrow for the missing couple who should have been sitting there. Jed forced himself to refocus. It was Abigail he needed to think about and his new life with her. Yet the empty pew was like a beacon of terror tempting him to break down . . . but he could not . . . NO, he would not. He turned his gaze and his full attention to the future that was right in front of him, about to come down that aisle.

The bridesmaids, Rachael Simpson and Sara Higgin, dressed in light pink dresses, came down the aisle first, slowly and elegantly. Their hair was tucked neatly under white bonnets. As Sara turned in front of Jed, she noticed his eyes locked on the empty pew. She stopped in front of Jed and whispered, "That pew isn't empty, you know. They're right there, Jed, and they're so very proud of you!" She smiled and winked at him as she took her place.

Jim Bridger and John Fremont were Jed's groomsmen, with Fremont as his best man. The wedding party looked dashing, and the groom looked sharp in a tailored tuxedo, although his long arms protruded far beyond the end of its sleeves.

The chapel was filled with members of the Society plus friends from Independence. A hushed silence fell over the guests as the organ began to play the wedding march. The entire congregation stood up, looking back at the beautiful bride arm in arm with her father.

Fez held on to Abigail firmly, as if guiding her across a frozen lake instead of down a wedding aisle. Although very nervous, Abigail was stunning in a white satin wedding gown with a light flowing veil.

Father and daughter slowly walked, her arm locked into his, step by step down the aisle as the soft folds of her dress trailed behind her as if she were a queen walking into her castle. As the two approached, Fez gave Jed a paternal look that hit a soft spot in the groom's heart, and he was suddenly flooded with all the kindness and affection that the two men had established over the past few years.

Pastor Higgin stepped forward and asked in a loud and emphatic voice, "Who gives this woman in marriage to this man?"

With an unintentional pause, then a nervous look from Abigail, Fez stuttered, "Her ah . . . her Mother and I." Fez turned to Abigail, gave her a soft kiss on the cheek, and said quietly, "Your momma would have loved this, you know?" He turned to take his seat on the front row pew, and it creaked as he nervously adjusted his position.

Clearing his throat, Pastor Higgin looked at the couple and then out at the seated congregation. "Dearly beloved, we are gathered here in the sight of God, and in the face of this company to join this man and this woman in holy matrimony . . ."

He paused at the part where he asked if any person could show just cause why Jed and Abigail may not be joined together. When Sara intentionally and unmistakably cleared her throat, Pastor Higgin realized that he had paused a bit too long. He smiled and lowered his head as he looked back to his Bible.

"Marriage is the union of husband and wife in heart, body, and soul. It is intended for their mutual joy and for the help and comfort given each other in both prosperity and adversity. But more importantly, it is a means through which a stable and loving environment may be attained."

"Through marriage, Jedidiah and Abigail make a commitment together to face their disappointments, embrace their dreams, realize their hopes, and accept each other's failures.

Jed felt a stab of guilt when Pastor Higgin said the word failure. *I am a failure,* he thought. *I couldn't even follow through on my father's wish for me to become a pastor.*

Jed shook his head slowly in an attempt to refocus on the wedding vows and the new commitment he was making to Abigail.

"We are here today, before God, because marriage is one of His most sacred wishes, to witness the joining in marriage of Jedidiah and Abigail. This occasion marks the celebration of love and commitment with which this man and this woman begin their life together."

Jed thought of the word commitment and the memory of the Oregon Trail consumed him. *Will I be able to commit to Abigail?*

"Marriage is an act of faith and a personal commitment as well as a moral and physical union between two people. Marriage has been described as the best and most important relationship that can exist."

Jed looked at Abigail, and though her face was partially hidden behind her veil, he could see those eyes that he loved so much. Just a quick glance at his bride's face behind the veil reassured Jed that all was going to be fine.

Pastor Higgin stepped up and turned to Jed and with a look of pride asked, "Do you, Jedidiah Monroe, take Abigail Wright to be your lawful wife, to live together after God's ordinance in the holy estate of matrimony? Will you love her, comfort her, honor, and keep her—as long as you both shall live?

Jed turned to look at Abigail. He realized that he had only heard part of what the Pastor had said, but he was sure of his answer.

"I will."

Pastor Higgin now turned to Abigail and could see that a few gentle tears had appeared under her veil—the tears of joy. He knew them well after conducting his share of weddings and being a part of the beginning of so many young lives.

Abigail listened carefully to every word Pastor Higgin spoke, and when he was finished and asked the same question of her, she said confidently, "I will."

Once they had placed the rings on each other's hands and the rest of the vows were completed, Pastor Higgin turned to the bride and groom and said, "May you always share with each other the gifts of love and be one in heart and in mind. May you always create a home together that puts in your hearts love, generosity, and kindness."

Looking at them, the Pastor reached for the hands of the bride and groom.

"You, Jedidiah and Abigail, have pronounced yourselves husband and wife, but above that, remember to always be each other's best friend."

Pastor Higgin turned and looked at the congregation, his hands still clasping theirs, and said in his loud voice, "What, therefore, God has joined together, let no man put asunder. And so, by the power vested in me by the State of Missouri and Almighty God, I now pronounce you man and wife, and may your days be good and long upon this earth."

There was silence in the chapel. Abigail and Jed stared up at Pastor Higgin with nervous looks on their faces. No one moved. The wedding party looked at one another and then back at Jed and Abigail. Muffled giggles could be heard coming from the congregation.

Enjoying the moment, Pastor Higgin cleared his throat deeply, looked straight at Jed, and with a fatherly expression said, "Jedidiah? Son, you may kiss your bride."

The kiss was gentle and loving, and with it came hope and adventure for the new Monroe family as it now took the reins from the Monroe family of old, never alone and never to be forgotten.

The newlyweds turned and began walking down the middle aisle of the church arm in arm. Abigail smiled, a smile so strong and so emotional that it radiated all she was feeling to everyone in attendance.

Jed took one last glance at the empty pew on the groom's side and knew that his parents were indeed sitting there, gleaming with pride. Knowing that, he joined hands with his new wife as they exited the church, destined for a life filled with security and love, as he vowed to himself to fulfill a promise he had made years earlier.

Chapter Ten

And Baby Makes Three

1839

The rock was hard and cold, but it was nice to finally find a place to rest. Jed sat behind Abigail and carefully rubbed her shoulders and lower back. The filtered sun felt warm across her face while she soaked her feet in the coolness of a pool of river water. She felt the roughness of his hands through her light blue cotton dress, which was soaked a few inches above the hem from dangling in the water. His hands, though rough, felt good on her lower back. That's where the pain usually hit this time of day.

Abigail sat staring across the river. The ripples of the current were determined by the gusts of wind whistling off the river and through the willow trees directly above them. Her eyes were glued on the mother duckling determined to cross to the other side while fighting off the force of the wind. Behind the unwavering mother were eight baby ducklings, each lined up in a perfectly straight line following its mother.

"How does she do it?" Abigail questioned, so softly that Jed didn't even hear her.

Her hands were in continuous motion rubbing her swollen tummy. "I'm scared, Jed," she said, this time loud enough to cause Jed to stop rubbing her back.

He leaned around her to give her a reassuring kiss on her cheek. "It'll be just fine; the doctor just said so, didn't he?" She didn't respond, so he added, "I mean, that's how I heard it, so you don't fret none and just enjoy this whole thing."

"Enjoy the whole thing!?" Abigail yelled, causing Jed to slip off his rock and land belly up on the muddy shoreline.

"Gosh darn it, Abigail, look what you made me do, now I look like a mudslinging pig farmer!"

Abigail broke out in laughter. Jed soon joined her, easing their tension as well as her lower back pain.

It had been ten months since exchanging their vows. They had just moved into their own little house, which was only two houses down from where the Higgins lived. It was a simple home with three rooms, one for the two of them, one for entertaining guests, and a kitchen. They planned on having the baby stay with them until Jed could expand the back side to add two more rooms. The front porch was large, like so many in the area, but didn't wrap around the side of the house like the one Jed had become used to at the Higgins' home.

Abigail had spent countless hours adding her womanly touches to their house. It had become their home, and they would soon be welcoming their newest family member.

Now Abigail adjusted herself on the smooth boulder while thinking about how the baby would look snuggled in its crib. She rubbed her swollen tummy lovingly, hoping her time would come soon.

Her husband's voice interrupted her thoughts. "Just think of it, Abigail, *my son* is going to be as big as a house and strong as an ox, so all of your carrying on like this will be well worth it."

Abigail glared at him. If stares could kill, Jed would have died on the spot.

Abigail abruptly shot up from her rock, turned, and stormed off toward Main Street and her father's mercantile store. She needed to make sure all the plans for the new baby were set in stone, but more importantly, she needed some time away from her husband. *Who does he think he is telling me that I was "carrying on and all"?*

"Now, Abigail, I do believe the entire town has their marching orders for when the baby comes," Fez reassured her. "You worry too much; trust me, it'll all be fine. Do you see Jed making all this fuss?" Abigail heard a noise and turned to see Jed. She was surprised that he had walked in right behind her from the river. He was trying to wipe off his mud-soaked pants with a new towel he had found on one of the front display racks of the Mercantile.

Fez saw the looks on their faces as they glared at each other. "Now, you two!" Fez cried out. "It's just a baby, for gosh sakes!"

Abigail turned toward Jed, hissing as she asked, "And what makes you so sure that this baby will be a boy, smart aleck?"

The air was thick with the silence of prelabor tension as Jed and Abigail bid farewell to Fez and walked up Main Street. Jed hoped that Abigail would return to her normal self once she became comfortable within the walls of her own home. He couldn't even imagine what she was going through, but knew that it was his fault that her demeanor had turned sour. *I should just keep my big mouth shut at times like these. I'd be madder than all get out too if I had to go through what she's been going through. And to put up with my mouth to boot. That takes the cake . . .*

* * * * *

The night was still as they sat quietly rocking on the wooden front porch, overlooking the town. It was their favorite spot to enjoy the quiet, despite the ongoing chirping of crickets. It was there in their rockers that they planned, on their many talks, the family decisions to come. The porch was painted white with a large wooden railing wrapped around its front. Two steps came off the front and met a brick walkway in the front yard that was lined by a tall green hedge. The tension from earlier in the day at the Mercantile had since subsided, and Jed was thankful that he hadn't made things worse with his careless words.

A cat was meowing around the corner of the porch, but the creaking of the screen door opening must have scared it away, as the feline talk abruptly stopped. Jed came back out after refreshing his lemonade, but after looking at Abigail, he knew she was ready to call it a night.

He assisted Abigail back into the house. As they entered their bedroom, Abigail crouched over in pain and frantically grasped for Jed's sleeve to steady herself.

"I think something's . . . I think something's happening, Jed," she said.

The jolting pain shot threw her again and she yelled, "Put me down on the bed, Jed, and get the doctor . . . . Quickly, Jed!"

Jed laid her down, covered her with the comforter, and turned to leave. "Jed? . . . Jed!" He turned quickly at the sound of her frantic voice, and the look on her face frightened him. "Please hurry . . . I'm scared" was all he heard as he sprinted down Main Street to get Doctor Andersen.

When Jed returned with the doctor, Abigail was drenched in sweat and breathing hard. "Jed, I need you to go down the street and get Sara Higgin," the doctor said in a matter-a-fact tone.

Jed hurried for the door, but was stopped by the doctor's voice when he said calmly but quite firmly, "And Jed, this baby's coming fast and it won't wait for you, so if I were you . . . "

"I got it, Doc!" And out the door Jed went at a sprint to get more help.

The doctor and Sara were busy inside. Jed paced frantically in front of the porch, and Fez sat on the porch steps with his ears geared for any sound from inside.

"Why does it take so long, Fez?" Jed asked, wiping nervous sweat from his brow. "What is happening in there . . . is something wrong?" Jed's questions were asked without expecting answers, and his pacing began to make a path in the front yard. Fez was trying to ease the strain, but was a bit of a wreck himself.

A loud scream startled Jed and raced to the front door, thinking something terrible must have happened. Having helped Abigail's mother with the delivery of their daughter, Fez knew the noises were expected. He stopped Jed from entering.

Another loud scream could be heard, and sent shivers up and down Jed's spine. Moments later, he could hear the high-pitched cry of a baby, and then it was eerily quiet. Jed couldn't stand it much longer. He froze when the door opened, and out came the doctor, wiping his hands with a fresh towel from the basin.

Jed rushed up to the doctor, almost knocking the poor man down. "Well?"

Looking a bit drained after his latest of many deliveries, Doctor Andersen said slowly, "Jed, everyone is doing just fine. A little tired, but just fine."

The doctor took off his wire-rimmed spectacles, wiped them, and continued. "You can go in once Sara finishes cleaning up the place and dressing Abigail. I'll be back in the morning to see how they're doing."

Doctor Andersen put his hands on Jed's upper arms. "Jed?"

"Yes, Doc," Jed answered, feeling distracted.

"You haven't asked," the Doctor hinted.

"Asked what, Doc?" Jed's voice rose. "Is Abigail alright?"

With a chuckle, the doctor shook his head and started for the front steps.

"What is it, Doc?" Jed asked, slightly annoyed at this point.

"Jed, it's a boy." The doctor said quietly with a grin.

Fez grabbed Jed's arm. "Come on, Son, let's go take a look. Sara should be done by now!"

Jed had never seen such a sight in his life. There in front of him lay his beautiful bride and his newborn baby boy. He had a puzzled look on his face and muttered dumbly, "It's so small."

"*He's* just perfect," she whispered, "and *he's* not an *it*."

Sara reappeared and instructed Jed to wait in the next room for a spell so that mother and baby could get some feeding time.

"I can't believe it. I've waited forever outside and now that I have my son, I have to leave him again. What's with you two women, anyway?" Jed complained.

With a soft nudge on his elbow, Sara whispered. "Now you go on, and keep your voice down, Jed. You don't want your little boy growing up thinking of you as a bully, do you?"

As Jed turned to leave, Sara caught his arm. "He's a fine-looking boy, Jed. Your folks would have been very proud."

He walked out, and as the door closed behind him, he realized he had a lot to learn and a lot to be responsible for. He was panicking with the fear that he wouldn't be able to care for his new family. He wished he still had his father so that he could ask him the numerous questions stirring in his mind.

* * * * *

Just four weeks after becoming a father, Jed ignorantly asked Abigail, "He never sleeps—he just cries. Is that ever going to end?"

Jed looked down at his boy, who was wrapped tightly in swaddling clothes and an oversized hat that made his ears turn down. He had a full head of hair, dark brown eyes, his mother's tiny nose, and the smallest fingers that Jed had ever seen.

"He can barely wrap those tiny things around my little finger," Jed said with a proud smile.

Jed and Abigail stared for hours at the new creation they had brought into the world.

There was a knock on the door, and in walked Fez to see his grandson. Sara had left just an hour before, and was kindly coming by several times a day to help Abigail get used to her new role as a mother.

Abigail, looking down at her son, remembered what Sara said as she left. "Don't worry, dear. You'll have all this down after your fifth one comes, so don't worry if you are struggling now. It's quite normal."

"Fifth one?" she whispered to herself as she brushed the tiny cheeks of her first child, not even able to imagine going through the experience of childbirth four more times.

"How's everyone doing in here, and—" looking to Jed, "when are you coming back to work?" Fez asked joyfully but with a hint of anxiousness.

Fez had been very gracious in allowing Jed time off from work to be with Abigail and the baby. He was hoping that by doing so, the two would hurry up and come up with a name—well, one that would stick. "Okay, so what's his name today?" Fez asked with a playful huff.

"Now, Papa, you know we don't want to rush in on such an important decision. He's going to have that name for the rest of his life, and besides, just 'cause you want it to be 'Fester' doesn't change our minds about taking our time," Abigail jokingly scolded.

"I just keep hearing all kinds of different names each time I come by—I just figured one of these days, one was going to stick," Fez shot back.

"Well, and it's not just because you asked, but yes, we have come to our decision," Abigail confided.

"I knew it!" Fez yelled, as he sat down with excitement. "I just knew it would be Fester! I mean, I'm all right with Fester Jedidiah or something like that, but either way, I knew you would see it my way!"

Abigail and Jed rolled their eyes.

"Okay, Papa," Abigail continued. "First, I need you to understand, it isn't going to be Fester, though we know how much you were hoping it would be." She paused and waited for him to register and accept this decision.

"Papa—we would like to officially introduce you to our first son, your first grandson, William Zachary Monroe, named after your father and Jed's father.

Using a few seconds to compose himself from the initial hit to his ego, Fez recovered and stood up. He went over to them and reached out for a family hug.

The little boy let out a wail. Fez backed away and said, "All . . . right . . . and with that, I do need to get back to the Mercantile."

Fez slapped Jed on the back and gave him a look.

Recognition suddenly registered on Jed's face. "Yea . . . uh . . . me too, Fez, I'm right behind you. I think my wife needs to use her magic to calm this little fella down. Right, Mrs. Monroe?"

Jed, about to follow his father-in-law out the door, stopped and bent down. He put his head inside the bassinet and whispered, "You take good care of your momma, too, William Zachary. She did mighty good bringing you into our lives, ya hear?"

The two men, arms around each other's shoulders, headed down Main Street as the cries of the newest member of their family faded in the distance. As they entered the Mercantile, Fez turned to Jed. "Okay, I get it now, you two are waiting for the next one to name after me, right?"

"Yea, that's it, Fez," Jed said as he laughed.

Chapter Eleven

Uncertain Expansion
1844

"Willie! Go get your brother before he goes in the street!" The loud order came from Abigail as she attempted to hang fresh laundry on the clothesline. The wet laundry hung over a tight rope, one side attached to a large maple tree and the other nailed to the house. It was quite a sight, with undergarments of all shapes and sizes now that they were a family of five.

She eyed two of her boys as the breeze blew gaps between clothes on the line. The two were arguing, but Abigail was used to it. Seeing that Willie, now five, had seemingly settled their current dispute, Abigail waddled inside the house to check on her youngest, Micah, who was sound asleep in his crib. She sat down in the rocker next to the well-worn crib to rest for a moment. She looked around the room, and noticed the chipped paint on the crib and boys' clothes littered throughout the room. Thinking to herself just how fast the years had gone by, she rubbed her tummy and felt the all-too-familiar kick coming from her soon-to-be-born fourth child.

Daniel was the first one to break her from her trance when he came tramping into the room that combined as a baby's room with Abigail and Jed's. "Willie hit me, Momma!"

"I did not, Momma!" yelled Willie in response. "He was in the street, Momma, so I grabbed his shirt and yanked him back into the yard."

With a deep sigh of exhaustion, Abigail rocked for a moment before replying. "Now, now, boys, let's just get along, and yes, Daniel, Willie was doing what I'd asked him to do. I don't want you playing in the street. There are way too many horses and wagons coming from both directions. You both need to stay in the side yard or in the back, do you hear me?"

"Yes, Momma," they replied in unison.

To Fez's delight, his second grandchild carried his name. Daniel Fester Monroe was a wild and energetic four-year-old and seldom followed directions unless it was after a stern scolding from his father. He resembled Jed more than Abigail with his light brown hair, deep-set dark brown eyes, and dark complexion.

He tested the patience of his parents, as he was doing at that moment. Abigail noticed that Daniel was climbing up the side of the baby's crib, but before he got to the point of climbing in, she said, "Daniel Fester, what are you doing up on that crib?"

"I want to see my little brudder!" Daniel shouted.

"No, you go back out in the yard and play with Willie," Abigail demanded. She pulled Daniel off the crib and placed him securely on the floor. She smiled as he ran out the back door, then reached into the crib to retrieve Micah, who was waking prematurely from his nap thanks to his brother.

"Okay, there, Micah Jefferson, come on up here to your momma." His eyes locked on hers, and he knew it was mealtime when the two of them sat down on the rocker and she pulled him in closer to her.

Abigail glanced out the window at the crowded front porch. She could barely hear Jim Bridger, John Fremont, her father, and Jed discussing the latest news from down South in Santa Fe. From this section of the room, she could almost keep up with the conversation while she tried to keep little Micah from wiggling off her lap.

The sun warmed the porch as hummingbirds enjoyed the nectar of a blooming honeysuckle. It was a relaxing Saturday, and Joe Carter was watching the Mercantile, giving Fez time to rest and spend time with his grandchildren. The mood was amicable, but those on the porch were not in complete agreement about the subject at hand.

"I know, I know, John, and I hear it all the time down at the Mercantile," a heated-up Fez stammered. "But it just doesn't make any sense, and why push the matter? It'll just send us all into a war, or is that exactly what President Tyler wants?"

Fez paused for a moment, it seemed to Abigail, in an attempt to calm himself before continuing. "I mean, business is good right now, so why mess it all up with talks of annexation and war?"

The entire group chimed in their agreement with Fez. Each talked at the same time as the other, so no one could hear what the other said, until it seemed that Bridger had finally had enough.

"President Tyler!" Bridger yelled, and immediately the porch became quiet. "Our beloved president, if you call him that, is in cahoots with his secretary of state John C. Calhoun, who is pushing to have Texas annexed!"

"I just don't see that as a problem, Jim," interrupted Fremont. "I mean, all the talk I'm hearing is how much everyone wants this nation to go from one sea to the next. So what's the big deal?"

"I'll tell you what the big problem is, my friend," Bridger responded. "Down there in Texas, and it's been going on since before '37, is this huge republic and the enormous debt it carries. Two problems exist there. One, if we annex Texas, then we assume all its debt, and two, Mexico declares war on us."

Abigail watched as Bridger stood up and adjusted his chair to get out of the afternoon sun. "I do know that Tyler tried to negotiate with Texas to leverage some of its land to pay off its debt to us. I've heard that he even suggested that Texas split up its Republic into four separate states, but his good buddy Calhoun was set against that. In Calhoun's opinion, if Texas split up its Republic, then half of the land would be above the Mason–Dixon Line, hence half would be free and half would be slave, and Calhoun, being a firm Southerner, would have no part in having a Free State entering the Union. If you ask me, fellas, that darn Calhoun is going to take all of us straight down to—"

"Do you boys really think Mexico would declare war on the United States over Texas after getting whooped at San Jacinto?" Jed asked as he interrupted Bridger midsentence. "I mean, even their General Santa Anna fled his country and is hiding in Cuba. Why in the world would Mexico even think twice about wanting a war with us anyway?"

Jed waved his friends closer and lowered his voice. "I tell you boys, if we do go to war with Mexico over this, I'm saying right now that I'm all in."

His voice may have been low, but Abigail heard every word. Micah had fallen asleep in her arms and she pulled him close. She felt her chest tightening as tears streamed down her cheeks.

Abigail took a moment to regain her composure before going outside to join her husband and the others on the porch. She glanced at her boys, who had made their way to the front yard. They were playing stickball with a piece of bark from the maple tree and a broken piece of porch railing. She thought of her sons. *Wouldn't it be nice not to have a care in the world and just play stick ball or dig holes looking for rabbits, instead of talking about wars? Why do adults have to complicate everything anyway?* She was hoping the sadness didn't still show on her face as she sat next to her husband, who had no idea she had overheard everything.

* * * * *

Before Abigail's arrival on the porch, Pastor Higgin had stopped by the Monroe home on his way to the Mercantile and had taken a seat with the rest of the group.

"Pastor, we were just talking about the issue down South toward Santa Fe, and all the talk about annexation." Fez attempted to get the Pastor caught up with the discussion while pouring him a glass of tea.

"Well, boys, that's a coincidence," Pastor Higgin said. "I just met a gentleman coming off the riverboat who heard a speech from one of the candidates running for president this year. The candidate's name is James K. Polk. Any of you ever heard of him?" After seeing all of their shoulders shrug, indicating no one had heard of Polk, he continued. "It seems from talking to this man, that if elected, Polk will be pushing to grab up every bit of land from sea to sea and up North as well."

"Well, I don't know about up North," Bridger replied. "But if I were president, or running for president like this Polk character is, I would think that ol' England is a bit stronger than little ol' Mexico, so if I were Polk, I'd probably try for one but not the other. If you know what I mean?"

"Yea," Fez added, trying to look serious with his comments. "You're probably right, Jim. I mean, you probably hear all about that issue up North with all the folks coming and going out of your—what do they call it now? Your fort?"

"Hey, Jim, they named it after you, didn't they?" Jed asked. "Fort Bridger—what a name! And here I am sitting right next to you. I guess I'm a bit famous, too. Right, boys?"

"Ow!" Jed yelled in response to the friendly punch in the arm he received from his good friend.

As the laughter at Bridger's expense quieted down, Pastor Higgin continued. "It seems that President Tyler just about has the annexation of Texas wrapped up, and I hear he plans on using that as the namesake for his presidency."

He finished up his glass of tea, gave Abigail a friendly pat on the forearm, and got up from his chair. "Well, I had best be going. See you all tomorrow at church, *right*?" the Pastor asked over his shoulder as he walked down the porch steps. He stopped at the walkway and turned full to the group. "I'm sorry—I didn't hear you, *Mister Fester Wright*—I'll see you at church, *right*?" Without waiting for Fez's reply and anticipating none, the Pastor turned and was off to the Mercantile.

They all watched Pastor Higgin walk out of sight up Main Street, and then Jed turned to his father-in-law and said with a wide grin, "Boy, Fez, he sure knows you well, doesn't he?"

"Well, Jed, I wouldn't talk there, Son. If I recall, you were supposed to be doing a lot more with the good ol' Pastor and that church than what's been happening?"

Jed looked away from his friends as his finger began to tap on the porch railing. Abigail could tell that the guilt was likely rising in him again.

"Okay, let's change horses a bit and talk about the good out of all this," Bridger said cheerfully as he changed the subject. Abigail excused herself to get the boys cleaned up for their afternoon Bible studies.

"Look at you, John," Bridger continued. "You've been pretty quiet the past hour, just doodling on that tablet of yours. Looks to me like another one of your maps. I'm telling you, my friend, you've practically drawn up every map known to man regarding the land from Independence to Santa Fe. And don't forget the maps you did for the army up the Oregon Trail as well."

Fremont put his notebook down and looked at his friend across the porch with a sly grin. "I'm not the one who has a fort named after me!"

"Now come on, it's not a fort, gentlemen!" Bridger tried to downplay the group of houses, livery buildings, and warehouses that many were indeed calling "Fort Bridger." "I mean, I'm not the one who will probably have a statue built for me for all the maps I've drawn up of this country. Yes, I can see it now: 'The John C. Fremont Memorial.' Yep, it couldn't have happened to a better fella!"

Abigail came back out. The screen door crashed closed behind her. She had a toddler in one arm and a fresh pitcher of tea in the other. "Jed, when are you going to fix that gosh-darn screen door, or just take it down, you know?" Fez scolded his son-in-law, while Jed jumped up to grab his youngest child.

"Here honey, sit down. I'll pour the tea," Jed said as he helped his very pregnant wife to her seat.

"Jed, I do think you're gonna be making good use of Doctor Andersen real soon now, don't you all think?" Bridger said, observing Abigail's state. "When are you two gonna call it quits and settle on what you have?"

Abigail looked at the burly man seated next to her, the faint scent of a dead animal on him—though she was used to that by now—*that's just Jim*, she thought to herself.

"Now, Jim," Abigail said, with laughter in her voice, "we haven't had a boy to name after you yet, so we just might have to keep trying until we do just that." The porch exploded with laughter.

* * * * *

Abigail sat in silence on the porch, but her mind was racing. She listened to her oldest son, who was working on his times tables out loud in order to memorize them. The worry in her chest continued to boil the more they talked of war. She knew her husband well after six years of marriage, and she could tell by his tone that he was stirring up something that she was not going to like.

The memory of his voice came back to her over and over. *I tell you boys, if we go to war against Mexico over this, I'm there.* Her gaze was not at the porch, but her children. She had a family now, and she knew that she had a responsibility to keep them all safe, and most of all—together.

Bridger, who had been quiet for a few minutes, slapped his hand on his leg, raised himself off his chair, and bid everyone a good day. "I reckon we'll be talking about all this for some time, but I best be getting up to the diner to get some grub. Thanks to all for an enjoyable afternoon, and Jed, don't be making any rash decisions any time soon, you hear?" He started down the steps toward Main Street and then yelled without turning around. "Oh, and Abigail, you can name him James or Jim, it doesn't make no difference to me—you know what I mean?"

The rest joined in laughter, but Abigail barely heard him. She was thinking of his earlier statement. *Jed, don't be making any rash decisions any time soon, you hear?*

One by one, each bid his farewell. The last one to leave was Fez, and he pulled Jed aside. "Son, I know what you're thinkin', I can see it in your eyes. It's the same look I seen back in '37, and I know you got that restlessness again. But this time it's different, Son, you got a family. So think real hard, you hear?"

"I got it Fez," Jed said. "But sometimes a man has to put his beliefs and his nature ahead of everything, and trust in the good Lord to carry him through, right?"

Jed looked around to see if Abigail was within earshot before he continued. "I feel really strong about what Mexico is doing down South, and yet on the other hand I can hear my momma tellin' me to forgive and be forgiven. But Fez, I just don't have that in me, and I need to follow my conscience toward the direction it's taking me."

"Again, Son, you have a wife and family now," Fez said, turning his face away and staring out at the yard.

"My life and my love are right here with Abigail and my sons, Fez," Jed said firmly. "But sometimes my sense of duty outweighs the luxury of being complacent."

The two men walked in silence out to Main Street. Fez had his head down and his voice was barely audible when he said, "You know that I look at you as more than just the husband of my daughter, don't you? I mean, I never had a son and all, and well . . . I'll be praying for you, Jedidiah Monroe."

Fez turned to face Jed, then grabbed his shirtsleeve tightly. "I know the good Lord will guide you to make the right decision when that time comes. But please do me a favor—pray about it and think about it before making any quick decision. Talk with Abigail, spend some time with her—heck, give me the kids, and the two of you go and enjoy a day together—God knows you could use it."

Jed looked toward the house and could see Abigail standing in the doorway, the broken screen door barely hanging on. "You know, Fez, you're absolutely right. I think I will take you up on that. If it's all right with you, I'd like to do it real soon."

Once Abigail and Jed's friends were gone, a quietness fell over the Monroe home. They stood together, watching their three boys peacefully playing on the living room floor, the sounds of Pastor Higgin's church bell tolling in the distance. Abigail reached out and held Jed's hand, and for that short moment at least, they felt a comforting sense of peace and security.

Chapter Twelve

Short-Lived Joy
1845

The air was thick with the coming rain as Jed made his way in the early morning light down the front steps of his home and then to the Mercantile. As he crossed his front yard, he passed by the wagon of one of his boys. He stopped as he noticed a small stuffed bear at the wheel. It had only one arm and one eye. He smiled lovingly at the condition of the unfortunate animal, and he felt a sense of gratitude for all of the Lord's blessings on him and his family. His nights had been restless lately, and he spent most of his time tending to Abigail and the children, or lying awake thinking and praying. He pictured his family inside, and he thanked the Lord for his three boys sleeping soundly in their beds, and the newest and smallest one in her bassinet just an arm's distance from her mother. Doctor Andersen had delivered their baby girl, Millie Elizabeth Monroe, earlier in the year. The Monroe family was indeed growing, but with each new delivery, the concern over Abigail's health rose. Abigail told Jed that all was good, but he could see in her eyes that this last delivery had been a hard one.

A block from the Mercantile, Jed stopped and looked ahead at the sign—Wright Mercantile. He could hear the morning frogs croaking along the riverbank. Jed stopped in his tracks. He turned and walked quickly back up Main Street with a determination to get something off his chest, deciding that it was time to tell it all to Abigail. As he approached the house, he had second thoughts and decided to walk a bit farther. He stopped at the front gate of Pastor Higgin's church.

Jed could hear the distant rumble of the town of Independence waking up. The front door of the church was unlocked as usual, and Jed walked in. The smell of cedar from the pews filled the air. Each pew was perfectly clean, thanks to the painstaking efforts of Sara and the women's auxiliary. He stood at the back of the church and looked up at the man hanging on the cross. His sad face was turned down and to the left, but in Jed's mind, he was looking right at him.

In deep thought, Jed walked down the center aisle and chose a pew near the front, the only sound the creaking of cedar as Jed sat down. His eyes focused on the despair in the face of the statue of his Savior Jesus Christ. In that moment, Jed felt as if it was just his Savior and him in that room—nothing else existed. The tears flowed freely as he sat and stared up at the image on the cross. The turmoil inside him, tearing him apart, had reached the breaking point, and he felt he needed the help of providence to pull him through his nightmare.

He saw an image of his parents standing before him, disappointment in their eyes as they looked down at him sitting in the church alone.

I should have written.

I have four children and a beautiful wife and you'll never see them, hear them, or know them.

I let you down, and I'll never have the chance to ask for your forgiveness . . .

Jed was lost in a state of guilt and he wished his parents could somehow join him and his own little family. He wished they could tell him that they forgave him, were proud of him, and loved him.

Those words would never come and he knew it, understanding that he would feel that guilt for the rest of his life. He had his wife and his family, but he also carried with him the burden and guilt from disappointing his parents, and he made a vow that day that he would strive to mend the wound he had caused and regain peace in his heart and soul, no matter what it took.

Jed had tried to relieve the guilt years before by traveling with wagons on the Oregon Trail, and now believed that he could only be absolved by taking it out on a Mexican enemy that he knew very little about. *Something, someone has to relieve this massive guilt.*

Jed felt that he couldn't bear his guilt alone. He loved his wife so very much, and he needed to involve Abigail with these feelings he was having. He had to find that peace he was searching for, and who better to help him find it but his soul mate and the mother of his four beautiful children?

He sat there motionless for a long time. He heard the whistle from the riverboat down at the dock, and it brought him back to reality. The vision of his parents was gone, and the only sight before him now was of Christ hanging on the cross.

He brought himself out of his gloom and proceeded to walk down the middle aisle of the church and out the front door. Pastor Higgin had seen

Jed leave the church and could see the troubled look on his face as he walked down the street. He bowed his head in prayer for the young man who came with him from Wheeling so many years earlier, the young man who had become more like a son to him than a friend.

Returning to Main Street, Jed passed by his sleeping house. It looked warm and welcoming from the street as he stood by a maple tree just a few feet from its wooden fence. He could see the kids' toys scattered throughout the yard. The paint on the wood siding needed touching up, and he chuckled a bit when he looked at the screen door, half on and half off its hinges. He could sense the stillness inside as his family slept, and quietly thanked God for such a blessing.

It had been more than a year since that afternoon when the men had lounged on the front porch of the Monroe house and talked politics. Fremont had enlisted in the army to continue mapping the western United States, and Bridger had left Independence to continue to develop his outpost on the Oregon Trail.

* * * * *

The 1846 New Year brought with it a sense of hope and excitement, hampered by anxiety and fear borne of the constant talk of war. Ever since President Tyler had attempted to negotiate an annexation treaty for Texas, an event that caused Mexico to sever diplomatic relations with the United States, tension along the Santa Fe Trail had been fierce. Small skirmishes on the trail and along the Rio Grande River were escalating, and everyone in Independence was waiting for Mexico to declare war on the United States over rights at the border.

Tensions grew even stronger when newly elected President James K. Polk announced his intention for the greatest territorial expansion of the United States to date. He mapped it out and called it "Manifest Destiny," a plan that extended the rights of the United States to its natural borders at the Atlantic and Pacific Oceans.

Those living in Independence were becoming nervous that this would not only intensify problems with Mexico, but also invite England into a possible conflict over rights in the Oregon Territory. Travel on the Santa Fe and Oregon Trails was down sixty percent. Without a military escort accompanying each train, most emigrants canceled their plans to travel west.

Business at the Mercantile suffered from the decreased number of trains traveling the two main trails west and south. Supplies weren't needed, and inventory piled up while Fez and other merchants suffered from reduced cash flows.

"We can weather this storm, Fez," Jed said while attempting to comfort his father-in-law.

"I don't know, Jed," Fez replied as the two walked outside and sat on the termite-infested bench under the Mercantile front window. "We have so much inventory, and the need for supplies on the trails is not what it was ten years ago." They propped their feet up on the horse trough in front of them. The air was still with the warmth of summer, and the streets were bare and quiet. There was little they could do but wait.

"It's just strange around here, ya know?" mumbled Fez.

"I tell you, Fez, ever since Polk took over the White House, everyone is either gunning up for a battle or running scared," Jed said as he brushed a fly off his ear. "I wouldn't hesitate joining up and teaching them Mexes down South to stay on their side of the river and let us take what's ours."

"That means war, Jed!" Fez cautioned. "Are you ready to march off and leave Abigail and the children in order for you to prove yourself a man? Does that stuff down South bother you so much that you're willing to give it all up and risk everything for a cause you have nothing to do with?"

"Nothing to do with?" Jed shot back. "I have everything to do with what's going on. We live in a country that we fought for, and we have another country telling us what is their land and what is ours!"

Jed got up from the bench and leaned against the wood siding of the mercantile shop. He looked at the dirty water in the trough and brushed another fly away. "We have a right to fight for what is ours, Fez!"

Jed became agitated with the subject they were discussing, and his anger was now spilling out on Fez. "I tell you, Fez, it's just a matter of time, and whether it's Mexico or England, there's gonna be a war, and I am going to be a part of it. No disrespect, Fez, but I'm not going to be a mercantile clerk the rest of my life!"

Seeing the hurt look in Fez's eyes, Jed sat back down next to his father-in-law. He regained his composure before continuing. "Fez, you know I promised my folks that I would be a pastor, and look how that turned out." He shifted in his seat as he thought for a moment about that statement and the many other promises to his folks that he hadn't delivered on.

Attempting to ease the tension, Fez said, "Come on, Jed, it's getting hot out here. Let's go back inside the Mercantile and try to rally some business around. What ya say, partner?" He gave Jed a hard slap on the back and a friendly shove, and the two went back to work as they waited for their next paying customer. But the Mercantile remained quiet and empty for another hour.

The stillness was quickly erased by the thundering sounds of horse-hoofs and wagon wheels churning down Main Street. Jed and Fez dropped what they were doing and rushed to the front door of the Mercantile.

"What in tarnation is all this about?' Fez questioned out loud, as he saw a division of blue-coated soldiers come to a stop in front of the Mercantile. A burly man with thick gray whiskers and flowing gray hair climbed down from a dark brown stallion. He looked up and down the street, handed over the reins of his horse, yelled out orders to a couple of his lieutenants, and crossed in front of the horse trough as he made his way toward the open door of the Mercantile. He had gold bars on his shoulders that could barely be seen under the inch of trail dust that covered his uniform.

He looked at Fez and Jed, and without a cordial greeting belted out, "I'm Brigadier General Zachary Taylor of the United States Army of the West." His eyes never completely made contact with theirs, but instead darted about as if he were familiarizing himself with his surroundings before making his next move.

"How do, General?" the older Fez replied in a calmer and more civilized tone. "What can we do for you boys? We have plenty of supplies, and the livery stable has plenty of room if you need a place for your horses."

Jed reached out his hand to the general. "I'm Jedidiah Monroe, and this here is my father-in-law, Fester Wright. We are the owners of this here mercantile store."

The general showed no interest in small talk or formalities. Fez whispered to Jed, "*We* . . . are the owners?"

"Oh, get over it, Fez," Jed whispered back, "this could be huge! I wonder if it has anything to do with all the commotion down South, or maybe even up Oregon way?"

Fez saw the excited look in Jed's eyes.

"Gentlemen," the general continued, addressing Fez and Jed in a deep baritone voice, "I'm going to assign my quartermaster to come see you. You must fulfill quite a large order of supplies for us."

"That sounds great, General!" Fez responded, forgetting all about his recent conversation with Jed about how slow their business had been lately.

"How long do you plan on being in town, General?" Jed interjected, trying not to sound too excited as they made their way further into the Mercantile.

"We have orders to resupply here and then we'll—"

The general sized up Jed and Fez, then looked each way to confirm that they were indeed the only civilians in the Mercantile. He hit his sleeves with his hat, attempting to remove as much trail dust as possible, and then found a chair to sit on. "We'll have to wait for two more divisions to arrive before we head on down the Santa Fe Trail to look into the trouble that's been brewing down there."

The general nodded to one of his young officers, who looked barely old enough to shave, then turned his attention back to Fez and Jed. "I'll wait to hear from my quartermaster over yonder to figure on the length of time needed to resupply, feed, groom, and rest our horses. Once I get an idea and we're reinforced by the other divisions, we will be on our way."

Jed eagerly asked, "General, what are the chances that the other divisions are gonna need some extra help down Santa Fe way?"

Fez dropped the kettle he had been trying to place on a display case. He looked at Jed with a scowl and said, "Jed, I'm sure the general here has much more to think about than someone wanting to join up with them midstream."

"I was just asking out of curiosity, that's all, Fez," Jed replied. "In fact, General, we have a friend in the army. Do you think by chance he might be in one of the divisions coming this way?"

General Taylor turned and faced Jed squarely and said, "Son, to answer your first question, we are always looking for good men to join us, and second, I'm sure you wouldn't know either of the commanding officers coming this way. One of them is Major General Stephen Kearny, and the other is Lieutenant Colonel John Fremont."

Fez suddenly felt queasy. He heard the eagerness in Jed's voice and saw the fire in his eyes. Fez's throat tightened, he couldn't swallow, and the only thing he could think of was his daughter and grandchildren. He looked hard at his son-in-law. *Please don't even think about it, Jed!* But Fez could see that his mind had already traveled to some other, distant place.

With a forced smile, Fez slapped Jed on the back and said, "So, we're going to have our good ol' friend John back with us again, at least for a little while, huh?"

"Hey, wouldn't it be something if big Jim showed up as well?" Jed replied. "We haven't seen either of them for over a year now, Fez—isn't that right?"

Without waiting for an answer, Jed continued. "Man, we could have so much fun in town if all four of us got together again—*you know what I mean?*"

Fez's head snapped up and he looked intently at Jed. They burst out laughing as they remembered Bridger's favorite saying. In unison, they chanted, "Yea, it would be great—'YOU KNOW WHAT I MEAN?' "

Their laughter came to a halt when the young officer handed Fez a list of needed supplies.

"Not a problem, Corporal," Fez said. "We'll take a look and give you an estimate within the hour. Sound good?"

Fez gave the list to Jed and asked him to start collecting the needed items, then excused himself. Jed continued to replay joyful memories of his good friend Jim Bridger in his mind, and the excitement of possibly joining up with the Army of the West, especially now that he knew his good friend John Fremont would soon be in Independence.

Fez walked outside, trying to shake the edginess that had returned. His feelings were the opposite of Jed's. He was filled with fear and worry, the temporary reprieve afforded by a little teasing at the expense of their mutual friend long gone.

He knew it was just a matter of time before he would see Jed and his daughter saying good-bye to each other once again. Jed's good-bye would be to fight in a war he knew nothing about, except the thrill of it all and the hope of ridding himself of some nagging guilt. Abigail's good-bye would be said instead with a choking voice and a hopeful heart. Neither scenario looked good to Fez, and though he loved his son-in-law dearly, he also felt, for the first time, some level of anger at Jed's desires, natural as they might have been. But mostly, he worried about his only daughter. His worry increased when he returned to help Jed fill the army's supply list.

Chapter Thirteen

Delight and a Painful Decision

1846

It was cold, it was wet, and the rain came down like sheets of feathered ice against their backs as they made their way to the buggy. They proceeded with determination and purpose. He knew he had to do this. She, seeing the weather and feeling the dampness, was a bit more skeptical of his purpose and agenda. But her trust in her husband allowed her to agree to whatever he had up his sleeve. The children were safe and sound at home under Grandpa Fez's care.

Jed wrapped another blanket around Abigail and pulled the cover of the buggy up high to prevent the icy rain from getting them overly wet. "What are we doing out here, Jed?" stuttered Abigail, her teeth chattering in the cold despite the warm wool blanket draped around her.

"I need to talk to you, and I don't think it can wait," replied Jed as he led the mare away from Main Street and down toward the Simpson Farm.

"I've got a place in mind where we can talk, and I promise it's a lot warmer," Jed said encouragingly.

Jed drove the buggy past the Simpson Farm about a half a mile and came to a familiar spot. It was hard to recognize with the rain, now turning to light snow, camouflaging the scene. The vines of honeysuckle all but stripped clean during its dormant period hung helplessly along the riverbank. The crashing of the river against the rocks could be heard now that the pounding of rain had been replaced by the silent flow of snow.

"Jed," she gasped with recognition. "Jed, this is our spot!"

"It'll always be our spot, Abigail, and it's the place where I've always felt the most comfortable when I've wanted to talk with you."

Trying to be kindhearted, but with her teeth still chattering, Abigail gingerly replied, "I know, honey, and I know you have a lot on your mind, b-b-but Jed, I'm f-f-freezing out here, and I don't know if I'll be able to hear a w-w-word you s-s-say."

He didn't seem to hear her as he tied up the mare and came around to offer his hand to help her down from the buggy.

She held on to his hand as she looked around. It was so peaceful with the calmness of the snowflakes as they began to turn the grassy area white, while a fine veil of snow settled on the trees and bushes. She was worried momentarily when she noticed the faint smell of smoke lingering in the air. "Jed, why do I smell smoke?"

He didn't immediately answer, but then with a smile said, "Shh, Abigail—just hold on to my hand and follow me."

"What are you doing, Jedidiah Monroe? There is nothing out here but trees, bushes, a river, and now a lot of snow . . . and I'm freezing!"

Jed pulled her along. "Trust me," he said.

Hidden in the thickness of the evergreens, a little cabin came into view. A thin line of smoke rose from the chimney. As they drew closer, Abigail could see a warm crackling fire inside.

"Jed, this wasn't here the last time, was it?" Abigail asked.

"No, the Simpsons built it just last year, and I've borrowed it for the night from Herman," he replied. "Surprised?"

"Mr. Monroe, if you keep on surprising me like this all my life, I'll just have to keep smothering you with love," she said. "But right now, let's get inside, cause I'm really, r-r-really freezing, and that fire looks very inviting."

When they were inside, Jed noticed that the fire had begun to smolder, so he put on another piece of wood, rubbing his hands together to bring some feeling back into them. Abigail draped the wet blanket over a chair in the corner of the room and came over to join her husband by the fire.

The cabin was simple, with one table and a small bed stacked with several quilts that made it look twice as big. Two rocking chairs sat near the fireplace, with a small side table between them. A vanity with a porcelain bowl and pitcher sat on a wooden dresser with an oval mirror attached to the top that reflected the blaze of the warming fire. The room was warm, and the mood was peaceful and loving.

"Jed, this is wonderful," Abigail said softly as she slowly came closer to him.

She hugged him gently and kissed him with a passion that reminded him of their wedding night. "You think of everything, don't you?" she whispered in his ear.

The room was glowing from the fire. All the desires they had suppressed while raising a home full of children came alive, and they melted into each other as they slipped under layers of quilts and into each other's arms. The two lovers became one in heart, soul, and flesh, reigniting the flame that they knew was there, but that they rarely exhibited.

The sounds of the crackling fire and lovemaking were all that could be heard, and then there was a moment of shared bliss before they separated and laid back in exhausted delight. They lay together, his arm around her, her head on his chest, both content with the love they had shared. Resting together, no words, no sounds, just the feel of their bodies nestled as one.

Jed got up to put more wood on the fire. He realized that after the heat of the moment, the coldness of the room was beginning to return. He grabbed a quilt that had slid to the floor, placed it back on the bed, and crawled under the covers to his loving and waiting wife.

Two more times did their love overtake their senses throughout the night, until exhaustion and satisfaction overtook them and they fell asleep in each other's arms.

The morning sun peeked through and was reflected by the vanity mirror as Jed lay on the bed and gazed out the window at the snow-covered tree limbs. He had gotten up a few minutes before to restart the fire and then slipped back into bed with Abigail. He noticed the serenity of the scene outside the window—the snow-covered grounds and pillows of snow on the branches of every tree. The sun reflecting off the snow and the sight of the flowing river a hundred yards from the cabin reminded him of the tranquil life he lived. He looked at his wife, the love of his life, and thanked God for blessing him with such an angel. She looked so peaceful and loving with her eyes closed, her lips parted slightly, and a soft hum coming from her rhythmic breathing.

He lay there, contemplating how to put his thoughts into words, even though he didn't exactly know himself what was in his heart. He had always recognized that Abigail knew him better than he knew himself. She had a sense about her that enabled her to know what he was thinking and feeling far sooner than he came to realize those things himself. He thought of last night and the lovemaking they had shared, and he thanked God again for blessing him with such a gift as his beloved Abigail.

Thoughts of the last ten years filled his head as he lay on the bed deep in thought. He reflected on his dreams and the promises he had made not only to his parents, but also to Pastor Higgin and the Society. So many promises to so many people, and he realized how many promises on which he had never really followed through. *Am I really such a bad person?* He was beating himself up inside.

I was supposed to help Pastor Higgin develop his church and then someday start one of my own, he thought. *I even promised Father that I would be a pastor someday, and Pastor Higgin was just the man to help me with it. How did that pan out, Jed? I basically left the Pastor and Sara in the lurch when I became so involved at the Mercantile. I wonder what they even think of me after all this time?* He judged himself harshly but believed that he deserved it.

He knew the Society had moved farther west years before, but he asked himself whether he had done all that was expected in helping them with their mission, or if he had only been looking out for himself.

Reflecting, he asked himself, *Do I still want to be a pastor? Come on, Jed—right now you don't know what you want. Well, I know that know that would make Father happy.* His mind was seemingly going a million miles an hour. *Maybe someday, who knows? But right now I have that restless feeling again that I can't quite put into words. Why can't I settle down?*

He was beginning to squirm in the bed because of his stressful thoughts. He didn't realize that he was actually talking out loud. "I have no idea how anyone could love a person like you, Jedidiah Monroe. I know I sure wouldn't."

"I sure do," Abigail's said quietly but emphatically as she looked quizzically at her husband.

"You sure have a lot on your mind, Mr. Monroe. I've been watching you the past half hour, and if your facial expressions are any indication of what's on your mind, well then, you and I have a lot to talk about, don't we?"

Turning herself to face him in bed, Abigail rubbed a hand through Jed's hair, and with loving compassion said, "You know you can talk to me, my darling, and you should also know that I will always support you."

She raised herself up on her elbow and looked her husband directly in the eyes and said, "You say you don't know who could ever love you? Well, my dear, I think I showed you last night how much I can love you."

Jed felt the memories of the previous night and laid his head back on the pillow. He stared up into the rafters of the room as Abigail continued. "We always will be one spirit, one mind, and one body, Jed. God brought us together, and only He can pull us apart, and I don't want you to ever doubt that, you hear?"

Abigail rested her head comfortably on Jed's chest and as she pulled the quilt up to keep herself warm. She tried to think of what could be tormenting her husband so. All kinds of thoughts crossed her mind, and she became anxious not knowing.

"I have no idea what's going on inside me, Abigail," Jed finally started to say. "It's like in '37 when I had that restlessness to get out on the trail."

Abigail, as she so often did, stayed silent and let her husband bare his heart to her.

"There is just so much going on around us right now, and I feel like I'm a man on an island and can't get near the action. This country is about ready to explode and expand its territory, and in doing so make history." Jed repositioned himself to look more directly at Abigail.

"Abigail, I want to be a part of that history," Jed confessed. "I want to be involved in the reshaping of this country. I don't want my children to grow up and only know that their father wore an apron and worked in a mercantile store. I want them to be proud of me, to be able to tell their children what kind of grandfather they had, what kind of a man he was."

They lay in silence, the only sound made by snow dripping from the cabin eaves. The temperature in the cabin began to cool as the heat from the fireplace faded.

"You know, I can lie here and tell you what you should or shouldn't do, but you also know that is something I will never do," Abigail said comfortingly. "I didn't do it in '37, and I'm not going to do it now. I love *you*, and your children love *their father*. We won't love you any differently because of what you do or don't do, or what you accomplish."

Abigail sat up, turned toward Jed, and said, "I won't lie and say that I understand exactly what you're feeling, because I don't. I want you to feel good about who Jedidiah Monroe is, and if that means that you pack up and leave us for heaven knows how long to go off and fight—then so be it."

Abigail paused to try to hide a sniffle before continuing, " . . . you go and do what you need to do, and then you come back to me."

She paused again and lowered her head back down onto his chest. His eyes, transfixed on the beam above, filled with tears.

"Jed, my husband Jed, my soul mate. Jed, the father of our children. Je . . . "

She choked on the last word as a crying convulsion caught her off guard. She rose again onto her elbow and looked at Jed's teary eyes. "You do what you need to do, and *when* you come back—not *if* you come back but *when* you come back—your family and your wife will be right here to welcome you. You may not think anyone loves you Jedidiah Monroe . . . "

Her crying started to take over, and her emotions made it much more difficult to speak. With her best effort she cried out as she said, "But I'm right here to tell you, Mister Monroe, that your family and your wife love you dearly and will always love you."

Jed's eyes overflowed with tears and his heart ached. He felt guilty and blessed at the same time at having been given such a gift as his Abigail.

"You know me so well, my love. You have always known me better than I know myself."

"That's why they call it love, dummy," she said, trying her best to relieve the tense emotions that had filled the room, and to ease her feeling of sorrow about his ultimate decision.

Abigail wrapped a quilt around her shoulders, walked to the window, and stared at the snowy country outside the cabin. She was considering that she might have given her husband permission to get himself killed in a war that meant nothing to her. But she loved him so much that she would not stand in the way of him somehow finding peace within himself. How he was going to find peace in the middle of a war was beyond her comprehension, but she told herself that no matter how many more times he did this, it didn't matter as long as he kept coming back to her.

She looked up at the falling snow coming off a branch from the tree outside, and could no longer hold back after that last thought of him coming back. As tears flowed and the knot in her heart became unbearable, she felt Jed's arms around her, and the flood of her emotions released as she melted into his arms.

They didn't speak during their trip back home from the cabin. He sat with the reins in his hands, navigating the wagon while digesting his guilt and second-guessing his plans. She sat staring straight ahead, pleading with God and asking Him to keep her husband safe and bring him back to his family.

As they were coming to their home, Abigail looked up to the sky and whispered softly, "Please God . . . take care of him and bring him back home to me again . . . will you please?"

She wiped tears from her cheeks as she climbed down from the buggy.

Chapter Fourteen

Tearful Good-Byes before Duty

1847

Independence had turned into a mass of soldiers, horses, and wagons. The usually calm commercial ship docks were bustling as military supplies were unloaded from deep in the bellies of timber-hulled ships. Two new divisions had arrived and were camped just outside of town. The waterfront saloons were overflowing with activity as soldiers indulged in drink and female companionship.

Fez had requested the help of Pastor and Sara Higgin, Herman and Rachael Simpson, and Willie in order to keep up with the enormous demands from the army. Jed watched with pride as his son, who was about to turn eight, worked as hard as all the others at Wright Mercantile. Three division quartermasters and Fez worked tirelessly as they collected the supplies needed for the army's upcoming deployment.

Jed helped out where he could, but he knew his time was limited after meeting with General Taylor. He had not been given his official orders, so he anxiously waited for one of Taylor's officers to find him and tell him where destiny would take him.

"Well there ol' friend, I heard from a little bird that you were joining up with us!"

Without looking up, Jed knew the sound of the voice and replied, "If it isn't the famous map artist of the West, right back here in his home away from home." Jed stood up from packing boxes, and reached over to grab the outstretched hand of John C. Fremont.

"I heard you've been given a division of your own. Is that true?" Jed asked.

"You heard that right, *Private*. Oh—I'm uncertain whether your official rank has been announced yet, but so you're aware. It sounds good, does it not?" Fremont joked.

"You know, John, to be quite honest, I don't know *what* I am. Since meeting with General Taylor a week or so ago and asking to come along, I've been sent around the mulberry bush and back more times than I can count. Sure could use some help."

"Let me see what I can find out for you," Fremont answered assuredly. "You just let me work on the details, and I'll make sure you get to where you need to be, and in plenty of time before we head out, all right?"

"That would surely be lifesaving, John. Just saying good-bye is going to be hard enough, but I have a feeling there's more that I'm not being told. If you can help me out with my orders, maybe I can find out before we leave."

"Speaking of Abigail, how's she taking it, Jed?" Fremont inquired, thinking that Abigail probably wasn't real happy about all this.

"Ah, you know, John, we talked, and I mean we talked for a long time, and . . ." Jed paused to regain his composure. "She's a good woman, John, and I certainly don't deserve her."

Jed paused, trying his best to suppress his guilt. "She's so supportive, John, even though I'm sure it's eating her up inside."

"Kind of reminds me of a few years back when you got that itch to see the West, huh?"

"Yea, but this time it's quite a bit different, my friend. We didn't have four children back then, and I wasn't going into a fireball of hostilities like we're facing down South," Jed countered.

"Ah, you'll be all right. As for me, I wouldn't have it any other way," Fremont said. "And as for Abigail, just think—in no time, you'll be right back here with that pretty little lady making babies all over again," Fremont continued in an effort to lighten up the moment.

"Let me head over to Taylor's tent right now, and I'll see if I can retrieve those orders for you. After reading them, you'll feel a whole lot better."

Jed thought about that comment for a moment. *"You'll feel a whole lot better." How am I going to feel a "whole lot better"? I'm leaving my wife and family to go fight a war I have no business being in.*

Jed placed his apron on the metal hook nailed to the wall above the pickle barrel in the back room of the Mercantile. He turned, intending to say good-bye to Fez, but was pleasantly surprised to run into his little son Micah, followed by his older brother Daniel. The boys ran right past Jed to a shelf where they grabbed their favorite lemon stick candy, ignoring their father as he stood over them and waited for a much-needed hug. He chuckled to himself, and thought about how candy would always outrank him when it came to his kids' affection. While he watched them, he got a lump in his throat, and he realized just how much he was going to miss them.

"Papa!" screamed little Millie, startling Jed and causing him to turn around abruptly and knock over the cans of coffee that had been displayed on the counter. Millie, now a toddler, was in a beautiful blue dress and matching bonnet that covered her curly blond hair. She was squirming in her mother's arms, clearly wanting to be let loose.

"Mama, down!" she demanded.

Abigail carefully put their daughter down. Little Millie, her eyes bulging wide, ran straight toward her father. Jed leaned down to catch her in his arms, but instead she went right past him to join her brothers, who were now getting their second lemon sticks from the candy jar.

Jed looked admiringly at Abigail as if he was seeing her for the first time. Her hair was placed high above her head with tiny ribbons. She was wearing a pink dress that looked new to Jed. Her eyes sparkled, and her cheeks were flushed from the walk to the Mercantile. She looked on with delight as their children actively devoured the lemon sticks and the boys helped keep a watchful eye on their little sister so she wouldn't choke on her stick.

"You look beautiful," Jed said softly. Her eyes stayed glued to her children, afraid that if she looked him in the eyes, she couldn't contain the pain and heartache boiling inside her. She said all she wanted to say during the past few days, and now it was time to enjoy what little time they had left as a family.

"Hey there!" yelled Willie, realizing his entire family was in the back of the Mercantile, and worse than that, all of his brothers and his sister were getting a treat and he wasn't.

"Now, that's not fair, give me that jar, Daniel!" Willie demanded of his younger brother. Willie grabbed the jar and retrieved a lemon stick of his own.

The four children were now sitting behind the wooden shelving that partitioned off the sections of the storeroom. Jed moved Abigail to the front of the wooden partition and out of the children's sight, pulled her close to him, and kissed her gently on the lips.

He slowly pulled away from her lips, looked into her moist eyes, and proclaimed, "This is exactly why I'm certain that I'll be back." He could feel the lump in his throat as he continued. "Abigail, God has given me a gift in you and these children. This family is what any man would fight to get back to."

As hard as she tried, Abigail couldn't contain her emotions, and with the children out of sight, she fell into Jed's arms and cried. They held each other tightly for several minutes, until Abigail felt a tug on her dress.

"Momma, why are you crying?" little Micah asked in a soft voice, looking up at his mother and then over to his father.

Jed got down on his knees and reached for Micah. "Son, your momma is crying tears of joy because she's so happy to have you, your brothers, and your little sister." Abigail sat down next to them on a small stool at the end of the counter.

Jed and Abigail knew it was time to let their children know what was really happening. Abigail held her youngest son close to her and said, "Micah, did you know that your papa is going to go and be a soldier?" Micah looked in astonishment at his father.

"Papa, you gonna be a soder?" Micah said in a loud voice that made the other two boys come out from around the partition.

"Papa's going to be a soldier?" asked Willie, standing behind Daniel and looking down at the rest of the family sitting on the floor.

"What rank are you going to be, Papa?" Daniel asked with excitement. "A general? A president?"

All three boys now looked at Jed, who was still sitting on the floor with them. He didn't know how to reply to his son. "No, Daniel, I'm not going to be a general, and I'm definitely not going to be the president," he said with a chuckle.

"Your father is going to honor his duty in protecting all of you and our country," Jed explained to his three boys.

Jed realized that they were all too young to really understand. He knew that Willie probably had the best grasp of what he was doing, but he didn't think any of them understood why. *Heck, I can't even explain my own need to join the army, so how can I explain it to my children?*

"Let's put it this way," Jed said, "there are gonna be a lot of soldiers helping to make this country bigger and stronger, and I'm going to be one of them."

He paused for a moment and then continued. "Now, while I'm gone, I'm gonna rely on all three of you *men* to watch over your momma, you hear me?"

He looked at them as they all nodded their acceptance in his direction. "I won't be gone long, and I am counting on all of you to do your chores and your verses."

He waited for their replies, and when he noticed them all staring at the ground, he asked, "Can I count on you?"

"Papa, you can count on *me* to make sure these two mind their manners," Willie declared, feeling much older than his seven years.

"Willie, I don't need lookin' after—I'm six you know!" Daniel announced. "Papa, I'll be good, you'll see."

Jed looked at his two oldest boys. "I'm counting on both of you to work together and look after your momma."

"Micah?" Jed turned to his soon-to-be-four-year-old sitting on Abigail's lap. "Will you be a good boy for Papa?" Micah nestled his head into Abigail's bosom and didn't say a word.

"He doesn't understand, Jed," Abigail whispered to Jed. "He'll be fine. He'll be too busy with his brothers to remain sad for long."

They all embraced as best as they could while awkwardly sitting on the floor in the back room of the Mercantile. The moment was broken up when they heard a tiny voice.

"Papa?" was faintly heard around the corner of the partition as two-year-old Millie Elizabeth came around holding six lemon sticks in her right hand and six orange sticks in her left. From the look on her face, she must have eaten a half-dozen already.

They all looked at Millie, and in unison exploded into laughter. Jed got up to get his daughter, and wrapped her into his arms. He turned, and with Millie in his arms, looked at his family and said, "I love all of you so much, and I am so, so proud of all of you. You remember that until I get back, you hear me?"

Jed looked down at his beautiful wife, who was still embracing their son Micah. Their eyes locked, and without words, they knew that their family and their love would survive. Their hearts were bound together, and no country or war could ever break that bond.

They all left the Mercantile together. Jed held Abigail's hand as they walked up Main Street in silence, Jed contemplating his next step toward deployment, and Abigail praying that he would change his mind.

* * * * *

The next morning was clear, and the air was crisp. The town's shops and businesses were all closed for the morning. The ground was still moist from a passing February storm that had just blown through. The three-month encampment of the army had broken. Supplies, armory, ammunition, and personnel were ready for the long march ahead.

From the outskirts of town and all the way up past the Simpson farm, army personnel struck their tents and collected the supplies that were needed. The area quartermaster had to collect more than a thousand wagons, three hundred horses, a thousand draft mules, four hundred pack mules, and a thousand oxen, all of which had arrived by way of steamers. The steamers had also brought food, cannon, and the personal armory that each soldier would need before heading out.

By midmorning, the townsfolk had lined up along Main and Front Streets, waiting for the military parade that would consist of thousands of men marching down the street. Ahead of them would be wagons, animals and columns of cannon.

Fez stood outside his mercantile store, proud that he had been so involved in the success of the army's operation. If it weren't for all the mercantile shops in Independence, the army would have been forced to wait another three to four months to get set up.

Abigail and the children, all dressed like they were going to Pastor Higgin's Sunday school, stood next to Fez as they waited for their chance to see the army go by.

"This kind of excitement doesn't happen too often around here, does it, Abigail?" Fez yelled over the noise of the crowd.

"Willie, get Micah out of the street and hang on to him!" Abigail yelled out to her oldest, then added, "Where's Daniel?"

"Right here with me, Momma. I've got 'em both," Willie yelled back while shaking his head in frustration. "Don't be frettin' so much, Momma—we're fine!"

Abigail wasn't feeling like her usual self, but she chalked it up to nerves at seeing her husband march by in his blue uniform. Even though she was scared for Jed, she gleamed with pride.

"Papa, take Millie for a second—I think I'm gonna be sick," Abigail said to Fez. She barely made it to the backside of the Mercantile to relieve herself of that morning's breakfast.

Feeling better, she returned to the questioning eye of her father as she reached out for Millie's hand. "Feeling a bit under the weather, Daughter?" he asked with a concerned look on his face.

"I'm fine, Papa," she replied, avoiding her father's eyes as he raised his eyebrows.

"Did you tell him before he left?" Fez whispered into his daughter's ear.

"Papa, stop it; it's nothing." Abigail concentrated on the upcoming parade.

The wagons went by, then the animals, and finally the cannon. The crowd stood, pushed, and maneuvered for better views as they watched rows upon rows of men in uniform march by.

Abigail, Fez, and the children frantically looked up and down each row, trying desperately to find Jed. They were about to give up when the last column came into sight, but still with no Jed. Abigail gave Millie to Fez so that she could run out into the street to get a closer look. *No, it can't happen, I can't have him go without one last look, one last good-bye.* Panic started to well up within her.

"Momma, there he is!" shouted Daniel, who was pointing and jumping up and down. Abigail looked frantically for her husband in the last few rows of the parade. There he was, much to her relief. *Oh, he's so gallant,* she thought as tears welled up in her eyes.

Their eyes met for a moment as he marched by. His heart connected with hers, and she wanted so desperately to tell him, just to let him know before he went out there. *No, there's no time,* she thought. *Why didn't I tell him before?* she scolded herself.

She stood in the street when he passed by, then watched him turn the corner out of sight. She spoke out loud, "You listen up, husband, we're going to have a baby, so you best come back to me, you hear?" As she wiped the tears from her cheek, she turned back to where Fez and the children were standing. Even though she knew Jed didn't hear her, she felt a little better because in her heart she did tell him. It gave her a sense of peace that he would be safe, and he would come back to her and his ever-growing family.

Abigail corralled her children with the help of her eldest, Willie, and then they started up Main Street and proceeded to their home. As she walked with Millie in her arms, Abigail noticed the street with its always-growing elm trees, which were getting larger and larger, with the end of the street stretching more than twice as far as it had when they first moved to Independence.

I wonder why I haven't noticed that before, she thought. She was sure there was much she would realize she had never seen before, now that she was alone and without her husband. The thought of being alone made her feel numb, and when she approached the front steps to her home, she put Millie down, turned herself around, and sat on the top step of her porch.

Who's kidding who, Abigail? she thought and smiled softly. *There's no feeling alone here at the Monroe house, not with four children and another on the way.*

Willie and Daniel sat down next to her on the steps. The two older brothers laughed and teased their two younger siblings who were playing in the grass below them. Abigail was in a vacuum, hearing no one, seeing nothing, and feeling empty.

"Momma, did you see how great Papa looked out there?" Her trance was broken by the excited comment from Willie.

"Yes, your Father was a sight, all right," Abigail muttered, trying her best not to ignore her children.

Snap out of it, Abigail! she scolded herself. *Your life for the time being is about these children, and you need to snap out of it.*

Abigail drifted back to her last view of Jed marching proudly down Main Street. He had been dressed in a blue coat and blue trousers with a dark blue stripe down each side. He had a dress cap, a light blue flannel shirt with his insignia and rank emblems stitched into the sleeves and pins in the collar. His shiny black boots reflected the sun while keeping perfect rhythm with his steps, marched stride after every stride.

Jed had taken his long flintlock smoothbore musket, which hung over his left shoulder along with a black powder bag tightly attached to his suspenders. Abigail didn't like looking at the musket, especially knowing that it was an old 1822 model, and she was afraid for her husband, *especially if the old thing quits working for him.* She instead focused and tried to concentrate on how handsome her husband was, and how proud he looked.

Her husband was fortunate to have friends in high places. John C. Fremont was able to get Jed assigned to the upgraded rank of sergeant rather than private, which meant he would be receiving monthly pay of $13 versus the $8 that most privates received. Abigail planned on working at the Mercantile to make additional money to offset the partial loss of Jed's usual monthly wages.

"Hey there, Monroe family!" yelled Pastor Higgin and Sara from the street, abruptly bringing Abigail back from her thoughts. "Mind some company?"

Abigail waved them over, got up from the front steps, and dusted off the wooden chairs on the front porch.

"Come on up. I'm sorry that I don't have anything to offer. We just got back here ourselves, but I sure would appreciate the company," Abigail said.

As the children played in the yard, the three adults made themselves comfortable on the front porch.

"Boy, that was quite the sight, wasn't it?" Sara commented in reference to the military parade they all had just witnessed. "I bet you're quite proud of your Jed, dear," she added with a soft and caring pat on Abigail's forearm.

Abigail could barely speak, still feeling the emptiness of seeing her husband leave. "I . . . I'm very proud of him, Sara," she said brokenly. "I . . . I'm just going to miss him so, and I don't know if I'll ever feel the same until he's back here safe."

"Why, that's quite normal, Abigail, and I wouldn't expect you to feel any different," Pastor Higgin said as he tried to soothe her. "Always remember, child, you have family right here, and folks who love you and the children. We'll always be here for you, so you'll never be alone, nor should you ever feel alone—all right?"

"He's right, Abigail," Sara added. "Anything you need, and I mean anything, you know we're just a few homes away."

Abigail nodded, then put one hand to her mouth and the other to her stomach. "Excuse me," she said hastily before rushing into the house.

Pastor Higgin excused himself to join the children, who were trying to corner a lizard between a rock and a tree trunk.

When Abigail returned, Sara put a hand on one of hers and gently said, "When are you due, dear?"

"Is it that noticeable?" Abigail said shyly.

Pointing to Abigail's children in the yard, Sara replied, "Remember child, I was by your side each time as you brought those four little darlings into this world. I've seen that look on your face before. I saw it at the parade, amongst other things, and I see it now."

Abigail looked a bit embarrassed that she had been unable to keep her breakfast down, and Sara continued. "Jed must've been so happy to know he is going to be a father again. I just hope he can be back in time for the baby. I would hate for him to—"

"He doesn't know!" Abigail interrupted.

"Oh . . . uh . . . I see . . . I'm sorry. Please forgive me if I sounded as if I was intruding in your private affairs, dear," Sara replied apologetically.

"No, no, it isn't anything like that. I . . . I just never . . . I just couldn't tell him," Abigail answered. "You see, I tried to get the nerve to do it so many times. But he was so excited about his deployment that the right time never came up."

Abigail paused for a moment and looked at her children. "It's funny in a way," she said, "but as he marched by, we looked at each other, and when his gaze left mine, I voiced the words to him, thinking somehow he would hear them or feel them. I don't know, call me crazy, but for some unknown reason, I believe he knows."

Abigail looked to Sara with tears in her eyes. Sara leaned over and pulled Abigail close. The two hugged, and Abigail released her fears into the shoulder of her dear friend.

Chapter Fifteen

Papa's at War but the Battle's at Home

1847

The marching, the dust, the food or lack thereof, the cold nights and warm days, and the endless drilling were taking the glamour out of Jed's idea of soldiering. He learned from other soldiers that it was all needed if they were going to stand against the well-seasoned and veteran Mexican Army.

John Fremont met up with Jed during an evening of rest. They sat on boulders, and their fire blazed after the small dry kindling caught fire and ignited branches gathered from nearby fallen trees. They were excited and restless over what the next few weeks might bring. The fire warmed them nicely, in contrast with the briskness of the night air. Fremont was calm, his experience showing through, while Jed couldn't hide his anxious demeanor and need to know what was going to happen.

"It appears, Jed," Fremont began, "that we are splitting into three different divisions, each of which will be going in a different direction."

He took a sip of coffee from his dented tin cup and continued. "It's a bit ironic, however. I always wanted to continue my work mapping a new and shorter route from here to California, and now I'll have that opportunity and be able to fight off Mexican intruders at the same time."

"Have they decided who will be placed in what division yet?" Jed asked with anticipation.

"Yes, they have," Fremont said, his voice echoing from inside his tin cup as he took another sip. He set his cup down and stirred up the fire burning in front of them.

"Jed," Fremont said, keeping his gaze on the flames, "I tried to get you with me, but they would have nothing to do with it, knowing that we are friends and have been acquainted for some time. I even tried, unsuccessfully, to tell them that I hardly knew you, but somehow

Old Rough and Ready knew all about us as far back as when we were encamped in Independence. There was nothing I could do, Jed."

"Oh, I'm not second-guessing you, John, and I understand it's out of your hands. But did you happen to hear where I'm being sent, if not to California with you?" Jed asked anxiously.

"Jed, you're going with Kearny to Santa Fe."

Fremont knew that Jed would be disappointed, since his heart had been set on the Rio Grande. The word amongst the ranks was that the Rio Grande was where the real fighting would happen.

"From what I've heard," Fremont continued, "it's become pretty testy down in Santa Fe, so I anticipate that you are going to see quite a bit of action. I say that assuming it's what you are looking for."

"I just want to be involved, John, and not on some expedition trip—been there, done that, you know," Jed began to argue, but settled down when he realized that Fremont's calm and sympathetic demeanor had not changed.

"When do we move out?" Jed asked.

"The day after tomorrow, so I suggest that you get organized and meet with Kearny's staff to get your specific orders."

Fremont looked at Jed. "Jed, I will always consider you a great friend. I still remember being best man at your wedding—that day was quite special. I hope we see each other again, my good friend, but we may not. And you might want to take this time to write Abigail. You may not get another chance to do so for some time. There's no way of knowing what you will run into out there, or when you'll have another chance to post a letter."

After a pause to shuffle the last of the embers and put the fire out, Jed turned to Fremont and extended his hand, saying, "I'll do that, my friend, I will. You take care of yourself, John C. Fremont. And I *better* see you again, you hear me?"

They shook hands, and as Fremont walked away, he said over his shoulder, "Give that pretty wife of yours my love, won't you?" Jed smiled in return, tipped his hat toward Fremont, and hoped him the best.

With the evening detail finished, the soldiers had the freedom to sit around fires and talk, play musical instruments, sing, or write. Most of the soldiers usually wrote home with the sounds of a hymn or two in the background. On this particular night, as Jed leaned his back against an old weathered log, a soldier in the distance with a beautiful soprano voice was alternating his singing of two songs, "Many and Great, O God" and "Amazing Grace."

Jed reflected on his childhood and hearing his mother sing "Amazing Grace." She would say, "Jedidiah, we should always be thankful for the grace of our Lord," and would sing the words as she held him close to her.

The mood and sounds of the distant singing took his mind to Abigail and the children, together but alone at home. He positioned himself against a tree trunk, then removed his paper and charcoal pencil from his pack. He stared straight ahead, and after a short pause to reflect, began to write.

My dearest Abigail,

It has been quite a few weeks since we both held each other, yet I can still feel your warmth and smell the sweet floral scent of your skin in my memory. The softness of your touch, and the gentleness of your eyes every time they meet mine, will always be the inspiration for me to keep going one foot after the other as we march into unknown territory.

We will be breaking camp tomorrow, and I pray this letter is received by you in due time and is not delayed, as my voice and my heart do not delay in telling you of my unwavering love. My wife, I do miss you so, and I want you to know before I go into any conflict in the weeks ahead that I'm determined to come home to you and the children. You are my saving grace and will be my guiding star to bring me home when all this is over.

You'll get this long after the secrecy of our orders has passed, so I don't worry about jeopardizing anything here. I will be in the division led by General Stephen Kearney headed for Santa Fe, Mexico.

I'll have a group of ten under my immediate command, but will be reporting to Colonel Alexander Doniphan with the Missouri Volunteers. It seems they all are good fellas, a little rough around the edges, but when it comes to getting their jobs done, I feel they will. I was given a darker uniform yesterday; I guess the darker the uniform, the higher the rank, but I just do what they say.

My old musket won't be of much use to me here. The colonel announced that we're all going to be given new '41 percussion muskets and a set of flintlock pistols to go with our sabers. I'm looking forward to having the newer model of guns. I wasn't too sure how long the old '22 musket was going to last. It's still good for shooting our turkeys every fall, but that's about it. My understanding is that I will be in one of the lines to advance when we come closer to Santa Fe. Again, I'll do what I am asked, and I pray to God that I perform with honor and dignity. All of the men are well conditioned by now after the many miles of marching and the drills we perform every evening.

John Fremont will not be with me, to my dismay, but for his benefit, he will be going toward California, and as he tells me, he couldn't be happier.

Abigail, I do hope I see him again, and I pray to God to keep him away from harm's way. Please do the same for our dear friend.

The trail is just like the one I traveled on in '37, but with fewer green hills and rivers. I'm looking forward to seeing the land of upper Mexico, and after that, possibly California. I've heard that California is lush with golden hills of grain, a vast mountain range, and fertile valleys ripe for farming.

It's disheartening to hear that war is right around the corner, but we all knew it was going to come to this. I do pray it isn't long and that I return to you and the children posthaste.

Abigail, I anxiously await our homecoming, and I pray that the days don't grow into years. I know we have plans for our family to grow, and I look forward to the day when you bless me with our fifth miracle, another child to call our own.

I realize that my being away is a hardship for you, especially taking care of the children alone, but I want you to know that my love for you grows stronger each day. I wake every morning, look at your picture inside my pocket watch, and long to hold you and tell you how much you mean to me.

I go forward, my love, into whatever the good Lord puts in front of me, and I go with confidence and a feeling of assurance that I will have you by my side in my heart and my soul.

You will always be my shining light and the beacon that guides me nearer to the safety of your arms.

I love you my Sweetness, my Wife, my Abigail,

Jed

* * * * *

By the time the letter arrived, Abigail was nearly to term with their fifth child. The women in town were taking good care of her needs while Fez helped with the children. Abigail read Jed's letter several times a day and wished he were with her, especially as she came closer to her delivery.

"You need to sit down, get off your feet, and let me and the other women from the church do what we do best," Sara had directed. Abigail tried her hardest to keep a cheerful disposition while others helped her with the household chores.

Fez noticed it first, then Sara concurred, and both mentioned their concern. Abigail knew she looked pale, and was also aware that her stamina was declining, though she had done her best to hide it. To some these conditions might be expected in the eighth month of pregnancy, but it was new to Abigail and to those who had been around her during her previous four deliveries.

After the other women had left, Sara approached Abigail with concern in her voice. "Dear, you're about ready to have that baby, and it's not going to do you any good trying to do too much. You need to let us help you more, and just put your mind on that new baby that's knocking on your door."

Abigail conceded the advice of her dear friend. She had to admit, she was feeling a bit tired and had a funny feeling in her belly. She believed it was due to Jed's letter and had nothing to do with the baby.

She sat down in her rocking chair and attempted to catch her breath. "It's not fair, Sara. It's been five months, and I've only received one letter from Jed," Abigail wailed. "I don't even know if he received any of my letters letting him know he is going to be a father again," she said in hope and desperation. "It just breaks my heart thinking that he is out there fighting some Godforsaken battle he has no place to be in, while his family needs him right here standing by us . . . standing by me!" Abigail, frustrated, pounded her fist into the arm of the rocking chair.

"Now, now, dear, you're going to get that baby all riled up and cause yourself more problems than you ever intended," Sara said.

Abigail's breathing was becoming difficult and her skin was turning even paler. "Let me get a real good look at you, dear," Sara said as she knelt down next to Abigail.

Abigail's skin was pasty and damp. Her cheeks, normally lightly flushed, were now a grayish blue. Her eyes were bloodshot, as if she'd been crying for days, and her hair was soaked with sweat. Sara knew that there was a problem, but she didn't want to alarm Abigail for fear that it would exacerbate her already elevated emotional state.

Sara felt Abigail's forehead. "You've got a fever, dear." She gently guided Abigail into her bed. Sara sat next to the bed and placed a cool cloth on Abigail's forehead. The doctor was out of town and wouldn't be back for three days.

Oh, dear Lord, thought Abigail, the baby can't be coming now; I'm not due for another month.

Abigail's children could be heard playing in the yard without a care, unaware of what was happening inside their home.

Sara calmly approached Willie and gently tugged on his arm to get him to follow her away from the other children.

"Willie," Sara said quietly, "your momma and I need you to go down to the Mercantile and get your grandpa." Willie frowned in response. "Your momma just needs him to help her with something. When you come back, you can continue playing with your brothers and sister, all right?" Willie's concerned expression relaxed, and he turned and ran down the street while Sara hurried back inside to Abigail's room.

"How are you doing, dear?" Sara asked quietly.

Trying her best to assume a calm voice, Abigail replied, "I'd like to say that I'm doing just fine, Sara . . . heck, I've done this plenty of times before . . . but it's just—"

Abigail stopped midsentence as a gripping pain shot through her like a train slamming into her full force, causing her to grab her belly, curl up into a ball, and scream.

It was an uncontrolled scream that came from the depths of her belly as the pain shot out in cascading bolts as if something had just exploded inside her. Fear gripped her as she looked around the room in confusion.

"Jed!" she yelled automatically, as if she were calling him while working together at the Mercantile.

Realizing what she had just done and knowing that her husband was not there nor would be, she lay back on her pillow and turned her head to the side. Her eyes stared straight ahead at some unknown spot beyond anything and anyone in its way. She tried to focus her eyes on Sara, who had a cool cloth in her hand. She then felt the coolness on her forehead, closed her eyes, and tried her best to stay calm.

The baby was coming fast even as Abigail's strength was slipping away. Sara sat quietly beside her, holding one hand firmly on the cool cloth on Abigail's forehead. Abigail could make out the shape of Sara's face, and could feel how tightly she was gripping her hand—at that moment, Abigail realized that they were in over their heads.

Sara got up and walked to the front window, gazed out, and began to pray. The tears flowed freely down her cheeks.

Abigail heard her quietly say, "Amen," and then more softly, "Thank you, God."

Heavy, quick footsteps could be heard on the walkway. Fez rushed through the front door and went straight to his daughter's side. Sara left to prepare for what was coming next and to give Abigail some time with her father.

Sara was in the kitchen preparing clean cloths and heating water on the potbelly stove when a loud outburst came from Abigail's room. "Sara?" Fez yelled. "Can you come in here, please?"

Sara returned to the bedroom.

The pace of Abigail's decline was shocking. She had soaked her nightgown all the way through to the bedsheets. Her hair was stringy and tangled from all the sweat. The room smelled musty and humid, and her eyes were sunken. Abigail was losing her battle, and those around her were beginning to sense it.

Abigail bolted up at her waist, sitting straight upright, her face tight with excruciating pain. Her scream was fierce and loud. Her hands gripped tightly to the bedsheets. As she fought to keep from slipping back under the surface, Abigail burrowed her eyes deep into her father's. Fez was panicked—he saw little resemblance of the Abigail he knew. She was being transformed by pain and anguish, and what energy she had left was being rapidly consumed.

Abigail collapsed back onto the bed. Her head bounced off the pillow and then rested helplessly, her exhausted and drained body now limp. In her foggy and delirious mind, she asked herself how much longer she could do this. She knew she was close to giving up, with all of her energy and strength gone. She lay sick, weak, and scared, thinking only of her four children and Jed. *How can I endure much more? Why won't the baby come? Why is there so much pain?* Her thoughts made her feel even weaker.

Time seemed to stop, and then the tremors began again. Her moans and cries echoed throughout the house. The exhaustion stole her remaining energy, her speech, even her ability to cry. Her body was drained and beginning to quit on her.

The shots of pain came again, daggers shooting their way from baby to ribs, her mind playing games as it too lost more energy and control. She could feel someone trying to cut her baby out, slicing her with knives. With each cut, a scream came out as a roar of pain, the cutting pain of slicing, of tearing.

She thought she could feel a blanket, sheets, and some sort of cloth beneath her. She also thought she could feel the fluttering touch of angels, but thought again. *No, those are the hands of the devil bringing me all this pain,* she thought. *God would never hurt me like this.*

She grasped for something, anything, and her father's familiar strong hands were suddenly there, giving her feelings of hope. She began to sense something or someone digging out her insides like a shovel digging out a large hole. Her head was up off the bed again, her back was straight upright, and she muffled out a soft plea to God.

She had the sensation of being stretched to the point of breaking. The shovels and knives were gone, but the stretching was endless. How long could she bare the stretching?

Oh God, it's pulling me apart!

She collapsed back again, her head landing on the bed, the pillow long discarded. A sense of emptiness filled her. There was a dry taste of blood in her mouth from endlessly biting down. Her limp wasted body lay as a bundle of exhausted body parts, tired and empty inside.

Sara and Fez did their best to comfort Abigail, but they knew it was all in God's hands now. Fez held his daughter's hand firmly, holding back his own need to cry out. Pastor Higgin had rounded up the children some time before, and they were now playing at the Higgins' house.

It was eerily quiet. Sara and Fez focused on what needed to be done. They worked as one, quickly and efficiently. Both were shedding tears, but remained quiet as they attended to their tasks.

Fez held his daughter's hand.

Why does it feel so empty? Abigail thought.

Abigail was starting to sense her surroundings again and the familiar feeling of relief after giving birth. All her senses were returning to normal. She focused on her hearing and listened for the proverbial baby's cry. Except the familiar sound was not there.

She tried to concentrate, tried to hear. *Where is the crying?* Her anxiety rose.

She felt those strong masculine hands around hers again, felt the cool cloth on her forehead. Everything returned to normal except one thing, and she began to panic. *Where's the baby's cry?* she asked herself, a deep frown appearing above her eyes. *There has to be crying, there's always crying*! she told herself.

She looked into the familiar eyes of her father, but what she saw were not eyes of joy, but rather eyes filled with sorrow. "Papa, where's the baby?" she asked, her voice barely a whisper.

Her father's eyes flooded with tears. He wrapped his arms around her tight and pulled her up to him. Resting in the security of her father's arms, she could see the baby resting quietly at the foot of her bed, wrapped in white.

Fez held her close and tight, loving her as only a father could love a daughter. "He put up a bold fight, Abigail, a strong fight!"

"No . . . no, Papa, get him to start crying, that's what we need him to do, he just needs to start crying . . . *please*, Papa . . . *get* him to *start* crying!" Abigail begged as she began to weep.

She looked around the room, still in her father's arms. With what energy she had left, she pleaded to anyone who might be there. "Please . . . please, he *has* to cry." Abigail clung desperately to her father and sobbed uncontrollably for her dead son.

Fez silently prayed for the strength Abigail would need in the days to come, and he too wept for his dead grandson as he held his daughter tight.

Chapter Sixteen

Heavy Hearts in Independence

1849

It had been more than a year since Abigail had laid her little newborn to rest. Abel Christian Monroe would have been her fifth child, but the good Lord had other plans. The grieving was long and hard, and Abigail still was unable to erase the painful memory of her loss from her mind. The physical damage from her dangerous labor had healed long before, but it would take more years to recover from the emotional damage , if she ever did.

Abigail visited Abel's gravesite once a week to replace the flowers she had left the week before. The cemetery was small and next to the Higgins' church. Abel's resting spot was nestled near the back side of the cemetery just a few feet from a slow-moving creek that fed into the Missouri River. The heavy limbs of two large oak trees gave cover to his resting spot despite woodpecker damage encircling the trunk of the larger one. Perennial shrubs and vines stretched out behind the base of the tombstone, and the sound of the bubbling creek made the area eternally peaceful, quiet, and serene.

Abel's Grandpa Fez, needing to place a memorial of his own next to his grandson's resting place, had built a wooden bench. It was handcrafted from a fallen oak and sanded down smooth with hours of soul-wrenching dedication to ensure that his grandson would never be forgotten. He had added a touch of glaze and varnish to bring out a finishing polish that would withstand the hardest of winters. One last touch, to secure its legacy and the eternal connection between grandpa and grandson, was the inscription Fez carved on the back of the bench:

HERE LIES MY GRANDSON, ABEL. WE SIT HERE
AND WILL ALWAYS REMEMBER THAT HE LOOKS
UPON US AS MUCH AS WE LOOK UPON HIM.
WITH LOVE AND REMEMBRANCE, GRANDPA

He was named after Adam's son Abel, the first of God's children to die. Abigail was certain that the good Lord's eyes were on little Abel Christian and that he would welcome him with open arms up in heaven.

On this particular day, sitting on "Abel's bench," Abigail held Jed's latest letter in her hands. His letters had been infrequent and usually with very little description of his daily life.

She had come to the conclusion after his last letter that for some reason he was not receiving any of hers. She was told by the postmaster that most letters to soldiers rarely made it to the front lines because of problems with the chaotic logistics of this new army of theirs, and also because mail was only delivered to locations when secure, not while under active combat.

Abigail looked down at Abel's tombstone and read the inscription her father had cut in the stone. She dreaded the day when she would have to share her grief with Jed. She closed her eyes, prayed for strength, and read his letter one more time:

My dearest Abigail,

I count the days until I see your face once again and feel the sense of family around me. The days grow long and tiresome, though we strive to stay strong and push on. I pray the end is soon.

We moved on from Santa Fe months ago, and met up with our dear friend John in California. The sights, smells, and rigors of my daily routine have been a terror that I wish on no man, but it has been a pleasure to see John again and speak of pleasantries instead of gloom.

My dear, we have lost so many good men, and I thank our Lord that He has spared me thus far so that I may write you once again while I wait for that glorious day when we are reunited. I do so tire of the smell of death and the constant battle against impending illness that the bullet does not carry. So many have fallen not by the sword or the musket ball, but by the filthy and inhumane conditions we must suffer through endlessly.

I fear not, my love, the chance of death by battle, but for my care if I were to be wounded on the battlefield. Please pray for my safe return and my search for the peace I am still without.

Abigail, I cannot express the words nor do I have enough paper to write how much I miss you. I miss your touch, and even the way you brush your hair hundreds of times a night. You are my soul mate, my love, and my best friend. I can't even imagine a world without you in it.

You fulfill my every desire and need by just being close to me, talking with me, and letting me look at you with admiration and thankfulness in my heart. We were never meant to be apart like this, and I will soon renew my commitment to you to always be by your side, as you will always be by mine.

I love you my Abigail, my Love, my Wife,

Jed

Abigail put the letter on her lap and looked at Abel's tombstone again:

Here
lies our
little Angel,
In Peace with
our Lord

She lowered her head, closed her eyes, and silently prayed for her husband to find his own peace with the Lord, and to come home safely to reunite with her and their four children.

Looking at the tombstone with Jed's letter in her hand, Abigail said out loud, speaking directly to her lost son, "Give me the strength, dear Abel, to find the courage to explain all of this to your father. I just don't know how I'm going to do it." She sat motionless and helpless to the all-consuming emotions that controlled her life these days, her lonely life.

* * * * *

At the same time as Abigail was spending precious time with Abel, a group of townsfolk were gathering at Stevens's Diner to discuss the latest news off the telegraph wire.

"Word has it that the negotiations President Polk initiated back in November are actually coming to a close," expressed Fez, sitting at a small table in the corner of the diner.

"You know, Fez, I heard the same thing," replied Herman Simpson, who was sitting at the next table with his wife Rachael. "He sent Congressman John Slidell to negotiate a while ago, but I hadn't heard much more of it until a few days ago. Some say we could have a peace treaty as soon as next month."

Fez cleared his throat and took a sip from his coffee cup, then added, "I still don't understand why all this has taken so long. I mean, Jed and Kearny's group took care of the Santa Fe area rather quickly, Taylor and his army whipped them down in Texas, and then we read from the wire that General Winfield Scott conquered Mexico City back in September. So why is it taking so long to get it finished?"

The news had indeed come to Independence that the almost two-year-long nightmare should be over soon, but "soon" was not soon enough for the families with loved ones still holding muskets and sabers for the cause of "Manifest Destiny."

John C. Fremont had been busy in California with his own "Manifest Destiny" cause. He had long before defeated what little resistance could be found from Mexico, and in his own words had "liberated the entire area of California."

When he and Kearny met and the two armies became one under General Kearny, the two feuded about the future of the newly liberated countryside. Kearny, outranking Fremont, had him arrested and hauled before a court-martial.

Word of this made its way to the folks in Independence, and Stevens's Diner was abuzz.

"Who do they think they are, telling such lies and stories about John?" Fez demanded to those sitting around him.

The diner was packed that sunny but cool January day, and by the looks of Patricia Stevens, everyone was ordering everything on the menu. The loud talk combined with the rattling of plates, coffee cups, and silverware rose to a such a din that Patricia became a bit frazzled. Inside, it was comfortably warm with the fire blazing in the rock fireplace. Outside, snow from the previous week's storm hibernated against the diner's walls under a glaring but cold winter sun.

Fez was creating quite a stir inside the diner, grabbing the attention of Herman and Rachael Simpson, Pastor and Sara Higgin, and Doc Andersen and his fiancé Nellie Watson. Not paying much attention to the clatter, however, was Sheriff Daniels, who was sitting by himself in the corner and quietly eating pot roast and whole potatoes while sipping his second cup of coffee.

Doc Andersen added, "Yea, and did you hear about the trial? I heard that when the order came down from the army to court-martial John, he made such a fuss that it was heard all the way to President Polk."

Herman Simpson, not wanting to be left out of the conversation, added, "Not only did it make it all the way to Polk, but the president made the army change the verdict and drop all charges against John. Whatcha think about them apples?!"

"As it should be!" exclaimed Rachael Simpson as she frowned at her husband. "With what John has done for his country, and the way he's fought for us, well, they should be giving him a medal instead of threatening him with a cell."

Dropping his paper and taking a last sip of his coffee, Sheriff Daniel stood up to leave. On his way to the door, he suddenly stopped, turned to the group, and said, "Didn't mean to eavesdrop, folks, but I couldn't help but hear you talking about John. The last laugh was John's indeed. I just read that he resigned from the army, and he's now the talk of California. Our John C. Fremont is indeed a national hero, what do you all think of that?!"

As the Sheriff stepped out of the diner, Fez turned to the Higgins and asked, "Pastor, Sara, you two have been awfully quiet about all of this.

What are your thoughts on our newfound hero and the town's dearest friend?"

The Higgins, who had just finished their meal, rose from the table and looked at the other folks who were still seated. "No—Sara and I don't have much to say about what's going on with the army or with John. As a matter of fact, we just keep praying that all of this—and I mean all of this talk of war—is over real soon," said the Pastor.

John Fremont's activities weren't all the townsfolk were talking about. News of a pending peace treaty had everyone in great spirits; business was good, and more and more emigrants were heading out West again, making Fez a happy man.

One of those emigrant families entered the Wright Mercantile, accompanied by Pastor and Sara Higgin. The Higgins had been entertaining the visiting family for the past few days as they gathered supplies to continue their journey across the state to southern Missouri.

"Hey there, Pastor, and good morning to you, Sara!" exclaimed Fez as he greeted them with a joyful tone.

"Good morning to you, Fez," responded the Pastor as he and Sara walked to where Fez stood by the front counter of the Mercantile. "Fez, I would like to introduce a good friend and colleague of mine in the ministry." The Pastor called his friends over. "Fez Wright, I am pleased to introduce the Reverend Robert James and his wife Zeralda Cole James. They are passing through on their way to southern Missouri, where the Reverend James is opening up his own church."

"Well, good day, folks, and welcome to the best mercantile store in town!" Fez boasted with a huge grin as he bent down to speak to the children. "And who are these little ones you have with you? I bet they're being groomed to join you in raising up their own flock, in the footsteps of their papa, right?"

Reverend James held up his oldest as Mrs. James picked up their toddler. Reverend James looked at Fez and said, "Mr. Wright, I sure hope to God you are correct in that prediction. Nothing would make me and the missus prouder than to see your prediction come true. Here, let me introduce you to our boys. This is my oldest boy, Frank, and Zeralda is holding our spunky Jesse in her arms. And doing a better job of it than I ever could, I might add."

The Reverend continued, "Yes, sir, I do hope our children will follow my calling someday. But you never really know with boys these days."

After more small talk, the group left the Mercantile and headed back to the Higgins' church. Fez went back to restocking canned goods. A large man came in off the street. His huge build was silhouetted in the doorway, making it difficult to see him clearly, but he appeared to be wearing a large animal and a huge feathery hat.

"Fez Wright, you old fusspot you!" yelled the man from the doorway.

Fez, taken aback a bit, moved in closer for a better look at the man in the shadow, then suddenly grinned and picked up his pace toward the door. The two embraced like brothers who hadn't seen each other for ages.

The bear hugs and backslaps between Bridger and her father were a welcome sight to Abigail as she stood in the corner of the Mercantile, unpacking crates of newly arrived merchandise. It had been a long time since she had experienced any pleasant feelings.

"Jim Bridger, you old geezer!" Fez exclaimed with happiness. "What in the name of Benjamin Franklin are you doing back here? In need of civilization or something?"

Bridger physically looked about the same as he always had, and he gave off the same smell, too, which was something Abigail had never gotten used to. He was dressed in a scrappy fur coat and wearing a coon's hat. His beard was full with more gray than black, and his face had weathered over the years, especially his eyes—once filled with the passion of the wilderness, they were now hollow and filled with some unknown misery.

"Come on, let's get you up to Stevens's Diner, and I'll buy you the biggest steak this side of the Mississippi," Fez demanded as he eyed his friend's out-of-character appearance. As he took off his apron, Fez yelled to Abigail that he'd be back in an hour or so, and the two bolted out the door. Fez was anxious to find out what was on the mind of his bear-fighting friend, who now wore an extremely long and sad face.

The steak was hot and juicy, the potato was big and drenched with butter, and the coffee was hot. Fez had just finished filling Bridger in about all that had happened during the few years since they had last seen each other, including Jed's departure into the army and the loss of Abigail's son Abel.

"So, you say Jed knows nothing of the little one yet?" Bridger asked with a look of concern for his friend. "Man, I feel for him, and for Abigail too. Boy, what a horrific experience you all had to go through. I'm sorry I wasn't around to help ya all out," he consoled Fez even though he knew there was nothing he could have done for his friends.

Fez looked at Bridger—whatever was troubling him had not gone away while they'd been talking. Even after eating a hefty meal and having Patricia refill his coffee, Bridger had none of the happy-go-lucky look that Fez remembered, and it was beginning to cause him some real concern.

"Hey, you doing all right, my friend?" asked Fez.

"Well, you do know me pretty well, don't you, Fez?" Bridger said. He took another sip of his coffee. "Fez, you've always been a good friend, and I've always known that if something were a-botherin' me, I could come to you and you'd lend an ear."

Bridger hesitated while looking out the side window at some unknown demon lurking around an unseen corner. "I've been battling the devil himself the past year, and I can't seem to lose him. He haunts me daily, and no matter where I go, what I do, or who I talk to, I'm reminded of the horrors of the winter of '47."

"The winter of '47?" Fez asked, tilting his head to one side. "Other than the war, we haven't paid much attention to anything written in the news, so I'm at a loss as to your meaning."

"It all started in the summer after I left this here town," Bridger started out. "I had just arrived at my encampment at the Fort, and there was a wagon party that was supplying for the trip over the Wasatch Mountains, around the Great Salt Lake Desert, and then up over the Sierras and toward Sutter's Fort. They were concerned about their route, so they had planned ahead for the exact number of days it would take to get them to their destination, plus a little extra for good measure. All their spirits were good, and they were eager to move on westward toward their new home. Their only concern was that they were supposed to have met their trail boss Lansford Hastings, but when they arrived, he had already left with another wagon."

Bridger stopped and poured another cup of coffee, pausing for a few moments to gaze into the distance. Fez could see that his friend was visualizing the event as he described it. "Hastings left a week before I arrived, so because I have a bit more experience than most in these sorts of things, I got myself involved in resupplying them. I actually became good friends with many of them in a short time, and I knew they would be moving out in a few days, after reading Hastings's note for them to follow his route. The leaders of the group met with me for supper, and they asked for my advice on the best route, since they knew I was the 'expert' of the mountains."

"Expert, huh, what a joke," Bridger said as he stared out the window, but seemingly at something that wasn't there. He shook his head slowly, and his voice began to crack.

Fez just sat there with his friend, knowing that what Bridger had to say was pressing hard on his mind, and in some way seemed to be controlling him.

"Fez, they asked me for my 'expert' advice!" Bridger said again, tears filling his eyes. "I knew Lansford Hastings, alright, and even though I thought he was an idiot, I knew his newly found cutoff through the mountains was solid and could cut three hundred fifty to four hundred miles off that kind of trip."

With a pause, Bridger confessed, "I went ahead and told them that the cutoff was fine, level roads with plenty of water and grass and all. I estimated that they should be in Captain Sutter's Fort seven days after leaving my little 'getaway.'"

"You mean 'Fort Bridger,' right?" Fez asked for clarity.

"Yea—I still can't get used to that name though," Bridger remarked as he continued. "We all met one last time to bid our farewells. I especially remember the children and the women; they were all strong and willing to work right by the sides of the menfolk. I thought to myself that this party was gonna have an easy time with their travels because of how prepared and organized they were. When they finally left, other emigrants had joined them, so the total to leave my establishment was about ninety folks and twenty wagons."

"My guidance to take Hastings's cutoff turned out to be wrong, and it cost the party an extra eighteen days!" Bridger said with anger in his voice. "That's eighteen precious days, Fez. That delay caused the party to cross the ever-dangerous Sierra Pass far too late in the season, and . . ." Bridger couldn't continue and sat motionless, staring into the distance as he attempted to compose himself before continuing.

"Jim, we can stop if you'd like," Fez offered.

"Nah, I need to talk about this. I need the demons to go away," Bridger said quietly with pleading in his eyes. "Fez, that party . . . that party got themselves trapped in the Sierras because of an early October snowstorm!"

With tears now streaming down his cheeks and landing in his woolly salt-and-pepper beard, Bridger tried to finish. "Forty-one out of 'em died out there, Fez. They couldn't make it through because they listened to me."

Fez listened compassionately to his friend, trying to ease his pain. "Jim, you can't blame yourself. I know you became close to them during their short stay with you, but you can't blame yourself."

"Look at it this way, Jim," Fez said as he attempted to show Bridger another side of the story, "if Hastings had come back and led them in a timely manner as he had agreed to in the first place, they would not have lost those eighteen days and would have made it over that mountain."

Fez looked at his burly friend and could see signs of recognition and self–forgiveness in his eyes. "Jim, you're not to blame for that party's disaster, and in a way, neither is Hastings. It was God's plan, and we can't understand His reasoning, we just have to have faith that He was there and in charge. It's the only way you, me, or any of us can have peace in anything we do. Jim, you have to trust in God and take that burden off yourself, you hear me?"

"It seems like me and God need to do a bit of talking ourselves, you know what I mean?"

"Yea, Jim, I know exactly what you mean, my friend." Fez stood up, gave his friend a big slap on the back, and said, "Come on, let's get on out of here."

"No, first I just want to tell you that it's been a long time that I've been carrying this on my back. You're a good friend, Fez, and just getting it out and having someone listen means the world to me."

Fez nodded his understanding. "I've got some mending to do, but now I do believe I got me a starting spot, thanks to you."

Fez reached over and squeezed Bridger's arm, and their eyes met. Each man knew that healing would take time. But Bridger felt some of the heaviness lifted, and Fez felt a special warmth embracing him because he had been able to help his tormented friend. It was a feeling that he too needed after months of grieving over the loss of his grandson.

As the two were leaving, a young boy came running up Main Street, yelling at the top of his lungs. In the distance, they could see his hands waving frantically and his oversized hat flapping in the wind. His words were not recognizable at first, and it was becoming ever more apparent that the boy's excitement was blocking his ability to announce the news that was consuming him. "What in the—can you hear what he's saying, Jim?" Fez asked as he crooked his neck in a futile attempt to hear the boy.

The closer the boy got, the louder he got, and his words finally began to make sense.

"The war is over! The war is over! The war is over!"

Chapter Seventeen

Anxious Homecoming

1849

The results of the Mexican–American War varied in size and scope. Nonetheless, all of the events were important in shaping the history of Mexico and the United States. The aftermath of the war included geographic gains for the United States, but it also widened the door for an increase in the internal conflict over slavery that had been building for decades.

Through the signing of the Treaty of Guadalupe Hidalgo, Mexico ceded California and the area that was renamed New Mexico. Together, these two areas included the entire southwestern continental United States. It also opened a debate about what to do with the newly acquired land.

To the citizens and commerce of Independence, the expansion of land was enormously important, because it opened up the trails to safer trade and travel. Unfortunately, it also sparked a silent flame that had been brewing the past thirty years over the rights to slavery in unsettled territories. This highly debated topic became very divisive throughout the country, and it was felt within the community of Independence as well.

"Please, folks, please." Pastor Higgin said to the large congregation that had gathered at his church. Hot tempers were brewing over the latest news of compromise coming out of Washington, DC.

The chapel was packed. Every pew was filled with angry and anxious citizens. The air reeked of cigar-soaked clothing and stuffy still air despite having all the doors and windows open. Men lined the back of the room and stood at the sides of pews, their loud voices and sweaty palms raised high to get the attention of Pastor Higgin. He had been nominated, along with his church, to hold the "Citizens' Voice of Reason" town hall meeting. Pastor Higgin was chosen because he had the biggest church, and in the opinion of most, he had the best chance of keeping the meeting civil.

"We all know our senator from our neighboring state of Kentucky, and we can appreciate his steadfast effort to look for solutions to this long-standing issue," announced Pastor Higgin as he tried again to get the citizens to settle down and allow themselves to listen to all sides of the arguments set in front of them.

The afternoon was warm, the last rain having come more than a month before. The horses tied outside the church were restless from standing straddled to their posts for what seemed like hours. Men had their hats drawn and were fanning their faces to pull whatever breeze they could muster from the stillness of the air. Between the heat of the weather and the heat of the topic at hand, the mood of the congregation was not pretty, and Pastor Higgin had little hope of seeing a happy adjournment.

"Henry Clay is a blue-blooded capitalist with only one agenda on his mind," yelled out Jonathan Braxton, the local blacksmith, who was seated in the fourth pew on the left side. "He tried back in '20 to keep the balance in check between Slave and Free States, but now it seems like we're at it again, and this time with much more land at stake!"

"I agree with Jonathan!" yelled Joe Carter, taking a break from the Mercantile to attend the meeting. "I'm telling you, we should take all of Texas and half of California and make them both Slave States. I mean, look at it, folks, it makes perfect sense and follows the compromise made in '20." Carter paused for a minute to gauge the reaction he got. He noticed through the crowd that Fez, Abigail, and little Millie Elizabeth had just walked in. Millie, holding her momma's hand, was six now and sternly preferred to be called Lizzy.

Carter hesitated for a moment as he wondered what his boss would think of him at center stage, but continued in his loud baritone voice. "Listen to me, folks!" Carter looked at the Pastor, and then to Braxton the blacksmith for support. He knew that the Pastor supported Clay, and it didn't sit well with him as he tried once again to get the crowd's attention. "People of Independence, Missouri, we are a Slave State, and we have the rights and ability to speak out in support for our other Southern brethren in the cause of sustaining slaveholders' God-given rights to—"

Carter was caught off guard and his oratory cut short by a commanding voice from the back of the room. "Mr. Carter!" All heads turned toward the bellowing voice of Jim Bridger. "You and all of you in this room have no idea what is at stake, here in Independence and in this country. If—and I mean a big if—we as a country adopt this highly debated compromise that the good man Henry Clay proposes, I stand here before all of you and tell you that you, your children, and your grandchildren will see blood spilled like you've never seen before."

Gasps were heard from the women in the room as Bridger made his way through the crowd in the back and up the center aisle to speak at the lectern, as the Pastor moved aside to give him room. "Let me tell you the two sides, and then and only then will we be able to really talk about this ordeal we are about to face." Bridger looked around the room at the anxious faces. He nodded acknowledgment to Fez and Abigail, who were leaning against the side wall, with Lizzy trying her best to stay still.

"Henry Clay, Daniel Webster, and that loudmouth from the South, John Calhoun, have been debating this issue for months now." Jim paused, fully aware that his comment about his distaste for Calhoun would probably spark an emotional uproar from the crowd.

"Here it is, folks, and hear me out," he started slowly and calmly. "There had to be a compromise for admitting the entire area of California, New Mexico, and the Utah Territories into the Union, and adjusting the size of Texas to border the Rio Grande. That compromise was the enactment of what they call the 'Fugitive Slave Law.' "

Bridger paused again, to see if the people in the room understood what he had just said.

"What's the fugitive slave law, and what does that have to do with us anyway?" a cooling-down Joe Carter asked as he looked again at the blacksmith to assess his demeanor.

"According to that leader of the lost, Calhoun," Jim stated, not resisting the chance to mock the Southern politician, "while conceding what land we won from the war to free territory and reducing the size of the land of Texas, his constituents demanded that the Fugitive Slave Act to be passed."

"You still haven't told any of us what exactly that law is supposed to mean, Bridger!" Braxton yelled from across the room.

Bridger looked at the burly man, all dressed in black with coats of charred coal still on his face. "I'll tell you plain and simple, and I'm sure most of you will get the gist of it all, but I'm also sure some of you still won't." His eyes met Braxton's directly as he spoke.

"This law outlaws any runaway slave, no matter where found and how long away, so that said slave is caught and returned to the 'rightful owner.' "

"So you're saying, Jim, that if I'm a runaway slave and I make it into free territory, I can still be caught and brought back to my master?" asked Fez, standing along the side wall.

"Yea, that's exactly it, Fez," Bridger answered. "And there's another big part of it I need to add. There's no time limit neither, meaning you could have escaped twenty years ago, and you can still be caught and returned to your master."

A mixture of applause and angry outcries came from the group, while the Pastor raised his arms in an attempt to keep people civil.

Jonathan Braxton stood up in a haste, causing all around to turn their heads his way. "Are you a-tellin me, Bridger, that in order for us to get all that land, all we have to do is pass some kind of law that tells us we *have* to return any runaway slaves to their owners?"

Braxton puffed out his chest at the encouraging cheers he'd received from his comment.

"Yes, Braxton, that about says it," Bridger yelled over the crowd, frowning and shaking his head slowly at the burly man's ignorance of what this truly meant.

"Well, I for one don't see what the big deal is," Braxton remarked. "I mean, we keep Texas as a darky state, and we keep all slaves where they belong, back with their rightful owners."

Braxton stopped and looked around the room again. When he had decided that more were in agreement with him than not, he continued. "Them there slaves are the legal property of their owners, just like my steel and iron are to me. They ain't people anyway, they're property, and if that's all we got to do to keep peace, then so be it."

"Mr. Braxton, I am appalled to even hear you or any of you consider another human being, one of God's creations, mere property," Abigail said out loud, giving Lizzy's hand over to Fez and walking toward the front of the church.

When she reached the front of the church, she walked up to the lectern, her face bright red with anger. She turned and paused for a second to compose herself as she held tightly to the wooden stand. She could see her knuckles turning white from her attempt to withstand the temptation to unload all the emotions she'd kept inside the past several months. She didn't care that her hair was out of place or that her forehead gleamed with perspiration. She cleared her throat, scanned the audience, and began.

"We are all here today in this house of God, and a lot of you are saying that a man created in the likeness of his Creator is not a man, but a piece of property?" She paused to catch her breath, then continued after her nerves settled a bit. "All this, just because of the color of his skin?" she asked as she examined the room to gauge the firmness of their opinions on the subject. Many looked down to avoid her piercing eyes.

"Mr. Braxton, you don't own any slaves, do you?" Abigail asked.

"Nope, I don't Mrs. Monroe. But I don't see where that has anything to do with me agreeing with the laws of the land and my fellow Southerners," Braxton argued, beginning to feel confident in his stand. "I mean, isn't all of these rights of slave owners and the great 'manifest destiny' hogwash the whole reason that your husband went and got himself killed in that hell-bent war?"

The room went silent; the assembled townsfolk spun their heads from Braxton to Abigail to see her reaction. Abigail felt a hot flash of anger sear through her spine as she tried her best to stay calm and composed.

More than a year had passed since her last letter from Jed. The war had been over for some time, but news about his whereabouts, or even if he was alive, hadn't gotten to her yet.

Her chest felt tight, her breathing became rapid, the walls seemed to be closing in on her, and all she wanted to do was run.

Fez looked at her with a concerned expression on his face while holding Lizzy's hand. Lizzy looked up at her mother, not understanding the emotions of fear and terror that she saw on her mother's face. She smiled at Abigail, and gave her an innocent gentle wave that magically brought Abigail's focus out of her prison of worry and back into the church. She sensed that the room had become filled with apprehensive and uncomfortable neighbors and friends after hearing the comment from Braxton.

"Mr. Braxton—Jonathan, if I may." Abigail started slowly, the room quiet as the crowd tried to anticipate what Abigail would say next. "My husband fought for what he believed in. He believed it was right to fight for his country. He didn't fight for the black man or the white man, but for all men who have the God-given right to live in this free country. He fought to defend this great country against any foreign oppressor that feels it can tell us what we can or cannot do. And if you say one more word about my . . ."

She tried to continue but couldn't, her voice broken, her eyes filled with tears. The room remained silent except for the sounds of shuffling feet and the creaking of church pews. Some people cleared their throats, some sniffled, but most looked down in a moment of reflection, not just for their country, but also about themselves and who they were. And for some, the greatest motivation was still to avoid Abigail's piercing eyes.

A voice was barely audible from the back of the church, behind four rows of standing people. "And this country will always stand for freedom, just as it did when it fought for its freedom more than seventy-five years ago!" The voice grew louder as a man maneuvered through the crowded back aisle. He made it to the middle aisle and began to walk toward the lectern.

His face was dirty and his long beard peppered with black-and-gray strands of coarse hair that was long and unkempt. He wore a dirty pair of blue torn trousers, and his jacket had the front pocket ripped out. His eyes bore down on the front of the church with a determination so fierce that no one spoke a word—they just let the man move forward.

"War is hell, people!" he yelled. "It is up to all of us to ensure that no more blood is dropped, and that freedom, fought so hard for and with so many sacrifices, is never taken for granted!"

His eyes were fixed on hers, and hers on his. She could see him plainly, even through the lake of tears forming in her eyes. Abigail knew that voice, knew that determination and conviction.

He made it halfway down the aisle and then stopped. "Freedom is a right, and we cannot take that for granted. Family is a privilege and a gift, and we should cherish it with each new child born. Marriage is God's way of telling us that His love will prevail, and we should be so thankful that we have that love that endures all madness and chaos." He continued to the pulpit.

They were within arm's length now, and the room was silent. She looked up at his bearded face, seeing his own tears flowing.

"You're home," she whispered to him.

"Yes, I am," Jed whispered back. "And we have a lot to catch up on."

Abigail smiled wide, the smile that had been absent for so long. They embraced, and the crowd quickly acknowledged that Jed Monroe had returned.

Jed and Abigail walked out the side door hand in hand, leaving the crowd behind as applause from the townsfolk surrounded them.

Once outside, they embraced tightly, no words, just the warm feeling of security and completeness. Jed, never wanting to let go, felt a tug on his torn pants. He looked into Abigail's eyes, and then down to his side into the teary eyes of his little six-year-old. He gently leaned down and swooped his baby girl up into his arms and hugged her tight.

Fez quietly approached and put his arm around the shoulders of his son-in-law. "I'm might glad to see you, Son."

Jed gripped Fez's arm, and without a word their eyes spoke loudly. Fez gently nudged Lizzy away from the tight reunion and up into his soothing arms. He knew all too well that the two needed some time alone to reunite.

Abigail was ecstatic beyond words to have Jed home, but she knew all too well that before they could begin celebrating his homecoming, she had to show him something, and with God's help, try to have it all make sense to him.

She pulled away from him and her eyes glistened. "I need to take you somewhere, Jed." Her chest ached. "And I need to share something with you, something that's going to hurt, but it needs to be done before we move on." Abigail's eyes looked into his with a plea to trust her and to follow her without asking.

She held on to his hand as she led him away from the church. She nodded to Fez to watch Lizzy as they began to walk down the street. Jed looked puzzled, but was curious about what was so important that Abigail would rush him off just as they were reunited.

He soon found out . . .

They sat on the bench with their heads down in silent prayer, their hands clasped together. The grounds were well kept, as they usually were, with weekly care by Abigail and Fez. She talked and explained everything to him. They sat on Abel's bench for hours, holding each other's hands, crying, and embracing well after the sun had set.

"The bench is nice, Abigail," Jed said, breaking the silence. He looked into her eyes, trying to reach that faraway place where she had gone to be lost in her thoughts.

She had come here so often that it was like a normal routine to go through her emotions, thoughts, and trances, but it was not normal for Jed. Jed's emotions from the loss of his child were hard, but the guilt associated with never knowing he was going to have another son bit into him far more harshly than anything he had experienced in war.

Trying not to upset Abigail and recognizing that she was fragile at that moment, he asked the question several times. Each time, he knew that she was on the verge of breaking when the discussion of their son came up. But he too had some healing to do, and the question had to be asked.

"Why didn't you tell me?" he stuttered, bracing himself for her emotional reaction.

She stayed poised, staring at the letters on the tombstone, letting the name of her son give her the strength that she needed to talk about him. Lacking the courage to look at Jed, she stared at her son's name and tried to explain. "It happened so fast, and I really wasn't sure, and once I had a pretty good idea, you were marching out of town." She felt a pang of guilt for letting him go off to war not knowing that she was pregnant. "Then I wrote, and I wrote, and I wrote. My goodness Jed, I wrote until my hands were raw, and each time I would describe to you the feelings of our child growing inside me and wishing you were with me, living it with me."

She looked up at him now and confessed, "When I was told that most, if not all, of your mail would never get to you, I was beside myself with grief. I couldn't get over the fact that you would never know that you were going to be a father again, after reading in your letters how you longed for that day to come again."

Her gaze returned to their son's tombstone. "I had to come to an understanding with myself that you would never know, but I had a sense of peace knowing that you would be so surprised when you came home and . . ." She couldn't talk anymore, and her guilt for not telling him and for losing their baby overwhelmed her.

"My God, Abigail, none of this . . ." Jed stopped, put his hand on her chin, and turned her head toward his. "None of this is your fault, and you have to stop beating yourself up."

They held each other. They cried, not just for Abel, but to help them heal from the effects of war and loneliness and despair. Far after dark, they continued to sit on the bench that had been built out of love, and they began in their own way to mend.

"You did real good with his name, Abigail," Jed broke the silence and consoled her. "Adam felt his own grief when Abel was killed and God comforted him, and He will do the same for us. We will always have our little Abel with us, right here." He placed his hand on her heart. "And you know you always have a special place right here." He moved her hand to his chest.

Her tears flowed freely, and she didn't try to hold them back. He held her tight, her back now to the words etched in stone, and he read them again. *You rest well, my little son, you rest well,* he thought.

She had her eyes closed, feeling the comfort and security in the arms of her husband, the husband she missed dearly. She made an oath to herself at that moment that she would give her husband another child to make up for losing Abel. She told herself that she would never tell Jed of the severity of her hard labor. *I will give you more children, Jed, I promise.* She wept into his shoulders while she thought her words of committed sorrow.

The sounds of children laughing brought them out of their embrace, and in the distance beyond the gates of the church, they saw their four children playing with Grandpa Fez. The three older ones were running around him, trying to grab the little feet of Lizzy, who was sitting on her grandpa's shoulders.

Abigail and Jed watched their family and smiled. "Abigail, I thought I was going to come back and describe all of my hell that I went through, but I am so humbled to realize how much worse you had to endure, and I'm so, so very sorry that I wasn't here for you," Jed said as he helped her up from Abel's bench. "I've seen enough in this country, Abigail, and I've adventured enough. My life is here with you and those youngins over there."

Hand in hand, they said their temporary farewells to Abel, turned, and walked out of the cemetery toward their family. Jed paused for a moment and turned to Abigail. "You know, you've never spoken about the delivery, just that we lost Abel," he commented, momentarily catching her off guard.

"It was a little hard, but not bad. You know I've been through five of these, so I think I should know what is bad or not—right, Mister?" She hid her deception from him as she glanced away. Yes, she would be fine in time, and yes, she would give him more children.

Chapter Eighteen

Calm before the Storm

1852

"I am not about to watch my boys go through what I just went through, Abigail!" Jed declared loudly. "I'll move us as far away as possible if I need to!"

"Sit back down, Jed. You're going to scare the children."

He stepped back from the porch railing and sat down abruptly next to Abigail, his face fiery red with fear and anger. He wanted to continue his outburst, but her calm demeanor quickly defused his rage. He let out a long forced sigh that brought a smile to the corner of Abigail's mouth. She took a mental snapshot of her children, who were playing joyfully in the yard with their Grandpa Fez, and then turned back to Jed to let him know that he should continue.

"You don't understand, Abigail," Jed pleaded. "I've seen what war does, and I won't let that happen to our family."

Abigail leaned over, gently touched his cheek, then placed her hand on his. "You know, dear, you said the same thing when you walked through the middle of that crowded church more than a year ago. What did you mean when you said that 'bloodshed will be the only cure'?"

Jed's eyebrows furrowed as he slowly exhaled and let out an abbreviated sigh, but he softened up when he looked into Abigail's genuinely caring eyes, which were pleading with him to explain. "You see, honey, it's like this—the North is so angry about this fugitive slave law that it wants nothing to do with any state in the South. And the South is fed up with the North always telling its states what they can and cannot do with their slaves."

Jed settled back into his chair, his face returning to its natural color. "I'm sorry, Abigail, but I just get so darn upset whenever I talk about this. I heard enough angry talk from both sides during the war that I was to the point of pulling my hair out. Each side stated its case over and over, and you know, the odd part is, I kind of came to agree with both sides, especially over the past year."

"Now don't get me wrong about this slavery issue," Jed quickly interjected, noticing that Abigail had raised an eyebrow. "I'm completely against a man being held as a slave by another man. But what I'm talking about is each state having the right to decide what's best for itself."

"Can't the states have their own rights and the United States still be one country?" asked Abigail as she made one of her occasional peeks to check the status of her father's endurance with the children.

"You would think so, huh?" Jed answered. "I really think the big unresolvable problem is the issue about slavery, and I don't think that can be fixed by talking or compromising. It will take bloodshed, and I'm afraid it will be a lot of bloodshed. That means United States blood—brother-against-brother, uncle-against-uncle, father-against-son type of blood."

Jed stood up and continued as he paced the porch, looking half at Abigail and half at his children playing. "Abigail, I do see both sides with the exception of slavery, and I vow to you and to this family that we will be as neutral as the good Lord allows us to be. I will not take a stand on either side of the fence that could be a danger or stress to you or the children, and I think we should teach our children the same thing. I can't fathom the thought of my sons taking up arms against each other—it just can't happen!"

"I'm right there with you, Jed," Abigail said as she poured him another cup of coffee.

"I just hope it doesn't go on forever," Abigail said. "We can control our children at the age they're at now, but how successful will we be once they're grown up with views of their own?"

Jed and Abigail each looked at the other with worry, then to the yard to watch their children play. They were looking for a way to change the subject to something other than war.

"Your father's been real good for them, hasn't he?" Jed asked.

"Yes," Abigail answered thoughtfully. "In fact, while you were gone, I don't know how I would have survived without him. He's always been there for me and the children, and he's always supported you as well."

Jed looked at her questioningly.

"He's still waiting for the day when you decide to follow your father's dream," Abigail confessed, keeping a close eye on her husband's reaction.

After his return from the war, Jed spent endless nights with Abigail, talking about his future. It would thrill her to no end for Jed to make the change and become a pastor; she hoped the change would put an end to the demons that haunted him. She still worried about the memories he brought back from the war, and she confided in Pastor Higgin from time to time in order to reassure herself.

What Abigail didn't know was that Jed had come to realize, halfway through the war, that he was ready to make true on the promise made to his parents. He had vowed on a lonesome hilltop near Santa Fe that upon his return he would learn the trade of ministry once and for all.

Jed's successful return to daily life in Independence took longer than he had envisioned. He frequently experienced nightmares of the battles in which he had fought, and these often included vivid images of fallen comrades. Many nights, Abigail would wake him from anguished sleep to find that he was soaked in sweat and delirious to his surroundings.

"It'll take time, Abigail," Pastor Higgin counseled her. "He'll need to fight through all those demons, and with the good Lords help, he'll find that peace for which he's been searching."

Jed's mind was constantly filled with memories of death, and his vision for the future of his country was glum at best. These feelings carried over to his life at home, and Abigail and the children felt it. Although it was tense at times, Abigail knew that she and the children were the best cure to help him out of the morose state into which he often found himself falling.

Jed turned toward Abigail.

"I really think I made up my mind during the war, Abigail," he began. "It's time, and I know it. Knowing that your father's kind of expecting it takes a huge load off my mind. I was worried that I'd be putting him in a bind if I left the Mercantile."

"Oh, I don't think it'll be a problem," Abigail said with a laugh. "I see a couple of growing kids out in the yard who will be happy to take your place."

Jed laughed along with his wife, and the feeling that came with it was nice and long overdue. He began to plan how he would break the news to Fez.

* * * * *

"I've actually been waiting for years to hear those words from you, Jed!" Fez said happily. "It would have made your folks awfully proud, and I'm sure you'll have no disagreement from your wife about your decision. In fact, knowing my daughter, she's likely already started looking for a church for you to start." The two laughed at the idea of Abigail searching all over town for a suitable spot for her husband's first church.

Abigail was pleased when she heard that Jed had spoken to her father; it seemed to bring a sense of warmth into their family, a peace that had been missing since the start of the war.

Jed loved his family and adored his Abigail. His greatest joys were seeing his family grow and watching his children with their beautiful mother. He couldn't fathom the thought of her not being by his side.

One evening while the children were sleeping, Jed and Abigail sat on the porch. The air was crisp and the stars filled the night sky. They talked about their ever-growing tribe.

Willie led his class in reading and writing. He boasted to his father of his knowledge of the country's current affairs. Jed had to admit that his eldest son had an independent mind of his own and was quite astute on most subject matters. Jed had also noticed that Willie was becoming increasingly more interested in the abolition movement, and despite Willie's young age, Jed believed that would ultimately be God's calling for his bright young son.

Daniel admired and idolized his older brother. He often tried to emulate Willie's mannerisms, beliefs, and convictions. Many times, Jed had found Daniel attempting to read Willie's books by candlelight so that he could try to keep up with his older brother's way of thinking. The latest book making its way under Daniel's covers was also Willie's favorite, *Uncle Tom's Cabin*, written by a woman up North named Harriet Beecher Stowe.

Micah was as opposite as any sibling could be from his two older brothers, and he seldom was seen with them. He wasn't considered a bully at only ten years of age, but townsfolk had spoken to Jed and Abigail repeatedly about his outlandish behavior. Micah once told his father that he was his own "man" and didn't need his brothers' help with anything. Although this concerned his parents, they considered his age and figured he would grow out of his currently rebellious state of mind.

Their only daughter, Lizzy, was an independent and opinionated young lady of eight going on twenty-two, and never hesitated to tell her big brothers a thing or two. Jed and Abigail always found humor in observing Lizzy with her brothers. They saw that not only did the boys listen to their young sister, but they also usually abided her demands.

She had a kind heart and was a nurturing soul to anyone in need. All too often, Lizzy would bring home an injured or stranded animal, be it a bird, frog, or even a lost squirrel to care for. She would stay up all night to ensure that the poor animal was protected against any harm the world might try to bestow upon it.

* * * * *

A week had gone by since Jed and Fez's discussion about the future of the Mercantile and Jed's pending new career. It was a Saturday, and the day was filled with the sweet scent of corn, squash, and pumpkin. Crows were busy in fields, scooping up the fallen harvest of local farmers' crops. All four Monroe children were helping Grandpa at the Mercantile, and getting a shiny penny each for their efforts.

Fall was Jed's favorite season, and he loved to watch the leaves turn from green to red, orange, yellow, and brown. Unsettled air was all around, emanating blustery warmth during the day and briskness at night. The fields on the outskirts of town were filled with the last of the cornstalks, which were aged to a golden yellowish-brown. The river level was down, which opened up secluded spots along its banks where visitors could put down blankets, and picnic baskets typically filled with the best meals from town.

Jed tried to hold down the blanket, which threatened to escape with each sudden wind gust that came off the river. "You were right all along, Abigail; it's been far too long since we did this. If I could just get this last corner secured—"

The strong smell of freshly cooked chicken wafting from the picnic basket was driving Jed crazy, but Abigail's attention was on a vine of beautiful morning glory located twenty feet from the shoreline, from which she later took home more than a dozen shrubs. The bright blue flowers fascinated her.

"I have never seen this spot as pretty as it is today, Jed!" Abigail cried in amazement. "Forget about lunch, I'm going to lie right here on the blanket and just embrace what nature has given us today."

"Whoa there, Mrs. Monroe," Jed said as he put up his hand. "This ol' boy is mighty hungry, and you've been torturing me this whole ride with the smell of a chicken that is just asking to be eaten."

With a laugh and playful nudge, Abigail arranged two sets of tableware on the blanket. The two enjoyed a delicious meal together while absorbing the beauty of nature and the sound of the river crashing against the rocks just a few yards from them. They were alone, at peace, and very happy.

After eating, Abigail lay back on the blanket, mesmerized by the sights and sounds around her. The blanket felt warm against her back, and with her husband by her side, she gazed into the bright blue cloudless sky. Occasionally, a hawk would fly by in search of food near the river.

"It is so nice here, Jed," Abigail said softly. "I was just trying to count how many times we've been at this spot, and how many important talks we've had over there, too." Abigail pointed to a large granite boulder on which they often sat.

Jed didn't reply, agreeing silently with his wife while staring into the vast openness of the sky. He had become much more relaxed and at peace since he'd made the decision to pursue his ministry. The nightmares had decreased, and flashbacks of battle had diminished. Now he focused on his and his family's future. He was haunted by thoughts about what kind of father and husband he had been and would be. *Do I support them enough? Do I support her enough?*

Over the prior few months, Abigail had confessed to Jed more about what had happened on the night of Abel's delivery. She didn't disclose the full severity of the situation, only saying that it was a "tough labor" and "I had to work harder" than when giving birth to the other children.

But despite the emotional toll her last delivery had taken, she was still willing to go through it again to give Jed more children. Her blindness to the danger of delivering another child had been brought to her attention by Doctor Andersen, but when she asked him point-blank if she could have more children, his answer was a quiet but reluctant yes.

"Jed?" No answer. She tried again, this time nudging his side—"Jed?"— but still got no answer. "Are you awake?" she said teasingly.

"I'm awake, woman!" he said jokingly as he brought himself out of his trance.

"Jed, there's something I've been wanting to talk about," Abigail said, still looking upward and not at Jed.

"It's been a long time since we lost Abel." She paused to listen for a reaction. Hearing none, she turned on her side and held herself up on an elbow. "I want to give you more children, Jed!"

She watched his face carefully. Still not seeing a reaction, she continued. "I want at least two more, maybe three, and since Abel, I feel that I could—"

Jed cleared his throat, still staring at the sky, and said, "There's nothing I would like more than to have another child, Abigail, believe me."

Jed turned to face her, his body mirroring hers. "I've wanted that for so long, and now that I'm home for good—I mean really home for good—we can plan the life that I promised you. He sat up straight and pulled her to him. He looked deep into her eyes and held her tight as he said, "You are the best thing that's ever happened to me, Abigail. Being together, raising our children, and enjoying the birth of another is . . . well it's . . ."

Jed's voice cracked, and he tried his best to continue speaking despite his emotions. He looked deeply into Abigail's tearful yet sparkling eyes and found the words he yearned to tell her. "I vow to be by your side, be the husband you deserve, and be the father that my four children deserve."

Abigail put her hands gently on Jed's cheeks, and with her loving eyes reaching out and locking on his, she said, "Part of the love I give to you is having your children, Jed. It's love, and it's my love *for* you and *to* you." Her tears began to well up in her eyes, tears of love and endearment for her husband.

They looked into each other's eyes without a word, each knowing the other's thoughts. They knew each other so well that words were rarely needed.

She softly whispered to him, "One more?" and waited for his reaction.

"One more," he said in reply.

Her eyes sparkled with tears of joy. Her smile was radiant against the sun, and her hug tightened, forcing the air from his lungs.

Jed put his hands on Abigail's cheeks, slightly lifting her head so he could look into her eyes. He knew he would be lost without her. To him, they were soul mates destined to live out the rest of their lives as one.

Jed had found peace, and knew it as he looked into Abigail's eyes, the tears trickling down her cheeks and over his palms. "Did I ever tell you that you are beautiful when you cry?" he said, holding back his urge to cry as well.

"Ah . . . You only say that because you have to, you know."

They both knew that God had been good to them, giving them their life together to cherish for years to come. And now they were about to add one more Monroe to the family. Life couldn't be sweeter.

Chapter Nineteen

Beginning's End

1853

In early 1853, the Independence newspaper announced the inauguration of Franklin Pierce as the fourteenth president of the United States. The front page stated that he was coming in at a difficult and unsettling time, with the senate debates concluded and the Compromise of 1850 bill now becoming law. There was a mixture of hope and despair running through the emotions of the folks in Independence. Many were hoping that the new president would soothe hostilities and bring a sense of goodwill and security back to the land, unlike his predecessor Millard Fillmore.

Fillmore had been no more than a lame-duck politician. The turmoil and uncertainty of the times were held together by the voices of Daniel Webster in the North, John Calhoun in the South, and Henry Clay in the middle. Each tried his best to guide the nation through heated debates in the hope of securing a future for the country.

But by the end of 1852, only a sliver of hope remained for a peaceful solution to the slavery conflict, as all three statesmen had passed away and left the republic helpless to negotiate a permanent and peaceful compromise. In Independence, this news was unsettling. Without political voices capable of calmly and evenly debating the issue of slavery, tempers grew thin.

Jed had learned, through his recent pastoral training, to be impartial and nonjudgmental toward others and their views. It was a difficult test at times, especially when differing views were heard all over town, including in his own home.

Since returning from the war, Jed had made a promise to himself to remain neutral in all political issues, having seen enough bloodshed and bitterness to last a lifetime. He was determined to find his own peace while fulfilling his father's wish that he become a pastor.

He and Abigail had always encouraged the children to think for themselves and discuss their views and opinions with others. Jed enjoyed listening in when his children debated current affairs affecting the country.

Willie had become involved with the local abolitionist group. He was one of the more vocal members in Independence when it came to the treatment of slaves and free black citizens throughout the country. He read articles written by the late Daniel Webster, and would sit down and argue with many townsfolk about the rights of Negroes and the audacity of slaveholders.

Jed admired his oldest son's ability to voice his opinion with persuasion and conviction. He told Abigail that he could see Willie becoming a political leader for slaves' rights someday, but admitted that the whole subject worried him. Worry frequently consumed Jed's mind in those days, and he prayed for insight and for the safety of his family.

Daniel was never far from Willie's side—the two brothers were inseparable. He shared his brother's sentiments, and while not as strong in his activism, he was always there to back up whatever Willie was saying.

Micah didn't yet fully understand the concept of slavery, but usually disagreed with anything his two older brothers believed. He was stubborn to a fault and mean as a bull.

Lizzy often listened to her brothers argue. Though she processed everything, she would usually just sit and watch, not indicating what side she was on.

"You've given me quite the family, Abigail Monroe!" Jed exclaimed after the four children had been excused from the dinner table to finish their studies.

Jed moved around the table to sit next to Abigail. They listened to Willie and Daniel debating with Micah, although they couldn't hear the specific subject of the night. Lizzy gathered up her dolls in the corner of the sitting room and pretended not to listen in, but Jed and Abigail could hear her chuckle from time to time over some comment the boys made.

"Can you remember when we talked about having seven or eight?" Jed jokingly said, breaking the silence between them.

"I'll be just as happy with the five after this one comes," Abigail replied, rubbing her tummy to soften the latest kick of her unborn infant.

Abigail knew that her time would come soon, and faint memories of Abel's delivery had been creeping into her mind. She kept those memories to herself, never wanting to alarm her husband or worry the children. She looked at Jed and gave him a reassuring smile.

From the time she told him that he was going to be a father again, Jed had pampered Abigail nonstop, to the point that she literally had to ask him to leave and spend more time at the church.

Still sitting at the dining table, they discussed what their life would be like when the new baby came. They were excited to welcome the newest Monroe into their family, especially now that it looked more likely that Jed would take over the church from Pastor Higgin.

"Do you really think Pastor Higgin will retire at the end of the year?" Abigail asked, still rubbing her tummy. "I've seen you work, Jed. I mean, you really show how genuinely you care for others." Abigail smiled slightly as her husband blushed. "You're modest about it, but I see how people respond to you. You're going to make a great pastor, honey, and your parents would've been so proud of you."

"Well, I don't know about all of that. But you know, Abigail, I do enjoy it, and it gives me a real sense of purpose. It's kind of funny, though, when I really step back and think about it. I've been searching for this feeling of contentment for so many years, and yet the very peace I've been searching for has been right here under my nose the whole time."

Jed put his hand on top of hers and looked deep into her eyes. He blocked the noise of the children from his mind and said, "Abigail Monroe, I've never been so happy in my entire life, and I thank God for blessing me with you."

Abigail's eyes were locked on his, inviting him to continue. "I fell in love with you the first day I saw you on the *Nebraska*, and my love for you just keeps growing stronger. We're going to grow old together, watching our five children as they find their own soul mates in life and start blessing us with grandchildren. I will never be able to thank God enough for where we are right now and what we have to look forward to."

Abigail listened intently as Jed spoke. She thought about how right he was, and how lucky they both were to have the blessings that the good Lord had provided them. She couldn't wait to see where their future took them.

Jed leaned over, and without caring if the children saw, tilted his head toward Abigail's and gently kissed his wife softly on her lips. He held his lips there, not wanting to ever separate, never wanting this loving moment to end. He was in love and at peace with his soul mate, and nothing was going to change that.

Abigail sat back in her chair and wiped a few stray tears away with the side of her apron. She looked down at Jed's hands, gently caressing hers, and as she looked up, she was gripped by a stab of pain. She knew what it was instantly, and tightly grasped Jed's hand for support.

Jed could tell from the look on her face. He got up and helped Abigail into their room. They worked as a team to get her changed and as comfortable as possible. Jed then nodded to Abigail that he was going out to talk to the children; she shook her head in agreement before closing her eyes.

He gathered the children together and spoke calmly and comfortingly to his questioning family. "Children," Jed started, "your momma and I are going to need your help."

They all knew from the tone of his voice what was happening, and all were eager to help.

"Willie, I need you to get the Doctor," Jed told his oldest while resting his hand on the young man's shoulder. "Daniel, you run down and get Grandpa Fez."

"Someone get Sara Higgin, too!" Abigail cried out from the bedroom in rhythm with the start of another contraction.

The boys ran out the door to perform their duties. It was decided that Willie would also notify Sara. Micah and Lizzy moved into the front room and stood in the doorway of the bedroom. They both looked frightened at the sight of their mother, not fully understanding why she was in so much pain.

"Micah," Jed said to his son, "I need you and your sister to put some more wood in the fire pot. Then get the big black kettle, fill it up with water, and place it on top. You two keep that fire burning, you hear me?"

Seeing fear in their eyes, he tried to reassure them. "She'll be fine, kids. Just think, in no time at all, you are going to have another brother or sister, but for now I just need you to do as I ask, understood?" His confident tone gave them the sense of ease that moments before had escaped them.

With the older boys out getting the needed help and Micah and Lizzy busy with the fire, Jed returned to Abigail. "You doing alright, Mrs. Monroe?"

Jed forced an encouraging smile while he wrung out a wet cloth from the washbasin and wiped it gently across her cheeks. "Help will be here shortly, so you just lie there, rest, and look beautiful as you always do." His presence gave Abigail comfort and the sense that all would be just fine.

"You just say that because you have to, you know," Abigail joked. "I'm not going to look very pretty in a short while, so keep your compliments coming until then, all right, Mister?"

Contraction after contraction surged through her like a knife cutting and splitting. The memories of the pain from Abel's delivery returned, and the outcome of Abel's fate plagued her like an endless nightmare.

Despite the physical agony and suffering she was experiencing, she was mentally prepared for the long haul. She was more determined than at any other time in her life, telling herself with utmost certainty that she was going to hear *this* baby's cry.

Doc Andersen arrived with a kind smile and his black medical bag, which was worn thin on the outside and had a broken buckle. He handed his coat and hat to a nervous Jed and then proceeded to the bedroom. En route, he inquired about Sara, and Jed assured him that she was on her way.

Upon her arrival, Sara went straight to the bedroom and saw Abigail lying on the bed holding on to Jed's hand. The two women looked at each other with loving familiarity from the many deliveries they had shared. Abigail's face was red, and her nightgown was beginning to soak through. Her breathing was quickening and the contractions were coming close and fast, and Jed knew that he would soon be asked to leave.

"Okay, lovebirds," Sara announced, "you two know that we have some work to do. So you, Papa Monroe, need to step out so the good doctor can tend to the new momma here."

One last kiss to her forehead, a soft touch to her cheek, and silent words from his eyes said everything as the couple parted. Jed slowly backed out of the room and closed the door behind him. He stood facing the door with his head down, silently praying to God to protect his loving wife and new baby. Then, wiping tears from his eyes and cheeks, he turned from the door, knowing that his Abigail was in good hands.

Outside on the porch, Fez waited with excited anticipation for his fifth grandchild to join them. He did his best to keep the children's attention away from their momma, telling the youngest two the familiar stories that they loved to hear from their grandpa. The older boys were staying busy in the yard playing stickball. Fez loved to hear their laughter, and it soothed his painful memories of his daughter's last tragic birth.

Jed was surprisingly calm, believing that all would be fine as he waited and listened for sounds from the newest arrival to the Monroe household. He strolled to the corner of the front porch, reflecting on how blessed he was and what a wonderful loving woman he had in Abigail. He listened to the sounds of joy coming from his children as they spent time with their grandpa, and felt at that moment that he was the luckiest and happiest man alive. He smiled at the thought of holding his newborn baby.

Jed was shocked by the sound that startled him from his reflective trance and brought him quickly back to reality. The scream was horrific, its vibrations rolling through the house in sonic waves.

The second scream was even more agonizing. Jed felt it engulfing him, squeezing his heart like a giant fist. The tightness in his chest grew as his pounding heart attempted to escape. He rushed from the corner of the porch toward the front door, passing by Lizzy, now sitting on her grandpa's lap. He failed to notice the frightened look on her face.

"Papa?" Lizzy begged, trying to attract her father's attention as he dashed by. Jed stopped just inside the door, turned quickly, and saw Lizzy's frightened eyes looking up at him.

He went to her, bent down, and kissed the top of her head. "Stay here with Grandpa for now, honey. I'll be right back."

Jed turned, entered the house, and knocked forcefully on the bedroom door. Sara stepped out, immediately seeing the terror in his eyes. She put a steady hand on his shoulder to comfort him, working to reduce his anxiety.

Sara's apron, which had once been clean and white, was now covered in blood. Sara saw the look of fear on Jed's face, and before speaking, she pushed back several strands of hair that had been stuck to her cheek by the heavy perspiration that covered her face.

"Jed, we need to refill this water decanter," Sara ordered, knowing that keeping him busy would help him to stay calm. "More hot water too, and more rags, and . . ." Not finishing her sentence, she began to reenter the bedroom.

"Wait!" Jed demanded, putting his hand firmly on Sara's forearm. "There's a problem, isn't there, Sara?" His eyes were pleading, desperately trying to understand what was happening. "Is the baby alright?"

"Jed, please . . . get the water and cloth," Sara repeated calmly. "It won't be long before you're holding your new baby in your arms, but I've got to get back in there."

Feeling slight relief, Jed let go of Sara's arm and stepped back. He went to get the water and cloth rags, yet wondered, *The blood. Why is there so much blood on her apron?* He began imagining the worst, causing his finger to twitch uncontrollably and the tightness to return to his chest. The anxious terror of not knowing consumed him.

Jed tapped on the bedroom door, more calmly now, providing Sara with the water and additional rags. The room was quiet now, and Sara conveyed to Jed that Abigail was between contractions.

As Sara closed the door behind her, Jed tried to remember how much blood there had been during the other deliveries. He couldn't, but then again, he hadn't paid particularly good attention other than listening for the crying of the baby. That wonderful sound that happens each time . . . except last time . . . and he wasn't there. *No, it can't happen again . . . not again.*

Oh dear God . . . He prayed, as hard as he ever had, for the well-being of his unborn child. How he yearned to be in there, by Abigail's side, holding her hand, wiping down her forehead. He leaned his ear to the door and tried in vain to hear, but could only hear muffled voices and erratic whimpering like a wounded animal pleading for help.

All the children were up on the porch now, the older boys no longer interested in stickball. Fez spoke to the children in his usual relaxed tone. Each listened carefully to their grandpa's instructions, taking careful note of what they were to do when the baby came. His affection created such calmness that not one of them sensed that anything was wrong. Fez had other thoughts, though, and kept a keen eye on his son-in-law for signs of what was really happening just a few feet away.

As the hours passed, more agonizing screams were heard from Abigail, mixed with shouts of encouragement from Sara and the doctor. Jed imagined how tired and fatigued his beautiful wife must be.

How much longer? Jed wondered. Oh, God how much more can she endure?!

His prayer was answered by the joyous sound of a baby's cry. After hours of labor and worry, the beautiful sound was like a signal from Heaven.

At last the door opened, and Sara came out holding the baby, who was tightly wrapped in a bundle of wool blankets.

"Jed, meet your new son."

Jed reacted as if this was his first-born child, and was overwhelmed by emotion as he gazed upon the beautiful miracle of a healthy baby. He thanked God as his children surrounded him to see their new baby brother.

Sara turned to leave and said, "Jed, I need to go back in to help the Doctor with Abigail—I'll be back shortly for the baby."

Jed noticed the concern in her voice and asked, "Is everything alright?"

Sara pulled him away from the children and said softly, "Jed, this was by far Abigail's hardest delivery, and she's lost a lot of blood." Jed froze—he looked at Sara, but didn't say a word.

Sara, aware of Jed's deep concern, tried to reassure him by putting her hand on his arm. "Jed, she's a strong woman and in good hands with the doctor. I'll come get you once we get her all cleaned up. It shouldn't be long."

After Sara had gone, Jed could only stare at the closed bedroom door and hope. Jed felt a firm comforting hand on his shoulder as he was turned slowly around. "Well, do I get to hold my newest grandson?" Fez's calm voice brought Jed's attention back to his newborn baby.

Jed watched Fez as he held the baby, cradling him in his husky arms while soothing him with the soft humming of a lullaby. His father-in-law was in his moment of glory. Fez portrayed pure joy while holding his fifth grandchild. Jed looked at his other children, who were now circling around their grandpa, and he wished that Abigail were out here with them.

Jed took his eyes off of the tranquil scene in front of him to glance back at the closed door. It had been far too long since Sara had come out. He couldn't wait any longer. He had to see Abigail, even if it was just to hold her hand while they finished getting her ready.

Jed quietly entered the bedroom and closed the door behind him. He immediately became dizzy when he looked before him. He leaned back against the door to steady himself. Thinking it wasn't real, he forced himself to contain his emotions.

The room was stuffy and rancid. Bloody garments of clothing were sprawled on the floor beside the bed. The dirty water in the washbasin was crimson red, while the sheets on the bed were soaked through with blood. The smell of blood and sweat consumed the room and nearly suffocated Jed. Two candles, barely giving enough light to work by, shone on Abigail. Her limp body lay still in a pool of her own blood.

Jed slowly walked forward, his eyes locked on the figure in the bed. He could see that Abigail's eyes were open but swollen. Her lips were cracked, her face was pale, and her hair was plastered against her forehead.

Exhausted, Doc Andersen stopped for a moment, turned to Jed, and with what energy he had left said, "Jed, she had the same complications as last time, but this time, thank God, we were able to get the baby out in time." He paused, took off his spotted spectacles, wiped his face with his sleeve, and cleared his throat.

Jed, in shock and denial, looked at the doctor and then at Sara, who was speechless. Sara's face was flushed, and she suddenly began to cry uncontrollably. Her hands and arms were covered with the blood of her dear friend.

Jed moved closer to the bed and looked down at his wife. Her eyes were partially opened and her lips were trying to form words, but nothing was happening. Now aware that Jed was in the room, she tried to raise her head up from the bed.

Doc Andersen sighed in exhaustion, and in a cracked voice said, "I'm so sorry, Jed."

Placing his hand on Jed's arm, he tried his best to look him in the eye as he continued. "She's just lost too much blood, there's just . . . well, there's nothing I can do, son."

"Jed tried his best to understand, but comprehension was beyond him. His beautiful wife, the same wife who just hours before had sat next to him at their dining table as they talked about their blessed family and the plans they had for their future. *What happened? Why did this happen?* Jed sat down on the bed and tried his best to make sense of it all.

Sara put a hand on Jed's shoulder, and then went over to Abigail and squeezed her hand gently. No words were spoken, only a tearful look of good-bye as she turned back to Jed. "I really thought we could save her, Jed. I . . . am . . . so . . . " Sara couldn't finish her words and left the room.

Doc Andersen followed Sara out of the room after a soft touch to Abigail's cheek. He had no words to say that could make any difference, and he knew it. He left quietly, and when Jed heard the click of the door, he turned toward Abigail.

The bedroom was quiet and still. Jed held her hand as he brushed a strand of hair from her face. He leaned down and gently kissed her cheek, her forehead, her nose, and finally her lips.

The words inside him, so many, so jumbled together, would not come out. He feared that he would break down at any moment, and had begun to realize that his time to speak was becoming ever shorter. Jed felt empty inside, and he could not understand what was happening to his world, his world with his Abigail, his world that had suddenly and inexplicably collapsed.

He leaned over, picked her limp body up into his arms, and held her tight. He lost the will to control his emotions, and he unleashed his sobs with abandon. When he lay her down on the bed again, she reached up and put her fingers to his lips to quiet and comfort him as best she could.

"Oh Abigail . . . I can't . . . I don't know how I'll . . . ," he stuttered, unable to finish his words as he began to sob again.

She patted his hand softly, but slower now, her eyes never leaving his despite being filled with tears.

"I will always be thankful to God for blessing me with you," Jed whispered, and then wiped her cheeks before adding, "You are the most beautiful girl God ever placed on this earth, and I want you to always know that, you hear me?"

"Shhh," she whispered. "Remember, you've always said that 'cause you have to." She tried to ease his pain with her own attempt at their familiar humor.

With what little energy she had left, she said, "My dear Jed, the love of my life . . ."

She paused, trying to summon the courage and energy to continue. "You need to be strong, my love. You need to be strong for the children and for me."

Her voice had been reduced to a faint whisper and she tried her best to keep her eyes focused on his. “You’ve given me a life full of love and happiness.”

She tried to clear her throat and winced in pain. Jed felt a dagger going into his heart at the sight of her in such pain, and he opened his mouth to speak. She hushed him with a finger to her lips.

“ . . . it’s the love and happiness that I want you to remember about us, and for our children to remember about me.”

Abigail used what energy she had left to move her hand up to his chest and placed it on his heart. “I will always be right here with you.”

Her voice faded and was weak but she tried her best to continue. “Don’t spend your energy in grief, my husband, spend it in building up a life for our children, and in them you will remember me.”

Her voice was barely audible now, her breathing short and weak. Jed lay down next to her on the bed, his head in the nook of her neck, his arm around her middle, his tears flowing freely.

Her eyes closed now, and with the breath she had left, she whispered, “I love you, Jedidiah Monroe. I love you so very much.”

The sound of her breathing ceased, and Jed lay still, holding his wife and wanting so much to be able to tell her just one more time that he loved her too. The room was quiet except for his uncontrolled sobbing for the loss of his soul mate, his love, his Abigail.

Chapter Twenty

Unhinged

1854

"What's in Lecompton, and for that matter, where in the heck is Lecompton?" asked Fez in frustration.

"Fez, I told you before, it's a small town just seventy miles or so west. Pastor Higgin spent a lot of time there years ago and knows the departing pastor well. He's also familiar with the town."

Jed was trying to avoid the same old argument he and Fez had been having for several months now. It had been a year since losing Abigail, and the grieving had not eased a bit for Jed, nor for his children. The effects from the traumatic experience of losing their mother were still evident to Jed in their behavior.

Jed felt he had no choice but to move his family away from the painful memories that surrounded them in Independence. To that end, he had found another town, with new faces, that could possibly save his family from what he saw as an impending internal destruction.

He admitted that the change would be hard at first for the children, but he believed that in time they would be much better for it. His processing of Abigail's death was still excruciatingly painful. He went from being extremely angry to depressed, and then back to angry again. It took him months just to heal from the shock of how sudden and unexpected Abigail's death had been, and grief still consumed him.

He realized he would never understand why it had happened. God had his reason, and though Jed tried to play the pastor role in understanding it intellectually, his heart was taking longer to soften. He knew all too well that being angry at God was not the answer. He realized that he needed God far too much, and it made no sense to be mad at Him, or anyone else for that matter.

His memories of Abigail would be forever burned into his mind. He worked hard to be strong in his faith, but the grief was still there.

Fez excused himself from helping to tie down Jed's belongings in the last wagon, and he turned and walked down the street. Jed watched his father-in-law, knowing where he was going, where he went every day at this exact time. Jed continued to prepare the wagon, after which he would gather his children and head out to their new home.

Jed felt bad for Fez, and knew that he was completely brokenhearted. The two had spent hours upon hours letting out their emotions, to the point that they were now both raw, and there was nothing left inside either of them.

Jed had asked Fez to come with them so that he could be close to his grandchildren, but knew that Fez would never leave. Although his wife had been gone since '29, Fez had special and happy memories in Independence, and the place meant much to him. The bench he'd constructed in memory of his grandson was close to the more recent sacred spot where his own daughter now rested.

Fez loved his grandchildren, and loved Jed as a father loves his son, but Jed acknowledged that Fez would never leave Abigail's resting place. Jed had gained new respect and admiration for the man. He was relieved to know that Abigail and Abel would have a caretaker long after he and the children moved on.

With Fez gone, Jed thought of his children and how each was processing and healing. He had thought Lizzy would be the one most affected by the loss, but surprisingly, she had responded more like a surrogate mother. She nurtured the boys as well as Jed, and especially cared for little Johnny Russell, who had just celebrated his first birthday.

The three other boys dealt with their loss in varying ways. To Jed's mind, Micah was taking it the hardest. He had always felt like the outcast of the family compared with his two older brothers. What once had been an obstinate and rebellious temperament had recently developed into a more aggressive and militant personality.

Jed worried about his son, and hoped that his grief and anger would one day be healed—he could only put it to prayer and ask God to heal Micah in His time. He loved his son, but there had always been a barrier between them that Jed could not break. He had often asked God for the same kind of bond with Micah that he shared with each of his two oldest boys, but it had never materialized, and this bothered Jed because he didn't know how to fix it.

Willie was the one who had demanded to see Abigail on that fateful day, and respecting his wishes, Jed had escorted him in. Willie had stood next to Abigail's bed, motionless and speechless, showing no emotion. He held back his tears, saying his farewells before leaving the room.

Daniel had displayed the most emotion. For weeks, he could be heard crying himself to sleep. As he usually did, Daniel depended on his older brother for emotional strength. Jed learned through that experience just how dependent Daniel was on the rest of the family.

Jed knew innately that his children would be all right in time, but still felt the need for a change in scenery that would hopefully accelerate the grieving process. Pastor Higgin had retired and had offered the pastorship of his church in Independence to Jed. Even though Jed was extremely grateful, he had had to turn it down.

Jed couldn't fathom standing at that pulpit and preaching in "their" church without Abigail in the room. Luckily, Pastor Higgin had made some inquiries of old friends and learned of the vacancy at the Lecompton church. Jed had met with the Lecompton elders a few months back, and after a short deliberation, they offered him the position. He began immediately with plans to take his family to Lecompton, Kansas to begin a new life in his very own church.

The melancholy of it all sent shards of pain through his heart. Tears welled in his eyes and a lump formed in his throat, as he realized that neither his parents nor Abigail would be there to share this new stage of his life with him.

He would have to be strong if he were to fulfill the promise he'd made to Abigail on her deathbed. He still remembered her words: "You need to be strong, my love. You need to be strong for the children . . . and for me." Jed's mind still held the image of Abigail looking up at him and saying, "You have given me a life full of love and happiness, and that's what I want you to remember, and our children to remember."

Gathering his thoughts and trying to keep his composure, he remembered her last words: "I will always be right here with you." Thinking of those words, Jed instinctively placed his hand on his heart and let out a short moan. He quickly regained his self-control when he saw Fez rapidly approaching the wagons. His father-in-law always looked happier after spending time on Abel's bench.

"The flowers look great, Jed," Fez remarked, referring to the flowers Jed had left next to Abigail's tombstone earlier in the day. "I know in my heart that she's real happy to be resting there next to her Abel."

"You know, the offer still stands, and there's plenty of room. I've seen the house that the church is giving us, and you wouldn't be any trouble at all, Fez," Jed pleaded one last time.

"Nah—as much as I'd love to come with you and the children, you know my roots are here. I mean, who else is going to look after those two if it's not me, right?" Fez said, trying to convince himself.

"Anyway, when you think about it, seventy miles is not that far," Fez continued. "I'm sure I'll need a break from time to time, especially during the off-season, as I'm sure you well remember. Besides, I couldn't think of a better reason for me to come visit than to see all of them youngsters," Fez said as he motioned and looked toward the front porch. Fez let out a loud bellow of laughter that caught Jed by surprise.

Jed looked at the porch and saw that Johnny Russell was letting everyone know that he was ready to go. He had taken off Willie's hat and crawled behind Daniel, and now was attempting to pull his hair. Lizzy's voice could be heard as she feebly attempted to control the little one-year-old.

Jed, briefly enjoying the scene, couldn't help but notice that Micah was sitting by himself on the other side of the yard. His look of disgust and obstinacy convinced Jed that he was doing the right thing by moving his family from Independence. He believed that Abigail would have told him the same thing had she been there.

"You know, Fez," Jed began as he turned his attention back to his father-in-law, "Abigail's favorite spot was always down by the river next to that giant granite rock. You know, the one close to the covered bridge. Well, when you sit on Abel's bench and look down toward the river, you can see that very spot in the distance. Now it might sound crazy, but when I've gone down there, I hear her voice along the river, and she's the one who's telling me to move on and take care of the children."

"Fez . . . you need to make certain that you do visit us often, 'cause the children will give me all kinds of grief if you don't. You got that?" Jed said as he tried not to get choked up.

* * * * *

Having said his good-byes to the townsfolk, Jed gave a nod to Willie to take charge of the first wagon, while Daniel took control of the second. Jed was comforted by knowing that the Higgins were going to visit them in a week to help with settling them into their new home and Jed into his new church.

Lizzy, with Johnny Russell in her arms, got up and sat next to her oldest brother in the first wagon. Jed hopped up on his saddled mare and gave out the order for his family to move out. Fez stepped away from the wagons to fond and loud farewells from his grandchildren.

As they left Independence, Jed's chest tightened and his eyes filled with tears. No words could capture what these townsfolk had meant to him and his family. He had an odd feeling like he was running away, but knew it was the best thing, the only thing, to do. As they moved farther from the river, he listened intently for Abigail's voice giving her approval and encouragement. Even in the wind, Jed could hear her say, "Go, find that peace, my love, and start again . . . for me."

Turning away from town, ensuring that the boys had the wagons secure and straight, Jed turned his horse around to take one final look. He had come a long way since arriving there in 1832. He had made lifelong friends and started a beautiful family.

No, he wasn't running away, he told himself, he was running ahead, and Abigail was leading the way.

III

Turbulence
1855–1865

UNITED STATES AND

The Confederate States of America surrendered on April 9 1865.
The process of Reconstruction took from one to five years.

RITORIES, 1864–1865

Chapter Twenty-One

Jed's Values Tested

1855

A portly man, stuffed into a starched white shirt and dark black trousers held up by a pair of struggling suspenders, poked his head inside the opened front door. "Hello, anybody home?" Thinking that maybe the family had stepped out, the man tried again, this time a bit louder. "I say, is anybody here?"

"Can I help you?" Jed answered as he came around the corner with a box of groceries in his hand.

"Well actually, Pastor, you can."

Jed, still not used to the title of pastor, didn't immediately acknowledge that his visitor was speaking to him. Pastor Higgin had advised him that it might take him a while to get used to being called "Pastor." Even so, Jed didn't think he would ever feel really comfortable being referred to as a "man of God."

Sara and Pastor Higgin had helped Jed out immensely by getting the children enrolled in school, and Sara spent a lot of time making sure that Lizzy knew exactly how to manage a house—especially the kitchen. Despite their help, Jed couldn't help but worry about whether his children were acclimating to their new environment.

Willie maintained that he was too old for any more schooling at age seventeen. Jed felt that he couldn't argue with him on that point, but knew that Abigail would have demanded that he attend school until he was at least eighteen.

Daniel was excited about attending school, especially after seeing the little redhead who would be sitting next to him.

Micah told his father that he had no need for schooling and would go only to honor his mother. He added that when he believed he had satisfied that obligation, he would quit and move out on his own.

Lizzy had a hard time with the entire school concept. She believed that her main responsibility was to look after Johnny Russell. As much as Jed wanted her to continue in school, he reluctantly admitted that his daughter definitely was needed at home. She had the talent, patience, and instinct to care for Johnny Russell and the rest of the boys, as well as Jed. But every time Jed found himself thinking that way, he could sense Abigail's scowl.

Wondering if he could live up to his promises to Abigail and his new role as "Pastor," Jed suddenly realized that his guest was still standing in the front room, hat in hand, with a questioning look punctuating an almost perfectly round face peppered with whiskers.

"I am so sorry, Mr. . . . uh . . . you know, I don't think we've been introduced," Jed said awkwardly.

"No, we haven't, but don't you fret none, I can see that you have a lot going on right now, but—" the man said as he stretched out his hand to Jed, "I'm Wilbur Moonbody, one of the members of the Lecompton town council. I was asked to come by and see if you could cover a few topics at this Sunday's church service."

"Well, I see, Mr. Moonbody—or may I just call you Wilbur? I'd be happy to listen to your ideas, but as a rule, I do my own sermon writing."

Jed offered Moonbody a seat in the parlor as he continued. "Since you made your way over here, please do sit down. Let me know what you all have in mind for these fine folks here in Lecompton to hear . . . in addition to the teachings of the gospel, of course."

Jed proceeded to sit on one of the armchairs next to the dining table as Moonbody continued. "Pastor, I know you're new to these here parts and all, but I—I mean we—think you need to know a few things about what's happening around here."

Jed, seeing that this was likely to be a long ordeal, moved his chair a bit to get himself more comfortable for the long haul.

"Pastor, you see, most of the folks here in Lecompton voted for Franklin Pierce in '52, and when he was inaugurated in '53, well, he told all of us—no, he promised all of us—that he would prevent slavery from becoming an issue. Well, Pastor, it's becoming a bigger issue than any of us ever thought it would, and growing every single day!"

"Wilbur, would you like a glass of water?" Jed asked in an attempt to calm the poor old man down.

With a wave of his hand to indicate that his answer was *no*, Moonbody continued on. "He even said that he regarded the Abolitionists as a bunch of lunatics and that they should be ignored in order for them to just, well, you know, go away!"

Jed looked at the old man with interest now. Though he knew that he wasn't going to take anyone's side on this matter, he was still intrigued enough to let the man continue. "I don't know if you know this or not, Pastor, but this area here is partial to the Northern views. It's those hooligans from over Missouri way that continue to give us all grief over here on this side of the river."

Moonbody noticed the frown that appeared on Jed's brow, and realized that he might have insulted him with his comment about Missourians. "Oh gosh, Pastor, I wasn't referring to you or your friends. We at the council all know that you come from Independence, but we also know that you come with outstanding credentials and recommendations from our dear friend Pastor Higgin." Jed made no comment, figuring that Moonbody would continue on with his rambling soon enough.

Feeling a bit more relaxed after his attempt at flattery, Moonbody continued. "It's actually all of those . . . those . . . what do they call them?" Moonbody tried in vain to think of the name of the group that he and the council so desperately despised.

"Border Ruffians!" he finally blurted out, excited that he could recall the name that had momentarily escaped him. "That's what they're called, and they'll stop at nothing to sway the thinking of the good people on this side of the Kansas River, especially here in Lecompton, and all the way down to the fair town of Lawrence." Moonbody stopped to take a drink of water from the glass Jed had brought him despite his earlier refusal. He was so engrossed in his speech that he didn't realize that he now had an audience, as Willie had entered the room and was listening with a gust of enthusiasm.

"Pastor, we need you to tell the congregation that we're all against slavery, but we're not against this great country. You see, that's exactly what the Ruffians are trying to make us all to look like."

Jed, who had anticipated Moonbody's request, and whose sentiments on the subject were quite definite, hardly hesitated before answering. "Wilbur, I need you and the rest of the council members to know that I'm a man of God, and I speak about God in a very impartial manner. Believe me, sir, I have seen my trials and tribulations, and as God is my witness, I, more than anyone, want to have peace." Jed spoke right from the heart and didn't sway one way or the other, no matter the grunting sounds from Moonbody, whose cheeks were now flushed red with emotion.

What Jed didn't notice was the look his son gave him as he listened to his father's comments. Willie had been quietly sitting at the dining table, taking in the passionate concerns of the local politician.

Jed thanked Moonbody for coming by, and reassured him that he would speak on the subject the coming Sunday, but reminded him that it would be through the words of the Bible and not from the words of the city council. He closed the door and turned with a slight smirk on his face as he thought about the portly man, and found himself standing not two feet from a red-faced and heated seventeen-year-old.

"Please don't tell me that you're not going to take a stand on that issue? You, of all people, have to tell those folks out there that slavery is evil and needs to stop!" Willie exclaimed, nostrils flaring. He was zealous in his position on the bondage of one human by another.

Since reading *Uncle Tom's Cabin*, he had become obsessed with following the Abolitionist cause. He had written several letters to the editor of *The Liberator*, a famous newspaper circulating in the North, and had had the good fortune of starting up a regular correspondence with its editor, William Lloyd Garrison. Unbeknown to Jed, Willie had several letters from Garrison and the American Anti-Slavery Society tucked under the mattress in his bedroom. The only persons in whom Willie had confided were his brother Daniel, and a new friend he had made soon after arriving in Lecompton by the name of Louis Carpenter.

All the quietness and passivity that Willie had learned from Pastor Higgin's many sermons was about to end. In Willie's mind, it was time for everyone to know why this disgusting and repulsive way of life must come to an end.

"Papa, you're a preacher now, a pastor of your own church," Willie continued. "You have a duty to preach the truth about this outrageous treatment toward other human beings. I just don't understand how you can tell that Mr. Moonsomething that you have to stay neutral in your sermons." Willie took a hasty but deep breath, then continued. "Papa, that is a cowardly way of turning your back on what your position stands for—what Momma stood for," Willie finished. He stepped back when he realized he had gone too far by mentioning his mother.

"William Zachary!" Jed countered, feeling his face flush. "You have no idea what I have seen, or why I choose to remain impartial about this. Yes, I agree with you emphatically, and if I could change it by myself, I would do it in a second. But I can't—just like I couldn't stop the killing in Mexico, or the death of your brother or your mother. I can't change the things that happen or the way people live. I became a pastor to bring peace to others, to this family, and yes, to me—not to become a political zealot."

Willie, his shoulders slumped and head down, turned and began to walk away. He stopped midstep and looked back to his father. "And what kind of peace have you found so far? We've left our home; we've left Grandpa Fez; we've left Abel and . . ." He couldn't continue without breaking down, and he definitely did not want to do that in front of his father.

Jed could see only Willie's back as he left the house without looking back. Jed went back to the front room and sat down to consider the confrontation he had just had with his oldest son. He thought of all the words he could have taken back, and realized that much of what Willie had said was true.

The room was dark and the fireplace unlit. The mahogany mantel displayed an antique clock that chimed only every few hours, to his dismay. Looking at the broken clock, Jed thought about what Willie had said. What am I running from? Where is the peace I'm searching so hard for? How many more have to die to find that peace, and is it that important anyway?

He tried to clear his mind. He decided that he would speak to Willie on the subject again, but first he needed to take some of the lessons he had just learned and put them to paper for his first sermon, which he was giving in just two days.

* * * * *

Willie walked down Fifth Street and admired the ash trees mixed in with the willows. His mind wandered back to their home in Independence, with a backyard that ran from the house to the edge of the Kansas River. Their new home had a large kitchen area with a walk-in fireplace that he knew his mother would have loved. The front part of the house had a large parlor and an adjacent room that his father used as a study. As he walked, he noticed that the smells were different here, with wild garlic fields mixed in between the house lots.

He turned from Fifth Street onto Boone Street, walked past several more houses, and then tuned left onto Woodson Road. At the corner of Woodson Road and Elmore Street was the town's mercantile shop, its giant window etched with the words **LECOMPTON MERCANTILE**. Willie paused, looked through the windows, and thought of his Grandpa Fez, his friends in Independence, and his mother. He sat down on a bench next to the mercantile shop, and while he looked down at it, he wondered how "Abel's bench" was holding up. He was glad that they all had a say in deciding whether to change the name of the bench, now that their momma was up in heaven with their brother. *No—"Abel's bench" it is, and always will be,* they had all agreed.

Willie got up and walked another half-block to a large two-story brick house that had a huge front porch with freshly painted white railings. He walked up the steps, then looked up and down at the large front door that, in his estimation, was twice as big as necessary. He knocked, waited a few seconds, and a man dressed like he was going to church answered. He was followed closely by a young man who looked to be about ten years older than Willie.

"Hey there, Willie!" roared Louis Carpenter, excusing the family's butler and escorting Willie outside to sit on the front porch. Willie pulled up a wooden chair that smelled of fresh paint.

"I was hoping you'd come by today," added Louis. "I'm just busting with news, or as my father would say, *hearsay*, about the current affairs that you and I have been talking about ever since you moved in."

The butler came out the front door with a tray of bread, cheese, two glasses, and a carafe of light orange–reddish liquid. Willie put his nose to the carafe and backed off like he'd been bitten by a snake.

"So, I take it you've never had whisky before?" Louis asked, poking fun at his new friend while pouring himself a glass two fingers deep. Willie was so agitated that he hardly noticed.

"Yea, I need to talk to you too, Louis," Willie said. "I just got into it with my father, and the first person I thought to talk about it with was you. You understand how important and vital it is to get the news out and fight the audacity of what the slaveholders are doing, but my father . . . well, he . . . well . . . he just doesn't get it, Louis!"

Willie sat back, feeling quite comfortable sitting on the flowered cushions that rested on each chair. *We sure didn't have anything like this on our porch in Independence,* he thought.

"This is where we need to make the biggest statement ever!" Louis began. "When that pompous Douglas got the Kansas–Nebraska Act passed a few years ago, it gave the power to the people to decide for themselves which new territories would be slave and which would be free. So your father can't be neutral . . . he has to choose a side!"

Looking deep into Willie's eyes after downing his third glass of whisky, Louis challenged his new friend. "Well, what side is your father *really* on, free or slave?"

Knowing that he had Willie right where he wanted him, he continued. "We know we won't have a problem up in the Nebraska Territory, it's just too far north, but right here, right in the Kansas Territory, well—that's where the heart of the matter is, and where the line will be drawn."

Willie shot Louis a look of confusion that caused the older man to snicker in amusement. "When I say the line, I mean the line for the entire country, and when that line is drawn, the sides will begin to separate, the bloodspilling will begin, and Providence will win out! It's just perfect!"

Louis's speech began to slur from the whisky. Even so, Willie was convinced that he had only one choice, and that was to pursue the abolitionist cause, even if his father was too much of a coward to take a stand next to him.

Unbeknownst to Willie, Jed was busy in his study writing his first sermon. He was going to address the compassion and love of Christ, and the sacrifices He made for the benefit of all His children. Jed was going to tell his congregation that he had his opinion, and he was against slavery, but he also was a servant of God, and in Christ he was to love all, which meant both sides. In Jed's mind, neutrality was not cowardice, but instead a way to show Christ's love to all His children. He was adamant that as pastor of the Lecompton church, he must be open and welcoming to all in the love of Christ.

Jed supported his son in his beliefs, but worried about his readiness to fight for his cause. He reminded himself of how zealous he was at the prime age of seventeen, so he could understand Willie's passion. From a father's perspective, however, Jed worried and prayed constantly and without end that his oldest son would be kept safe and out of harm's way.

Jed was aware, as he sat at his desk with a feathered pen and paper in hand, that the tempers of most local citizens were hot and on the verge of boiling over. Rumor had it that thousands of armed Southerners, mostly from the lower portion of his previous home state of Missouri, had poured over the border to vote for the latest proslavery congressional delegate. Most settlers from outside the area who had come to Kansas from the North or South only wanted to homestead in peace. They weren't interested in the conflict over slavery, but unfortunately found themselves right in the middle of it.

As he continued to write his sermon, he felt the Christian responsibility to preach for peace and not bloodshed, compromise but not bias, but most of all, about the hope that only God could give.

He prayed that on the day that he was to give his first sermon in his new church, the congregation would fill the church to capacity. He welcomed the thought that his five children would be seated in the front row and witness his commitment to peace through dignity and faith, not violence, mayhem, and carnage. *They will hear that their father is far from being a coward.*

Chapter Twenty-Two

Willie's Stand

1856

It had been more than a year since Jed's first sermon, and the town of Lecompton had been designated as the territorial capital of the Kansas Territory. It was now considered the center of the proslavery movement. Lecompton was only fifteen miles from Lawrence, which was well known as a Free State stronghold. Support on both sides was beginning to gain ground, and steam had begun to blow, but Willie and Louis remained strong in their conviction for the freedom of the colored.

"This might sound good, Willie, but those 'Free-Soilers' are almost as bad as the proslavery folks. I'm telling you—we need to stay firm with what Garrison and the American Anti-Slavery Society believe in."

The two young men enjoyed the coolness of the living room in the Monroe house while they discussed the latest social movements of any party that could jeopardize their cause. Lizzy had just left to take Johnny Russell, now three, for a much-needed walk. He'd been a terror in the house all morning, and by the looks of the toys scattered about, was up to his usual mischief.

Daniel, now sixteen, the same age as Jed was when he left home, sat next to Willie, partly listening to the two talk while reading the latest letter from family friend John Fremont.

Micah was poking around in his father's office, looking for something he could use to widen the rift in the father–son relationship or, in Micah's opinion, the lack of one.

Louis sat across from Willie and Daniel, wishing he had a glass of whisky by his side and kicking himself for agreeing to meet at the Monroe house instead of his own. He was eleven years older than Willie, but looked twice that due to the effects of liquor on his body. He still was the only friend who could relate to Willie and his passion regarding the issue of slavery. Daniel did his best to support his older brother, but found it difficult to keep up with what the two discussed. Others in the area were more like the Free-Soilers or completely neutral, and none had the same passion for freeing the slaves that these two young men had.

"You all realize that the Free State settlers, or as some of them like to be called, Free Soil settlers, demand free territory for free *white* people." Louis preached like he usually liked to do, his lips unusually dry and his hands shaking. "Oh yea, they hate slavery all right, but not out of concern for the slaves themselves. They hate it because the plantations have taken over so much land, and have prevented white working people from having their own homesteads."

"Now you'll see what I have been saying for years!" Micah yelled from the other room. "Everyone is going to do their own thing, whether it be free land or slave land, black or white, it doesn't matter. No government should be able to tell any of us what we can or cannot do. We have our own rights, and if that means it comes to someone dying during the fight, well then, let it happen. And I, for one, will be the first to join up!"

Willie and Daniel looked at each other, and both raised their eyebrows simultaneously. They were used to Micah's independent outbursts, which recently had been coming out more frequently and passionately.

Louis tried to regain his composure after hearing Micah's outburst. He brought his attention back to Willie, looked around the room in obvious distaste to his surroundings, and with a condescending tone asked, "Don't you all have any kind of, you know, spirits in this, uh, this cabin?"

Willie and Daniel shared a glance, scanned the interior of the house with comic intensity, and then acknowledged with raised eyebrows that it was indeed not a cabin, before breaking into raucous laughter. From the next room, Micah yelled, "Hey there, Mr. Fancy, you want to get some liquor, you might as well go on back to your plantation and have your *own* slave get some for you."

Willie looked at Louis in expectation of a rebuttal, but Micah was too quick, continuing before Louis could open his mouth. "Tell me, Mr. Abolitionist, what's the difference between the bondage of your so-called *butler* and the bondage of a black field hand? And don't say money—I've seen how he lives, so I know the money isn't all that good."

Willie looked apologetically toward his friend, but at the same time tried to suppress laughter. "If it's all the same to you, Louis," Willie said as he nodded Micah's way, "why don't we go back to your house, and you can show me that letter you received from the Anti-Slavery Society."

Louis looked insulted, but readily agreed. As he and Willie began to collect their belongings, Daniel asked, "Mind if I tag along? I think I'd like what you two are up to instead of—you know—" The three looked in the direction of the office, where Micah could be heard sifting through his father's belongings as he continued to look for something to cause a ruckus later on.

Back at Louis's house, Willie and Daniel sat down and watched as Louis poured himself a drink with shaky hands. "I'm not a prophet or anything, but if I were to guess correctly, I would say that your brother back there will be trouble to someone someday."

Louis's butler came into the room and asked if they needed anything before he started working on the night's supper. Louis put a hand on one of the butler's shoulders and asked him to fill his whisky decanter and leave it on the table with a few glasses.

Willie and Daniel noticed the kindness in Louis's tone and were impressed to see such tenderness displayed toward a Negro. The exhibit left a lasting note in Willie's mind that reinforced why he was so passionate about following through with his abolitionist ambitions.

It was the first time Daniel had seen a butler, and if he hadn't known better, he might have thought he was just another slave. The butler was in his early fifties with balding gray hair. His eyes were large, just like his belly, and he walked with a limp that made going up the stairs look awfully painful to Daniel. His uniform was immaculate, with black pants, black polished shoes, a well-starched white shirt, a black vest, and a floppy black tie. His jacket was tailored nicely to fit his portly waist, and he carried a white towel draped over his left forearm.

After the butler had delivered the requested carafe of whisky, he turned to Willie and Daniel and asked them if he could be of service to them as well. Daniel, enjoying this experience and looking at Louis's glass, was about to answer when Willie abruptly interrupted. "We'll both have a glass of lemonade, thank you."

Daniel had always wanted nothing more than to be just like his older brother, so he was in his prime sitting with Willie and Louis and discussing the rights of slaves.

"Willie," Louis interrupted apologetically, "we need to start making our plans for the rally coming up in Lawrence. You know, it's the biggest get-together the Anti-Slavery folks are putting together this year. I'm just itching to put something together that's good enough to make it center stage. If we can do that, then maybe, and that's a big maybe, we could get asked to speak about it in person."

He took a sly look at Daniel, crooked his neck, and tilted his head back to Willie. "You are planning on going with me, right?"

Willie put his glass down on the well-polished dining room table, then looked over the shoulders of his brother to make sure that Louis's butler had left the room. Seeing that it was only the three of them in the room, he pulled his chair closer to the table and gestured to Louis to pass him his paper and pen.

"You talk and I'll write. Let's give 'em something that will make their heads spin."

Daniel looked on; the corner of his mouth curved upward as he slowly nodded his head in silence. He poured himself another glass of lemonade and sat down next to Willie, opposite Louis. He couldn't have been more proud of his older brother.

Thinking out loud while writing the rally plan, Willie said, "You know, Louis, we could even suggest a plan to start our own Underground Railroad right here in Lecompton. I heard the ones up North are doing a real good job of passing along the runaways."

Willie looked for a reaction from his more experienced friend. "Actually, my father told me that it's not Lecompton but Lawrence that's a stopping point for the Underground Railroad," Louis replied. "But you're absolutely right, Willie, it would be great to see if we could help them out while we're in Lawrence for the rally. My father can make all the connections for us."

Louis's father was Jonas Carpenter, a well-known judge in the Kansas and Nebraska Territories, who from his lavish living conditions appeared to have quite a successful career. He had high aspirations for his son, securing top-rated law tutors to prepare him to take the bar in a year or two. His goal for his son was that he become a judge before his thirtieth birthday and carry on the campaign against the practice of slavery. Jonas Carpenter and Wilbur Moonbody were leaders in Lecompton, and influential in political and business arenas. Both men had conducted several meetings at the church to discuss what impact the new pastor could have on their cause.

Willie said few words to Daniel on their walk back home. He was visualizing the rally and what impact he and Louis could make. *If we can just get our message to center stage.*

When they arrived home, Willie went straight to his room while Daniel, still beaming with excitement, plopped down on his favorite oversized chair in the living room. He put his head back and stared up at the ceiling beams, unable to contain his excitement.

Jed, seated in his chair and reading the day's news, noticed the look on his son's face. "Boy, it sure looks like you've had a good day, Daniel. What big adventure did you have to cause that glow I'm seeing all over your face?"

"It was great, Papa!" Daniel said excitingly. "Willie, Louis, and I have been talking about it all day, and it's going to be perfect when I see what Willie puts together for the event down in Lawrence in a couple of—"

Daniel stopped midsentence when he noticed the shocked look in his father's eyes. "What big event in Lawrence, Daniel?"

"Well, I'm not really supposed to say anything, but I guess there's going to be this big rally to bring everyone's attention to the slavery issue." Daniel couldn't restrain himself from telling Jed all about it.

Jed froze and listened intently while Daniel continued. "There's also supposed to be this really important man coming to speak at the rally . . . uh . . . um . . . I think I heard them say his name was John Brown or something like that—not quite sure, but it sure had Willie and Louis all fired up."

At supper that night, with the scent of pot roast lingering in the air and the fireplace still blazing from the preparation of their meal, Jed sat in his usual spot at the end of the table. He looked at Lizzy, amazed that such a young girl could have all the right instincts to take over the role that once was Abigail's. She had assumed the tasks of cooking, cleaning, and taking care of little Johnny Russell, and Jed knew how proud Abigail would have been to see her so responsible—and grown up.

His three older boys, seated two on Jed's left and one on his right, were a different story altogether. The two oldest wanted to save the enslaved, and Micah wanted to keep them enslaved and as far away from him as possible. Such a division, and at such a young age, and yet Jed looked at the boys and could see how his family probably wasn't much different from most. Each family undoubtedly had its divisions to be borne, and unfortunately to Jed's mind, it wasn't going to be getting any better in his case. He hoped and prayed that his family would be spared the potentially tragic consequences that might occur in the not-so-distant future.

"So, tell me, Mr. Monroe," Jed said as he looked right at his oldest son, "what is all this talk about getting involved in the rally for the antislavery cause?"

Willie shot a look of anger at Daniel for his brother's perceived disloyalty, then paused as he tried in vain to come up with a response to his father. "Papa, you know my feelings about this cause." He paused to gauge his father's disposition. "I've heard so much from William Floyd Garrison and have read Stowe's book so many times that I've practically memorized it. The practice of slavery is uncivilized and un-Christian, and it must be abolished. If that means that I go to hundreds of rallies, make a thousand speeches, or if I could, write my own articles, I will do it. Papa, it's our duty as Christians, as fellow human beings, to rise up against the audacity of that practice!"

Lizzy, feeling uncomfortable, excused herself to attend to the needs of her little brother, who was getting fussy. She gave her father a feeble assurance that she'd return later to clean up, although Jed barely acknowledged her, his attention centered on his eldest son. Daniel sat glued to the encounter in front of him, while Micah shuffled his feet and gazed around the room as he searched for some excuse to leave.

"Why Lawrence, William Monroe?" Jed asked, trying to stay calm but using Willie's proper name. "I do realize it's the headquarters of the Free-State Party, but of late, it's also been the center of a lot of bloodshed, Son, and I forbid you from going."

"Papa, I'm eighteen years old and soon to be nineteen," Willie said as he stood to meet his father's glare. "Your father and mother allowed *you* to move thousands of miles away from home when you were *sixteen*. You took up the reins of a wagon train and blazed the Oregon Trail at twenty-one. All of which you felt a need to do, and your father and mother had enough trust in you and faith in our Almighty to let you go, right?"

Remaining true to his principles and feeling confident in what he was defending, Willie continued. "Sure, not everything turned out like you wanted it to, but don't use that as a reason to block me from sowing my oats and expressing my own beliefs!"

The two now sat alone as the other boys excused themselves, with Daniel sitting close by in the next room but still within earshot, and Micah leaving out the front door, having no interest in any topic that had to do with freeing the Negroes.

"Son, I . . . I . . .," Jed said, trying desperately to find the words to show support for his son's beliefs while shielding him from any harm that could come his way. "Willie, I admire and respect your feelings and your passion. Son, I do agree with your cause, but I cannot sit back and allow you to walk right into a situation that could very easily turn bad on you. I just don't know what I would do if . . ." He couldn't muster any further words.

Willie understood his father's reluctance. "Papa, nothing is going to happen to me—I promise. You have to understand that I need to do this, just like you needed to find what was at the end of that trail or at the end of that river. You found it, and I need to find what purpose I have out there, too."

Willie could see the kindness in his father's eyes as he continued. "Papa, you've taught all of us real well. We know to rely on our faith and to trust in God to keep us safe. You see, that's why I know I'll be just fine. I need you to trust me and trust in my beliefs. Your blessings would mean the world to me, Papa, but even without them, I am still going to Lawrence."

Jed's head was tilted down as he stared at the table. He was thinking of his Abigail and what she would have done. He knew his son as he knew himself when he was his age.

After a moment's pause, he said, "Son, I'm not going to stop you, but I do need to ask you not to get Daniel involved. He admires you so, and I wouldn't put it past him to want to join you. I just couldn't bear to see both of you go into that fire together."

Willie's thrilled expression reminded Jed of what his own expression must have been when he jolted out from under the front porch after he heard his father ask Reverend Spaulding and Paster Higgin if they would take him west. A mixed sense of pride for his son, along with silent terror, filled Jed's heart as the two embraced.

Daniel, quietly sitting on a stool around the corner, heard the entire conversation and did not plan to be left out of the coming historic moment. He would be at that rally standing proud and strong beside his big brother. He just had to figure out how.

* * * * *

The middle of May was usually a welcome time of year in Lecompton, with most of the winter snow and chill long gone for the season. This day was icy cold with a chill wind that slithered into and down the back of Willie's jacket.

He and Louis had just finished hitching the horses to the wagon and were ready to head out. Willie instinctively grabbed the reins, and was about to give the horses a whistle, when Lizzy suddenly bolted out the front door. "Willie, hold on! Willie!" Lizzy had scooped up Johnny Russell on the way out and stood defiantly beside the horses.

"Dear God, Lizzy, you startled us half to death with that yelling. My word, girl, I thought something had happened to Johnny Russell or worse. You do have a set of healthy lungs on you, that's for sure. I wouldn't want to be Johnny Russell when you get mad."

"Oh, knock it off," Lizzy said as she interrupted his teasing. "Willie, I just . . . well . . . you know, I just wanted to tell you to have a good time, and bring me back something nice, something really nice, all right?"

"Uh, all right Lizzy," Willie answered his sister, a peculiar look on his face as he wondered what kind of shenanigans she was up to. "We'd best be going now, if it's all the same to you. You tell Papa that we we're really sorry we missed him, but we need to get these books to the rally before the crowds get there."

With a final wave, Lizzy shifted Johnny Russell back on her hip, went up the front steps, and eased back into the house, taking one last look at the back end of the wagon where Daniel had quietly snuck in during the ruckus she had caused. By the time they realized he was in there, it would be too late, and the only person Daniel would have to square with would be his father when the three of them returned later that night.

Their short journey was quiet, and the wind was to their backs, which made it much more pleasant for their faces. The road was fairly empty—a few horses and buggies were coming back and going forth, but nothing was out of the ordinary. Just outside of the Lawrence city limits, they spotted a camp with a half-dozen horses tied off to the bushes. The large group had a fire blazing to keep them warm, and there were empty bottles of whisky tossed around.

"Mighty early to be hitting the ol' bottle, but I guess some will do anything to take the bite out of the chill in the air," Louis observed.

Two men came away from the fire and attempted to halt the wagon with their arms in the air. "Hey there, friends!" A large burly man approached the wagon. His speech was slurred, and he carried a half-empty bottle of whisky. He was joined by a scrawny man who looked as though he hadn't eaten in weeks. "Where you all going this time of morning?" the burly man asked.

Willie paused for a minute. He blinked his eyes as he tried to focus on the man. "Mr. Braxton? . . . Is that you, Mr. Braxton?"

The man spat out a wad of chew that had been tucked in his cheek before replying. "Do I know you, boy?"

"Well, I don't know if you know me, but I'm sure you know my father and my . . . my mother. I'm William Monroe, and my father and mother are . . . uh, were . . . uh, are Jed and Abigail Monroe. We lived in Independence for years, but recently moved back yonder to Lecompton."

A look of scorn immediately filled Braxton's face as he turned to his companion. "Now look what we got here, Jeb, we have right here in front of us the son of the great pioneer and war hero Jedidiah Monroe. I was hoping I'd run into your father again after he had me run out of town."

The two young men sat motionless, looking at Braxton and not knowing what to expect next. "Yea, that's right," Braxton continued. "It happened right after he returned from the war fighting them Mexes, who, if you ask me, are one step lower than any of them blackies we are here rallying against. I guess if I can't get even with the senior Monroe, I'll just have to settle with one of his kids, ain't that right, Jeb?" He slapped his partner on the back, nearly knocking the man off his feet.

"Mr. Braxton, I'm sorry for whatever caused you to leave town, but my friend and I are just going to Lawrence peacefully to deliver some books for the rally, and we aren't looking for any trouble. So, if you'd just be so kind as to step aside so we can pass, we'd be most obliged," Willie requested calmly. At the same time, he yanked the reins hard to the right, causing the horses to jerk into a full gallop.

The back end of the wagon knocked Braxton and his sidekick Jeb onto the hard-packed dirt road, allowing Willie and Louis to make it several hundred yards down the road before the two men were back on their feet. Willie shuddered as he heard them yelling in the distance.

Holding tightly to the reins, Willie guided the horses swiftly down the road. Daniel, holding on tightly under the canvas of the wagon, was jostled about with each movement of the wagon. He was busy trying to stay concealed, but the incident he just overheard sent shivers down his spine. Willie and Louis were speechless, deep in thought over what had just happened, as they made it to their final destination. Willie didn't fully understand the immense hatred that man Braxton held for his family, but was glad he wasn't around him anymore to find out.

Chapter Twenty-Three

A Cause at What Cost?

1856

A bald man with a walking cane approached Willie and Louis as they hitched the wagon next to the center stage. He introduced himself as Justin Stone. He was the husband of the keynote speaker, Lucy Stone, who was going to be on center stage in just a few hours to rally the audience behind the abolitionist cause.

Willie and Louis, their nerves tempered a bit since running into Braxton, proceeded to the back of the wagon to unload the books and pamphlets donated by Wilbur Moonbody in Lecompton. Stone thanked Louis and Willie for the much-needed material, which he planned to distribute in advance of his wife's speech.

Louis lifted up the flap of the wagon, and he and Stone were startled when a man's face looked right back at them. Daniel was sitting in the back of the wagon with a mischievous smile, which grew even larger when he saw Willie come around the corner of the wagon.

"What in tarnation are you doing here, Daniel!?" Willie yelled, in disbelief that Daniel would do something like this. His mind raced as he frantically tried to figure how he would ever explain this to his father, and he shivered as cold ice flooded his veins.

Back at home, Lizzy was trying her best to get out of her own uncomfortable predicament. "He did what? And you did what? And you weren't going to tell me because of what?" Jed yelled, completely beside himself upon hearing the plan that Daniel had sweet-talked Lizzy into.

"Do you realize what kind of danger those two have just gotten themselves into, young lady?" Jed yelled again.

As he tried to figure out what to do, he looked around the room as if anticipating someone else, or another surprise, coming his way. "Don't tell me, Daughter; please don't tell me that Micah went, too?"

"Nah, you're not gonna find me a stone's throw from that thing," Micah's surly voice came from the other room. "I heard they were going to do somepun' stupid, so I stayed as far away as I could. Besides, I'm the last person they would want around. Nope, freeing slaves, well, that's just not something up my tree, so you won't have to worry none about me, Papa. At least not this time, anyways."

Jed, trying his best to ignore the sarcasm coming from Micah, asked Lizzy for more information about the whereabouts of Willie, Daniel, and Louis. Jed quickly packed up his gear and saddled his mare. He knew that he had to leave quickly for any hope of finding his two sons safely. Darkness was settling on the land, and the new moon would give him zero visibility; realizing this made his already anxious heart beat even faster.

* * * * *

As Jed approached the town, he could hear the horns and drums far sooner than he could actually see the festivities. As he got closer, he could see a large stage at the town's center, with what looked like several thousand people gathered around. An old man yelled through a long megaphone as he attempted to quiet down the crowd, but the noise seemed to just get louder. Jed could hear yelling and chanting for the freeing of the slaves. At the same time, he could hear chanting from the proslavery side. Jed remembered what Wilbur Moonbody had told him a few months before and could see why he felt as he did. It seemed everyone was taking sides, and it was frightening to think that the entire country was doing the exact same thing as the few thousand right in front of him.

No, he thought as he fumbled with the reins of his horse in his attempt to tie it to the hitching post, *I still don't have to pick a side. My side is with the Lord.* Jed reminded himself that he had already made it through many trials, especially Abel's and Abigail's deaths, so he quickly prayed that this too would pass: *Lord, please help me.*

Jed's mind raced as he began searching through the mass of people. He was beside himself with the recurring thought that each time he pursued some kind of peace, something happened to throw him backward. He focused his eyes as he scanned the crowd. He jumped up on a wooden crate with a cross symbol painted on its sides. He could tell by the commotion that the crowd was getting fairly riled up.

Something or someone was doing their best to create mass confusion in order to stop the rally, but Jed couldn't quite figure out who or why.

He jumped up onto the edge of the stage and held on to the reins with one hand, frantically surveying the crowd as he looked from one face to the next. His chest tightened with fear and a sick feeling filled his stomach, as his sons were nowhere to be found.

Jed's heart skipped a beat when he spotted his oldest son on the far side of the stage. He yelled as loud as he could, but the crowd noise was overwhelming. He whistled, and the high pitch caught Willie's attention as he turned his head and spotted his father.

"Papa?" His mouth formed the word but it couldn't be heard. He looked surprised and gave his father a questioning look. Willie looked to his left to someone Jed could not see, and then nodded back toward where Jed stood. *Must be Daniel,* Jed hoped as he jumped down from the stage to run to the other side. *Got to get to them.*

Jed ran past a mob of men carrying torches and chanting an unfamiliar song. His anxious and wary feelings about what could have happened began to fade, and he was filled with joy at finally finding his sons.

As he swung himself around the last corner of the stage, the sound of gunfire stopped him in his tracks. Along with the screams, it turned him around like a spinning top. Jed panicked, as he could tell that the shot had come from near where Willie had been standing just a few seconds earlier. He shoved himself through the madding crowd in terror and fright.

"Willie! . . . Daniel!" Jed screamed, his head spinning. He pushed himself to the edge of the stage. Terrified spectators were quickly clearing the platform.

Maneuvering to the back of the stage, Jed was pushed abruptly into a burly man. Jed looked up at the man, his eyes mad with anger, his face dripping with sweat, a menacing grin forming from his all-too-familiar yellow-stained teeth. Jed's eyes quickly moved down from the man's face to see the smoking gun he was holding in his shaking hand.

"Braxton?" Jed said in disbelief.

"It should have been you, Monroe!" Braxton spat out, then ran down a back alley and out of sight.

With Braxton out of sight, Jed returned his attention to finding his boys. The noise of the crowd was completely muffled in Jed's mind as his focus turned to the scene in front of him. Louis Carpenter lay motionless on the ground, blood pooling beneath his body. Jed knelt down and reached out a hand to the young man. He touched Louis's still fingers, and when he tried to look into the man's eyes, lifeless orbs stared back at him blindly.

Jed leaned over in the pale light from the torches and closed the innocent eyes of his son's good friend, silently promising to Louis that he would be kind to his family when telling them of their loss. A sense of relief swept through him, a guilty relief that he wasn't closing the eyes of his own son.

The crowd had pushed away from the scene. Jed, still kneeling, looked around. His whole body was numb from what just happened. He still heard nothing as he searched the area, and he began to become uneasy again. The stage was now empty. The grounds around him were littered with useless rally cry prompts and speaker notes.

He once again spotted the wooden crate with the symbol of a cross on its sides, three men huddled next to it. He bowed his head; tears filled his eyes as he silently thanked God for sparing his boys. He lifted his head and found Willie. An elderly man in a black jacket and black shirt with a white collar, wearing a cappello romano, held on to Willie tightly. Jed could see the terror in his son's face, and it made his heart melt.

Jed stood slowly and walked over to his son. Their eyes never separated, both filled with tears. Jed thanked the priest, and reached out to take Willie into his arms.

"Papa," was all he said, but it was the most beautiful sound that Jed could have heard. He held Willie tight to his chest, and his father's love caused Willie to break down.

Jed lifted another arm and welcomed his other son into his embrace. Daniel had watched the whole ordeal. He was the last one to see Braxton before he disappeared down the alley. Braxton had stopped briefly to stare down Daniel to ensure that the young man had no intention of following him. Daniel was still shaking from the incident and the loss that he knew filled his brother with grief.

"Let's go home, boys," Jed said quietly as he glanced upward to the heavens and thanked God for protecting his boys.

* * * * *

Jed held tightly to the reins of the wagon, silently pleading with the horses to take them all home safely. His and Louis's horses, tethered to the back of their wagon, obediently followed behind. Louis's father never made the trip to the rally as he had planned, and it was a blessing that he had not been there to witness the horrific scene.

It should have been you, Monroe! The words and Braxton's twisted face revealed a warped mind that somehow blamed Jed for all the misgivings bestowed upon him over the past several years. The words stuck in Jed's mind like glue, and the bitter promise of vengeance on Braxton's face was committed to Jed's memory.

"It should have been you, Monroe!" But why? What happened prior returning from Mexico in 1849? What do I represent to mark me as a threat to the likes of the Braxtons of the world? And if it should have been me, then why target my boys—why not come right for me? Jed's mind raced faster as he drove the wagon farther from the center of town. *Will I always be looking over my shoulder, worrying whether my powder is dry and my gun is clean?* The thought made him shiver.

"You think we'll see him again, Papa?" asked Daniel.

Jed looked at his son and his heart ached. Daniel was still shaking, his face pale and eyes frozen wide open with fear. His voice had the high pitch it assumed every time he was upset. Jed knew well the signs of fear coming from his son. Jed began to answer, but Daniel cut him off: "His eyes looked right into my soul, Papa! Right into my soul!"

The three sat on the buckboard together; tight as it was, they felt a need to sit together. "There's a good lesson here, boys," Jed began, still holding firm to the reins, "no matter where you go, what you do, or who you meet along the way, there will always be 'Braxtons' in this world. You need to trust that you'll always have God as your protector. That's much more powerful than anything you will ever face, and He will always be there for you. You both need to believe that."

Willie had been quiet since leaving Lawrence. He sat motionless, listening to his father and thinking. Jed saw that he was staring far ahead at nothing in particular—his eyebrows tightened in concern for his oldest's recovery. Willie had just been through a horrible ordeal, and his silence was worrisome.

Jed turned to speak, but suddenly Willie blurted out, "We need to continue, Papa!" Jed tilted his head quizzically in response.

"We need to continue with the cause. The cause that Louis gave his life for!"

Jed, knowing that his oldest son was hurting and filled with guilt, tried to reason with him. "No cause is worth dying for, Son. The true purpose is to continue living so you can touch as many lives as possible and change wrongs into rights when you can. I believe you and Louis had the right motives, but it's wrong to say you would die for them. Your cause, or whatever you call it, needs you to support it, but not die for it."

"Does that include without slavery, Papa?" Willie asked angrily. "Because the last I heard you say, you were going to stay neutral and not take sides. What kind of cause is that? You might not think of yourself as a coward because you fought in a war years ago, but I say that not taking a stand, one way or the other, constitutes cowardice regardless of one's position in life. Besides, Papa, when you fought in the war, you risked your life for a cause you believed in."

Still driving the wagon, but at a slower pace now, with torches lit on both sides of the buckboard, Jed thought hard about how to respond to his son.

They were about halfway home when Daniel broke the silence. "Papa, do you think we will actually go to war over this slavery issue? I'm always hearing people talk about it, and even hear about opposing views within families. Does that mean that family members would fight against each other over it?"

"Come on, Daniel!" Willie yelled out at his brother. "Look right under your own roof for that answer. You and I believe in freedom for the blacks, but our own brother would just as soon see them rot away with chains on. Does that mean we would fight against each other over it? I don't know, but I can see how some homes could end up splitting into sides."

"Well, for your mother's and my sakes, I sure hope and pray that never happens with us," Jed pleaded with his sons. "I promised your momma that I would do whatever I could to raise you to love each other and grow up having fond memories of each other. To tell you both the truth, that was your momma's last request. She wanted her family to find the peace and love that she could only hope for. You boys need to think about that, and her wish for you to know God.

Jed stopped the wagon for a time to rest awhile, the flames of the torches illuminating the trees and bushes on both sides of the road. The night-blooming jasmine gave the area a sweet smell as a chorus of crickets and bullfrogs exchanged rhythms.

After several moments of silence, Jed felt a sense of closeness to his sons as he turned to face them. "Listen to the sounds of nature out there, boys. Now that's the sound of peace, that feeling that when you close your eyes, you can feel the presence of the Almighty all around you. The spiritual peace will need to come from inside you, you know, and that's up to you and your God. The key is that you need to want it. Then, as God has promised, He will give to you abundantly."

"Papa, you really are starting to sound like a preacher, you know?" Willie joked, finally breaking from his emotional turmoil.

"Just think, Willie, we're sitting on the same buckboard as one of God's chosen ones, huh?" Daniel chimed in, and all three burst into much-needed laughter.

"Okay, *men*, and I say that with some reservation after the last couple of wisecracks aimed at me," Jed said, "let's get this wagon home and call it a day. Don't know about you two, but I'm mighty hungry, and I can just imagine how worried Lizzy's getting."

Before Jed could gather the reins, a loud crack of gunfire pierced the night air. The horses, shocked and frightened by the loud noise, bolted down the road. The sudden jolt caused Willie to fly off the buckboard and into the bed of the wagon as it began to slide and bounce out of control.

"Grab the reins!" Jed yelled. "Get the horses to stop, for God's sake!"

This can't be happening again, Jed thought, *not to us, not to this family, not again*! His thoughts suffocated him and logic momentarily escaped him.

"Get down!" Jed cautioned. He finally managed to get the horses under control. He scrambled to the back of the wagon and found the gut-wrenching sight of a lifeless body. Tears streamed down his face—he tried desperately to stop the bleeding.

"No . . . no!" he cried out in vain.

His mind raced. Thoughts of Abigail, thoughts of all the talks they had had. The many talks he had had with his children about asking God into their lives. Yes, the God that loved us so. This he had to forcefully remind himself as he looked down at his son. He thought, he hoped, he prayed that his son did just as he was taught. *But did he ask?*

Worry and fear filled his mind. *Oh God, why? . . . why? . . . what more can I give? How much more will you take?* He picked up the bloody body and held Willie tightly to his chest. His arms wrapped around his dead son, shot through the heart by a vengeful man aiming to hurt the father, but instead killing the son.

Jed's body was limp, his chest tight, his heart empty and lonely.

At that moment, as Willie lay in his arms, Jed's oldest child was not a man. He was once again that little toddler, barely walking, talking as best he could, and his first words were "Papa, Papa, Papa."

Jed looked at his son lying so peacefully in his arms, and for a moment his heart beat in unison with the faint thread that was his son's. Then one was gone.

He was sure that his son had asked God into his life and was walking into the open arms of his momma, then through the pearly gates with Jesus by their side.

Jed could see Abigail's reassuring look, letting him know that she would take good care of their son . . . William Zachary Monroe . . . dead at eighteen, and resting peacefully in the loving arms of Jesus.

Chapter Twenty-Four

Torment Too Hot

1857

"No, I don't understand, Jed, and as many times as you've explained it, I just don't understand why so far away," Fez pleaded. "Trust me, I shared your pain when we lost Abigail, and understood why you felt you needed to move your family, but Lecompton was still a stone's throw compared with this!"

Jed, confused but committed, said, "With what happened to Willie, Fez, I don't think I could ever get my family far enough away to ease my worry."

"Jed, I know it's been a tough year," Fez said more calmly. "Heck, it's touching on several years if we include Abel and Abigail, but take a minute and ask yourself, what would *she* be saying to you right now?"

Looking down at the tombstone of his oldest boy, Jed was speechless and immersed in futile deliberation over what he would do next. Willie had been laid to rest next to Abigail and Abel close to a year before, the service given by Pastor Higgin on a gloomy and rainy day. It had been a long while since Jed had stood by the resting spots of his wife and sons. Seeing the third tombstone again nearly broke his resolve.

He had to admit—he hardly remembered the service Pastor Higgin had given that day. Jed had still been in shock, plus there were so many questions from the local sheriff that his attention was diverted from the pastor and given only to his concern for the welfare of his family.

Just days after the shootings of Willie and Louis, the Kansas territorial officers brought in the Pinkerton Agency. Jed was told by lead detective Aaron Dobson that the two incidents were definitely connected. Wearing a spotless striped three-piece suit and round derby hat, the detective was a small man, barely taller than Lizzy. His thin wire-rimmed glasses had thick lenses that gave him huge froggy eyes. He spoke with a high pitch and had a strong lisp. As hard as it was to focus on Detective Dobson, Jed knew he must if he expected to procure any additional information about Braxton and the murder of his boy.

Jed learned that key suspect Jonathan Braxton had become an outspoken leader for the proslavery movement and had organized a mob to put an end to the lead speakers at the rally. The actual targets had been Lucy Stone and John Brown, but Louis Carpenter had unfortunately walked into the path of the bullet. Stone and Brown had emerged unharmed.

Jed inquired as to why Dobson believed the incident at the rally was connected to Willie's death, and what the detective conveyed caused Jed great alarm and concern for his entire family.

Based on a confession from one of Braxton's accomplices, during the chaos after the missed shot, Braxton had run into Jed, his gun still smoking, and threatening words were shouted at Jed about some kind of vengeance from years past. Apparently, Braxton and two accomplices followed Jed's wagon as it headed for Lecompton. Just outside the Lawrence town limits, Braxton and the others passed the wagon in the darkness of the woods before stopping to set up an ambush point. Jed's wagon had stopped for a moment, which gave Braxton time to pull out his rifle and take aim at his new target. When the shot was made and he realized that he hadn't killed Jed but his son instead, Braxton quickly fled. He departed suddenly, leaving his accomplices in the lurch when the posse showed up moments later. Braxton was still at large, and when Jed discovered this, he was consumed by fear, forcing him into the decision to move his family.

"You've taken real good care of Abel and Abigail, Fez," Jed said as he finally looked up and took a seat on "Abel's bench." He gestured to Fez to join him for a much-needed "father–son" talk.

They sat together on the wooden bench, which Fez had recently given a fresh coat of paint. The last of the snow had melted away, leaving puddles of water scattered about that reflected bright blue sky between each ripple. The two men were the only ones in the cemetery, which seemed odd for a Saturday. Jed noticed, glancing around the cemetery, that the number of tombstones had doubled in the three years since he'd left Independence.

"I'm so confused right now, Fez," Jed began, trying to funnel a year of thoughts into one intellectual conversation. "I've prayed until I'm blue in the face, and I've written down ideas and the pros and cons of every move I've contemplated. And believe me, Fez, there've been quite a few since Willie died."

"Just take your time, Son" Fez said, feeling the pain entrenched in the heart of his son-in-law. The weather was mild, but both men still needed the wool jackets they wore to keep the chill wind off. The sights of the cemetery were familiar to Jed. The tree that was just a few feet high on his last visit was now twice as high and beginning to bloom. He had always enjoyed the spot Abigail had picked for Abel, now home for two others including herself. It was peaceful and far from the other plots, giving them the tranquility they treasured when they came to give their respects.

"All I've ever wanted is to have the peace of mind of knowing my family is safe. I thought I had it here, but I destroyed that concept when I rushed off to be a hero in a war I should never have gotten myself into," Jed said. "Not being here for Abigail when she lost Abel is something I will never forgive myself for. Then, when Abigail and I started to rebuild our lives, we . . . I . . . I mean . . . I lost Abigail."

Jed leaned forward, head in hands. After a pause, his head came back up—he was gritting his teeth, his eyes outlined in red, and Fez thought he saw a thin line of blood on one of Jed's lips as they parted and he continued. "I'm telling you, Fez, I was through with living at that time. I told myself to give up and find the only place I wanted to be and that was with her, even if I had to kill myself to do it."

Fez sat in silence, giving Jed the time he needed. "But you know, Fez, I took one look at my family, and I realized then that Abigail is truly still alive in each our children. I feel her presence each day. So my life began again, and revolved around making Abigail happy by raising our children the way she would have wanted and always remembering her wishes for them."

Jed paused for a minute, took his handkerchief out, wiped his nose, and took a long breath before continuing. "Fez, that night . . . that night with Willie, that gun blast in the darkness . . . oh God, Fez . . . that horrible night!"

Jed brushed his cheeks with a hand and looked skyward. "It was so dark, Fez, and I was holding on to one of my sons, and only when I heard Daniel's voice did I know that . . . that the one . . . I . . . I was holding was . . . my boy Willie."

Fez put his arm around Jed, allowing him to relieve himself of the pent-up emotions that had built up inside him over the past year. His sobbing tears flowed freely as he and Fez sat together as son and father, looking down at the three headstones, each one engraved by Fez's caring hands.

Jed now had four children to care for. He silently wished his father-in-law would tell him what to do, where to go, and how to raise those four, but knew that the answer had to come from him alone.

He bowed his head and silently prayed to God for His love, His guidance, His protection, and most of all His peace.

With one parting gesture, Jed kissed the tops of each tombstone. He and Fez left the cemetery and walked slowly down the street to the mercantile shop to find his family.

Halfway to the Mercantile, Fez put his hand on Jed's arm, and the men came to a stop. "I'm still not sure I understand—why are you choosing a place so far away, Jed? I understand why you feel you need to move, and I'm all for that, but what makes you feel that you have to go a thousand miles away?"

"Listen," Jed said. "Let's check on the children, and if they're alright, we can sit outside on the boardwalk and talk some more. Because to tell you the truth, Fez, I'm not completely convinced I'm doing the right thing either. I just know it's what my heart is telling me, and I have to trust that it's God answering the many prayers I've sent His way lately."

The two walked into the mercantile shop to see the children before heading back to the boardwalk. Daniel was busy helping his grandfather's newest assistant to restock the dry goods. Lizzy had her hands full with Johnny Russell, now a happy and lively four-year-old.

Fez told Jed how much Lizzy reminded him of Abigail, and reassured him that he wouldn't have to worry about Lizzy and Johnny Russell as long as they had each other.

Micah, on the other hand, was nowhere to be found. Daniel told his father that Micah had said he was going down to the waterfront to see the incoming riverboat and throw stones into the river in hope of hitting a few ducks. Upon hearing this, Fez reiterated his ongoing concerns about Micah and what might come of him as he grew older. Jed could only nod sadly in agreement.

Jed and Fez sat down on their wooden bench, still familiar to Jed even though he'd been gone from Independence for four years. "You know, Fez, I'm so tired of the fighting, the arguing, the . . . the killing." Jed repositioned himself on the bench to regain his composure before continuing. "I thought I left this place to go to a quiet town and start my own church. It turned out that Lecompton and the surrounding towns are anything but peaceful."

Jed turned and faced Fez. "You know why I left Independence, right, Fez? I couldn't stay here and see my Abigail everywhere I turned. I thought Lecompton was the answer, but I was wrong . . . so very wrong."

"That whole area of Kansas and Nebraska became a war zone between proslavery and antislavery activists, and the heart of the controversy is right between Lawrence and Lecompton. Once they started debating the Lecompton Constitution, that's when it all started—mass killings, beatings, threats. They call it 'Bleeding Kansas,' and it's brought out the radicals from both sides. Most in the country are saying it's just the beginning to much more violence and bloodshed, and I can see how true that will be if someone doesn't stop it."

Jed looked back into the Mercantile and saw little Johnny Russell playing with his big sister. He paused before continuing with sadness in his voice. "I just wish I had reacted sooner to move us far away from that mess. If I had, I would still have . . . my boy . . . it's my fault that he's . . ."

"Now you stop that right now, you hear?" Fez put his hand up midsentence. "You had no idea that the Lawrence rally would be so violent, and you surely didn't know how insane and vengeful Braxton had become. It was not your fault, Jed! You have to get that through your head. It was *not your fault*!"

Jed noticed a white bird as it swooped down to pick up a small twig from the ground before soaring back up to place it into a chick-filled nest. The sight made him think back to a passage in the Bible. The thought brought a small smile to his face as he turned to Fez.

"I know God will care for us, Fez. He told me not to worry about what we will eat or drink, or what we'll wear. I felt the Holy Spirit tell me that He will always be with us." Fez looked on, trying to understand where all this was going.

"Fez, did you see that little bird come down and grab that twig for her nest? Well, if God looks after the birds of the air, how much more is He going to look after us?" Jed chuckled at the puzzled look on Fez's face. "Don't worry, we're gonna be just fine."

Continuing, Jed said, "Hey, not to change the subject, but did you know that our good friend John Fremont was heavily involved with the Lecompton Constitution? Yea, he was so much against this slavery issue, and especially the state constitution, that he formed himself a new political party. They called it the 'Republican' party. He joined up with a Northern democrat named Stephen Douglas to try to kill the constitution. They actually became really good friends, although they were on opposite sides of the political aisle, Douglas being a Democrat and all. I really think that in the end, that constitution will fail to pass either way. When the dust settles around here, Kansas will come into the Union as a Free State."

"Boy, that's going to make people like Braxton really mad, and out for even more bloodshed than even *we* can imagine," Fez remarked.

"That's exactly it, Fez! That's why I have to do what I'm doing!" Jed exclaimed as he jumped to his feet.

As hard as he tried to fight off the image of Braxton confronting him at the rally, whenever Jed thought the name Braxton, it reaffirmed his decision to move his family as far away as possible.

"I'll tell you, Fez," Jed proclaimed, "I'll do anything to maintain peace and a safe haven for my family. I found a small town in Eastern Virginia that I remember my folks talking about. I remember they told me that I once had relatives there or something. Though I'm sure they're all gone by now, I remember my parents always talked fondly of that town."

"It's a small town far away from all the trouble in the Kansas and Nebraska Territories, from all the talking and fighting over slavery, and from dealing with the corruption of loaded ballot boxes to get something passed. It's just too ugly and unsettled out this way now for me and my family, Fez. I can still find the peace that I'm looking for in Virginia."

Jed looked to see how his children were doing, then added, "I have word from other pastors who've passed through that there's a great need for my work in that part of the country. I also hear that it's an area full of proper culture and genuine hospitality, which will be important for Lizzy—she's becoming quite the little lady these days."

The two sat in silence, each contemplating what to say next. For Fez, the thought of never seeing his grandchildren or Jed again was frightening. His daughter and two of his grandchildren were still with him, and that helped, but only slightly, in accepting the pending distance that would separate him from the rest of his family.

"I could always try to make it out there to visit," Fez said in a solemn tone. "*If* I can find a suitable assistant to watch the Mercantile," he added, trying to make a joke to ease the loss he had already begun to feel. "My good help just seems to be moving on and leaving me." Though his words might have conveyed disappointment, when his eyes met Jed's they showed only compassion and understanding.

"Papa!" Lizzy screamed loudly from inside the Mercantile, causing Jed and Fez to race for the door. Thoughts of their warm conversation quickly vanished as they darted into the Mercantile to find out what the crisis was.

Daniel and Micah were on the floor in front of them in a heap of entangled human flesh. At first glance, Micah had the upper hand based on the volume of blood dripping from Daniel's mouth. Daniel gained an advantage, however, when he threw a forceful right that landed squarely on Micah's left eye that caused him to sprawl backward, then followed up with a charge and tackle that threw them both into a table displaying a collection of the newest china sets from the East. China could be heard breaking as Jed and Fez sprang into action in the middle of the room, Jed grabbing Daniel and Fez grabbing Micah.

"You two are about to find out what a *real* beating is all about, if you don't cool your tempers down *now*. Micah, you *over there*, and Daniel, *there*!" Jed said as he pointed first to Grandpa Fez's rocking chair against one wall and then to a bench on the opposite side of the room. "I don't want to hear one peep from either of you—not one peep! Do I make myself clear!?" The two boys, despite their pent-up anger, obeyed their father and reluctantly sat on opposite sides of the room while they waited to see what their father would do next.

"Lizzy, take Johnny Russell outside for a walk," Jed told a wide-eyed and teary Lizzy. "And grab a couple of those hard candy sticks on your way out to keep him occupied.

"Okay, Papa," Lizzy said, trying her best to stifle her sniffles after witnessing her two older brothers attempting to take each other's heads off. She grabbed Johnny Russell's hand and guided him toward the door, stopping for a second to get a lemon stick before heading toward the riverfront.

Jed stood in the middle of the Mercantile, ignoring the two startled women who were finishing up their orders at the register counter. "What in the devil has gotten into you two? You know how I feel about my children fighting. There's no reason on God's green Earth that should ever cause any of my children to fight. I think I've made that perfectly clear over the years, haven't I?"

Jed stared at Micah and then at Daniel for acknowledgment of his family rules. Fez threw the boys some cloth rags to wipe their faces, and then began sweeping up the china that had been broken by the brawl.

"Pa . . . pa!" Daniel started, though with difficulty due to a swollen lip. "I just couldn't sit quietly and listen to Micah telling me that we were the cause of Willie's death, and if we had taken the right stand like everyone else at the rally, we would still have Willie with us."

"Now, just wait a minute, that is not—" Micah shouted before being scornfully reprimanded by his father and told to sit and hush.

Daniel continued. "He said that Willie died for a Negro, and that was a waste of anyone's life, especially Willie's. But when he said that Willie's better off dead than having to see the day when the Negro shares the same things we do, well I . . . I just couldn't take it anymore, and I clobbered him, and I clobbered him good, and I don't regret it neither!"

Jed stared at Daniel for a few minutes, trying hard to digest what he had just said. With a mixture of sadness and surprise, he turned around slowly and walked over to where Micah was sitting and still holding a rag to his swollen left eye.

"Micah . . . Son, is that what you said about your brother? More importantly, is that how you really feel?" Jed asked sternly.

"It's true, Papa—you know it's true!" Micah, only fifteen, had the intellect and radical views of a man twice his age. Jed knew that Micah had always had a rebellious nature, was always the one alone and adept at playing the poor victim. He wondered then if Micah would ever grow out of it, or if instead he was going to turn out just as Fez had predicted a few moments before.

"Papa!" Micah exclaimed as he stood up in front of his father in defiance. "Willie and Daniel have had these grand ideas for equality that they've been poisoned with by all the books they've read. This nonsense of equality for Negroes has to come to an end, and you know it, too. It's just not how it's supposed to be, and if that means a fight, then, well . . . I'm ready . . . even if all of you aren't!"

"And you're an expert on this subject, are you, Micah?" Fez interrupted with a roar louder than any of them had ever heard from their grandpa. "You, at the ripe old age of what, fifteen? You have it all figured out, do you? And that's the reason your brother was killed, huh?"

Fez angrily slammed the last of the broken china into the trash with a heave and abruptly turned to his grandson. "Micah, if you had said those things about your brother to me, I probably would have knocked your block off just like your older brother just tried to. Son, you just don't say things like that about family . . . ever . . . do you get my meaning, Micah?"

As expected, Micah was not about to back down. "The only thing I hear from all of you is the sound of a bunch of cowards being told what to do and what not to do by some big important government. You don't see it . . . none of you!"

Micah glared at Jed, then Fez, then back to Jed before continuing his outburst. "No one should be able to tell us what we can or what we can't do, and if I wanted to keep a slave as a slave, then I have the God-given right to do just that, and no one's going to tell me any different!"

"God-given right?" Jed thundered, not caring who else was in the Mercantile as he stepped in front of Micah. "What do you know about 'God-given rights'? God—*our* God—told us to love not hate, to treat others like we would like to be treated! My *God*, Micah! Don't you realize that your brother . . . my son . . . died in my arms without even a chance to say good-bye, to say he loved us or to hear that we loved him? You have the gall to sit there and tell us that he should have died for believing in something that you don't?"

Jed was fuming and pacing the floor. He turned again to his son. "Where is your sense of humanity, boy? There are no sides here, there is no fighting here! We are family and by God, we are the only family that any of us has left!"

Jed had to turn away to look out the window before he imploded. He caught sight of Lizzy playing with little Johnny Russell, and the sight made his heart ache for Abigail to be there, to show him what to do and say. He felt so alone. He told Daniel to come to the other side of the room and sit next to Micah.

"Boys, I don't know where this country is going with all this talk of slavery and all, but I do know that your momma would be crushed to see you both fighting amongst yourselves. Believe me, I do respect both of you for your personal views, but you need to make sure that you always remember that those are your opinion. Everyone has the same right as the other to be heard. Daniel, you have your view, and it's much the same as Willie's was, and I respect that. Micah, you have your way of thinking about how this country should be and about the rights people to decide for themselves what they will or will not do, and I respect that as well."

Jed quieted his voice and sat down between his two sons. "Listen boys, I'm not a politician or a lawmaker, but I do know that all those ideas and visions are necessary to make this land into the great country we know it can be. Hold on to your values boys, and work to build our next generation, but do it together, not against each other!"

Looking at both of them for a few seconds, Jed asked them, "Can I at least get your word that you'll think about what I just said."

Both boys, heads still down staring at the ground, grudgingly nodded their heads in compliance.

Jed, seeing that his latest so called family crisis was taken care of, decided it was time to tell his two oldest about their pending move.

Okay, you two, now that we've got that settled, I need to tell you about a decision I've made," Jed began. I've thought about it long and hard, and I've decided it's the best thing for all of us.

Daniel turned and faced Jed, his expression a mix of concern and apprehension. Micah stared straight ahead, detached from whatever his father chose to say.

"Tomorrow, we'll be going back to Lecompton to pack up our stuff. We'll be moving far away from all of this . . . all this . . ." Jed couldn't come up with the words that would make them understand the real reason he had chosen to move. He knew though that it was to get away from the hostility and danger they'd been witnessing lately.

"Let's just say it's going to be best for us to move on and start up in a new town," Jed tried again. "I know it's quite a surprise to throw at you, but after you think about it for a while you'll understand it's for the best."

Daniel was the first to ask. "Papa, where are we going!?"

Jed looked at Fez for moral support before he replied to his sons. "Boys, we're going east to a small town in Virginia called Fredericksburg where we can begin again.

Daniel understanding immediately the distance of the trip solemnly replied, "That's a long ways away from Grandpa Fez, Papa. Is he coming too?"

"No, Son" Fez interjected. "I need to stay here to keep an eye on your momma and your brothers, but I'll get out to see you as soon as I can, all right?"

Jed knew his oldest well and could see the hurt in Daniel's eyes as he processed that he may never see his grandfather again.

Micah stood up and shouted with his hands to the air. "Now were talking!"

Micah's sudden interest caught everyone by surprise as he continued. "That's right in the heart of the South, isn't it?"

Jed could only shake his head slowly with a look of hopeless despair as he looked at both of his sons. He realized that this latest scuffle was unlikely to be he last conflict that would occur in his family.

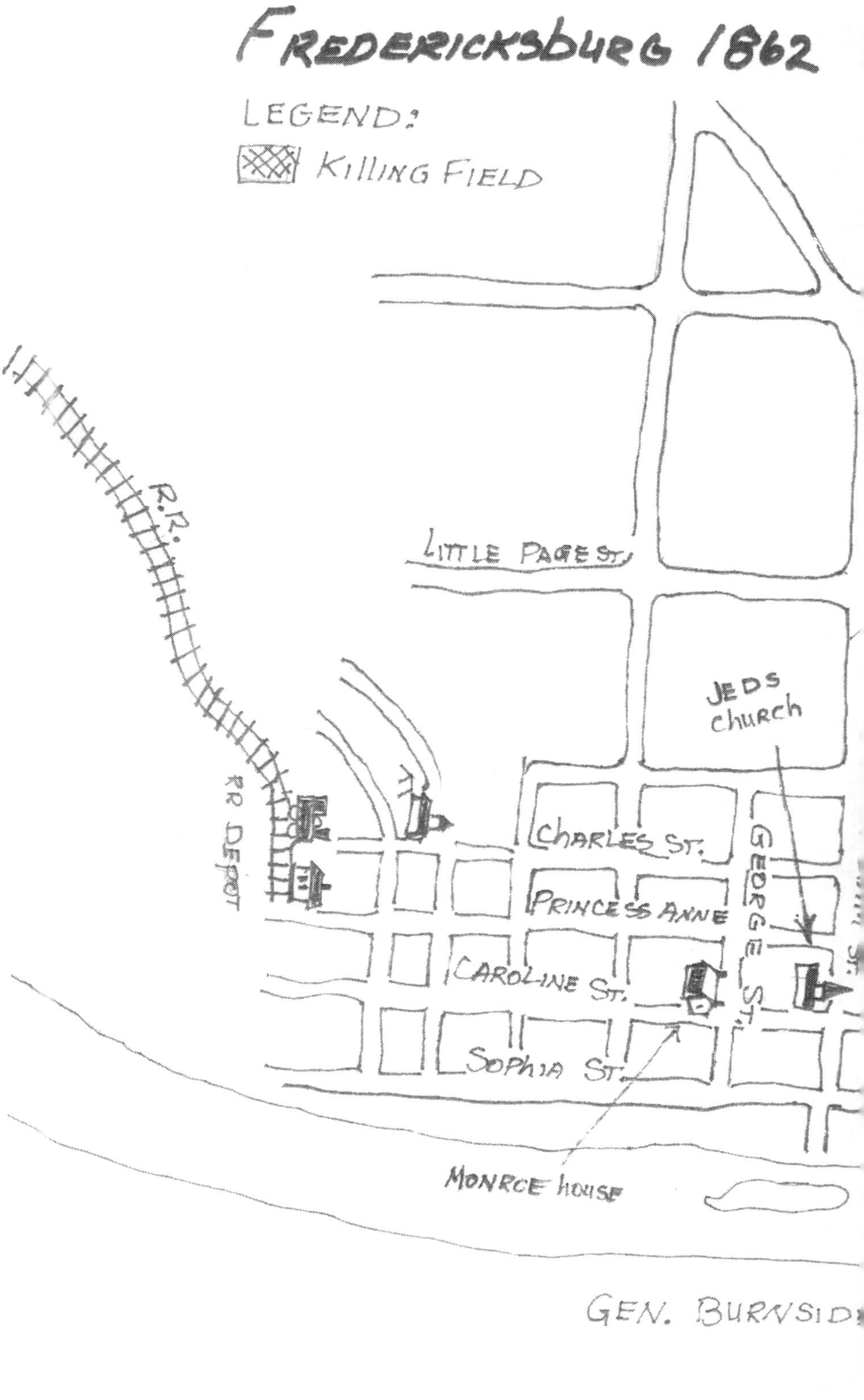
FREDERICKSBURG 1862
LEGEND:
KILLING FIELD
R.R.
LITTLE PAGE ST.
JEDS
church
RR DEPOT
CHARLES ST.
PRINCESS ANNE
GEORGE ST.
CAROLINE ST.
SOPHIA ST.
MONROE house
GEN. BURNSID

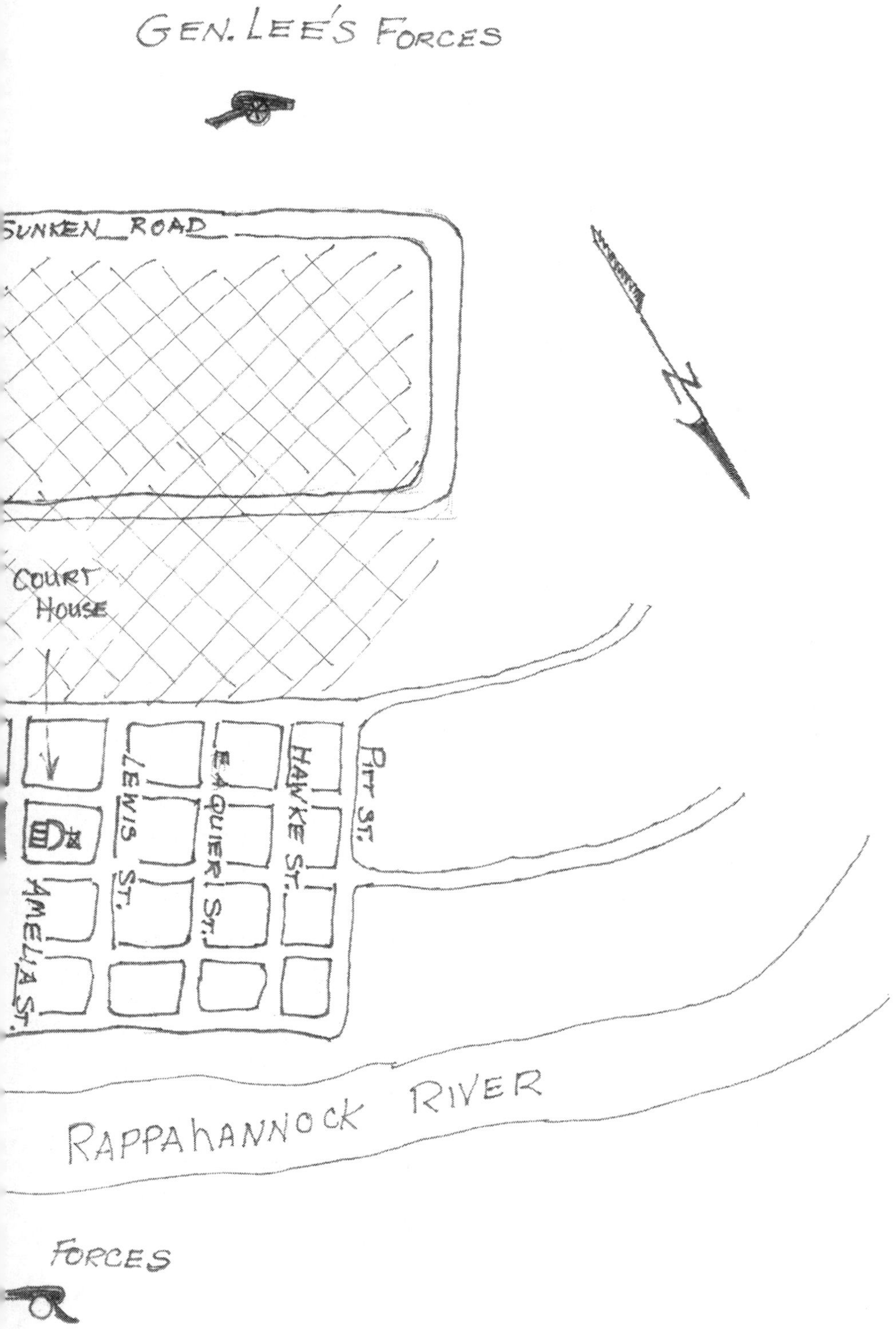
GEN. LEE'S FORCES
SUNKEN ROAD
COURT HOUSE
LEWIS ST.
F. AQUIER ST.
HAWKE ST.
PITT ST.
AMELIA ST.
RAPPAHANNOCK RIVER
FORCES

Chapter Twenty-Five

A Needed Friend

1860

"Whatcha gonna have tonight there, Jed, you warnt the special or yur usual?" the woman said, her flowery apron cascading in an ocean of color from her shoulders to the floor.

Jed felt he had come a long way toward becoming accustomed to Fredericksburg, but still felt at odds with the strong twangy accent carried by some of the locals. He didn't have anything against it, but had been embarrassed many times by his inability to understand it.

While waiting for Jed to answer, the plump woman fussed with her apron, trying hard to cover up stains from the night's special of biscuits and gravy.

The little diner was a convenient place for Jed to get a bite when matters at the church got to him. His usual table in the corner had a clear view of the Rappahannock River. Watching its swift current created a sense of peace that he welcomed during busy days.

"You know, Helen," Jed finally answered, "I think I'm just gonna have a cup of coffee and wait until a friend of mine shows up before I order any supper, if it's alright with you."

"Well, honey," Helen replied as she brushed a strand of hair from her eyes, "yous just let me knows when that there time is, and in the whiles we wait, I reckon I'll jussa keep the coffee coming."

Helen grabbed a pot of coffee from the counter and returned. "As you can sees around this here place, honey, there's ain't no hurry cuzza my account." Jed looked around at the empty diner, smiled at her, and moved his coffee cup closer to the edge of the table for his first of the night.

Sitting in his usual spot, Jed was hypnotized by the sight of the fast-moving Rappahannock. The quiet diner, serene river, and taste of the diner's fresh brew began to affect him, and soon he was daydreaming.

Jed considered how quickly the past two years had gone by. His worry and dilemma over the decision to move his family East had long been settled. It wasn't until the end of 1858 that Jed and his family had finally made their way from Lecompton to Fredericksburg. The plan had been to first go by train to Wheeling to settle some unfinished business with his father's affairs, look into the current status of his church, and show his children the area where he had grown up. The memories flooding Jed's mind seemed so distant, as if they had happened a hundred years before.

Departing Independence after Willie's funeral had been much more difficult emotionally than leaving Lecompton had been. Jed concluded then that he could never return to Independence because it would be too painful—perhaps for his children as well.

It had been difficult beyond words to bid farewell to his beloved bride and two sons, one whose hopes and dreams had been ahead of him, the other who never got the chance to dream at all.

Fez said good-bye to his grandchildren as was his usual: roughhousing the boys and tousling Lizzy's hair. When the boys ran off to play, Lizzy turned sharply and wrapped her arms tightly around her grandfather's belly. She seemed to sense that it was their final good-bye.

When Jed and Fez finally said farewell, both men understood that it was likely the last time they would see the other, because of the distance and Fez's age. Jed remembered the last words they shared. They were few but endearing, and though he felt a world away sipping coffee at his corner table, he could still feel the strong bond they shared. Jed reminisced that he and Fez had become closer than probably either of them had realized back in Independence, probably the result of all they had gone through together.

Jed stared at his reflection in the coffee and continued to think about Fez. He owed much to his father-in-law. Jed's heart hurt as he remembered watching Fez say good-bye to his grandchildren the final time. He had come to grips with that new reality, though, and knew that Fez had understood it, too.

"Yer friend here yet, Jed?" Helen asked as she refilled Jed's coffee. "I got here a delicacy of these here parts, and yur gonna love it." Jed looked down at the table as Helen placed a freshly baked batch of rolls in front of him along with a jar of apple butter. "Now, remembers, yous just flag me down when you's ready, all right darlin'?"

Jed lathered up a roll with creamy butter and thought about the first stop he and the children had made on their way East. The first leg of the trip had gone by so fast. Other than the commotion of Daniel and Micah chasing a rambunctious Johnny Russell up and down the aisle of the train car, the trip was uneventful.

Jed looked out the window of the diner, recalling his first look out of the window of the train as it arrived in Wheeling. His boyhood hometown had changed so much from how he had remembered it. The view out the train shocked Jed, but he tried his best not to show it as he and his children disembarked.

Jed and his family were met at the Wheeling train station by Pastor Albright. Once the luggage and personal belongings were loaded from the train to the pastor's wagon, Jed climbed up onto the buckboard with the pastor, and his children piled into the back of the wagon. They enjoyed the sights of the town, new to the children and still foggy in Jed's mind, as they made the short jaunt up Main Street to a small cottage behind the church that would be their home for the short stay before moving on to Fredericksburg.

Jed had noticed that Pastor Albright had changed, and not just a little bit—he tried hard not to betray this observation in his words or actions. After the death of Jed's parents, Albright, who had been Zachary Monroe's assistant, assumed the role of senior pastor at the church. Jed could still remember Albright as a skinny man with snow-white hair that was just beginning to thin, and a big wide smile, the teeth of which Jed remembered more clearly than any other feature. This new Pastor Albright was portly and completely bald, and the only thing that hadn't changed were the teeth, which were still pearly white and as big as a horse's grin.

Jed's mind flashed with memories of his parents. He questioned his earlier reluctance to see their gravesites. His answer had been swift and firm when Pastor Albright asked him if he wanted to pay his respects. The look on Albright's face when he declined had burned into his memory like a scolding angel from heaven, disapproving and disappointed.

Jed shook his head to clear it, stared out the window at the churning current below, and remembered how difficult it had been to decline that kind of offer from his father's former longtime assistant. Jed hoped that Pastor Albright had in hindsight come to understand Jed's decision, but didn't know if he had. *Only time will tell, right?* he asked himself.

"Still waiting, huh?" Helen came back to see that Jed's coffee cup had once again gone dry. "I see that ya like them rolls and apple butter." Noticing that the rolls were also gone, Helen refilled Jed's cup and then delivered more rolls to his table. "I surely hopes that yur friend shows up soon." Helen pointed to the empty chair opposite Jed's. "You keep drinking all this here coffee, it's only gonna do one thing to you, if you catch my meaning. If in fact you do have that need, you'd best grab your coat, 'cause its way back behind the last slave quarters next to the big house out yonder." Helen pointed Jed in the direction of the outhouse.

Jed, catching Helen's meaning completely, chuckled and said, "Well, my dear Helen, it would be well worth having to traipse out in that cold, 'cause I just can't seem to get enough of this great coffee, and that apple butter is the best I've had since I was a child!"

They were still laughing when the sound of the front door opening caught Helen's attention. She gestured toward the door while looking back to see if Jed recognized the visitor. When Jed did nothing, she persisted by raising her eyebrows, to which Jed shrugged his shoulders haltingly. Not until the man turned their way and Jed's face erupted with an acknowledging glow did Helen know the answer to her question.

"My goodness, if you didn't get here soon, this here gent was gonna have to go toe-to-toe with them slaves back yonder at the pig trough in order to relieve himself," Helen jokingly scolded the newcomer, who stared back at her in bewilderment.

"Ah, don't mind her, she's been taking real good care of me while we waited for you to get here. But I have to warn you, the apple butter here is contagious and habit-forming," Jed said while making his way to the open arms of his longtime friend John C. Fremont.

The two men embraced in a long overdue bear hug so strong that it might have crushed the ribs of its namesake, had it been an unsuspecting recipient. Fremont let go first, but immediately grabbed Jed's shoulders and looked him intently in the eyes.

"Damn, it's good to see you again!" Fremont finally said, his voice breaking with emotion.

"You too, John," Jed replied. "It's been way too long!"

Fremont removed his coat, hung it over an empty chair at their table, and they both sat down. Jed noticed that Fremont's beard and hair were much grayer than they had been the last time he saw him.

"I can't believe it's been over ten years! Jed proclaimed. "Now, I've tried to keep up with all of your activities over the years, and believe me, it's not that hard since you're usually in all the newspapers, but I want to hear it straight from you, not from some editor of a newspaper."

"Of course, my friend, but first tell me, how are you doing?" Fremont said as he redirected the focus to Jed. "I hear just bits and pieces out there, and I know what a great *letter writer* you are." Fremont paused to let the affectionate sarcasm sink in.

"I heard about Abigail, Jed. I also heard about Willie. I am so sorry!" He then added, "God, Jed, I should have been there for you."

"We made it through alright, John," Jed said, his head down and eyes lowered. "It was hard . . . I mean it's still hard with the children and all . . . but we'll continue to make it through, I guess."

"Yes, I heard you took up the robe and the Bible. I must confess, I personally don't read the good book nearly enough, but I am so happy for you. My dear friend, if anyone can find peace for his family, it will be you. That's something of which I am certain—"

"I'm just a bit worried, John. I don't know if I can do all of this on my own, without . . . I mean, without having Abigail . . ."

"You're a good man, Jed, and although I don't know much about the good book from which you preach, I recall it saying something to the effect that God has a reason for everything. So I think if you believe that, then you will be just fine."

Fremont sensed that there was a lot Jed wasn't telling him. He looked at his friend squarely and asked, "The real question is, Jed, do *you* believe that?"

Jed looked up at his friend as a well of emotions came to the surface. "Yea, I still do," Jed said reluctantly. "It's just . . . it's, well, John, it's just me out here, and sometimes it just feels so lonely, you know. There's just no one to talk anything over with, if you catch my meaning."

Fremont waited, knowing that there was more.

"Well, it's just that . . . so much has happened to me, to my family. Well, that's the problem. I say it's happened to me, or that it's part of God's plan, but if I'm truly honest with myself, much of the misfortune in my life is my own fault. I've brought it on myself by my own selfishness and by making choices that were my own, not God's and not those of others."

Fremont nodded, then said, "Jed, we all do the best we can. Men sometimes make tough choices, and sometimes wrong choices, but—"

Seeing that Helen was on her way back to their table, Jed wiped his eyes with his napkin and said, "John, I really am glad to see you. I hope you know just how much I mean that."

Fremont's face said it all. He looked at Jed with a comforting warm smile and clasped Jed's arms with his strong hands.

"Well, fellas, I knows my coffee's the best in town, but you boths gots to be famished by now, so what's it gonna be, the special?—or the special?" Helen asked, lightening the mood and causing all three of them to laugh.

Helen delivered their meals just as the two men finished catching up on the most recent eventful years in Fremont's life.

"You know, John," Jed began, "I would never have guessed that the best man in my wedding would be running for president of the United States.

Now, I know from talking with you that you definitely have a passion for freeing the Negro, but do you really believe the issue will never be settled except with bloodshed in this country?"

Fremont wiped the gravy off his plate with the last remaining roll, stuffed it into his mouth, and put a finger in the air while he chewed a couple times and then swallowed hard.

"That's not what I believed ten years ago, Jed. Back then, I thought Clay's compromise was likely to resolve the entire predicament. But as you saw in the Kansas and Nebraska Territories, the people of this nation are quite willing to take up arms against each other. What happened there was but a small example of what people are capable of when the scale is escalated. And I believe that happened last year."

"What do you mean, last year?" Jed asked.

Fremont motioned for Helen to bring more coffee before continuing. "Many Northern leaders thought that by capturing and hanging John Brown, proslavery advocates would get the message that slavery is a dead issue. Instead, it resulted in more tension, and most are now calling that lunatic a 'martyr of the North'!"

"Here ya go, hon," Helen said as she poured Fremont's coffee. "Sorry to overhear ya all, but if ya all would asks me, that man John Brown was the devil himself, and I'm not alone in that kind a thinkin'. In fact, if all them up yonder north of here knows what's best for 'em, they'd best leave us folks alone, and leave our slaves alone, too!"

As Helen walked away, Fremont turned to Jed. "You see? And that's just one woman who has that fire in her."

"Yea, but Washington must be aware of all this with the election coming in November—"

"That's another huge problem," Fremont interrupted. "The party is so split on almost everything. They asked me to run again, and I told them absolutely not. In fact, right after I relinquish my latest maps, I'm heading back to California to canvass what remains of my mining camp. I want nothing to do with any of this."

"Well, with what you know about Washington, who do you think is going to win the election?" Jed asked.

"I can't say with any certainty for the country overall, but I have personal knowledge of how some individual states have positioned themselves. Several have indicated that if Abraham Lincoln wins there will be hell to pay, including secession from the Union."

"They can't do that!" Jed said angrily. "That's got to be against the Constitution, plus it's against everything so many of us fought for . . . it's our country, for God's sake!"

"Hey, I'm with you, my friend," Fremont said as he tried to calm Jed down. "We fought hard in '46, and those who came before us fought even harder during the Revolution. But that's the whole thing, you see? Many Southerners consider their position just as valid as the struggles that came before, including the ones we fought for. They've even taking to calling this *inevitable* event a 'new revolution.' And I must tell you, if South Carolina had its way, it would already be out the door as we speak."

Jed looked across the diner at Helen, wondering how others in Fredericksburg felt about slavery and how the state might vote on secession if it came to that. Jed thought of his friends in Independence and Lecompton. He thought of Fez. Most of all, he thought of his remaining children.

They concluded their meal, then continued their discussion outside the diner as they hitched up their horses. The two had spoken for hours and reminisced about the many good times they had shared, but were still cautious about the future of their homes and the welfare of their families.

After they had saddled up, Jed turned his horse toward Fremont's and extended a hand. "I can't tell you how much I needed our talk, my friend," Jed said. "Like I said, it's been a bit lonely around here with . . . well, you know . . . without Abigail and all."

"Jed, I'm about to leave for California. But I will *always* come back from wherever I am if you need anything—a man shouldn't have to fight the world on his own." Fremont paused, putting a palm gently on his horse's neck before looking at Jed without blinking. "You know that, right? I know you're not a writing man, but if you ever get all knotted up again, you send me a wire, and I will come. Do you understand me, Jed?"

"John, from the way you explained it, I think I'd rather be going with you to California than facing what I think is going to be an all-out cat fight around here, if you know what I mean."

"Hey, did you just say what I think you said?" Fremont said boisterously.

"Yea, and we better never forget him, too, if—you—know—what—I—mean," Jed replied with a grin that belied the somber tone of his delivery.

The two men tipped their hats and then turned their horses in opposite direction. One was going as far west as was possible, while the other was traveling a mere mile to the east. One hoped to find more gold, wile the other hoped he could come up with a way to get his family through the the violence that was nearly certain to come from the conflict brewing in the country.

Chapter Twenty-Six

Childhood Ends
1861

"It's not your fight, Micah!" Jed yelled across the sitting room as Micah stormed out the front door with a slam that shook the entire house.

Jed could only stare at the closed door and pray that his son didn't go and do what most other men his age were doing—and when he thought "son," he feared for both Micah and Daniel.

Jed spun around to face Daniel, who was on the other side of the room, his faced flushed with anger. "What did the two of you say to each other to make him so mad?"

"Papa, I've told you over and over again that Micah has a streak of anger in him. He's had it for as long as I've known him, and you know it as well!"

"Come on, Daniel, sit down before you go out and do something stupid like I fear that your brother is about to do," Jed insisted.

The house was empty except for Jed and Daniel. They sat down in the large living room at the front of the house. Daniel sat quietly while Jed tried to come up with something to say to his oldest son.

Lizzy had made their home in Fredericksburg as comfortable as she could, using what they brought from Lecompton and what the church had supplied. The spring day was filled with the sounds of newly arrived birds singing in a maple tree a few feet from the house's wrap-around porch. Lizzy had been gone for some time; she had said that she had to run some errands after walking Johnny Russell to the single-room schoolhouse on Wolfe Street.

Daniel reluctantly took a seat on the refurbished Victorian sofa that had been given to Jed by the women's auxiliary of the church. Jed sat across from him in his wooden rocking chair, one constant that he had kept through all of his travels from when they had first arrived in Independence.

"You know he's gonna follow all the other rebels in these here parts, don't you?" Daniel said with disgust. "Ever since South Carolina shot off the first cannon on Fort Sumter, this whole town—heck, this whole country—has been in a state of chaos, and that goes for Micah as well."

Jed was well aware that conditions had deteriorated and conflict had escalated to the point of war, but he hoped that the situation could still be resolved quickly and without bloodshed. He had had several meetings with the elders at the church, the last one being the most vocal. Jed now realized that the conflict in the country had migrated down into the cities and small towns of every state, even as far down as his own congregation and family.

Jed paused to give himself time to think of the right words to reason with Daniel. "I know, Son. I do pray that it doesn't come to that and that Micah will somehow see that it isn't his fight to fight and will just let it go."

"How can you say that, Papa?! This *is* our fight!" Daniel shouted in frustration as he stood up, knocking over the side table next to him in the process. Jed frowned as Daniel continued. "It seems like you're the only one who still remains neutral and afraid to choose a side. Well, I'm not afraid, Papa. I too have chosen a side, and that side is my country. And I don't give a damn what my arrogant and selfish little brother thinks!"

The tension in the room was thick, and neither spoke for several minutes. Jed had noticed the emotions building up in Micah, but must have missed the signs from his oldest, and it broke his heart that he hadn't seen this coming.

"What are you going to do, Daniel?" Jed softly said, sounding defeated.

"I don't know, Papa," Daniel replied, becoming a bit calmer as he picked up the side table and placed the disheveled newspaper back on top. He looked at the front page as he put it down, then read the headline out loud:

SIX STATES HAVE SECEDED — IS VIRGINIA NEXT?

Seeing the look on Daniel's face as he was reading the headline, Jed felt worry and panic sliding down his spine. He knew he had two boys who were at ages that allowed them to join in any military activity that might commence, and what he had seen in Mexico came back to him in flashes of horror.

"It doesn't have to end in bloodshed, Son," Jed said. Daniel turned his gaze from the newspaper back to his father and sat back down on the sofa. "Those other states have elected to leave the Union, but many of the people here don't want that. I am praying that the current Virginia Convention votes to remain in the Union."

Jed saw the look of despair that covered Daniel's face, and he knew that he would have to act fast. He needed to convince his son that all was not already lost and encourage him to take a path other than joining in the fighting—any path as long as it wasn't that one. "Look at all the other states that have held their own conventions. Arkansas had one, and they rejected secession. Missouri had one, and they rejected secession, too."

Jed paused for a mere second to reflect on his old home in Independence, and was thankful that his friends and Fez had voted to stay in the Union.

"I know for a fact that almost half the state of Virginia, mostly on the western side of the state, is adamant about staying in the Union, so there's hope," Jed pleaded. "Daniel, there is hope, and we have to keep praying that we don't start to actually fight, and kill each other, over all this.

"You're right, Papa," Daniel said in an exhausted tone. "But Papa . . . if Virginia does secede, I will have no choice but to leave and fight against it, and I hope you'll give me your blessing if that happens."

Daniel paused, weighing his words before he continued. "Papa? What do you think Willie would do if he were here and we did go to war over all this?"

Daniel's eyes were fixed on a spot near where he sat—he could see a vision of his older brother as he continued, and thought that the vision might let him know if his argument was correct. "You know what I think he would have done? I think he would have been the first to enlist and fight. He was always so much against slavery, and I don't think he would've hesitated to stand his ground against it . . . and you know what, Papa? . . . that would have meant shedding blood if he needed to."

"Daniel, don't you think he's already shed enough blood for that cause?" Jed said. Though he was irritated that Daniel didn't see the irony of his brother's death, Jed was mostly sad as he felt his hope of curbing Daniel's intentions slipping away.

"It is so hard to watch, Daniel," Jed began. "You see, as a father, I am devastated by even the thought of more of my sons shedding blood for a cause that we have very little to do with. We don't own slaves—we never have and never will. We live our lives to teach and preach peace and trust in our Lord, knowing that He is in total control, and we need to believe in that and live by it."

"Do you ever think that maybe it's God who is causing all this?" asked Daniel with a sardonic grin. "You have to admit that God must hate slavery. Heck, you taught us that He saved the Israelites from the pharaoh. You don't think He's telling all of us that slavery in our own country is wrong, too, and He will prove His point, even with bloodshed?"

"Yea, I really do think Willie would have enlisted, and if it does come to that, Papa, so will I, in honor of my big brother!" Finished, Daniel stood and walked to the front door. He paused there as he reflected on what he had said, gave himself a nod of acceptance, and kept walking. Jed was left alone in the front room, hoping and praying that his son would choose not to fight, but fearing the worst.

Hours passed as Jed sat in his rocker. Darkness came, yet he continued to sit and rock. Thoughts of his family filled his head . . . his two sons and what they might do . . . what life lay ahead for his daughter if war broke out . . . what sort of future little Johnny Russell would have, surrounded by masses of soldiers and the killing that would certainly take place.

He couldn't deny what was about to happen, and realized that his family was about to embark on a future path that no one had ever experienced before. And yet his family seemed to be fragmenting, and he was alone, there in his house, alone without his Abigail to keep him strong.

Jed's thoughts consumed him. *Oh, how I miss her, especially at times like these. If she were alive, she would have nurtured and schooled the boys better than I have, and maybe Micah wouldn't have been so angry all these years. Why is Micah so angry? Is he angry at me for not keeping his momma safe and . . . and alive? Is he angry at her for not being here for him? Who knows, who will ever know? Micah has never talked about it—instead he chooses to be angry and distant.*

His meditation was interrupted by the front door crashing open. Micah erupted through the entryway, flailing his arms and yelling something unintelligible at Jed.

"Whoa there, Boy, slow down! I can't understand a word you're saying!" Jed yelled as he jumped up to try to gain control of the situation.

"They can't tell us what to do anymore, Papa!" Micah continued in a loud voice. Jed stood in silence, unable to decipher what Micah was so riled up about.

"I knew it all along, Papa," Micah yelled, a smirk on his face as he ran into the other room. "We just told that baboon in Washington that no one would tell us what we can or can't do, and if we want slaves, then by God we will have them."

"Micah?"

"Papa, don't you get it? Virginia has seceded from the *ol'* United States. We're going to be a part of a new country that will let us do as we please!"

"Do as we please?" Jed yelled back as he grabbed hold of Micah's sleeves. "Is that how you see it, Son?" Jed had finally lost his patience.

"Micah, do you understand what this means?" Jed's voice cracked and he was unable to hide his fear and anger. "You are all excited about what just happened, but what it really means is that our state has just proclaimed war on all the other states that are still in the Union."

Jed shoved Micah onto the sofa and hovered over him as he continued. "That means war, Son, which means bloodshed, which means that people we love are going to die! Is that alright with you? Because it's not alright with me!"

Micah looked up at his father with contempt and yelled back. "You have always been a coward in my mind, Papa. You just go back to your pulpit and preach for peace and harmony like all the other cowards. Me, I'm enlisting to fight for the protection of our new land, our new country."

Jed could only look at his son with sorrow and grief, still trying to understand where all that anger was coming from, and why Micah was so determined to fight a war.

They heard marching bands playing in the street, the faint sounds growing louder as the parade got closer. Fireworks raced into the sky, the armory of the local artillery unit sending whistles of acceptance and exoneration as Virginia was led into the next chapter of the country's bloodshed, one that promised to be more crimson than the one preceding it.

"There's an enlistment table down at Fed Hill, Papa, and I'm going to enlist. Whether you like it or not, I'll be gone in the morning and hopefully end up right where the first fighting starts."

Micah raced to the window to watch the parade go by. "I am ready! Yes, sir, I am more than ready!"

Jed watched his ecstatic yet misguided son run out the door, down the front walkway, and up George Street toward Fed Hill, and he wondered if he would even get the chance to say good-bye to his son before he left.

Thoughts of all that could possibly happen, that could go horribly wrong, overloaded Jed's mind. His finger twitched uncontrollably and his throat tightened into a strangling knot. He couldn't bear the thought of losing another child.

"Hey, Papa, we just passed Micah, and he looked like he just found Uncle John's gold. And what's with all the people in town?" Lizzy asked as she came through the front door and encountered her downtrodden father.

Jed tried to compose himself as Lizzy instructed Johnny Russell to get ready for bed before sitting with her father. They both watched the celebration outside, Lizzy confused and Jed terrified.

"It's like we just celebrated an early Independence Day, Papa," Lizzy commented. "The only difference is that this time, the people we passed were shooting their own share of bullets straight into the air, and whooping and hollering about secession. What's going on, Papa!?"

Jed sat in silence and watched the crowd in its lost celebration. He could only think about what the cost would be for everyone's stupidity. He noticed Lizzy's concerned and questioning look, and sat back down to try to ease her worry.

Jed recounted what had happened, starting with Micah and Daniel's fight. He finished with the last remark Micah had made before he lit out the front door.

"What will all this mean to us, Papa?" Lizzy asked anxiously. "If there is a war, where would we go? What would we do?"

Lizzy's voice trembled, and Jed's finger began to twitch again. "I just don't understand all of this, Papa. It just doesn't make any sense. Why has it come to this? Why couldn't they work it out up in Washington. Why fight? And why does Micah have to fight? It just doesn't make any sense, Papa."

"I know, Lizzy, and I wish I could give you a simple answer to a simple question. But none of this is simple, and I'm afraid there won't be a simple and quick solution, either," Jed answered, sharing his daughter's feeling of helplessness, but being careful not to let it show.

"No, there won't, and that's why the country's going to need all the help it can get to fight back the treason that states like this one and others have committed!" Daniel spoke loudly and suddenly from just around the corner of the front room, having walked in the back door before overhearing Lizzy and his father.

"Daniel," Jed said as he motioned for his son to join them, "I think Micah has another opinion on the whole matter."

"Oh, I'm fully aware of my dear little brother's intentions. He gave me an earful as he passed me on George Street. Yes, my big and bad little brother has gone and signed up, joining, as he puts it, 'the cause.' But if he thinks that everyone's going to just stand by and let eleven states decide for themselves to quit a country, then he has a lot to learn."

Johnny Russell came in and joined them after putting on his nightgown. He walked over to Jed and asked, "Papa, can I go play war with Micah?"

"Johnny Russell, there's not going to be any war, so no, you can't go play it, all right?" Lizzy scolded as she deftly assumed her usual maternal role. "I'm just glad that we'll all still be together, despite what Micah is about to do."

Lizzy pulled Johnny Russell onto her lap and held him tight as she looked for confirmation. "We'll all be safe right here at home, right, Papa?"

"Now wait a minute, Lizzy, no, no, no . . . I for one will not just lay low and let those people walk all over us while we do nothing," Daniel blurted out. "I know what Willie would have done, and that's exactly what I intend to do."

"Son!" Jed said in quiet desperation, knowing that he was losing control of his family's destiny. "You know that if you do that, you'll be going up against your own kin . . . your own brother."

Jed turned his entire body toward Daniel. He felt pain in his chest, and his heart was beating heavily. "Son, could you live with yourself choosing to go to war, if you knew you'd be fighting your own brother?"

"Just like the rebels have already done, Papa," Daniel insisted. "Micah made the first move, and I'm just defending what I believe is God's cause."

Jed felt defeated in his own home, his energy drained from him. He looked at his three remaining children and couldn't say a word. He longed for his Abigail, for he knew that she would be able to pull him from his endless despair. He looked pleadingly at Daniel, hoping to change his mind by thoughts alone, but knew it was not to be.

"Willie taught me to be strong and stay true to what I believe in," Daniel said with confidence and purpose. "He believed in the freedom of the slaves, and I was right by his side all the way . . . even . . . even to the end, and I, for God's sake, am not going to let him down now."

"Papa!" Lizzy screamed in protest as she turned to her father. "This can't be happening, Papa! Do something . . ."

Jed looked at Lizzy with despair, realizing that all his words to that point had been futile. His boys weren't boys anymore. They were nineteen- and twenty-one-year-old men. Both were capable of making their own decisions and were accountable for their own actions, even if those actions were against each other.

"Papa, there is going to be a war," Daniel said matter-of-factly. "I would like to hear your blessing of my intention to serve our country and stand for the rights of all men to be free."

Daniel looked straight into Jed's eyes and didn't blink. It was the coldest, darkest stare Jed had ever seen from his son.

Daniel, determined to get some sort of approval from his father, said, "I would like to go away knowing that I have your support, Papa. You know why I'm doing this, and you know why Willie would have been doing it, too. I can't speak for Micah—then again, I never could—but if by chance we meet down the road somewhere, I'll just pray that God, the same God that you taught all of us to trust, will be right there to do His will."

Everyone else in the house was quiet, and the father–son standoff was making them visibly uneasy as they exchanged furtive glances. Again Daniel asked, "Papa, do I have your blessing?"

"Daniel, you're asking me to give you a blessing to take up arms against your brother, and that I cannot do!" Jed said with a broken voice. "I'm proud of you, Son, for your conviction to a rightful cause and your patriotism, and for that I will bless. Most importantly, though, what I will do is pray. I will pray that the meeting of two brothers on a battlefield never comes, and that this moment in time quickly passes with little harm to all loved ones and all children of God. I will pray as I always do, for God to give us His peace that we can only find through His grace."

Jed stood up, walked over to his eldest son, and held him tight as his tears flowed freely and without shame.

After a time, he released Daniel from his embrace. He looked at Lizzy, then at Johnny Russell, then back at Daniel. "I want all of you to know how proud I am of all my children, and yes, that includes Micah. We don't know why God's will takes us here or takes us there, but we have to believe and trust that He always knows what's best. No, I won't give out any blessing when it comes to fighting each other. I will give you my love, your mother's love, and our prayers to keep you safe so that one day you once again come home to your family."

Jed watched the light go out of his son's eyes. He stood in silence, following Daniel's movements as he picked up his hat, walked over to his sister, leaning slightly to give her a soft kiss on the cheek. He moved on to his little brother, shuffled his hair, and gave him an acknowledging smile.

He turned one last time to Jed, hoping for the words and blessing he wanted so badly. Jed searched his son's eyes for the gentle love he had always seen in them, but it was not to be found. With a silent nod of respect, Daniel placed his hat on his head, tipped the corner to his father, and turned toward the door.

Daniel stopped one last time at the threshold, but did not turn from the world outside as he said, "I'm obliged for the prayers, Papa."

The last thing Jed saw as he moved closer to the doorway was the back of his son as he turned the corner and headed for the train depot to go north.

Chapter Twenty-Seven

Lizzy's Time and Cause

1862

The wind off the Rappahannock carried a much-needed reprieve from the unseasonably hot April day. Lizzy walked along the river trail, her mind twirling and confused. In one hand she clutched a letter from Daniel, while with her other she plucked flowers from the dogwoods. She knew she had time. She *always* had time. Johnny Russell wouldn't be out of school for another hour, and she had promised her father that she'd walk him home after school.

Lizzy was eighteen, and although she gladly helped with the raising of her little brother, she was beginning to have mixed feelings about many things, and he was just one of them. He was full of youthful energy, which admittedly she enjoyed. *But he's nine and not a baby anymore.* Her mind raced from Johnny Russell, then to her other two brothers, and finally to deeper thoughts about the things she had missed out on.

Her hair was waist-length now and pulled back with a ribbon. Lizzy had long abandoned trying to keep it pinned up, employing ribbons or braids instead. *To heck with the social ladies who meet with Papa, with all their noses in the air.*

The town was full of young men dressed in gray wool uniforms, and her mind raced at the thought of meeting one of them. Lizzy had become fond of her new home in Fredericksburg. The hill behind the house rose to scenic Marye's Heights, and the town had a mercantile store, a livery stable, a schoolhouse, a small hotel, and her father's church. But catching her attention lately were the dashing young men, who thankfully seemed to be everywhere.

She thought of Daniel and the blue coat that he wore instead of the gray that was the only kind she saw in town. She sat down on a brick bench that overlooked the fast-moving river and reached for the letter from Daniel that had folded nicely into the pocket of her cotton dress.

Firmly grasping the letter, Lizzy walked along the riverbank and noticed a group of ducks swimming in line, heard frogs croaking on a hidden lily pad, and watched a young family of quail marching in order as the chicks followed their mother. She thought of the young man she had met briefly in Wheeling. She had visions of him in his tailored suit, his hair combed neatly back and he had a closely trimmed beard. His eyes were a green that shot emerald fire at anyone who looked into them. *Or perhaps that effect only happens to me*, she thought.

She remembered that he had tried to speak with her about something that she couldn't quite understand. She gazed at the river and marveled at the movement of the water, deep in thought. *What was it that he was trying to tell me?* She had difficulty trying to pinpoint it so that she might fully understand what he had meant, but then she came up with what she considered a better idea. *Maybe he'll be clearer the next time we meet*, she thought. *When did he say he was coming this way again?*

Lizzy's focus returned to the duck and quail families swimming near her. *If you only knew what was happening all around you*, her mind sharing secret knowledge with her new feathered friends. *Neighbor fighting neighbor, brother fighting brother.* She frowned as her last thought hit her hard, unfolded the letter, and began to read it again.

She shifted on the brick bench, trying her best to stay comfortable while waiting for her little brother to appear. She looked at the letter. How she wished that she had been able to speak with each of her brothers before they raced off. Micah vanished right after a spiteful display in front of her and her father. Daniel quietly disappeared. Despite giving her a silent good-bye kiss, even he had left without the closure she desired. She still couldn't understand the passion each had, and why their visions were so polarized, but now they were gone and Lizzy felt alone.

Lizzy stared at the handwriting. Daniel had always had such an eloquent writing style, and his letters made her feel closer to him each time he wrote.

She found this particular letter much more pleasant to read than the one he had written a few months after leaving the year before. She looked up and stared blindly out toward the river, thinking back to Daniel's description of the horrors he had witnessed.

She still thought it odd, and painfully nonhuman, that a group of women and children would think it sensible to ride into the middle of a battlefield so that they could have a picnic lunch and watch. *What did they think they were going to see, anyway?* Thoughts flooded her mind, while pain for Daniel ached in her heart.

What was it that made him think that one battle on a creek just fifty miles from this very spot was going to be the one and only fighting to take place? She wondered. Then again—why couldn't he have been right?

Lizzy was lost in her thoughts, thinking about how wonderful it would be if Daniel were home right now to join her as she waited by the river for their little brother.

In his first letter, Daniel had been very descriptive and upset, and he placed a lot of blame on his fellow soldiers for running away from massive chaos. He wrote about a Confederate general who stood his ground and cheered his soldiers onward, demoralizing Daniel and the whole Union Army.

"Stonewall Jackson," she muttered out loud, quickly looking around to make sure that no one had heard her blurt out the words. She was all mixed up inside regarding her loyalty to her brothers. Should she be upset to read about this 'Stonewall Jackson' because of her allegiance to Daniel? Or should she be thankful for this general in order to support Micah? Her dilemma made her squeamish.

Lizzy slowly put the letter down on her lap. Her gaze at the river was blurred by memories. Where were her two brothers? Were they safe? Were they dead?

She shook her head violently. No, they are both very much alive.

She hadn't heard a word from Micah since the day he fashioned his uniform in the sitting room for her, her father, and Johnny Russell to see before he reported to Richmond.

The look of pride and spite on his face remained frozen in her memory, but she knew then, as she knew now, that she couldn't find it in her to agree with him, brother or not. To her, what he was doing was wrong, and it didn't help that he had cleared out of the house without a care, disregarding his family's feelings. *Especially Papa's.*

Lizzy's heart still ached from Micah's last words. "Not that this family cares much about it, but this fight has been a long time coming, and I'm going to make sure that it's over right quickly, even if I have to kill every last 'Blue Boy' who gets in my way! And if need be, that includes my no-good big brother!"

She could still see him racing out the front door and slamming the door behind him. She could only wait, hope, and as her father had always taught her, pray!

She thought back to the many fights and arguments her two older brothers had gotten into over slavery, and a sad expression crossed her face. She rarely got into the middle of those arguments; though she probably would have sided with Daniel, it seemed silly to continue an ongoing quarrel about an issue over which they had such little power.

Lizzy laughed quietly when she noticed two duckling siblings taking little bites at each other while their mother stayed as far away as possible. *That's mighty smart there, mama duck,* she thought.

How her father could remain so neutral was beyond Lizzy's ability to understand. She was beginning to sway to Daniel's way of thinking, and she attributed that to talking with the man that she had met in Wheeling. *What was his name?*

Lizzy adored her father, and she knew how much he relied on her and adored her as well. She believed he had his reasons for maintaining his neutrality, and she vowed to always support him, even though she knew she might have to break away from him one day to follow her own passion and cause. She had an idea that his stand for peace for both sides stemmed from his life with her momma. And the thought of that being his reason brought tears of pride to her eyes.

Would she stand by her father's side, or make her own stand and hope he would bless it? Thinking that she might need her father's blessing frightened her—she could still remember the day when Daniel had asked Papa to bless his cause. She was beginning to understand which way her loyalty was leaning and which brother she would be following.

It was in Wheeling, that's where I first decided. Her mind cleared, and she realized that she was still clutching Daniel's letter, and the quail and duck families were still about their business without a care in the world.

She started to gather her belongings and placed the letter back into her purse. With one last look at the sibling ducklings as they bickered, she stopped and thought, *Lizzy, it's about time you came forward and did something about it. That's what that handsome gentleman had said, too.* She tried in vain to remember his name, but she did remember how he made her feel and she knew what she wanted to do.

As she gazed at the tops of the ripples in the river, her mind wandered away from her brothers and to the encounter with her mystery man. She continued to rack her brain to put a name to the striking young man who had caught her attention from the moment she met him. *But what was his name . . . Martin McKeever, that's it!* Her laughter caused her to stumble over a rock embedded in the river trail.

Lizzy recalled that the encounter was brief but impactful. She and her family had stopped at Wheeling for a few days on their way to Fredericksburg. She had been introduced to a clerk who was assisting the pastor at the local Wheeling church while her father and Pastor Albright toured the various churches in town.

Lizzy felt a rush of heat fill her face and chest, and was confronted by an embarrassing awkwardness. Thinking of this young man was having an effect on her, one she had never experienced before. *Wonder if this is what Momma felt like when she first met Papa?*

She remembered him saying that he would be in town during the upcoming weekend. The thought filled her with hope. *But was he just joking when he said that he'd drop by?*

Johnny Russell had finished school and was approaching Lizzy at their meeting spot outside the schoolhouse. She noticed that he had that "I'm so tired of reading, writing, and arithmetic" look on his face.

To Johnny Russell's amazement, Lizzy said abruptly, "Let's go!" The look in her eyes was distant, and she had only one thing on her mind, and it wasn't to ensure that her little brother had a walking partner with whom to discuss the day's events.

Lizzy thought of the short but impressive discussion she had had with Martin about the ill treatment of the enslaved Negro. She recalled what he planned on doing, but didn't know how far he would go, and was eager to someday pick up the conversation where they had left it.

Could this be the weekend? Her pace quickened. *Could this be the day?* Faster still. *Am I more interested in the conversation or about, no . . . stop that kind of thinking, it's bad for me to think such thoughts.* At least that's what some of the women in church had told her. Now she was nearly running.

"Ya know, I'm nine years old, and I don't need a babysitter walking me home from school!" Johnny Russell complained as he tried to keep up with his older sister. "And besides, it just seems . . . hey, will you just slow down a bit? What ya all on fire about?"

"Knock it off, Johnny Russell, and keep up with me!" Lizzy yelled back to her brother, her eyes focused straight ahead and her mind swirling with endless thoughts of her previous meeting with Martin.

"Okay, smarty-pants, see if you can beat me home, if you think you're so fast!" Johnny Russell yelled as he whisked by Lizzy, running down Princess Anne Street and out of sight around the corner onto

Hanover Street. She knew that his aim was to beat her home, but she didn't care . . . she now had only one thing on her mind.

Johnny Russell turned into the front yard of their home on Caroline Street, and after skipping three of the four wooden steps, jumped up on the porch, turned around with his arms in the air to claim his victory in front of an empty yard that showed no signs of his sister Lizzy.

With a sigh of satisfaction and a victorious shrug, he turned at the front door. Out of the corner of his eye, he noticed a man sitting on the rocking chair at the end of the porch. The man had a wide grin, and gave Johnny Russell a congratulatory nod to indicate that he'd witnessed Johnny Russell's fictitious victory.

"Well done, young man!" the stranger said as he applauded Johnny Russell. "I'm assuming you just won a race, and whom may I ask were you racing against?"

A bit startled and hesitant at the unexpected visitor, Johnny Russell motioned to the front walkway and Lizzy, who was approaching on the walkway with her eyes fixed on the man on the porch, a surprised and prophetic look on her face.

"Now this is a strange coincidence, and if I do say so myself, a bit creepy too," Lizzy announced, her eyes wide open in disbelief. "You'll never believe it, but I was just thinking about you and trying to remember the last time we met and now . . . well now you're right here in front of me, on my very own front porch!"

He was just how she remembered him—tall and broad at the shoulders, well groomed with oiled jet-black hair, and deep fiery green eyes. She noticed the dimples that had caught her attention the last time, especially when he smiled. Her mind was now racing faster than her attempt to beat her brother home from school had been.

"Johnny Russell, this here is Mr. Martin McKeever, you remember him from when Papa was visiting those churches in Wheeling, right?" Lizzy attempted a reintroduction with her brother, but her eyes never left Martin's and unknowingly, Johnny Russell had already moved on into the house to find something much more entertaining to keep him busy.

"Wh . . . what . . . uh . . . how did you find where I lived?" Lizzy fumbled for the right words to begin their awkward reunion.

"Oh that was the easy part; remember . . . you're the daughter of the town's pastor!" Martin answered.

"Plus, I had the vision of this place set in my mind ever since we said our last farewell. Based on the description you shared with me of your dream house, I could see you in this Victorian house with its large front porch and white railings. Now what about the three or four little ones you also told me you were going to have?"

Fully blushing by now, Lizzy sat down on the porch bench. Martin followed her lead and sat in a chair in the corner of the porch next to a geranium plant that was in full bloom. A dog barked in the background, and they could hear Johnny Russell trying his best to find food in the pantry, but having no luck. Four small birds were perched in the beams of the porch and chirping away. The slight breeze carried the scent of blooming jasmine across the porch.

"No, there are no children, and this is not my dream home," Lizzy said, breaking the silence between them.

"Now that's a relief!" Martin joked. "But I have to admit, I noticed how good you are with children when you were in Wheeling. In fact, I noticed how caring you were with anyone who came in contact with you."

"I guess. Well, I probably got that nurturing thing from my mother. She was such a loving woman, and I've always hoped that I will be like her someday."

"That was but one of many reasons for me to come to Fredericksburg," Martin said warmly. "I saw the nurturing nature in you right away, plus I saw something else in you while you were in Wheeling. You made an impression on me, Miss Monroe."

"Mr. McKeever?!" Lizzy said melodramatically as she batted her eyes and gave Martin a scolding look. "We have just recently met, and you must know that none of that flattery will get you anywhere with me!"

Lizzy could feel her insides knotting up. Her rapid breathing was tightly concealed, and the expressions on her face remained neutral while her emotions were igniting a fire deep in her soul. She had never experienced anything like this and wasn't quite sure what to make of it.

"Mr. McKeever," Lizzy quietly continued as she tried to compose herself, "my father taught me to be a lady, and since, as I believe I mentioned and of which you are undoubtedly aware, we have just recently met, I would appreciate it if you could . . . I mean, if you could . . ."

And that's when all of her attempts at composure and concealment began to go awry.

"Don't we have any food in this house?!" Johnny Russell yelled as he came crashing out the front door, bringing the conversation between Lizzy and Martin to an abrupt end.

"I do need to start supper, Mr. McKeever," Lizzy said, sounding disappointed at the unexpected end to what felt like a splendid beginning. "My father would be overjoyed to see you again. Would you do us the honor of joining us for supper?"

Never the defeatist, Martin agreed. "Yes, that would be great, but you must stop calling me Mr. McKeever, all right? I do insist on you calling me Martin, and I also insist on you letting me help you prepare our supper. Do we have a deal?"

"Deal, and please, call me Lizzy," is all she said, or more accurately was all that she could manage. The butterflies were swarming in her stomach, and each time she glanced Martin's way, she saw that he was looking at her like no other man ever had, unflinching, unwavering, unstoppable. She didn't know what to make of the feelings she was having. *Is this what love is?* she wondered. *Oh Momma, where are you when I need you?*

Lizzy escorted Martin into the kitchen and instructed him to gather the kindling wood from the stockpile behind the backyard shed. "Martin, you will be in charge of getting the stove nice and hot while I get the fixins ready," Lizzy ordered comically.

"I believe I can handle the single task that you have perhaps assumed to be the extent of my manly abilities, but if you need me to handle any of the makings, I am quite good in the kitchen—if I do say so myself."

With the stove prepped and burning hot, the two stood across from each other at the butcher block, cutting up vegetables, pulling apart chicken pieces, and adding spices where needed. The room smelled of a mixture of oregano and spiced apple from the cutting block, and smoke from the stove.

Their conversation was casual, mostly talk of her town, then his town, her family, then his. "So, how are your brothers doing, anyway?"

"Haven't heard much from either one of them lately," Lizzy answered. "I wish all of this would be over so we can get them back here again. It seems like they've been gone forever, and it's been just a year and a half. I dread thinking of what they have seen, and more so what they have had to endure."

Lizzy put the final touches to supper, then placed it on the stove with a lid to allow it to simmer and stay warm until her father got home. She grabbed a towel and wiped her hands.

"Martin, what made you decide to stay out of it? It just seems like everyone felt that they had to drop everything and run off to get themselves killed—and for what? I just don't understand what kind of 'cause' could so intoxicate a man that he would leave his family and home to go out like that."

Wiping his hands and wrapping the towel around the dowel next to the washbasin, Martin turned to Lizzy with a soft expression in his eyes. "Lizzy, sit down and let me see if I can explain it to you."

They both sat at the kitchen table, listening to the simmering of onions and chopped chicken parts in the iron skillet. The scent of onions in the air made Martin's stomach ache for the taste of the upcoming meal. Johnny Russell could be heard playing "army" in the backyard. He didn't care which side was good and which was bad.

"Remember we talked briefly in Wheeling about my concerns for the enslaved?" Martin started slowly and cautiously. "Now, I know you, or at least I think I've gotten to know you in this short time, and you have always kind of sided with your brother, uh . . . Daniel, right?"

"Yes, Daniel," Lizzy said.

"Right. It seems to me that you still love your other brother, but you don't agree with his beliefs," Martin continued.

"Well, to be honest, I don't really know what his beliefs are," Lizzy replied. "In fact, I don't think Micah himself knows what his beliefs are. He's really tormented about something, and it's been eating at him for years. I just wish I could figure out what it is and take it from him. He's always been so, so angry and against anyone and everything. I think he's just using this as a way to fight against his demons, not to fight for some so-called *cause*."

"Okay, but nevertheless, Daniel is fighting for the North, for the Union, and against slavery. Micah is fighting for the South, for states' rights, and for the bondage of human beings," Martin generalized.

"Yes, I think you've got it right, but . . . ," Lizzy attempted.

"The key phrase that I just described is exactly what I am against," Martin interrupted.

"What key phrase?" Lizzy asked puzzled.

"For the bondage of human beings!" Martin said, his voice rising with a mixture of conviction and passion.

"Sure, I want our country to remain a Union," Martin said. "I know for a fact that the South doesn't have the resources to outlast anything the North has for them. This war will end with the North winning it, I'm sure of it, but in the meantime there are many innocent people who are or will become the real victims in this whole nightmare."

Lizzy had her full attention on what Martin was saying, so neither one noticed the lessening smell of onions in the air or the sizzling of the simmering meal on the stove.

"Lizzy, I'm talking about the bondage of Negroes, and the audacity of the slaveholders in holding other human beings in chains," Martin said, leaning forward and taking Lizzy's hands in his.

Lizzy didn't back away, flinch, or hesitate from Martin's passionate statement. Instead, she looked him in the eyes with the same conviction and determination that he wore.

"Martin, I do sympathize with the treatment of the Negroes, just like you do, and yes, I would side with my brother Daniel and with the North . . . but . . ." Lizzy had to pause to regain her train of thought. "But Martin, what can people like you and I do in a case like this? I mean, I surely can't pick up a gun and go fight to free the Negroes, and by the way, you still haven't told me what's stopping you from doing just that."

"Exactly my point!" Martin said with confidence, now feeling that he could speak freely with Lizzy about the sensitive nature of his work. "Lizzy, I, well, I'm involved in helping out the Negro."

"What do you mean, helping out the Negro?" Lizzy backed up in her chair, cautiously looking around the room to make sure that their voices could not be heard by anyone nearby.

"Have you heard of the Underground Railroad, Lizzy?" Martin asked.

"Well, sure, I think. I mean, isn't it a group that helps Negroes run away?"

"Yes, in a way that's true. It's not the whole caboodle, but you've got the gist of it," Martin confirmed, his smile widening and lighting up his face. His green eyes were practically sparkling.

Lizzy slowly got up from her chair, walked to the back window, and watched Johnny Russell play. "Sounds dangerous and very illegal," she said matter-of-factly.

"Lizzy, we're in a time in our lives that requires us to take a leap of faith to do what is right. Dangerous or illegal it may be, but it is the right thing to do, and we are doing it," Martin said assuredly, as he got up from his chair and joined Lizzy at the window.

Lizzy thought of her two brothers. Where were they? Were they still alive? What would they think if they heard that their little sister was thinking of getting involved in something like this?

She was eighteen, and here she was in her father's kitchen talking about breaking the law, and maybe, just maybe, falling in love. *Momma, I sure need you now!*

The room fell silent other than the sizzling of the now well-done chicken and shriveled-up sliced onions.

"Hello? Anyone home?" Her father's boisterous voice startled Lizzy back to her senses.

"We're back here, Papa," Lizzy yelled out.

"*We're* back here? I just passed Johnny Russell in the front yard playing some kind of game with a ball and a long wooden stick, so who are you with?" Jed queried.

"Papa, you remember Martin McKeever, don't you?" Lizzy said abruptly as she met Jed at the doorway leading into the kitchen, blocking his way and giving him a "please don't embarrass me" look before letting him pass. She knew that she could endure the scolding she might receive for the impropriety of having a gentleman caller in their house unannounced and unchaperoned, but it was unlikely that she could endure being embarrassed by her father in front of this fascinating man with piercing green eyes.

"Well, why yes, I do remember . . . back in Wheeling, right?" Jed said.

"Yes, sir," Martin replied with confidence, getting up from his chair and reaching out his hand to Jed.

"Yes, of course," bellowed Jed, easing Lizzy's worry about having had a gentleman sitting in their kitchen unannounced. "And how is your father doing these days? I must write to him and Pastor Albright to see how the church is doing. It does seem like forever since we last spoke."

"Papa, we were just discussing some of the work that Martin, I mean Mr. McKeever, was doing in Wheeling with his father, and he was hoping to have a word with you to hear what you think."

"Oh, the Underground Railroad is still keeping your good ol' father occupied, and keeping him away from helping poor ol' Pastor Albright at the church, huh?"

Lizzy and Martin both looked at each other in surprise. The temperature of the kitchen seemed to drop ten degrees and get ten feet wider and taller at the same time. A sense of ease filtered through the room as Jed continued.

"Yes, that was a concern of mine when we passed through—"

Both Lizzy and Martin felt the room contract again as the temperature began to rise, and Jed saw the panicked looks on their faces. He grinned slightly as he suddenly understood the confusion, and said, "Oh, no, I didn't mean the *Underground Railroad*, but rather the lack of support for the church." Lizzy and Martin breathed simultaneous sighs of relief. "You do know, son, that I have an avid interest in and a personal connection to that particular church, and I hate to think that something could happen to stop its growth."

Lizzy watched carefully as her father looked Martin up and down, eyeing him closely and sizing him up, but for what she did not know.

"Martin," said Jed, "you and your father have a reputable cause, and I do believe in the sanctions of equality and Christian values, but I hope you're not here to solicit the help of my daughter."

"Papa!" Lizzy burst out. "First of all, Martin is my guest here, and you have no right to—"

"It's all right, really," Martin interrupted. "Sir, if I may be frank, my father and I, along with many, many others, are working together to spread God's love and God's protection, and yes, we are in need of help, and yes, I am asking, but not just of your daughter, but of you as well."

Lizzy watched her father carefully, not knowing what reaction would come of this. She knew his stand on peace and that he strove to keep all around him safe. She loved him dearly, but like her brothers she needed to make a stand for what she believed in. She had always hoped that her father would support her in her beliefs, whatever they might be, but after Willie's death and then Daniel and Micah leaving to fight their own battles, her confidence was waning.

"Papa, I've always done what you wanted, and I will always love you and value what you have taught me. Knowing the difference between right and wrong is a value that you taught all of us. Willie believed in it . . ."

"Yes, and Willie died for it, too!" Jed interrupted, becoming agitated with the direction the conversation had taken and concerned about losing another precious child.

"You wouldn't want any of your children to run from protecting those who are wronged, now would you, Papa?" Lizzy began to choke as she remembered a time far in the past.

"I can still remember that Momma would always go out of her way to protect us and stand up for us when she knew we were in the right. She had a heart of compassion, but a will to protect what was hers, and I believe I have that, too," Lizzy proclaimed.

Lizzy watched her father slump down in his oversized leather chair, the arm still torn from a battle it had lost many years before. He had a faraway look in his eyes, which made her want to go to him, but she knew that following that pattern would jeopardize her goal. Instead, she stayed in her chair and watched to see what he would do.

"You know, kids?" Jed began. "All I've ever wanted was peace for this family." Lizzy listened intently to what her father was saying. "I wanted it for your momma, and I lost her. I wanted it for your oldest brother, and I lost him. And I still hope and pray for it for your other brothers, and . . ."

"Papa, we don't know that they're not all right," Lizzy responded.

"I will take my children to the ends of this world to ensure their peace and safety, if it's the last thing I ever do," Jed finished, disregarding Lizzy's attempt to interrupt.

The grandfather clock chimed five loud bangs, indicating the time but also making them aware once again that they were sitting together in their living room. For the time being at least, they all were safe, and it brought a sense of comfort to know that they were all family and friends during a time of turmoil and uncertainty.

"Martin." Lizzy listened intently as her father called upon her guest. "I know that you have come here to get support for your cause, and as much as I support it and the Christian motives behind it, I have to admit that I am reluctant to give my permission for Lizzy to go with you into harm's way, even if it is to save others."

Lizzy felt ill and confused as she looked at her father and then back to Martin.

"*However,*" he paused, remembering the joy it had brought him to watch his two strong women together, his Abigail teaching and his Lizzy learning.

"I also know my daughter very well, and she is the exact image of her mother. Martin, my Abigail would have taken in a wounded dove, cuddled it, nursed it, and protected it despite whatever dangers may have lingered around her. I fell in love with that kind of spirit, and I see it again in my adoring daughter."

"Papa," Lizzy said sympathetically. She knelt next to her father. "I grew up admiring what Momma stood for, and her love and compassion for any of God's creatures, but I also grew up loving and appreciating the values and principles that you instilled in all of us. You showed us how to love, and how to protect each other from any harm that could come our way."

Lizzy looked at Martin and then back at her father sitting next to her, tears dripping down his cheeks as he remembered the losses his family had experienced thus far.

"I want your blessing for what I think is my calling to help Martin and his father. I believe in my heart that Momma wouldn't have hesitated to assist the slaves. I want to be the one to carry her torch to more of the world, so she can look down on us and smile, knowing that we are doing all we can to protect those in need."

"Mr. McKeever!" Her father's booming exclamation was abrupt and unexpected, and Lizzy fell backward from her position next to him. "I love my daughter more than you or anyone else will ever realize!" Lizzy's heart erupted in a gulf of emotion as she wondered where her father was going with this latest remark, and whether her dreaded fear of embarrassment might come to pass after all.

"When I lost her mother, I was lost. But seeing Lizzy with her little brother, and watching her grow up, I got to see my Abigail every single day. It was Lizzy who got me through those rough times."

Lizzy's tears flowed, and she could see that the same was happening to her father, and her heart went out to him.

"I agree with and admire your cause, Martin. The actions you and your father are taking are admirable. I will never come right out and bless the actions that my daughter undoubtedly is about to take. But I know how strong my loving wife was, how proud I was of her strength and compassion, and what she would have said about all this. She would have given her blessing wholeheartedly, and I have to say that if Lizzy is half the woman her momma was at her age, then I would be mighty proud of her, too."

Lizzy could see her father's tears flowing down his cheeks, and her first reaction was to run to him and embrace him, but she stayed put and let him continue.

"The Monroe family has lost so much in such a short period of time, and as a father, I am scared to *death* of having to endure any more loss. Despite my own fears, though, I want to support my daughter's ambitions and convictions, just as if they were her mother's."

"Daughter." Lizzy looked at her father. "You have a conviction, and God is calling you to act on it, so if we look back and ask ourselves, did Noah wait? . . . did Moses wait? . . . did King David wait? No! Nor shall you, and I pray for the two of you to protect each other and rely on God's grace and protection no matter where you go. He's the one you need to know is leading your way—you both hear me?"

Lizzy took a few moments to regain her composure. She met her father in the middle of the room, her eyes red and swollen. Her smile told him how much she loved him, but she had one final concern.

"What about Johnny Russell, Papa?" Lizzy said, as she considered the extent to which her father relied on her to care for her brother.

"You mean, he's not going with you?" His stoic expression caught both Lizzy and Martin off guard until he showed his wide grin and the sparkle in his eyes. "I'll put him to work around here. Besides, someone has to do the cooking, and it surely isn't going to be either of you after what you just did to our supper!"

Lizzy and Martin laughed as they glanced at the shriveled-up chicken and onions still simmering over the open flames of the stove.

Chapter Twenty-Eight

Moving In, Moving Out
1862

He had never been so cold. The mood was glum at best. Daniel checked to make sure he had all the gear he needed for the next march. *The next march . . . how many marches have there been?* The army had just celebrated what many had called a draw at the Battle of Antietam. It would seem odd to celebrate a draw, but the gathering gave Abraham Lincoln the opportunity to make his statement, by way of the Emancipation Proclamation, to free all slaves. Even though it would be a few months before the proclamation became law, word was spreading across the country, with joy in the North and disgust and denial strewn throughout the South.

We'll take any good news we can get,

Daniel had written his father in a letter filled with frustration and dismay. He described the endless marching, the latest being from Maryland to just south of Richmond. He told his father it wouldn't be so bad if he had confidence in the direction and purpose of his service:

I've lost track of who is in charge anymore.

His letters were bitter, and who could blame him? Daniel had experienced the lost battles at Bull Run, and barely escaped entrapment under the stone bridge at Antietam Creek in September.

We've gone from general to general, and some around me are questioning whether we are actually fighting for anything anymore. After Sharpsburg, I can honestly say that if this doesn't turn soon, I'm not going to have enough in me to continue.

The words were hard to read, and Jed wanted to rush to his son's side and encourage him—if he had it his way, he would bring Daniel back home. The good news from Daniel was that the army was moving toward central Virginia. Daniel sounded excited at the chance to slip over on leave and visit.

Jed was hopeful that he might get to see his son, but on the other hand was worried that the entire army could end up so close to their home.

If the United States Army was coming south, its only reason for doing so was to fight. Daniel wrote that the new commander of the army was General Ambrose Burnside, and from what Jed could decipher, there weren't many who respected him or trusted his judgment.

Heard anything from Micah?

The question was both melancholy and painful. No one had heard from Micah for more than a year and a half. He was not on the casualty or AWOL lists, though they grew longer with each new posting.

Daniel had written several times, and the arrival of his letters was a welcome event. Jed was alone most of the time now, with the exception of watching Johnny Russell as he played both sides of the conflict in the side yard. Lizzy had moved to a boardinghouse in Wheeling and was assisting the McKeevers with their efforts in the Underground Railroad.

Lizzy rarely wrote about episodes in her life that dealt with the Railroad, as all of those activities were dangerously covert. But she did write frequently about her activities at the church. She was actively assisting Pastor Albright with the operations of the church, and in her latest letter she had written:

> Pastor Albright says to tell you that he's only holding Grandpa's church warm for you until you get back here to take it over.

The thought of someday going back to his first home crossed Jed's mind from time to time. But for the moment, he had more pressing business to attend to. He picked up Daniel's latest letter, which he had received just the day before. He went out to the porch and sat in his rocking chair. He began to formalize a picture of what was coming soon, and as he looked at his youngest playing war, fear rose up in his chest as thoughts about his two other sons thrashed about in his head. Thoughts about the two brothers who weren't just *playing* war.

The first part of the letter was filled with a sense of excitement that had been missing in Daniel's previous letters. He wrote that he had been recognized at the Battle of Antietam and promoted to the rank of Captain of the First Infantry in the Third Division. He also shared that his immediate commander was Brigadier General Horace Henderson.

The name sounded familiar to Jed, and he laid the letter on his lap and gazed at Johnny Russell in the yard as he pondered the name. *Horace Henderson? No, it couldn't be. Corporal Horace Hendersen of the Second Infantry in Mexico? One and the same?* Jed chuckled at the thought, and wondered in amazement at how small his little world really was.

Jed picked up the letter again, and as he continued to read, the knot in his chest grew tighter and heavier. Daniel wrote that he was ordered to march from just below Richmond southeast to Falmouth. He was to wait there until all 110,000 men had arrived. Then they were to cross the mighty river.

Jed read the words over and over and still he couldn't believe what he was reading:

Papa they want us to take your town!

The boldness of the ink seemed to emphasize the emotions his son must be feeling.

Jed could only stare at the handwriting, so eloquent and fine. But the words were blurry to him now, and he had to put the letter back on his lap. He heard Johnny Russell laughing about his latest conquest of whatever enemy he was fighting.

When? Lizzy? Johnny Russell? What am I to do with him?

He pulled the letter back into focus, quickly scanning it for a date. *How much time do I have, Daniel?*

The letter was postmarked November fifteenth.

Daniel wrote that he couldn't say much more—in fact, what he had written could get him arrested—but he had to warn his father and encourage him to get out, and get out soon.

It all started to make sense. The increasing number of graycoats swarming up and down the streets. The mass of activity above the cemetery and at the top of Marye's Heights. Why hadn't he seen it more clearly before?

There were several thousand soldiers in town already. *Why didn't I see what was happening?* His mind raced. *Johnny Russell. I must get Johnny Russell to Lizzy. I'll telegraph her.*

More graycoats went by in front of his house. Wagons went by carrying crates. Was it his imagination, or were the townspeople moving much faster than usual? *Why didn't I see it sooner?* He had been blinded by his hope for peace, and in doing so, might have put his youngest son in danger. He continued to be scolded by his thoughts.

He picked the letter up from his lap and finished reading it. From Daniel's description, the troops were marching, and based on the postmark, they would arrive any day now.

"Johnny Russell!" Jed yelled out to his son. "Johnny Russell, get over here now!"

"What's going on, Papa?" Johnny Russell answered, crooking his neck.

Jed pulled his son to him and guided him to the front porch bench. "Son, I want you to go up to your room and pull your valise out from under your bed."

"My what?" Johnny Russell asked, not understanding the tone and expressions coming from his father.

"Johnny Russell, please listen carefully." Jed tried hard not to sound alarmed. His youngest was only nine, and was so dear to him that in Jed's eyes, Johnny Russell was even younger than that.

Johnny Russell had always been special to Jed. Not just because he was his youngest, but because when he looked at his growing son, he thought of Abigail. Jed would be the first to admit that he coddled and protected him more than any of the others, but he had made a vow years earlier that he would do everything in his power to protect the last memory he had of his loving wife.

"Something is going to happen real soon, something really dangerous, and I need you to go up and spend some time with your sister and the McKeevers for a while," Jed reassured his young son.

"If you're talking about the battle coming, I already know," Johnny Russell said matter-of-factly. "The soldiers up on the hill told me all about it." His knowledge surprised Jed. "That's why I've been practicing out in the yard, Papa."

Jed looked with loving amazement at his very grown-up nine-year-old.

"No, Son, I need you to go up and look after your sister. I need you to keep her safe until it all passes over down here. Can you do that for Papa?"

Protecting his older sister made the idea of leaving the impending battle site easier to take. He always had a special bonding with his sister, who had for so long filled the role of loving mother to him.

Jed had to wait an hour to get to the telegraph desk, and everyone around him seemed tense. Once he received the confirmation that his telegraph had been sent, he waited outside for a response. He knew it would take a while, but he needed to make sure that Lizzy got the message.

He leaned on a hitching post and looked around the town. He thought of his family. He knew that Johnny Russell and Lizzy would be safe in Wheeling, and that brought him some relief. He thought of Willie and wondered what he would have done during this conflict if he were still alive. He thought of Abigail, and he was relieved that she didn't have to witness any of this turmoil. *She would have been worried out of her mind,* he thought. *No, that was always my job.*

The response came and was handed to Jed by a tall man with a square black hat with gold laces hanging from its bill. He smelled of liquor and had tobacco stains on his gray beard. *I'm sure there's a lot of drinking and chewing going on right now,* Jed thought as he began walking home.

"How old are you now, seven?" Jed asked his youngest son as they looked through his valise for all the essentials.

"Come on, Papa, you know I'm nine," Johnny Russell teased back.

"Well, today you're going to be much older than that, and I couldn't be more proud of you," Jed stated. "When you get on that train, I want you to sit and not talk to anyone. Your sister will be at the Wheeling station to pick you up."

"Not even a little exploring from one car to the next?" asked Johnny Russell.

"No!" Jed answered before continuing, silently scolding himself for raising his voice. "It's a long trip, but you'll be there before dark. And I need you to do me one more favor."

"What is it, Papa?" Johnny Russell asked, his eyes bright with anticipation. "You need me to capture anyone and take 'em prisoner?"

"Johnny Russell, this is serious!" Jed said, trying not to lose his patience and silently scolding himself once more. "You have never done anything like this, but I know you can, and you're old enough to know what is right and what is wrong. So I know I can count on you to stay out of trouble, mind your manners, and only talk to the conductor of the train. You got that?"

"Yes, Papa, I got it," Johnny Russell answered, trying to hold back his excited grin.

The walk to the train depot was short, but to Jed it seemed to be the longest walk he had ever taken. He wanted to hold his son's hand, but knew that would make Johnny Russell uncomfortable. He had stopped wanting overt affection from his father a few years before, much to Jed's disappointment.

The depot was unusually busy. Women and children made up the majority of the waiting passengers. Their nervous expressions indicated that news of the coming altercation had become public, and many were leaving. The train was late due to the heightened activity and increased passenger volume at all of the depots from Richmond to Fredericksburg.

The train currently in the station was unloading soldiers, wagons and cannon. Hundreds of troops filed out of stock cars, and several troops helped unload crates of ammunition, wagons, and carts holding shiny iron cannons. The sight of it all changed the concept of the upcoming conflict into a fierce reality that made Jed's stomach turn. *Got to get him out of here.*

Jed looked at the train and wondered how many trains had transported both of his older sons all over the country. How many battles had they fought while facing each other?

Jed wondered if Micah was here. He knew Daniel would be here soon, but the thought of possibly having them both here at the same time, fighting against each other, made Jed even more nauseous. He didn't know if Micah was even still alive. He wished that Daniel weren't coming here and knew that his wish was shared by thousands of parents who were worried for their sons.

Thoughts buzzed in his head as the train began to move on down the tracks, opening up the depot for the train that would take Johnny Russell to safety and peace. He was glad that Abigail wasn't here to see any of this.

Johnny Russell heard the train whistle first and ran to his father's side. The two moved to the corner of the depot and shared a bench with a heavyset woman who had a large crate in front of her. Jed looked deep into his young son's eyes. "You go and make me proud, Son, you hear me?"

"I will, Papa, I promise," Johnny answered, sensing his father's concern for his well-being.

"And you take care of your big sister and make sure no harm comes to her."

"I said I will, Papa, I promise," Johnny Russell answered again, but this time he looked frightened by the sights around him and the anxiety in his father's voice.

Jed brought his youngest close to him and held him tight. He felt like exploding into tears, but he didn't want to scare Johnny Russell more than he feared he already had. When they let go of each other, Jed saw that his son had been crying, but he said nothing of it.

"Aaaaaallllllaaaaaboooooooooard!" yelled an oversized train conductor. He was dressed in a dark blue suit, and one end of a silver chain snaked from one of its pockets. The other end was attached to a pocket watch that he held firmly in his left hand. His moustache drooped over his lips so much that no one could see his mouth move when he spoke.

Jed introduced Johnny Russell to the conductor and explained to him his age and the circumstances.

"Yep, we're gettin' a lot of that here lately, mister, but don't fret none, this fine boy and I will become best of friends between here and Wheeling," the conductor said as he eyed Johnny Russell. "But only if that's all right with this nice young man. What are you, twelve?"

Johnny Russell smiled wide and looked at his father with a sense of comfort. Jed knew his son was in good hands, and gave Johnny Russell one last hug before he boarded. "I love you, Son!" Jed cried out.

"I love you too, Papa," Johnny Russell yelled back.

Stepping off the steps of the coach, Jed watched as the train began to move north. He knew that in Richmond there would be a change of trains before going west, and he was thankful that the same conductor was going all the way through to Wheeling.

Jed watched the back of the train disappear, then pulled Lizzy's telegram out of his pocket and sat down on the same bench that earlier he had shared with Johnny Russell. It was empty now. He reread her response:

WILL MEET JR STOP PAPA PLEASE COME I LOVE YOU= LIZZY

Jed felt a sense of peace knowing that at least one half of his family was safe. He would not leave Fredericksburg, not with Daniel coming directly into harm's way. He didn't know what he could do to reduce the danger, but he knew he would not leave Fredericksburg.

He put his elbows on his knees, bowed his head, and prayed. "Dear God, please watch over my Daniel, keep him safe, and offer your guardian angels to surround him and protect him as he ventures into this new battle, the battlefield I once called home. You are the grand master of everything, and I am blessed to have You to protect my children. I reach out to You once more to bring Micah to me. I don't know where he is, but I know that You do, and I just ask that You keep him safe and bring him to me soon. In Your Son's name, Amen."

He rose slowly and began the return walk home, but decided to go by the church instead. He wanted to be closer to God right then. He passed his home, crossed George Street, and approached his church on Caroline Street. It was quiet in town, even with wagons and horses and soldiers around. The air had an eerie stillness to it, and despite the coldness, it was rather comfortable.

Jed turned onto the walkway to his church, then took one last view of the depot where he had just said good-bye to his youngest son. As he looked away from the depot and walked up the church steps, a Confederate lieutenant on William Street crossed Caroline Street near the church as he walked toward his destination at Marye's Heights.

Jed walked into the church and sat in the front pew. He looked up at the Christ on the cross. He thought of his family. He thought of Daniel.

He hadn't seen the young Confederate lieutenant crossing the street behind him on his way to Sunken Road. Lieutenant Micah Monroe made it to the top of Marye's Heights and began digging trenches behind a big stone wall. He wasn't thinking of his family, but rather how many Billy Blues he was going to kill—*the sooner the better.*

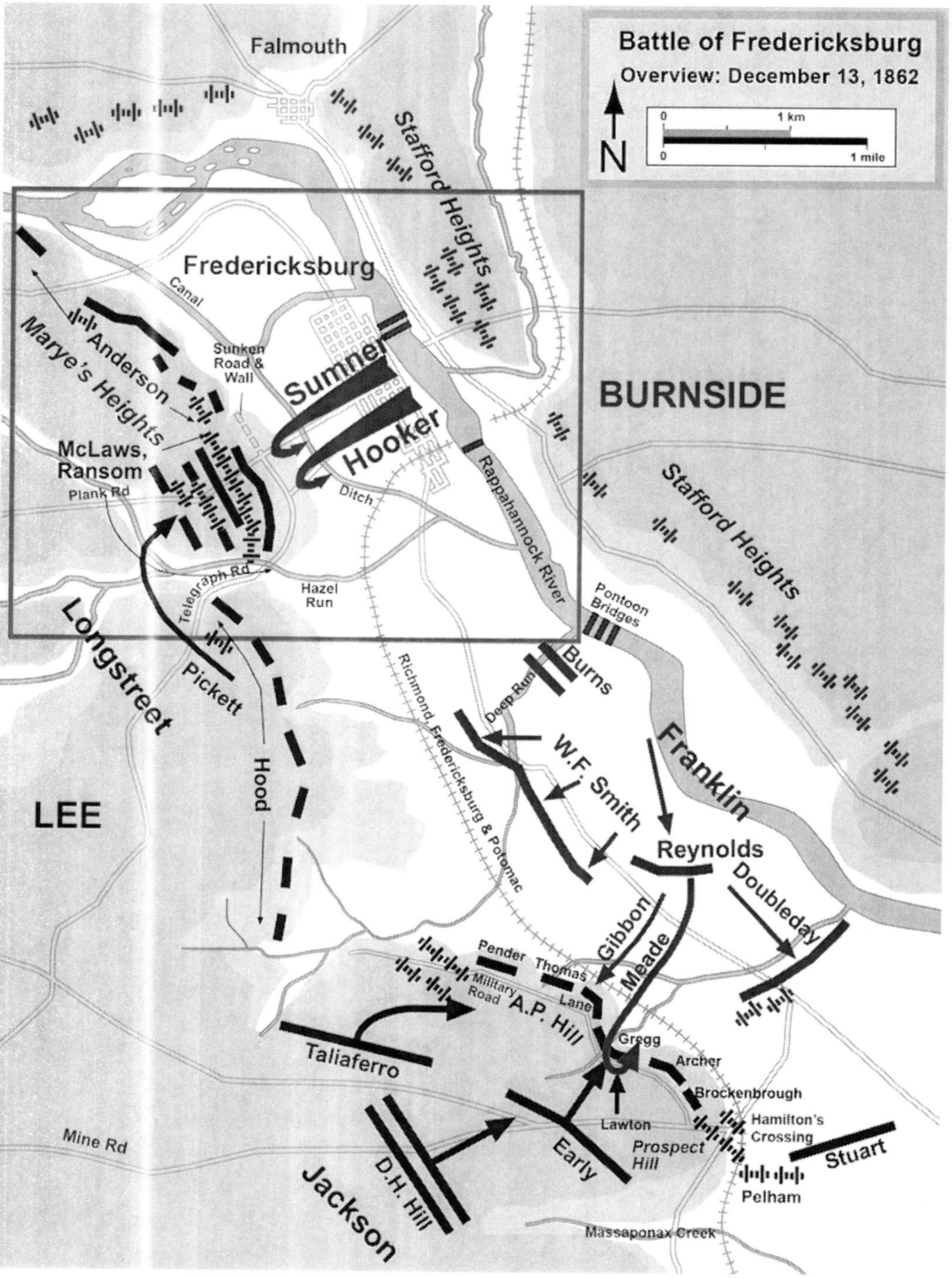
Battle of Fredericksburg
Overview: December 13, 1862
N
0
1 km
0
1 mile
Falmouth
Stafford Heights
Fredericksburg
Canal
Anderson
Marye's Heights
Sunken Road & Wall
Sumner
Hooker
BURNSIDE
McLaws, Ransom
Plank Rd
Ditch
Rappahannock River
Stafford Heights
Telegraph Rd
Hazel Run
Pontoon Bridges
Longstreet
Pickett
Burns
Deep Run
Richmond, Fredericksburg & Potomac
W.F. Smith
Franklin
Hood
LEE
Reynolds
Doubleday
Gibbon
Meade
Pender
Thomas
Military Road
Lane
A.P. Hill
Gregg
Archer
Taliaferro
Brockenbrough
Lawton
Hamilton's Crossing
Mine Rd
Prospect Hill
Early
Stuart
D.H. Hill
Pelham
Jackson
Massaponax Creek

Chapter Twenty-Nine

Brother against Brother

1862

The rock wall stood four feet high at the crest of the Heights. After two days of digging trenches behind it, it stood at nearly six feet. The open space beyond the wall was known as the Sunken Road. It could hold up to eight rows of soldiers, all equipped with enough black powder and Minié balls to stand for hours and pluck any turkey, deer, or rabbit that even thought of crossing the field in front of them, let alone tried to run up it.

Micah was given orders to place his infantry regiment between two Parrott cannon and two smoothbores twenty yards apart on Marye's Heights. He looked past his last cannon down the four-mile Sunken Road. He wished he had been assigned to the town of Fredericksburg instead of up on this hill far from where the fighting would likely take place. The only thing he wanted to do was kill as many Blue Boys as he could. His rage had not diminished over the past year and a half, and he was going to let it out against the enemy when he faced them.

Once he was set, he confirmed his status with his commanding officer, and then he and the entire Army of Northern Virginia waited.

He watched the river far below. The water was moving swiftly and reflected the muddy gray of the sky above. At the river's edge just beyond the city, the pontoons were almost complete. Sharpshooters had been busy for days picking off the enemy of the Gray one by one. Micah thought nothing of the sound of guns after months of fighting. To him it just meant one more Blue Boy dead.

Looking through his spyglass, he scanned the town: streets running north–south and east–west making perfect square blocks where a mixture of shops, offices, and homes lay in wait. He noticed that most of the townsfolk had left. *Better off not to be here to see it anyway.* He focused on the tall white steeple close to the water's edge, about a block north, and thought of his father.

He put the spyglass down on the wheel of the cannon and leaned against its cold iron, knowing that soon it would be fiery hot. He thought of his family. *Wonder if they still think of me?* Sadness, though guarded, filled his heart. He was the strong one, the only one who had the good sense to know what was right. Thinking about the past year and a half convinced him that his father and brother were wrong. *Wonder where they live now? Wonder where Daniel is now?*

A sudden thought crossed his mind, and Micah picked up the spyglass again and looked toward the river. *Are you down there, Daniel?*

"Arms up and prepare to fire long range at my orders!" The shout from his superior officer snapped Micah out of his trance.

"Orders up, stand and be ready!" he shouted to his men.

In an instant, the forty men under his command were up, guns loaded and standing tall, ready for the command to fire. Beside them, rows and rows of infantry fell into lines behind the rock wall, all looking down at the quiet town below.

"They're across the river, Captain!" a private in the next regiment yelled out.

"Hold your fire, boys!" The captain responded. "Don't any of you get antsy now, we want them right at the base of this here hill, ya all just sit tight and wait for my orders!"

Micah waited and watched. The fighting down in the town was fierce, but from his viewpoint it looked like they were being pushed back through town by the enemy, his army's cannon doing little to slow them down. He watched the explosions and destruction of the town's buildings, then turned his spyglass back to that white steeple, and saw that it was holding firm.

He thought of his father again, and of Daniel.

"Here they come, boys!" yelled the captain. "Wait for my order, then fire in volleys, step back, and row by row step up until you hear from me to stop!"

Micah watched the bluecoats stop at the base of the hill and line up. *They really are going to come up this hill after all. What fools!*

Row upon row of bluecoats marched forward up Marye's Heights as Micah waited, his elbows braced on the rock wall and his hands firmly gripping the rifle in anticipation of bearing down for the slaughter. *This is going to get ugly.*

"Fire!"

Daniel had made it across the river, one of the last to navigate the man-made pontoon bridges. He anticipated immediate gunfire on his position, but instead could hear that the battle was going on far ahead. The town looked as if it had suffered a fierce blow. Minié ball holes were everywhere, with homes and businesses in flames, but there were no signs of the enemy.

He looked down the first street he crossed and knew it wasn't the one. He ran to the next one and looked to his left—he saw the church and knew that he was close. He didn't have much time, knowing that he would be needed at the line on the ridge in the distance, but he had to try.

He turned down the street and past the church, the smell of burning wood and black smoke all around him. He ran to the church and opened the door. The pews were scattered and side windows were broken, but no one was around.

He raced outside and down the next block. He looked frantically for house numbers, street signs, a familiar building that might guide him. The volleys grew louder, and he sensed that he had little time left.

Finally, he found the address. He sprinted up the steps and flung open the door. "Papa!" No one answered. "Papa, are you here?" he once again yelled out, hoping desperately that his father would reply.

Daniel went from room to room but found no one. He tried the basement door, but it was locked. He raced toward the front door, grabbed a piece of paper from his father's side desk, and crafted a hasty note:

Papa,
Came by, but no one home. Got to go, needed ahead. Hope you're good. I am.
Daniel

Daniel dashed out the front door and down the street to make sure he met up with his regiment before it reached the base of Marye's Heights.

The house stood quiet, the sounds of battle now blocks away. A few seconds after Daniel raced away, the lock on the basement door made a tiny click before the door opened and Jed appeared. He slowly checked each room of the house, and other than the opened front door, everything looked secure and safe. He noticed a piece of paper on the table. He picked it up and read it, then sat down slowly and read it again—and again—and wept.

* * * * *

"Line up, men, arms at the ready!" Daniel shouted as he gave the order to his men.

In the chaos of battle, with Daniel's regiment the last of the reserves, he wasn't missed and was now in full control and ready for duty.

"Steady, men!" he shouted.

He looked past the regiment ahead of him and up the heights to the long rock wall at the top. He saw that the hill was littered blue with dark red accents—a macabre landscape using thousands of blue bodies as paint—and suddenly felt sick to his stomach. *This is not going to be good, Daniel.*

"Move up, men!" he ordered, trying to sound confident as he realized fully the futility of their charge. He watched as row after row of men attempted to reach the stone wall, each cut down right in front of him.

They've got to call us back, call a retreat. This is maddening! Daniel waited for the sound of the bugle blowing retreat, but nothing came. *We're next up. Be strong*!

"On my order, men!" he shouted. *Dear God, help me!*

"March!" The words came out automatically and his body moved on its own. He didn't look down his column for fear that his men would see him ghost white.

"On my order, men!" He waited. *Got to get closer.*

"Charge!" he yelled out in a raspy voice. His tired legs did their best to move. He ran—and he ran—hopping, zigzagging, up and around the dead and dying. He could sense others falling around him. He smelled the acrid scent of blood in the air and his lungs filled with choking smoke from the guns. He heard the cries of the wounded, but worse were the awful screams of the bloodthirsty rebels on the other side of the wall.

He thought he imagined it at first, but then heard it again. The blow of the bugle was a loud and welcome sound.

"Fall back, men!" His shout was hoarse, and his throat hurt each time he yelled. "Fall back to the base of the hill—now!" Daniel yelled the order and felt a sense of hope. *Maybe, just maybe.*

On the other side of the wall, Micah's arms ached from repeatedly holding, shooting, and reloading. It seemed as if he had been repeating the motions for hours, because he had. He looked down the hill at the slaughter below, and instead of the exhilaration he had expected, he felt only sadness and guilt. *Why are we doing this?*

He surveyed the piles and piles of bodies. He heard the screams of the wounded, their arms reaching skyward as they attempted to grab on to something, but only finding empty air. *Is this a truce?* It had been done before, and it was surely a good time for it with this . . . this . . . massacre taking place. But no, it was not. Micah looked over the wall, then yelled, "Here they come again!"

"Company up! Regiment at your ready!" The orders came from behind them as they leaned into the stone wall.

"Fire!"

A couple hundred yards from the wall, Daniel and what was left of his regiment were moved to the third line and given orders to charge again. His mind was blank and his stomach knotted up. He needed to vomit again despite having thrown up numerous times already. The acrid and putrid smells of blood, bile, smoke, and burned flesh mixed with the cries of the wounded to create an overwhelming horror.

He had given up trying to stop the deserters and actually didn't blame them. He tried to look strong and sound confident for his men as he waited for the orders to come, and his mind wandered. *God, why wasn't Papa home?* Memories of family dinners and picnics filled his mind. The smells of cooked turkey and baked pies replaced the gruesome reality surrounding him as he floated away on thoughts from earlier happy times in his life. Those times had been peaceful and loving: Momma and Papa sitting in their chairs reading; Lizzy playing in the corner with her dolls; Micah playing war with his toy soldiers; and Willie teaching him the importance of being honest and true to what he believed in.

His memories were tinged with melancholy—*Willie . . . boy, do I miss him—*

"Company fall in and form the line!"

He didn't care who gave the orders anymore. The hill ahead was a demon, his demon, and charging it was his destiny. Frustration welled inside him—his eyes blurred and he thought he heard soft voices. *Momma? Willie?* Click. Gone.

"March!" he yelled automatically. His feet moved on their own, and he gripped the butt of his rifle with his hand and leaned the barrel against his shoulder. His mouth was dry and salty, and his eyes burned. His ears became nearly deaf to the sounds of battle as he moved faster and faster behind the column in front of him, which was thinning ever so quickly.

He could see the stone wall just ahead, seemingly closer this time. He heard screams of encouragement from other officers. *Can we do it this time?*

The graycoats behind the wall were now close enough to be seen. Daniel continued running up the hill. The figure of one soldier in particular was a blur at first, his face blackened by powder, but still he recognized him immediately—*Micah!*

Daniel stopped, his regiment passing by him. He wiped his eyes and looked again . . . *Micah!*

The volley hit him and he was violently whipped around before falling hard onto his right side—then his mind went numb.

Daniel twisted around and looked for Micah, but the figure was gone. He tried to get to his feet but couldn't find the strength. He rolled until he was facing away from the wall, then began crawling down toward the base of the hill.

A second brutal blow hit him, and this time he recognized it. He tried to continue crawling, but couldn't find his left arm. His stomach wretched. He cried out for help, but none came. There was no one left except for thousands like him, and most were already dead. He looked down the hill for help, but saw only chaos.

With all his strength, Daniel made it back to his feet, stumbling over and around the dead, weaving and staggering and trying to kept his balance with one good arm. As he approached, he could see his regiment safe at the bottom. *So close . . . got to . . . get . . . there!*

He worked his legs one at a time, oblivious to everything around him. He thought he saw his father running up the street and toward the hill, and tried yelling to him to go back.

Papa?

Got to keep moving! But he stopped to look at the top of the hill one more time. *Micah?* He was dizzy and delirious.

The third and final blast flung him high in the air, and he landed hard on his back. His ears were ringing as he tried to focus. His mouth was caked with powder, dirt, and blood, and he lay still.

Must . . . get . . . up. Daniel could no longer feel his arms, his legs, or even pain. His head was so heavy. He tried to lift his hand to clear his eyes, but it wouldn't move. He lay flat and stared up at the sky, which he noticed was beginning to darken.

"Daniel!"

He barely heard the words, could not see the face.

"Oh, dear God, Daniel!"

Muffled sounds, but somehow familiar.

"Papa?" Daniel's hoarse voice was barely audible.

"I'm right here, Son!" Jed's voice cracked as he knelt and then cradled Daniel's head on his lap.

"Papa? . . . I . . ." He coughed up blood and Jed wiped it away with his sleeve. "Papa?" Daniel could barely speak. "I tried to . . . to find you!"

"I know, Son. I'm here now—I've got you!" Jed said, his tears falling onto Daniel's bloodied and tattered uniform.

Daniel summoned all the strength he could. "Papa?" came out in a tiny whisper.

"It's all right, Son," Jed said, his voice struggling for coherency through his sobs. "God has you now."

"I love you, Papa . . . I . . . love . . . you."

His whisper faded, and so did he.

On the hilltop above, Micah looked down on the carnage below and shook his head in disbelief. He had never experienced such a murderous act and was overwhelmed by enormous guilt. He no longer thought himself a soldier—only a murderer. He closed his eyes and they filled with tears. He thought about the God he'd left years before. He was guilty, he knew it, and no God would ever forgive him for what he had just done.

Then an eerie thought hit him. An unsettling possibility. He shook his head violently in denial. But he knew it was possible—the thought sent panic through his veins, and he shivered. He tried his hardest to remember how to pray. "Oh God . . . please God . . . tell me that Daniel wasn't down there. Tell me that I didn't just kill my own brother."

Chapter Thirty

Escaping from the Pain

1863

"With all due respect, Jed, it is your church, after all," Pastor Albright pointed out.

"Well, it's not that easy, Chester," Jed replied. "I'm still getting used to the idea of being back here and all. It's just kind of strange, you know, because this is where it all started for me. And to be quite honest, I'm not so sure that I'm ready to have my own church, especially this soon after losing Daniel."

"That's understandable, Jed, and I don't want to push any of this on you," Albright answered quietly. "I'm just letting you know that whenever you're ready, if *ever* you're ready, this church will always be yours to have."

"You've always been so kind, Chester," Jed said. "I mean, from the time you took over the church after Papa and Momma died, to welcoming my family and me back here after . . . what . . . after what happened . . ."

Jed choked up, then stood in silence as he tried to gain the strength to speak again.

"It's been so hard, Chester."

Jed felt as if he were about to break down, as he had done so many times in the months before. He took a deep breath, looked skyward, then looked back at Albright and continued. "It's been so hard with the loss of Daniel, then making the decision to move everything back here, and trying to start fresh again."

Jed paused, slowly shaking his head as tears welled up. "You know how many times I've said that, Chester? To start fresh again . . ." Jed could control himself no longer. He wept and fell into the arms of his longtime family friend.

Albright could see the agony and sadness that were ripping through his friend's soul. He held Jed tight as he released some of his pain.

"Let's make it easy for you for a while, Jed," Albright said softly, "at least until you figure out what you want to do. Let's just have you just help me out at the church for a bit as, let's say . . . my assistant pastor. That way we can take the time you need to reintroduce you to the town, get you acclimated to what's new around here, and reunite you with what's old."

Jed pondered the idea for a moment, then Albright added, "Time is on your side, Jed, so you needn't worry about moving any faster than you see fit, and I won't push you to do so either. Get yourself reacquainted with the town and the people, and spend some much-needed time with your children."

My children. His stomach twisted into knots. *How many have I lost?* He immediately felt guilty for not appreciating his two remaining and loving children, Lizzy and Johnny Russell, and a wave of nausea rolled through him.

I need to be there for them. I need to build a loving home for them.

Then there was Micah. He hadn't heard from him in more than two years.

Where is he? Is he alive? Jed's thoughts smothered him. I should never have chased him away. I should have loved him more. I should have been a better father.

Jed tried to shake the demons from his head as he thought again of Lizzy and Johnny Russell.

"That sounds great, Chester," Jed said in a muffled and trembling voice. "I really do appreciate your kindness and understanding."

He turned from Albright and looked to the valley beyond the church. His mind locked onto a distant place that seemed a lifetime away. He was playing with all his children. He saw his wife Abigail, watching on and encouraging her children to get the best of their father. He heard laughter, he felt happiness, and he immersed himself in the memory as he tried valiantly to ease the pain of the present.

Albright looked at Jed with sorrow and helplessness, then attempted to lighten the mood. "Don't you fret, Jed. One thing about Wheeling is that it's a small town, and people are like family to each other. In fact, several of the womenfolk have already adopted your little one, and I'm sure they'll welcome you back as if you'd never left."

Jed snapped out of his trance, and Albright could see a sparkle of hope in Jed's eyes. Continuing, he said, "Your father was my best friend, Jed, and we've always regarded you as one of our own. It's time for you to feel like you're home again, and home for good."

Jed took one more glance at the valley as he tried mightily to regain the vision of his family. Realizing that it was gone for good, he put his hand on top of Albright's, then nodded his head slowly.

Jed bid Albright a temporary farewell, telling him that he needed a good walk to clear his head. Though Jed was clearly still upset, Albright was optimistic because occasionally a glimmer could be seen in Jed's eyes—he had never seen that until recently. Perhaps Jed would pull through after all.

Jed began walking away from the church. He passed house after house—some he remembered and some he didn't. The flowers and plants in the yards were in full bloom, itching to show off the pure beauty of spring. He thought of the many times he had walked the same streets as a young boy.

After just a few blocks of walking, he turned and looked back. He saw his father's church on the left, standing tall with a new white steeple in place of the one he remembered from his youth. Next door was the home in which he grew up.

The home my parents were killed in. Will I ever have the courage to move into it again? Memories flooded his mind and he became dizzy and unable to breathe. As he looked at the boarded-up home, the memories of that horrible day flashed in his head as if from just the day before. He remembered receiving the letter from Albright telling of the tragedy that had befallen his mother and father. Looking at the house, he could only imagine the gruesome scene displayed that fateful night. He wasn't sure which was worse: seeing his childhood home or reliving that horrific nightmare on a hillside in Fredericksburg.

Fredericksburg . . . thinking of it made him sick. Jed's decision to leave that Godforsaken town was an easy one. He packed up and left right after putting Daniel to rest. Jed was required to pay a mighty penny to get a single gravesite because the Confederates were burying their *enemy* in mass graves and their so-called *heroes* in single ones. It helped that Jed had been the town's pastor, but unfortunately he and his family had also been labeled Union sympathizers. With accusations in many quarters that he was a traitor to the South's cause, the potential for harm to his family was evident.

He decided to leave immediately, and no one in the town tried to dissuade him. The same town he had served as pastor, spreading the word of God to hundreds, told him to take his family and get out.

Now back in Wheeling, Jed stood on a street corner, looking back at what might soon be his home and his church again, and waves of anxiety and fear pulsed through him. *I don't know if I can do this!*

Jed was hurting. He was tired, and he was out of ideas. All he had ever wanted was to find peace for his family, but all he ever found was disaster. No matter how many times he moved his family, it seemed that peace escaped them while heartbreak surrounded them.

He had just lost yet another son, a sweet boy who reminded him terribly of his Abigail. Jed was at his wits' end and didn't know what to do. He used to pride himself for taking his family under his wing and being in control. He had always thought he had the right plan, vision, and intentions. But it had all started to unravel around him.

Realizing that perhaps it had always been that way, but he had just been too blind to notice, he considered giving up for good. Jed looked to the sky. Tears began to flow and his throat tightened up as he yelled, "Oh, God! Why?"

There was no answer as he waited for a miraculous voice to tell him that everything would be fine. He wiped tears away with his sleeve, and with resignation, turned and walked on alone.

As Jed continued walking across town toward his rented home, he crossed a brick bridge and watched the water flowing swiftly and ferociously, energized by the spring snowmelt from the Appalachians. The water was clear and looked fresh and crisp as it bounced off the rocks below.

The war, his parents, his father's church, the family home, his friends back in Independence, his children—so many parts of life to consider. *So many decisions I have to make.*

"God, take these decisions from me!" he cried out loudly over the sound of the rushing river below. "Everything I try to do turns to despair, God! Don't let me destroy what family I have left with the decisions that I make."

Jed fell to his knees. He had never felt this alone at any time before in his life. He looked through the split rail fence on the bridge into the rushing water. He tried to clear his eyes of the tears that were partially blinding him. In the moving water below, he saw visions of Abigail, Willie, and Daniel. Behind them were Jed's mother and father, and in his mother's arms rested the baby, Abel. Each was looking at him with love that consumed his entire soul.

He shook his head, then looked again, but the vision was gone with only the rush of water remaining. Jed fell back against the side of the bridge and prayed.

"Oh God, give me the strength to know that my family is with you and that you are with me. Help me, oh God, to follow your path to the place you are preparing for my family and me. Let me find the peace I've been searching for in the place where you are sending me. Amen."

Jed slowly got up from the ground, looked again at the moving water, and whispered, "Thank you, Lord." He walked slowly off the bridge as he considered what had just occurred. He noticed that his spirits were lighter, and hope, which he had all but lost, had returned. He was excited to get to his rented home so that he could tell Lizzy and Johnny Russell that they were moving again, but this time only across town and into the old "Monroe House."

Crossing the street and heading for the town center, Jed thought about the town that he once knew and all the warmth he had felt from the town and its people. *Am I really home?*

Downtown, he was delighted to see that much had stayed as he remembered it. Shopkeepers congregated outside their stores, talking and debating about the current affairs of the country. The sight brought back fond memories, and his heart felt lighter at the idea that he just might have made the right decision by coming back. The thought grabbed him tight, and it felt true to him.

"Hey, Pastor!" shouted the local barber, wearing his obligatory white apron and cracking a wide smile. "Need a trim or a shave?"

Jed waved him off with a smile as he continued down the street to the center of town. He walked to the mercantile store and went in. He stopped at the entrance as he reminisced about the old Mercantile in Independence.

Thoughts of Fez, Pastor Higgin, Sara, Doctor Andersen, and the rest flowed through his head like gusts of wind coming off the south end of the Missouri River. Jed walked to the back of the mercantile store to the post office, to send a letter and retrieve any mail that might have been sent to him.

The young man behind the counter was pleasant and efficient. He was no more than fourteen, with dull razor marks across his jaw bones that indicated he had yet to develop a friendly relationship with his razor.

"How can I help you, Mr. . . . uh . . . ," the young man began as he looked at the return address on the letter that Jed was posting, ". . . Mr. Monroe. You have a package and these four letters here, but that's about all since you were here last week." He looked Jed up and down. "Is there anything you're a-waitin' on that I can be lookin' for?"

"No, I guess not," Jed said matter-of-factly. "But if you see a letter from Independence, could you flag me down?"

"Sure thing, Mr. Monroe, I . . . ," the young man said as he hesitated. "Come to think of it, there is a letter that I noticed two days ago with a return address of Independence, Missouri, but I couldn't make out who it was addressed to."

Jed perked up and said, "May I see the letter?"

"Surely, Mr. Monroe, and if it's for you, well . . . then my job is done!" the clerk said hopefully. "You can't believe how many letters come in here that we can't tell hide nor hair who to send them to. It's maddening, I tell you, and there's so many people who are waiting for letters each day, and they're just sitting here—right here, rotting in this here wooden crate and all, and I just can see how hard it would be for the writer to just write and wait, not knowing if the letter got to its final destination, and what seems even worse is that so many of the letters—"

"Can I please see the letter!?" Jed asked abruptly, his head spinning from the clerk's rambling.

The clerk found the letter and handed it to Jed. Jed looked at the envelope and immediately recognized the handwriting. "Yes, this is what I've been waiting for. Do you need me to sign anything?"

"Nah . . . again, I'm just tickled pink that I don't have to investigate to find where the letter goes to," the young man said.

Jed tucked his letters into his pocket, and the package under his arm, and walked out the front door. He wasn't ready to go home quite yet, because he really wanted to be alone a while longer. He figured that Lizzy and Johnny Russell were home, and that supper would be ready soon, but there was still time to spare.

He was still euphoric from what had happened at the bridge and that he considered a vision from heaven. He was certain that he had seen his loving family, and they were telling him that he was not alone, that they would always be with him.

Jed walked another block to an open park and sat down on a corner bench. He looked at the envelope and carefully tore it open. As he pulled the letter from the envelope, he marveled at its length. Fez had never written anything longer than a page or two in his life, and Jed was curious. *Fez surely must have something he needs to get off his chest.*

Jed read the first page and understood immediately why the letter was so long.

His right index finger tapped relentlessly as he tried his best to hold down the pages and keep them from falling from his hands. As he read on, his heart sank once again.

Chapter Thirty-One

News of Sorrow and Hope
1863

Staring in disbelief at the open letter in his hands, Jed was reminded of an evening in 1838, that fateful night so long ago when he learned that his parents had been murdered. The impact on his psyche was as awful this time as it had been then. His father-in-law, usually short on words but long on meaning, was this time long on both. Jed clinched his right hand in his left as he tried to stop his twitching finger and settle his nerves.

Fez wrote that the fever had come quickly and decimated the entire town within weeks.

Jed looked up from the letter for a moment as he caught his breath. He noticed two squirrels scampering from limb to limb, chasing each other as they played. *Such freedom from worry and stress,* Jed thought as he watched the little animals. *If I could just have one ounce of it, just for a minute, I would be downright grateful.*

He shook his head in disbelief as he resumed reading. He skimmed the first part of the letter, and the names blurred and pulsed and then seemingly jumped off the page like bizarre textual phantasms trying to get closer as they screamed at him: Patricia Stevens, Rachael Simpson, Joshua Simpson.

He turned the page. The letter slipped from his hands and onto his lap before floating to the ground. His body tensed and he choked convulsively as he started to cry: Pastor and Sara Higgin. While Jed was quickly catapulting into a state of utter despair and anguish, his imagination suddenly wrestled the wheel away from harsh reality and mercifully drove Jed into the comfort of fond memories. He sat motionless as he recalled all the wonderful times he had spent with his dear friends.

After some time, Jed picked the letter up from the ground and continued reading. The sun was beginning to set, and a cool evening breeze was chilling Jed's neck. He tugged up on the collar of his jacket, turning his body to get the last bit of sun to shine on his father-in-law's letter.

Fez believed that a family returning from the Oregon Trail brought yellow fever into the area. It went first for the Simpsons—their son Joshua died before the rest. Soon Rachael Simpson and Patricia Stevens had also succumbed to the fever.

Jed read faster, trying to learn more about the Higgins. Fez gave example after example of the whole town coming together in support and prayer. He indicated that Doc Andersen had worked day and night and saved as many as he could, but before it was over the town lost more than twenty-five souls.

Jed finally found more from Fez about the Higgins. They came down with the fever and were quarantined in the church for three weeks. Each day they battled the fever, the congregation outside grew larger. Prayer groups lined the front of the church both day and night, and in the end, both Sara and the Pastor survived.

Jed looked at the setting sun, took a deep cleansing breath of fresh air, and prayed. "Oh, dear God, thank you!" he exclaimed, not caring whether anyone heard him.

His most vivid memory of the Simpsons was of the time they offered their little cabin to Abigail and him, and with a smile he recalled Joshua's kindness in caring for Jed's horse in the cold blizzard of that wonderful night. His smile flattened as he realized once again how tragic it was to lose a child.

Patricia Stevens had always been kind to Jed, more times than he could count as he sifted through his memories. Many talks with his friends wouldn't have happened except for the peaceful and comfortable porch outside her diner.

Yes, they will all be sorely missed. Thank you, dear Lord, for sparing the Pastor and Sara—I don't know what I'd do if they were gone, too. Jed's sense of relief that his closest friends were all right was tempered by his sadness at the loss of the others.

His reading became more difficult as the sunlight faded. He struggled through the letter until he noticed another name.

Micah?

Jed squinted and tried to refocus his eyes, but the sun was gone. He grabbed his belongings and raced the five blocks to his home, hoping for news of his son. He hopped the steps of the front porch, opened the door, and quickly lit the lamp on the reading table.

The house was empty and dark except for Jed's thoughts and the lamplight. *Lizzy and Johnny Russell must still be at the McKeevers'.* He sat on his rocking chair, pulled the lamp close, and continued to read.

Fez's words were startling but reassuring. Jed learned that Micah had been writing to Fez the past few years and keeping him up-to-date with the happenings of the Army of the Confederacy.

I wonder why Fez never told me? He must have thought I already knew. But I could swear that I told Fez I hadn't heard from Micah. Then why . . . ? He frowned, confused, then shook his head and continued to read.

Fez wrote that Micah had been injured slightly during the Second Battle of Bull Run.

Jed looked at the jittery flame from the lamp, imagining how lonely his son must have been. *If I just hadn't . . .*

Returning to the letter, Jed's brow frowned more deeply. Fez wrote that the first of Micah's wounds was nothing compared with the injury he sustained at the Battle of Fredericksburg.

Fredericksburg? He was there?

Jed slowly put the letter down on the reading table. He looked beyond the flickering light of the lamp into the darkness. *Was he on the other side of that rock wall?* Jed shook his head in disbelief. *Oh God, I wonder if he knows about Daniel?*

He frantically grabbed the letter from the table and continued reading, hoping that Fez would have answers to the thousands of questions circling in his mind. The whoosh of Jed's breathing was deafening to his ears, and though the temperature in the house was comfortable, a chill was spreading through him.

On the fifth page, Fez wrote that he didn't think Micah knew about Daniel's fate. He said that in Micah's recent letters, he had been asking about the family more, and especially about Daniel.

Why couldn't he have written to me instead of his grandpa? Jed thought, beating himself up as he concluded that his own actions were the cause. *It's because you threw him out!*

Jed read more about what happened during the Fredericksburg battle. Toward the end, while pulling his men back, a Minié ball hit and penetrated the left side of Micah's chest, throwing him back against the hot barrel of a cannon.

Jed shook his head, angry at himself for allowing Micah to leave. *If I'd made more of a stance, he would've . . . no, he wouldn't have.* Jed forced himself to continue reading and learned that Micah lost the senses of hearing and touch after colliding with the cannon. A group of corpsmen had pulled him from the battlefield, placed him on a stretcher, and then onto the back of a wagon. That was the last that Micah remembered before waking in an army medical tent.

Micah wrote to Fez that the next thing he remembered was waking up in a tent, which he described in hellish detail. The putrid odors of sweat and rotten meat; the swarming of flies on his lips, nose, and eyelids; the condition of the other soldiers in the tent with their bulging eyes staring into open space, surrounded by their filthy bloody sheets; and pools of bodily waste everywhere.

Yet, he explained, the sights weren't as bad as the sounds. Despite a ruptured eardrum, he could hear the excruciating screams and the sound of sawing. He heard the deafening cries of men as they begged for death to take them away from all the pain. Micah had been forced to hum himself to sleep, with pillows stuffed over his ears to block out the grisly nights.

His memories of the battle and his wounds were a fuzzy memory. He didn't realize how long he'd been laid up until someone informed him that it had been more than four months since he had been carried off the hillside.

Micah had been recovering in a hospital tent for most of that time with help from a plantation owner's wife and the plantation's slaves. The plantation owner was a prominent member of the Fredericksburg Council and serving under Robert E. Lee. He also had fought in the Battle of Fredericksburg, but Micah didn't know where he was or even if he was alive.

Fez wrote that Micah's demeanor seemed to have changed, and was no longer the antagonistic and obstinate boy from years before. Fez wasn't sure how it happened, but he believed that Micah had fundamentally changed.

Jed contemplated the conclusion his father-in-law had reached. He couldn't remember the last time that he and Micah had argued, or even what about—it was just so long ago, a chasm too wide to repair. The two had always fought, he remembered that much, and cursed himself for never having put a stop to it. *What happened to my vow of unconditional love from father to son? What if Micah's lying on a bed somewhere in need of his family, in need of love from his father?*

Haunted by these thoughts, Jed prayed to God to give him the wisdom and courage he would need to find his son. Though the pragmatic part of his mind was convinced that he would never be able to repair the rift between them, and was unlikely to even find his son, the part that had faith and believed in miracles harbored the hope not only that he would find his son, but also that their relationship could be resurrected. He needed to bring him home.

Jed glanced at the lamp in response to its flickering light. *Need to add oil soon.* There was still enough to finish the letter—just. Jed moved the letter closer to the waning light and continued.

Fez went on to write that Micah had begun to question the merits of the Confederacy and the prudence of fighting for a cause he had begun to mistrust. He said that he missed Independence, his family, and—his father.

Why couldn't he tell me himself? Jed wrestled with the anger and pain competing for purchase in his mind. Have I pushed him so far away that he'll never return?

A picture of Abigail flashed in Jed's mind, and she was not interested in his anger and self-righteousness about Micah's shortcomings. He heard her say, "But he's your son, Jed, and that trumps everything else. You vowed to be a father—so be a father, not an angry victim. Stop judging our children by how closely they meet your expectations, and instead meet them where they *are*. Otherwise, you'll continue to lose them, and it won't matter anymore whether they're dead or alive. I love you—be strong."

I'm so sorry, Abigail. I promised to keep our family together, and I've failed you. Jed sighed at his overspoken and rarely acted-upon words: I promise. He shook his head slowly, disgusted with himself for continually failing to deliver on his promises.

He remembered the vision at the bridge and the love he had felt from those in his family whom he had lost. Warmth and hope filled his mind. He sat, holding the letter and thinking of Abigail, as he vowed to build a new life in Wheeling. *God willing, I will bring Micah back to help with the rebuilding.*

First he would have to find Micah and learn the extent of his injuries. He knew it would be difficult since he was now in Union territory. The western counties of Virginia had recently voted to secede from the eastern ones. Wheeling was now part of the new state of West Virginia and very loyal to the United States. To get information regarding a Confederate soldier would be difficult and risky. *But I will do it, by God, I will do it.*

The remainder of Fez's letter was about his health and his handing over of the Mercantile to a young family that had settled in Independence a few months back. He assured Jed that he was taking good care of Abigail's, Willie's, and Abel's gravesites and still visiting them each day.

The light from the now-empty lamp went out just as Jed finished reading the letter. He looked into the darkness of the room and thought of the little wooden bench that Fez had built for Abel. It now sat in front of three gravesites and allowed visitors a welcome area for reflection. He envisioned Fez sitting on the bench he built, holding flowers in hand, and gazing at his daughter and grandsons. *Oh God, do I miss her,* Jed thought, suddenly realizing something that again made him shake his head slowly as his eyes watered. *I can't believe it's been ten years.*

Jed's meditation was broken by sounds of heavy footsteps on the porch stairs. The front door flung open, and young Johnny Russell rushed in and ran right to Jed.

Jed took his youngest child in his arms and hugged him tight. He could see Lizzy and Martin standing just inside the doorway. "Why is it so dark in here, Papa?" Lizzy asked, bewildered.

"Oh, it's . . . uh . . . it's nothing . . . just reading a letter from your grandpa," Jed replied. "Let's get some light in here, and I'll tell you all about it."

After they filled the lamp with oil and started a fire, the four of them sat in the living room while Jed described the contents of the letter. Lizzy's reaction to the tragedy in Independence matched how Jed had felt about it, but her reaction to news of Micah's status was far more emotional than Jed had expected.

"I'm happy that he's all right, Papa, don't get me wrong," she said, putting her hands up in defense, "but I've seen a lot this past year. I have a problem with the South and how they treat the Negro, and that goes for my brother as well."

"Your grandpa seems to think that Micah has changed, and I'm going to give him the benefit of the doubt," Jed replied. "Plus, Lizzy, he's my son and your brother. I've vowed to bring this family back together again, and we're going to start fresh right here in Wheeling."

The room was silent with building tension. The only sound came from the other room, where Johnny Russell searched through the kitchen cupboards for something that resembled dinner.

"Lizzy, I need you to help me make us a family again," Jed said quietly. "This horrible war will be over soon, and everyone will need to heal. That includes us."

Jed thought back to his vision on the bridge and said, "The rest of our family depends on us becoming whole again, and I can't do it alone."

Jed watched his daughter intently under the bright lamplight. Her face softened, and Jed noticed that Martin was holding her hands to give her support.

"We are still going to help the Negro, Papa!" Lizzy declared. "But . . . but I will oblige your wishes and help you anyway I can, all right?" Lizzy's affirmation was shallow but a start, and Jed stood up and gave her a loving embrace.

"I know how much this has hurt you, Papa," Lizzy continued.

Jed looked at his daughter and she looked right back under the bright lamplight, paging through his thoughts and emotions as only one other woman had ever been able to do. "This difficulty with Micah is what causes you the most pain, isn't it?"

"I let him go, Lizzy," Jed answered with his head lowered. "I will always carry the guilt that I failed as his father, and by doing so I failed your momma too. She lived her entire life, short as it was, for this family. She never asked for much, only that I keep us all together, and what did I do?"

"Where is he, Papa?" she asked.

"I don't know, except that he's still recovering from his wounds in some hospital tent in Virginia," Jed answered. "I was hoping that your organization could get some information for me somehow. If I knew where he was, I would bring him back here and nurse him myself."

"Absolutely not! We will help you find him. And Papa—you can't go into enemy territory to find him. I won't stand for it!"

Jed smiled as he looked lovingly at his daughter. He was filled with pride listening to his daughter argue against the idea of going into Virginia. He was reminded of Abigail once again.

"You sound just like your momma, you know that?" he said joyfully.

"Hey, everyone!" Johnny Russell yelled from the kitchen. "I'm starved!"

Johnny Russell's cry for help was met by good-natured laughter, and the dark cloud that had surrounded them was lifted. Lizzy and Martin proceeded to the kitchen to rustle up some dinner.

Jed was the last to leave the living room as he once again contemplated the vision at the bridge and the family he had vowed to save.

Yes, we will be a family again—and Abigail, this is one promise that I will keep!

Chapter Thirty-Two

Micah's Transformation
1863

"Hey there Mista Micah sir, you be movin' around quite nicely these days." The voice was familiar to Micah after hearing it for the past seven months. Agatha was a house slave at the Applebee Plantation run by Colonel Justin Applebee.

Since the middle of 1862 it had been used as a field hospital, accommodating the needs of soldiers who needed more time to heal from the wounds of battle. Each room, once filled with fine china, crystal glassware, and expensive furniture, was now a sea of dirty cots upon which lay the deathly sick and critically wounded. The smell of stale air and urine filled the confines of each living quarter and despair was reflected on the faces of both the caregivers and those they cared for. The critical cases were kept inside, while those whose recoveries were more certain were hospitalized in tents on the great lawn in front. Micah had been one of the unfortunate residents occupying a critical care room until just a few weeks earlier. Now his dwelling was a tent that he shared with a boy barely old enough to shave, but old enough to have his left hand shot off in a battle not far away and not far enough in the past.

Micah was considered a mortal case when first delivered to Applebee Plantation. A bullet was lodged behind his right shoulder blade. After two surgeries, the doctors were able to extract the bullet, but the infection spread and took its toll. Micah had been in and out of consciousness for months, and for the entire time, Agatha kept watch over him.

Barely beyond her teens, Agatha was tall, thin, and lightly colored compared with the other slave women in the house. As a young child, Agatha had been fortunate to find favor with Mrs. Applebee. Most of the young slave women were sent into the fields along with the men, but Agatha had always worked in the big house for Mrs. Applebee.

Not long after the plantation's overseer, Hansen Withers, brought Agatha home from the Fredericksburg slave auction, Mrs. Applebee took her under her wing. The Applebees seldom agreed on the treatment of their slaves, but when it came to Agatha, Mrs. Applebee would have her way despite scowls from Withers.

Typically, younger slaves, being stronger, were needed in the field, while older slaves, being older and more acquainted with the workings of the plantation, were used in the main house for housekeeping chores. Mrs. Applebee made an exception in Agatha's case, and no one objected, or at least not enough to be noticed. Agatha was always by her mistress's side, even while she mended the menfolk of a war about which Mrs. Applebee herself was now having some misgivings. She had not seen or heard from her husband in more than a year, and the only thing that brought her comfort was helping the wounded, each one of them.

Mrs. Applebee had noticed that Agatha took an interest in Micah as soon as he arrived. She was far too busy to be concerned about it and was pleased that Agatha could bring some good to such a horrific situation. Agatha was never far from Micah's side, even if it meant the possibility of disappointing her mistress or upsetting Withers. One she didn't worry about, and the other she always stayed clear of.

"You ever hear back from your granddaddy, the one you's written that letter to when you first could sit up?" Agatha asked. "I's remember when you's first come to, and you's was mumblin' all sorts of crazy about your granddaddy, your papa, your momma, especially about your brother Daniel."

"Nah, I haven't heard a word," replied Micah. "But then again, none of them would have a clue where to send a letter. In fact, not even I know exactly where I am."

"Masta Withers came by, and I heard him saying of another fight up North ways. I couldn't hear much, but I did hear sometin' about that the colonel headin' one of the parts of the army in a big fight near a town calls 'Gettesburg' or sometin' like it. He spoke like if we win that battle, then this here war would be over."

Micah sat down on a bench next to Agatha and watched her fold linen taken from clotheslines hanging between two dogwoods. He looked at her, and was bewildered that this woman would have a positive interest in the South winning the war.

He looked around the grounds of the plantation, and at the fields in the distance filled with acres and acres of tobacco. Field slaves were spread out among rows and rows of the wide-leafed plants, chopping, pulling, and stacking the sticky leaves onto rickety wagons. When wagons were filled, other field slaves pulled them into one of three large barns for processing and shipping. He looked at the beautiful dogwoods that surrounded the large white house, its marble pillars standing majestically tall while upholding the second floor.

"Agatha?" Micah asked, "why do you do it?"

"Do what, Mista Micah?"

"You're a slave, and you treat me like you actually care for me. I don't understand why you—well, any of you—wouldn't rather take a hay pick and stick me dead while I sleep."

"We be Christians, Mista Micah, and some day we be in paradise together," Agatha proclaimed.

"If this is what the great Lord has us doin' until then, well then, we just do the best we can, and we just keep lovin'."

"I'm fighting to keep you a slave—you understand that, right?" Micah said firmly.

"Yessir, but we all be children of God, Mista Micah. And that be includin' you too," Agatha replied without looking Micah in the eyes.

Micah's mouth was agape, but no words would come out. While he watched Agatha fold linen and heard her soft humming, a feeling came over him that he'd never had before.

"You know, Agatha, I was taught as a young boy about God. Mostly from my mother, but when my father became a pastor, I fought him on every idea and way of life that he tried to teach me."

Micah lowered his head in thought while Agatha looked his way. "I remember my momma always told me dat it be never too late to ask Jesus in our hearts. It was a long time ago, and I was just a young 'un, but I's still remember her voice. You knows, Mista Micah, that means it's never too late for you, too, no's matters what you's done or who's you done hurt."

Micah slowly shook his head as he tried to decipher what was happening inside him. The ideals of the Confederate cause and the fight to keep slavery alive were no longer that important. In the abstract such ideas had always seemed easy to defend, but he was beginning to realize that only in the abstract could one argue that one group of human beings, against their will, somehow deserved lives of slavery and shackles. He realized that he was fighting to keep people like Agatha chained and in bondage, and that realization made him uneasy.

He pushed himself up off the bench and looked at Agatha again. She had gone back to humming something soft and soothing. The sound, mixed with the sweet scent of dogwood flowers in full bloom, brought him peace.

So many questions stirred within Micah, and he was confused. He started walking slowly down a path that was lined on both sides with bright-colored flowers. The path circled around to the front of the house, and Micah felt small next to the towering effect of the house as it glistened against the bright blue sky. He had much to think about, and some of what Agatha had said hit a fragile nerve. Micah, still weak from his wound, slowly made his way to his favorite sitting spot, which was a wide fallen log that had partially decayed over the years. He sat at its center and looked out over acres of tobacco fields.

Micah had just regained his breath when he spotted a soldier slowly riding in on a tired-looking mare. The soldier looked to be a lieutenant or courier of some sort, but Micah couldn't discern which because his uniform was torn. One boot was missing a heel while the other had the toe torn off, exposing a bare foot. *Boy, we are one sorry-looking army if I do say so myself,* Micah thought, and then wondered why he was still even a part of it.

The soldier nodded to Micah as he steered his horse toward the front of the big house. He twisted and hopped off like he'd done it thousands of times, and he probably had. Micah could relate, though he didn't miss the endless marching and riding.

The soldier walked up the marble steps to the front door of the house with difficulty. Micah wondered if he'd been injured or was just stiff from all the riding. He had a handful of papers under one arm and his hat under the other, which made it difficult for him to knock on the door. Micah thought about getting up to assist the man, but by the time he had decided he was too weak to be of any help, the man had entered and slammed the door behind him. Micah shook his head in disgust at what the army—his army—had come to, *and for what?*

Micah felt the need to rest and process what he and Agatha had talked about. He looked again at the front of the house, and noticed that the soldier had dropped several pages of whatever he had been holding. The pages began to levitate as they were caught in the warm afternoon breeze. Looking one more time across the fields of tobacco, Micah forced himself up from his log and walked to the front of the house where the papers had blown. He bent over gingerly to pick up some wrinkled papers. As he tried to put them back into some semblance of order before locating the soldier, he noticed the header on one of the forms: CASUALTY LIST--FREDERICKSBURG 1862 Micah's brows furrowed, and for the second time that day, he became quite ill.

Curiosity got the best of him. Rather than notifying the soldier, he decided he would wait outside until he reappeared. He sat on the marble steps and thumbed through the pages. Vivid memories of that horrific day, and the horrible stench of death, came alive as jerky images in his head. He looked at the pages briefly and realized that the casualties listed were just a portion of the total dead. He held only four pages, while knowing for a fact that thousands had died that day.

More memories of the battle assaulted him—the sickening thought of the hill caused him to hyperventilate, and an eerie chill crept over him. He put the stack of papers aside for a moment. He felt the breeze blowing and focused on the dogwoods to regain his senses. He saw Agatha on the far side of the house, and his sense of comfort returned. He shook his head slowly and let out a long breath, still not understanding what was happening to him. *What is she doing to me?*

He picked up the pile of papers again, aware that the soldier would reappear at any time. He glanced down and carefully skimmed the names of the dead, anxiously watching the door with his peripheral vision as he did so. He had the middle letters of the alphabet in his hand: KUGER, LANGSDON, LONGMOUTH, LEWIS, LUMPLY, MADISON, MARSDEN. He hesitated, thinking he might not be able to continue reading. "My God," he whispered, "so many": MILLER, MILTON, MONROE, NELSON, OSTERMAN, OTTERFIELD, OSTEEN—

Micah froze.

He stared out and focused on Agatha, still folding linen. A sharp feeling of despair overcame him, and he dreaded looking at the papers again. What he had read sent shivers down his spine.

That's impossible, it couldn't be . . . no, it can't be so . . . His mouth was dry and felt like cotton. He put his head between his legs and nearly passed out.

Once his anxiety had subsided a bit, Micah once again picked up the stack of papers, and looked carefully for the one name that moments ago had passed by just like all the others. He found it, then closely studied the full name: DANIEL MONROE, CAPTAIN, 2ND BATTALION INFANTRY, 3RD DIVISION.

The front door jolted open as the soldier reappeared. He stumbled down the steps, awkwardly mounted his horse, and left without a glance or a word to Micah.

Micah still sat on the top step, frozen in time. He had unknowingly dropped the stack of papers—they were scattered on the porch and tossing about in the breeze. He held on to one sheet with shaking hands—the one with his brother's name on it.

He thought of that day, the battle, and his rage—he had felt cold and hollow inside, just as he did now. *Was I the one . . . oh, dear God . . . did I kill my own brother?*

The thought made him panic and he scanned the grounds for Agatha while tears filled his eyes. He spotted her on the other side of the yard, and began to haltingly and uncertainly traverse the yard in her direction. He made it only halfway before falling to his knees. He put his head to his ground and began to cry.

Agatha looked up from her work and saw Micah just as she heard him crying out to her. She ran to him, knelt down, and cradled him to her bosom. All restraint abandoned him as he cried uncontrollably. Micah cried not just over the loss of his brother, but also for all the harm and pain he'd brought to his family.

She held him tight, rocking him gently, not understanding but not needing to. As she held him, she softly hummed a ballad from her youth. Memories of her momma holding her and giving her comfort filled her heart while she prayed to God that His Spirit would fill the man she was holding.

He surrendered himself, allowing her to calm him just as his mother had done so many years before. It didn't matter the color of her skin or what side of the war he was supposed to be on. Her reassuring embrace and the memory of his mother transformed Micah, and his outlook on such things became forever changed.

Agatha held him as she continued to hum the same soothing song that had always brought her the peace she felt in her heart. She prayed for Micah and asked God to come into his heart and cleanse him of all his guilt and pain. She too cried, but her tears were shed for him, this man whom she had nursed back from death over the past seven months.

When Micah became calm enough to speak, he told Agatha about happening upon the stack of papers and by chance seeing his brother's name on the casualty list.

"That weren't no act of chance, Mista Micah. That be God and he be talkin' to you. He wants you to believes in Him, to trust Him, and to shed all of yo's guilt and pain."

Micah sat with his head down as Agatha continued holding him. It was soothing to him, a feeling that he desperately missed. The words she spoke between hymns began to sink in and make sense to him.

"Agatha, I'm done with this war," Micah said solemnly. "I'm through with any more fighting, and I'm through causing so much heartache to people who love me."

Agatha gently released Micah from her embrace. They sat back on the grass, and Micah wiped his eyes and nose with his sleeve. Filtered rays of light from the setting sun made their way through the trees and then danced on the plantation grounds surrounding them.

Micah leaned on his elbow and looked at Agatha. "I need to go home, Agatha. I need to show them all that I'm finished causing so much pain to so many people."

"Let God leads ya, Mista Micah," Agatha said softly.

Micah slowly shook his head again. "But it's probably too late, Agatha. They're never going to accept me back after what I've done to them over all these years."

"Let God be the answer to dat, Mista Micah—follow Him and His will make it all happen for yous."

"I don't even know where to start. I haven't a clue as to where my family lives these days. We've had ties in Wheeling, Independence, Lecompton, and Fredericksburg, but I have no idea where to find them now."

Micah realized from the look on Agatha's face that none of the places he had just mentioned meant anything to her. He was a bit disappointed in himself for not having more compassion for all the people who only knew the plantation on which they lived. For them, the rest of the world didn't exist. He made a special vow to himself that he would do all he could to change that.

The first thing he needed to do was to work harder than ever to regain his strength so that he could travel. Once he was strong enough, he would find his family and then find a way to help Agatha and all of her kind. *All of her kind*—realizing that he sounded as if he were talking about a foreign species, he felt terribly ashamed.

Micah felt a new sense of purpose in life. There was a powerful presence running through him and pulling him to do what was right and reconcile for all that was wrong. He knew in time that he would have to forgive himself for all the wrong he had done and for harming those who had been affected by his actions.

The question was how to do that. As he pondered this, a revelation came to him. He knew he couldn't make amends with Willie or Daniel, and not even with his mother, but if he could just get closer to the God that Agatha lived by, the one his father preached about, maybe, just maybe, he had a chance.

He thought of his sister and little brother. He tried to picture Johnny Russell's face and his curly hair and big blue eyes. He wondered if Lizzy had gotten married or if his father was holding her at bay until she was an old maid. Micah grinned and chuckled at the thought of his father telling Lizzy that she couldn't get married. *Oh boy, that's something I'd love to see.*

Micah thought about what he should do and how to accomplish it. He was the oldest Monroe child now, and he was facing an uphill battle if he hoped to win back the love of each member of his family—he fully understood that.

"You know, Agatha?" Micah said when he finally spoke again. "I always thought I had it all figured out. I mean, from a very early age I thought I knew better than anyone—my mother, my father, definitely more than any of my brothers or my sister. I always just did my own thing and never felt like I needed to rely on anyone. Oh, they tried . . . yes they tried . . . and each time I'd shut them out. I lost my chance to really get to know my older brother before he was killed—I was always too busy bickering with Daniel to ever have the time to try to understand him . . . I mean, always . . . my own brother."

Micah stared out at the tobacco fields and then tried to continue, but the thought of Daniel choked him up. "Agatha, oh, dear God, if I had anything to do with Daniel's death, I would . . . I mean . . . I don't know how I would ever . . ."

"Mista Micah, don't punish you self for what's you's don't knows. Even so, it's always in God's hands, and it was God's plan for your brother to go. The more you's get to know the Lord, you will see what I is talkin' about."

"Yea, you're right, Agatha, and I know that by getting myself home and back with my family, I can learn all about God from my father, and then I'll make him proud of me again."

"If he be your papa, then he be already proud of you, Mista Micah. Dat something dat never changes," Agatha said confidently.

Micah considered her words, wondering if what she said was right. The mere idea that his father still loved him made him even more anxious to get well and get home.

"What about you, Agatha?" Micah asked. "We don't know how this war will end, but if the South wins, you'll be a slave the rest of your life."

"That's all I's know, so if it's to be, then it's in the good Lord's hands."

"I can't accept that, not after all that you've done for me. There has to be a way to get you free," Micah declared.

"I did hear of a railroad that takes some folks to be free, but I ain't never seen no train around these parts," Agatha said, shyly looking over her shoulder for fear of being overheard.

"Yes, I know what you're talking about, Agatha," Micah confirmed. "It's happening throughout the country. Folks will come and help you escape, hiding you through different passageways by train, boat, wagon, or all of them. They help folks like you, Agatha. It could very well be the answer we're looking for to get you your freedom."

"Freedom." Agatha thought about what that meant. In many ways it frightened her. "I done nothin' but this my whole life, Mista Micah," Agatha replied softly. "I be scared to do sompin' different."

"I could find someone to help you learn how to be free and teach you reading and writing," Micah reassured her. "I know you could do it, Agatha! Plus, as you said yourself, God will lead you and protect you all the way down the road to your 'freedom paradise,' so you'll have nothing to worry about."

Agatha was now the one looking out at the tobacco fields. Her eyes filled with tears as she nervously straightened her apron and attempted to clear her throat. "I thinks I like that, Mista Micah, I thinks I would really like that."

"Okay, then, it's settled," Micah declared. "Once I get stronger, I'll make my way back home and find a way to get you the help you need to bring you to me. Once we're together again, I'll do all I can to help you become a free woman, all right?"

Agatha thought about what it would be like to be free, to walk where she wanted, do what she wanted, and serve no one unless she chose to do so.

Meanwhile, Micah's thoughts were of home, Lizzy, Johnny Russell, and his father. He had always known about God, but not until this slave woman opened his eyes did he truly see who *He* was. This new light in his life was brighter than ever before, and his hope for a new beginning was a solid road lying before him. He was determined to make things right with his family and show them how much love he had for them. *If they'd have me back*—that was the constant demon that continued to dwell in his thoughts, ready to dash his hopes whenever he became optimistic or his confidence was on the rise.

Micah and Agatha were just getting up from the grass when a rider came down the roadway at full gallop, creating a gale of dust and choking anyone nearby. Micah looked on with stern curiosity as the rider made haste as he handed off the reins to a small slave boy and then hurried inside the house.

A loud scream was followed by blood-curdling cries; their source was Mrs. Applebee. Micah looked at Agatha with a stare that asked if she knew the reason for Mrs. Applebee's anguish. Neither had any idea, but her cries and sobbing continued, growing louder and more violent.

The rider reappeared on the porch and proceeded to his horse, but not before Micah intercepted him. "What news do you bring, soldier?" Micah asked.

"Gettysburg was a disaster, Lieutenant!" the young soldier announced with a panicked look on his face. "I hear Lee is turning back with his white horse Traveler's tail right between his legs . . . Sir . . . now please, if I may, I must proceed to my next hospital."

"But what of Colonel Applebee and the rest of the Army of Northern Virginia, Sir?" Micah asked as the rider mounted his horse.

"Sir, if I were you, I'd give up on this so-called 'cause of the South'. After the devastation of the army in Gettysburg, there won't be any Army of Northern Virginia much longer and besides, if you ask me . . . this whole war is lost!"

The soldier grabbed the reins and turned one last time to Micah. "It's just a matter of time, sir."

The rider paused a second to catch his breath and lowered his voice. "As far as the colonel—well sir, he died charging up a hill on the very last day of the battle."

As the rider turned, he gave Micah a forced salute before pulling up on the reins of his horse. He turned the horse with a harsh yank left, then yelled back to Micah one last time as the horse started to trot. "It's time for all of us to go home, Sir! And if I may suggest, you'd better do so right quickly!"

Micah looked at Agatha. His lips drew tight and his eyes narrowed. Without saying a word, they knew what they needed to do—and that their time was running out.

Chapter Thirty-Three

Hope for Peace
1865

Spring had arrived in Wheeling. Flowers and dogwoods blossomed along the Ohio River where it flowed freely near the outskirts of town. Cardinals flew carelessly along the slopes and nestled in the trees, enjoying the much-awaited sunshine of the new season. Not far from the river's crest, Jed walked along the well-worn path used by many of the townsfolk. Rhododendrons lined the trail with their vibrant purple flowers, and the sound of rushing water cascading over slippery rocks made it the perfect spot for him to clear his mind.

Jed had acquired the habit of going to the river every morning to walk and think. During the past several years, his hair had turned mostly gray, his hairline had receded more than he would admit, and the wrinkles in his face bore the turmoil of enduring years of war and family tragedy. He would be turning fifty the following year, but already felt twice that age. Weighing most heavily on his mind, though, was Micah and his uncertain whereabouts, and he longed for the day when he could tell him just how much he missed him.

While he counted his blessings daily—twenty-one-year-old Lizzy and twelve-year-old Johnny Russell—he also counted his tremendous losses—Abigail and three sons. Micah was now twenty-three, but no one had heard from him since Fez had written that long letter in 1863.

Jed was worried. Though Micah had caused him more pain than all of his other children combined, over time Jed's concern about his son's welfare had eclipsed any anger or frustration he once harbored. But as more time had passed without any news of Micah's fate, Jed's hopes had faded.

Jed often sat on a boulder located off the main trail that allowed him to be completely alone. This was "his place," and he sat on the boulder every morning before starting his day. Just to think . . . and to openly pray, since other people rarely walked by—today was no different.

"Oh, Dear God, I thank you for this day," he prayed out loud over the sound of the rushing river. "I thank you for all that you are and all that you offer me, Lord."

Jed paused as he usually did after thanking God for all that He had given him. He battled with the concept regularly. He had argued and fought with God many times about what God had taken from him, but knew better than to push the issue and believed that everything was in God's hands.

"I ask you today, Father, to help us with the rebuilding of our home and the remodeling of the church. Lord, the church needs so much work. It shows its wear and tear, and I ask you, Lord, to help us rebuild it to make it shine for Your glory."

He looked upward, peeking through branches and budding leaves and seeing the bright blue sky above. A warm calmness enveloped him as he continued. "My Dear God, I ask you to bless my Lizzy and my soon-to-be son-in-law."

Jed chuckled. Even though nothing had been announced nor had Martin asked for his permission, Jed could tell that it was just a matter of time. "And God, please bless my Johnny Russell. He is but twelve, and so much has gone on in his young life. Please help him sort it out and help him to make sense of it all, cause I sure can't Lord."

He choked up when he realized how much pain had come to him and his remaining family. He looked at the fast-moving river and watched the water crash against the boulders, which caused him to briefly lose his concentration. "Oh, and God, please Lord, I don't know where he is or if he is even alive, but God, could you show me some sign that Micah is either alive or with you?"

"There you are!" yelled Lizzy as she approached, bringing Jed out of his prayer. She was scurrying through the foliage of rhododendron and fern. "We've been looking all over for you, Papa!" Lizzy quickly caught her breath after making it to Jed's boulder.

"We have a bunch of people from the church, and they're all at the house ready to work. Papa, you got to come and see, it's amazing!" Lizzy's excited voice was full of intrigue.

Jed followed Lizzy back to the house, even though he felt that his prayer had been cut short. *I'll get back to you again tomorrow morning, Lord, if that's alright with you.*

Jed noticed that Lizzy was staring at him with concern in her eyes. "I'm fine!" he yelled.

"It's just that you always come out here to that same ol' rock, Papa!" Lizzy said.

"Yea, and it gives me a chance to clear my head and plan my day with the Lord—is that so bad?" Jed knew that his daughter had been worried about him for some time. The two spoke often about what had transpired in their family over the past fifteen years, and to Jed's delight, Lizzy had been very easy to talk with. She understood the impact it had had on her father.

"Papa," Lizzy said as they walked, "I just want to warn you that not only are the church folks at the house, but so are the mayor and Sheriff Hancock."

Jed thought of that bit of news for a moment. "I'm sure it's nothing, Lizzy," he said. "Those two, along with the entire city council, have been bugging me to join them to plan the celebration when the war is officially over."

"Do you really think it might happen, Papa?" Lizzy asked. "I mean, it makes perfect sense. Martin told me that the Underground Railroad has been shut down for months now, and not because of danger, but because those in charge don't feel there's a need anymore."

"Well that's one bit of good news." Jed stopped and turned to his daughter. "Lizzy, I've always supported the reasons for you and Martin to be involved in that operation, but I have to tell you that it eases my mind to know that you will no longer be putting yourselves in harm's way."

"Papa, we always knew you were with us all the way, even though you always acted neutral." Jed felt a nudge to his ribs and looked at Lizzy. She wore a big smile on her beautiful face, and they both laughed as they continued down the path.

They were a couple of blocks from the old Monroe house when Lizzy asked, "Papa, do you think we will ever see Micah again?"

Jed looked down, his heart throbbing in his chest as he continued walking. "I don't know, Daughter . . . but what I do know is that if God has it in His hands to happen, then it will." As they approached the house and before the crowd could get near, he stopped her, taking her shoulders in his hands as he said, "It would sure make this old man mighty happy though."

The crowd was enormous, and Jed couldn't believe that so many people would join together to assist him in rebuilding his family's old house and his father's church, but here they were. Most of the congregation was there, along with Chester Albright and his wife Madeline; Bill Hancock, who had been elected the new Sheriff of Wheeling just the previous November; and Mayor Homer Plunkett, the oversized bald man who spoke in a low baritone voice.

Martin and Johnny Russell were near the front porch talking with a woman whom Jed had never seen before. She was a slightly built woman with blond hair that was tied up with a ribbon. She wore a light blue bonnet and had an off-white shawl wrapped around her neck. She looked to Jed to be about ten years younger than he was, and he definitely would have remembered if he had seen her before. *It was the eyes, the deep blue eyes. Get that out of your mind, Jed,* he scolded himself.

He had always loved the ribbons Abigail wore. This woman's complexion was fair, unlike Abigail's, but it was her eyes that made Jed uneasy. He immediately refocused his thoughts on Abigail and away from the blue eyes and ribbons of the woman. Jed's reprieve was short-lived, however—while he was deep in thought, she and Martin had walked over, and were now standing directly in front of him.

"Jed, I'd like to introduce Marian Sutherland. She is Pastor Albright's niece from Ohio," Martin interjected into the awkward silence that the mystery woman had created.

"Uh . . . hello, I . . . I'm Jedidiah Monroe, and it's very nice to meet you, Miss Sutherland," Jed stammered.

"Please, Mr. Monroe, call me Marian. I feel like I know all about you from my Uncle Chester. He has told me so much about your family and how this church and house have been a cornerstone to this town for so many years. You must be pleased."

Jed could think of no words, so he just stood and gawked at this beautiful young woman until Lizzy came to the front porch and rescued him.

"Papa, do you remember Pastor Albright talking about his niece coming to live with him? Well . . ." Lizzy said, pausing to look first at her father and then at Marian, "well, here she is!" Out of the corner of his eye, Jed could see Lizzy flinging out her arms as she introduced Marian, but all of his attention was on the woman. He felt the temperature rise as a blanket of red crept up his neck and onto his cheeks. It had been many years since Jed had had such feelings, and at that moment they had completely overcome him, and we was bewildered. *It's not right . . . I'm still married . . . so knock it off.*

Pastor Albright approached the three of them as they stood under the ash tree in front of the house and immediately noticed the slight tension in the air. "Everything all right here?" he asked.

"Oh yes, Uncle Chester," answered Marian, "I was just being officially introduced to Jedidiah by his daughter. You didn't tell me the new pastor was such a handsome man, Uncle Chester. And it seems he also has attractive children who definitely get their looks from him."

Lizzy blushed and tried to correct Marian. "I still think I take after my momma, but everyone thinks that Johnny Russell over there takes after Papa."

Marian redirected her gaze to Johnny Russell, who was playing with the other young boys out in the street. "Well, you both are very handsome, and your father is very lucky to have such a beautiful family to come home to every night."

Lizzy excused herself, and Chester asked to speak to Jed in private. "Maybe we could talk again soon after we get everyone busy working, Marian?" Jed asked before walking away with his older colleague.

"Yes, Jedidiah, I would really enjoy that," Marian replied. "Uncle Chester keeps me locked up in his home and only lets me out on holidays and special occasions, so your invitation is most welcome."

The three laughed as Chester took Jed's elbow and directed him to the front room of the old Monroe house. He had something on his mind, and he looked concerned.

"You have a very beautiful niece, Chester," Jed remarked as they sat down in the living room. "Is she visiting with you for a while?"

"No, she's going to live with me permanently. She asked to work with me in the church, since her parents have been gone for many years. I always wanted to bring her here, but so many of the other relatives had to have their say in her business, so I was put on the family waiting list if you will." Chester looked out the window and watched Marian as she sat with Lizzy, drinking a cup of lemonade.

"I've told her all about the church, about your house, and forgive me, but also about you and your family. She asked about you the first time she was in town, and I felt like God was leading me to tell her all about you," Chester confessed.

"Now, Chester, remember, I'm a married man, and though Marian is a very beautiful woman, I need to be loyal to Abigail," Jed barked back in defiance.

"Jed, son, Abigail has been gone now for over twelve years," Chester said kindly. "She would want you to move on, son. If not for yourself, then by all means for your children. Lizzy has been taking on the mother role all that time, and by the looks of her and Martin, she won't be around much longer to mother you and Johnny Russell, you know."

Jed also looked out the window, first at Marian and then at Lizzy. "I don't know, Chester. I just don't know—it just doesn't seem fair."

"There are so many things that don't seem fair, Jed. Especially with the times we've all endured with the war and all." Chester turned to get Jed's full attention, which was becoming difficult with the distraction outside. "Jed, the war is going to be over in the next few weeks, I'm guessing, but nevertheless there is a lot of planning we need to do to prepare for when that happens."

There was a loud knock on the front door, forcing Chester to put his thoughts on hold. Jed opened the door and welcomed in Mayor Plunkett and Sheriff Hancock. "Come on in, gentlemen, we were just beginning to discuss some of the changes that inevitably will be affecting all of us real soon."

The four men moved to the dining table and sat down across from each other. "Can I offer you anything?" Jed asked.

They all declined, eager to get on with the conversation. Jed had heard many of their concerns before, but the looks on their faces indicated that the matter was becoming dire. He knew that even though Wheeling was on the far western border of the state, it still would experience considerable resentment from the other states after the Confederacy was dissolved.

Their state had been a part of Virginia and seceded along with it in 1861. But two years later they voted to leave Virginia and become their own state, and more importantly a Free State. Anger and retaliation from the war's losers could become fierce. The town council had discussed it several times and had set up a contingency plan that Jed believed was good.

"I heard there are talks going on as we speak at a small town called Appomattox Court House," Mayor Plunkett said.

"Let's pray that both sides come to terms and end this awful nightmare," added Chester.

"I wouldn't be so quick to say it will all end, gents," warned Sheriff Hancock. "Once Lee surrenders, all of those soldiers are going to go home. My guess is that most of them are going to be relieved to have the war over, but I'm also a-guessin' that there will still be a bunch of hotheads in these here parts for some time to come."

Jed listened carefully while thinking about Lizzy and Johnny Russell's safety and welfare. Discussion of the war's possible end brought back thoughts of Daniel and Micah. One was never coming home, and the other, well . . .

It would take years for the country to mend from the damage of the previous four years, but Jed wasn't thinking about the country, but rather his family, his friends, and now his refound hometown.

"Pastor Monroe?" Mayor Plunkett asked.

"Please call me Jed."

"Okay, Jed, and since we're all going to be tighter than a family on these town issues, please call me Homer."

"I would like to finish up on the work at your place of worship as soon as possible," Plunkett said. "I want a place in Wheeling where everyone can feel at ease and gather in peace."

Jed gave the others a look of agreement while being silently elated. "What all needs to be done to get your father's church back into tip-top shape in order to have it opened up for everyone in town?" Plunkett asked.

The four discussed what needed to be done and drew up a timeline for the completion of the remodeled church. To Jed's surprise, Plunkett notified him that the town council had voted to put up the resources to rebuild the old Monroe house as well.

"It's the least we could do to honor the memories of what your father and mother meant to this town," Plunkett said, receiving nods of agreement from the other two men.

The four came to an agreement on the timeline and the work schedule. Once they had shaken hands, Plunkett and the Sheriff excused themselves to congregate with the townsfolk. Jed and Chester stood at the door and looked out at the townsfolk, who were engaged in fellowship that neither one had seen in years.

"If that's not a peaceful sight out there, Jed, I don't know what is," Chester said, unaware of the impact his simple comment was having on his colleague.

"Peaceful . . ." Jed repeated it back to his longtime family friend. "Do you know how *long* I've been searching for peace? It sure has escaped me the past couple of decades."

Chester waited patiently for Jed to continue.

"Do you know how much I've *lost* while searching for peace? If it actually exists somewhere, then I've been looking in all the wrong places, Chester."

Jed opened the screen door and walked out, and Chester followed. They stopped at the railing and felt the coolness in the air. Jed felt Chester's hand resting on his shoulder. He tried his best to keep his emotions in check as he said, "You know, that's all I ever wanted for Abigail and myself . . . for my entire family, for that matter. But no . . . it was not meant to be."

Jed's chest tightened as he looked at his friend. "No, Chester . . . I don't believe peace will ever exist, and we are fools to think that we can ever find it. We need to just cope with what we are faced with and do the best we can."

Jed could see Chester's disappointment, even as he understood why Jed felt as he did. "Now, don't get me wrong, Chester, I believe we have a God and our Lord loves us, but he isn't going to give us the peace we are looking for—it just isn't out there. I've tried to find it, from east to west, from north to south. It isn't out there, trust me."

"Maybe you're just looking for it in the wrong area?" Marian's voice startled the two men, who were still standing near the doorway.

"Oh, uh, Marian . . . didn't know you were behind us," Jed stuttered, a bit embarrassed. He scolded himself for letting a moment of weakness get the better of him.

"No, don't be sorry, Jedidiah," Marian interjected. "It sounds to me like you need a good listener in your corner. Plus, if you ask me, I'd say you have a lot more on your mind that you'd like to share . . . someday."

Aware of Jed's awkwardness, Chester tried to come to his friend's rescue. "Hey, you two, I've got a splendid idea. Jed, why don't you come over for supper Wednesday night? We can continue this discussion, and to be honest, I could use some feedback on a sermon I've been working on. What do you think?"

Jed could only stare into Marian's blue eyes, as his head told him to say no while some unknown force allowed him only to say, "Uh, yea, that would be nice. It so happens that Johnny Russell will be at the McKeevers' with Lizzy, so I'd be all alone anyway."

Jed looked directly at Marian and continued. "I really do appreciate the invite, but no promises on me unloading and boring you two like I just did. I do apologize for my lack of self-control, and I assure you it won't happen again."

"Well then, it's settled!" Marian confirmed with her uncle. "But I won't accept your apology, nor will I honor your word of not sharing your thoughts. That's what the Lord made us for, to listen, care, and love, and if it's all right by the Lord, then it's my duty to obey."

Her smile was radiant, and Jed blushed at the thoughts that followed. Those hidden emotions, dormant so many years, were now coming to the surface, and he felt incapable of controlling them.

Their moment was interrupted by the faint sounds of horns, drums, and gunfire, which grew louder as they got closer to the church worksite. All the workers stopped and moved to the grassy area to the side of the worksite. The work of rebuilding the church and the old Monroe house temporarily came to a halt as all on hand looked to see what the commotion was coming down the road. The rumbling, which started out low, continued to grow louder as bystanders voiced opinions about what it could be. Expressions of bewilderment and anticipation crossed their faces. As the parade of music and gunfire got closer, Jed thought he heard chanting, but couldn't make out what it was.

Marian gasped and put her hand to her mouth in disbelief as the chants became recognizable. Jed's heart skipped a beat, and he felt his finger twitch against his pant leg as a result of the hope and excitement he felt.

After a few more minutes, they all could hear what was being yelled, and more and more onlookers joined in:

The war is over, Lee has surrendered,

The war is over, Lee has surrendered

Jed didn't know what to do—should he yell for joy, or should he kneel and cry? Both emotions took over as tears began to stream down his cheeks.

He thought about how hard Willie had worked in trying to persuade people against war by attempting to change a culture that wouldn't change without bloodshed. He thought of Daniel, fighting for his honor against impossible odds that would take his life. He thought of Micah and prayed that he made it through this nightmare, with or without his obstinate personality. He thought of Abigail and thanked God that she didn't have to live through the horror of it all.

Jed felt his knees buckle under him, and he knelt on the ground next to where Marian stood, not caring who watched him. He wept without shame not only for all the pain the war had caused, but also for the peace that now lay ahead. *Oh God, let there be peace once and for all.*

He felt Marian's arm around his shoulder. He turned his head to see that she had knelt beside him and joined him in tears. Jed wrapped his arms around her and squeezed tightly. He didn't want to leave the comfort of being within this woman's arms, and it was a feeling he hadn't had in ages.

Jed finally let go, but neither he nor Marian made any effort to move away from the other. They looked into each other's eyes, silently understanding. They hugged again, but this time in happiness rather than simply relief. Their war was over! Jed looked upward and said a silent prayer—*thank you, Lord.*

Jed and Marian joined their two families together the following day at a large feast set up on the grounds of the Monroe house. The house was still in its rebuilding phase, but worked fine for gathering family and Wheeling friends to celebrate on the grassy field behind the house.

Jed, Lizzy, and Johnny Russell, all in their finest; Marian, her Uncle Chester, Mayor Plunkett, and Sheriff Hancock; and Martin McKeever and his parents enjoyed the much-needed gala after hearing the news of Lee's surrender.

Martin took advantage of the joyful mood to ask Jed if he could have a word with him. The two men walked closer to the edge of the Monroe property and out of earshot of the rest of the guests. Jed could see that the young man was nervous, and he tried to hide his amusement at the difficulty Martin was having.

"Yes, Martin, you have something to ask me?" Jed asked while trying to keep a straight face

"Uh, uh yes I do," Martin stuttered. "Sir, I . . . I would like to ask permission to, uh, to marry you."

Jed choked as he burst out laughing. He put his hand on Martin's shoulder to put his soon-to-be son-in-law at ease. "My answer is no, Martin," Jed teased. "But—if Lizzy is the one you want to marry, well, my answer is definitely—yes."

The two men laughed and shook hands. Once Martin's blushed color had returned to its normal shade, Jed looked him right in the eyes.

"You take good care of her, provide for her, and most of all, you love her above anything else in this world, you hear me?" Martin could only nod as Jed continued. "Martin, I need to tell you that you are taking away my little girl—she's the image of my beloved Abigail, and I'm expecting you to treat her like the angel she is, do you understand?"

Martin gave Jed his word and was more serious than Jed had ever seen him before. Jed felt secure in knowing that his baby girl, his little Sweet Pea, would be fine. He squeezed Martin's shoulder and gave him a gentle fatherly shove toward where Lizzy was standing, and said, "Okay, son, now it's your turn to do the really hard job—you still need to ask her."

Jed watched Martin as he walked across the yard toward his daughter. He looked at her and saw the little girl who rescued him when he lost Abigail. He knew that she had had to grow up quickly at the time and had missed out on a lot of life's experiences. Jed was confident that now she would begin to create her own memories, and despite the tightness in his chest, he couldn't have been happier.

He wished Abigail were there with them, but could sense that she was smiling down on them from heaven. He took his eyes off Lizzy and they met with Marian's. She had been watching Martin and him the whole time and shared his enjoyment with a knowing wide smile.

The evening could not have been better, and Jed began to feel the peace he had longed for. The war was over, his daughter was getting married, he was starting to feel something for Marian, and he had hope of seeing Micah again someday. As he began walking back to the celebration, a loud scream came from near the front of the house.

Jed ran toward the noise, as did several others. Mayor Plunkett's wife, Helen, was beside herself as she approached the Monroe house, frantically looking for her husband. No one could understand what she was trying to say, and it took a few moments for her crying to subside enough that she could speak.

"The president has been killed!"

Chapter Thirty-Four

Recover, Rebuild, Grow

1865

The town hall meeting was loud and nerves were wearing thin. Presiding over the rambunctious crowd was the portly Mayor Plunkett, and next to him was his confidant, Sheriff Hancock. The room of the schoolhouse had been cleared of all the children's desks, which were replaced with benches. Normally the town hall meetings were conducted in the church, but because of the construction, it temporarily couldn't accommodate such a large group as the one in attendance.

Jed stood in the back, with Chester on one side of him and Marian on the other. Many were still loyal to the Confederacy and condemned the new state for breaking with Virginia and joining the Union in 1863. A growing panic over potential retaliation against West Virginia had consumed people since the end of the war. The threat came from those who remained loyal to a dead cause, and they swore revenge against any town or person who now pledged an oath to the new country.

After a couple hours of arguing and debating, the majority agreed that the town would be safe. There would be a few changes, such as increasing the staff of Sheriff Hancock's office and developing a neighborhood watch in case some stranger decided to come into town and wreak havoc on some innocent family or business.

Sheriff Hancock had a tall muscular build and long drooping moustache, and he tried to use his commanding presence to convince the town's citizens not to overreact to the crisis in Washington. "Booth was just one man, and he was caught and killed," the sheriff explained. "We are at the farthest northeast point of West Virginia, and I'm most confident that we are all out of harm's way. We cannot allow fear to change the course of this town or slow our efforts at moving forward. If the country can mend, then so can we, and my friends, mend we must!"

The sheriff was a bit taken aback by the grand applause he received. He tipped his hat and sat back down as the mayor proceeded with the final bits of the town's business. One of the top priorities was to finish the work on the church. He set the goal for completion at Thanksgiving. Jed looked inquisitively at Chester and then at Marian as he thought, *We have some work to do, don't we?*

Weeks passed after the town hall meeting. Most citizens of Wheeling took Sheriff Hancock's words to heart and continued to build up their town and the new country. They all were a part of a new United States and a new leader in President Andrew Johnson. Optimism filled the air and peace could be felt all around, except by Jed, who still had his reservations.

Chester had announced that he was taking a job on a missionary adventure in the Deep South. He told Jed that he had a calling to help with the Reconstruction, and the whole idea had sparked interest from Lizzy and Martin.

Jed remembered how involved Lizzy and Martin had been during the war in the efforts to help Negroes escape from bondage. He listened as they explained to him that this would give them an opportunity to continue helping the unfortunate and oppressed.

Martin had successfully proposed to Lizzy, and Jed was delighted and amused to hear that it had gone more smoothly than when Martin had asked for Jed's permission for his daughter's hand—well, technically, when he had asked for Jed's hand. The big day was slated to occur once the church renovation was complete. Lizzy had written letters to folks in Independence, and much to her delight, many would be able to attend. Jed was pleased for her when word came back from Fez that he wouldn't miss it.

Johnny Russell had become Sheriff Hancock's sidekick, and at twelve years of age was in his element while learning the ropes of what it was like to be a town sheriff.

Jed left the work of the church remodeling to the construction crew, which comprised many folks from the congregation. He often caught himself getting too close to the project and would back off so that work could be accomplished. The mayor had told him that the church was in good hands and that Jed need not worry about it.

The Monroe house was practically finished, with only the final touches yet to be completed. Jed stayed out of that business as well, and when he forgot and started making suggestions, he was immediately scolded by Lizzy and Marian. They often told him to go do God's work and let women do women's work.

He never really understood what they meant, but decided it was in his best interest to abide by their demands. Besides, time spent alone was good for Jed. It enabled him to prepare his weekly sermons now that he had officially taken over the pastorship from Chester Albright.

* * * * *

Jed spent most of his alone time at his favorite spot by the river. He had always felt more at peace alongside rivers, but this river was special. He could feel a presence with him there. He often experienced the Lord among the sounds of water and the sights of small animals as they scurried from tree to tree.

It was there at the river, while sitting on his favorite rock, that he had had the most recent vision of his family. He scolded himself for frequently coming down to the same spot, sitting on the same boulder, in case they appeared again. *It happened, and it could happen again*, he would justify himself, but he knew that it wasn't healthy and that he needed to move on . . . *but how?*

The rock seemed colder than before; he noticed that the season was changing and the sun was no longer shining on "his" spot, where he came to be closer to his God and . . . his family.

As Jed sat on the cold damp boulder, he thought about what was happening with his mind and contemplated the possibility that he was indeed going crazy. Here he was, venturing off along a riverbank to "his" rock to talk to a family that didn't exist and to a God that for some reason wouldn't allow him to ever find the peace he was desperately searching for.

"It looks like you could use some company."

Jed looked up with a start. Although his vision was partially blocked by the sun shining through the leaves of the dogwoods, he knew who it was.

"You're not leaving all the final details and womanly touches to Lizzy, now are you?" Jed asked as he reached out a hand to help Marian take a seat next to him.

"Ah, she's got it all under control, and I think you'll be impressed with how much your daughter knows," Marian answered.

"I've watched her in amazement ever since she had to take over for her mother," Jed said. "What I do know for certain is that any smarts she has are certainly not from me."

Jed and Marian laughed while they gazed at the rushing river. "Abigail was always the smartest of the family, and the prettiest!" Jed continued. "Lizzy definitely got her beauty from her mother in addition to her smarts."

Marian didn't reply to Jed's comment, which caused him to give her a questioning look. "Did I say something to offend you?" he asked.

"Absolutely not, Jedidiah," Marian responded quickly. "I'm just amazed by how much love you still have for your wife and the love you have for your family."

They sat quietly for a bit, both entranced by the water moving over the smooth rocks. "I'm actually a little envious," Marian said, breaking the silence

Jed looked at Marian, and his eyes softened at the thought of Abigail. "She was my soul mate, Marian. And my family, well, they're the only thing that keeps me putting one foot in front of the other. I've lost a lot through the years, and sometimes I feel like I'm losing my faith as well, and it's not a welcome feeling, I tell you."

"You'll never lose your faith, Jedidiah," Marian countered. "I can see what kind of man you are, and although you've been tested throughout your life, God does that to make you even stronger in your faith."

"But—" Jed began.

"No, Jedidiah," Marian countered. "You're a good man, and during the short time that I've gotten to know you, I can tell that Abigail was a very lucky woman."

Marian stared at the whitewater sluicing off the large boulder in front of them. Though excited by what was happening between Marian and himself, Jed was confused and felt disloyal. He looked around to see if any of his family were watching him, which made him feel a little silly. *They're not ghosts, Jed.*

Jed wished that he could see Abigail one more time just to ask her what he should do. He hadn't had feelings for another woman since her, and he still wasn't convinced that he should have them in any case. Here he was, sitting on a large boulder along a roaring river with a very attractive woman, and he felt guilty.

"I know you still love her, Jedidiah," Marian said, softly bringing Jed out of his trance. "I also know that no one will ever take her place, nor should they want to."

Jed had been kicked in the gut. Hearing Marian talk about his love for Abigail reassured him that she understood what he was going through. He wondered where the kick had come from, but disregarded any farfetched fantasy that it was Abigail telling him that it was all right for him to love again.

"You're right, Marian," Jed said, turning to face her. "Yes, I do still love Abigail, and yes, I always will love her. She is the mother of my children, and we promised to love each other until the day we died."

Jed realized with surprise that he had been holding Marian's hands in his—for how long, he wasn't sure. The sounds of the river below had disappeared—the only thing that mattered at the moment was the two of them. "But she's gone now."

He choked up at the words. "I've never said those words before, Marian," he confessed. "I know that she'd want me to love again." His voice cracked, and what he really wanted to say would not come out.

They both sat quietly for a moment, Jed looking at the river and trying to compose himself and Marian searching lovingly for a look of reassurance. "You have a lot of love to give, Jedidiah," she said softly. "I can see that in your eyes and the way you speak. Whoever is your next love will be a very lucky woman, just as Abigail was. I know you'll find it in you when you're ready, and I'll be extremely envious of that woman."

Jed looked at her with a questioning expression as she continued. "It's true, Jedidiah, the woman you undoubtedly will someday fall in love with will spend her life with not only a wonderful man and father, but also a man with great faith for his Lord."

Jed could see the tears flowing down her cheeks. He wanted to reach out to her and tell her so many things. He looked beyond her to the dogwoods, as if they would provide the courage he needed to say what had been locked up inside him for so many years. He held her hands tightly in both of his, and when he looked at her again, her eyes were fixed on his. He glanced beyond her to the dogwoods once more for some kind of permission. *Abigail, I will always love you, and you will always be my soul mate.*

He used one of his hands to gently wipe the tears from her cheeks. He looked deep into her eyes and said, "Marian, if . . . if you dare to take a chance with a man who is a little mixed up, I'd like to ask you, uh . . . "

She put her hands on both of Jed's cheeks and said softly. "We can take it slowly and see where God leads us, Jedidiah. There is no timetable with love, and . . ." Her tears welled up in her eyes again. "Abigail will always be a part of you and of your children, and I wouldn't want it any other way."

Jed felt the knot in his stomach begin to loosen, and though he hadn't finalized anything yet, he felt a loving spirit inside him that had been absent for some time. He reached out to Marian and held her tight, feeling security and hope for a future without loneliness.

With Marian in his arms, he once again looked out among the dogwoods, and in the distance he saw her. He blinked and tried to focus in on the image. There amid the trees was Abigail, and she was holding Abel's hand. She smiled at him, and Jed nodded and smiled in return, and then she was gone.

He helped Marian up from the boulder. They walked back to town in peaceful silence, her arm clasped around his. They wanted to see Lizzy's final touches and to tell everyone about the good news—news of *moving slowly.*

IV

Peace
1866

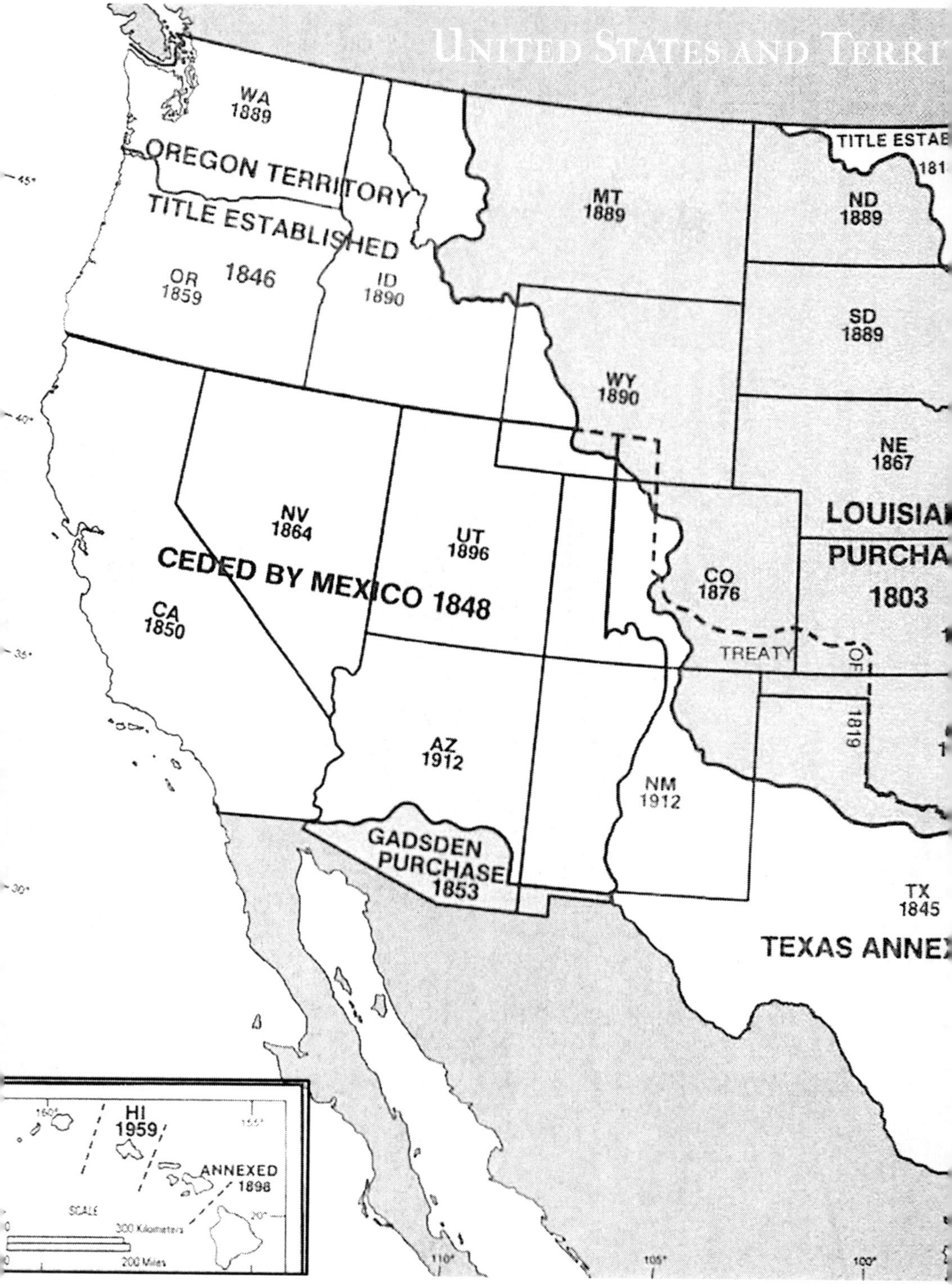

UNITED STATES AND TERRI
WA
1889
OREGON TERRITORY
TITLE ESTABLISHED
1846
OR
1859
ID
1890
MT
1889
TITLE ESTAB
ND
1889
SD
1889
WY
1890
NE
1867
LOUISIA
PURCHA
1803
NV
1864
UT
1896
CO
1876
CEDED BY MEXICO 1848
CA
1850
TREATY
OF
1819
AZ
1912
NM
1912
GADSDEN
PURCHASE
1853
TX
1845
TEXAS ANNE
HI
1959
ANNEXED
1898
SCALE
300 Kilometers
200 Miles

ES, EARLY 20TH CENTURY
ME 1820
VT 1791
NH 1788
MA 1788
CT 1788
RI 1790
NY 1788
PA 1787
NJ 1787
DE 1787
MD 1788
DC ORG. 1800
VA 1788
WV 1863
OH 1803
MI 1837
WI 1848
IN 1816
IL 1818
IA 1846
MO 1821
KY 1792
TN 1796
NC 1789
SC 1788
GA 1788
AL 1819
MS 1817
AR 1836
LA 1812
FL 1845
TERRITORY OF THE THIRTEEN ORIGINAL STATES 1783
CEDED BY SPAIN 1819
1845
SCALE
0
300 Kilometers
0
200 Miles
40°
35°
30°
90°
85°
80°
75°

Chapter Thirty-Five

Reconstruction from Within

1866

With the New Year, hope spread across the land and the dark cloud of hardship and despair finally began to lift. Time seemed to slow as the violence and discourse of the prior four years was left behind. Not long after General Johnston surrendered to General Sherman, the folks in the small West Virginia town began a return to prewar normalcy.

Wheeling settled back into its normal routines: picnics along the river with bands playing and barns opened up for dances instead of the storing of guns; Sunday morning gatherings at church to sing hymns of praise and thanks to the Lord for bringing peace; youngsters gathered with wooden sticks and balls, laughing endlessly as they ran around a diamond track playing a new game called baseball.

People smiled rather than giving each other furtive glances when they passed on the boardwalk. Voices in the mercantile store talked about the latest recipes instead of dire news of war. Laughter, long forgotten, was a welcome refrain after years of exploding shells and cries of agony from the many young men who now lay in grassy groves, in churchyards, and on the outskirts of family farms.

President Lincoln's vision had been that all soldiers would return to their farms and rebuild. Wheeling's new reality was not far off from the late president's vision. Even so, the Reconstruction would be gradual. Though it would not be easy, the nation would heal as its people did.

One quiet and peaceful Sunday afternoon Jed could be found lying on a blanket sprawled in the middle of a meadow, not far from an open field where families from his congregation gathered to fellowship and relax.

Jed enjoyed this spot among the wildflowers almost as much as his "special boulder by the river." He lay flat on his back and looked into the deep blue sky above while listening to the soothing sounds of the Ohio River, which were always nearby even when the river was far from sight.

He had just given a remarkable sermon comparing the vision of the late president's hope for normalcy and peace to that of Jesus's parables about the Kingdom of God.

He listened to the buzzing sounds of the bees as they gathered pollen from the foliage that surrounded him. The warmth on his skin felt nice, although he could feel a slight moist breeze coming off the river. It was here that he often came to spend some personal devotion time with God.

His thoughts were interrupted by the sounds of footsteps approaching through the tall grass. As the sounds grew closer, Jed launched himself onto his elbows and saw Marian approaching. She was carrying a straw wicker basket that was quite heavy, judging by the look on her face.

"What do you have in there, a whole side of beef?" Jed said, laughing and offering her a hand.

"You get out of there, Mr. Monroe!" Marian smacked Jed's hand as he tried his best to open the delicious-smelling picnic basket.

"Aw, come on!" Jed whined. "I'm starving—how did you know where to find me anyway? In fact, how do you always know where to find me?"

They both laughed at the question, realizing that it was so very true. Marian did have a keen awareness of Jed's whereabouts, and more importantly, Jed's thoughts.

During the time Jed and Marian had been courting, they had been doing what they had promised and taking their relationship slowly. Jed was becoming more comfortable lately with the idea that he could have feelings for a woman other than Abigail. His children had encouraged him from the very start to do what he needed to make himself happy.

Lizzy, for one, even encouraged a future wedding, but she treaded lightly. She had watched her father spend years in loneliness, and though she respected the memory of her mother as much as anyone, she now realized that her father should not be alone. That belief was more real now than ever before. Her own wedding day was coming up in a few weeks, and she was worried about how her father would survive without her around to help him.

Today, Jed and Marian rested on the blanket after enjoying a leisurely lunch. The two lay side by side on their backs as they stared into a cloudless sky. They had developed a nice sense of ease around each other. Jed appreciated Marian's compassion and kindness, and quickly found comfort in expressing anything to her. Marian derived the same comfort from confiding in Jed, and the couple who had been moving so slowly were now gliding easily into a lasting relationship that they both relished.

"Your sermon was good today, Jedidiah," Marian said, turning to look at him for a reaction. "I was just a little curious about why you disappeared so quickly after the congregation departed?"

"It was not unusual, Marian," Jed replied. "I like to come out here to the meadow or to the boulder by the river after church services to, you know, to think and listen."

"Listen?" she asked inquisitively

"Yes, I like to listen to what God tells me and to ask what He thought of my sermon," Jed said. This time it was he who turned to her to see if she thought that was odd.

"Well!" Marian said, pleasantly surprised. "I like that! In fact, you know both my Uncle Chester and my father were pastors together in their younger days, but I never heard either one of them reaching out to God for approval after any of their sermons."

"It's not so much that, Marian," Jed said. "I, well, I just want to make certain that what I say to the people is what God is putting in my heart. If I'm missing something out there, I'm just afraid they are too."

Marian looked at Jed with concern on her face. She understood what he was talking about and had heard it several times before, but she still couldn't understand why he didn't feel God's peace inside him.

On the day she had first met Jed, she fell in love with him. From the endless talks they'd had, she felt that she knew him and understood him well enough to spend the rest of her life with him. Somehow and someway she had to help him fight through the demons that haunted him.

Marian looked back at Jed and saw that he had laid his head back down and closed his eyes. The two lay in silence for several minutes. Marian could hear Jed's breathing become heavier, and giggled lovingly at the thought that he'd fallen asleep.

She propped herself up on an elbow, brushed a butterfly off of Jed's cheek and looked at him inquisitively. She knew of the loss of his parents, of the guilt he still carried for not writing them and never going back home when they were still alive. She knew about the shame he carried for wanting to go with the emigrants and leaving Abigail behind, of leaving again to fight a war that Abigail was against. Jed had told her of the demons he still carried over the loss of his first son Abel.

The thought of Jed losing Abigail was horrible in itself, and Marian still got chills whenever she thought of the way he had described that fateful day. She saw the pain in his face when he told her the story, but it didn't compare to the sound of his voice when he told her about holding his sons as each died in his arms.

Marian couldn't imagine all that Jed had gone through, yet as she looked at his face while he slept, she saw peace and comfort. She hoped that by some miracle, God was talking to him right there and giving him comfort.

She gently brushed a leaf that had fallen on his shoulder, and shifted to continue watching him as he slept. As she crooked her neck in thought, she wondered why he took on so much of the blame for the pain his family had endured. She prayed that if she could take anything away from him, it would be the one thing that haunted him the most.

Jed told her that there wasn't anything more painful than his uncertainty about Micah. He had sworn at himself for not being a better father. Jed declared that he would never forgive himself, and that serenity would remain elusive until the day came when he held his son in his arms and pleaded for his forgiveness.

Jed's eyes fluttered, and his nose twitched when he opened his eyes, sensed the emotion in the air, and looked at her. He shifted up and lay sideways next to her, holding himself up on one elbow. He used his hand to wipe a tear from her cheek, not knowing why she was so sad.

"You were sleeping so peacefully, I was hoping you'd sleep awhile," she said, trying to answer the questioning expression that arose with him. "I'd love to see your face shine like it does when you sleep, Jedidiah, so serene and calm. I'd give anything to help you find that peace that you feel escapes you. But—"

"It'll come someday, Marian," Jed replied softly, still trying to wake up.

"I want to be with you while you search for it, Jedidiah," Marian said.

"And I want you with me, too, Marian," Jed reassured her.

He stretched his neck from side to side, looking up and around as he struggled to regain his bearings. Marian was very quiet—concerned, he returned his gaze to hers before adding, "You know it'll all work out once I know that everyone will be alright."

"You mean Micah, don't you?"

Jed stared past her and felt his gut ache. "Especially Micah."

He sensed the seriousness of her concern, and a deep stab of guilt hit him. "Marian, I just can't quit praying that someday, somehow, I will once again hold him and hear him say that he loves me . . . and forgives me."

They sat and gazed at each other. Emotions were strong, but at the same time fragile, as Jed propped himself up to sit across from Marian. He knew he had to do something to lighten up the moment. "So, do you still want to join me and all the stuff that I carry with me?"

"Quit teasing, Jedidiah!" Marian pulled up a clump of grass and flung it at Jed with one hand while wiping her cheek with the other.

"You know very well, Jedidiah Monroe, that God has control over all this, and you know better than anyone that you'll just have to trust Him to reveal it to you."

Jed stared at Marian, his eyes burning into hers. "You didn't answer my question."

She looked past him, diverting her glance toward the far sounds of the river, and then looked into his eyes again. "I'm in love with you, Jedidiah Monroe, so yes, silly, the answer is yes!"

He was speechless and didn't know how he should respond. He paused, cleared his throat, and reached for her hands. "Marian, I think you know how I feel—heck, it seems like you know everything there is to know about me in such a short period of time.

Jed looked down, shuffled his feet, and cleared his throat. "Marian, I'm in love with you, too, and if you'll have me . . . I—"

"Yes, oh yes!" she interrupted as she flung herself onto him, toppling him and throwing them both off the blanket. They grasped each other's sleeves and held on as they rolled back and forth in the tall grass. They were lost in their own little world, not caring who might be nearby.

"I . . . I do need to ask you one thing, though, Marian," Jed finally asked after they had collected themselves and finished brushing the grass from their clothing. "Are you ever going to call me, uh, you know, just plain ol' Jed?"

After a moment to process the question, Marian said with a mischievous grin, "I don't think so. I like the properness of it all, and from what you've told me about your father, I think it fits well."

Jed noted the irony that years before, he had believed that shortening his name had made him independent and confident, but he was now finally confident enough to use his given name if it made Marian happy.

"Then Jedidiah it will be," he said, grinning widely as he shook his head slowly, but affirmatively, and brought Marian closer to him. Jed held her tight and felt the warmth of her embrace. He brushed her hair away from her ear and whispered, "Mrs. Monroe—now how does that sound to you?"

Chapter Thirty-Six

Something New
1866

On the way back into town, Jed and Marian agreed to wait until after Lizzy and Martin's wedding to announce their own wedding plans. Their excitement was overwhelming them, but they didn't want to take any joy or happiness away from Jed's daughter and soon-to-be son-in-law.

The next few weeks were busy as the final details for the young couple's wedding came together. Marian was on a cloud of her own while helping with Lizzy's dress and all the reception plans.

Marian developed a whole new appreciation for the wedding preparations, in comparison with her perspective from just a few weeks before. She now had a vested interest in the happiness of the bride, even while Lizzy had no idea that the woman helping her would soon be her stepmother.

When the big day came, Jed woke from a wonderful dream that he and Marian were walking hand in hand under a gushing waterfall. The sounds were so vivid, and he swore that he felt the mist from the cascading water. As he shook himself awake, he realized that his dream was real. The moisture was the rain dripping from the windowsill and drenching his nightgown.

Lizzy was devastated by the rain and wouldn't come out of her room. The wedding ceremony was to be inside the newly finished church, but the reception had been planned for outside, and now in Lizzy's mind, those plans were ruined. The black cloud hanging over the Monroe house was much darker than the rain clouds hovering over the town of Wheeling, West Virginia.

"Oh, come on out, Lizzy!" Jed coaxed as he tried to convince his daughter that everything would be okay. "Look at it this way, it's just God cleaning up everything so we can have a nice cool celebration after you say your 'I dos'."

Lizzy ignored her father's efforts at humor and stayed behind her locked door in silence. After patiently waiting outside her door, Jed said quietly, "Come on, baby girl, it's going to be alright."

The door to her bedroom creaked open a sliver, and her eyes peeked out at her father's, which were staring right back at her. She let out a soft sniffle, cleared her throat, and said sadly, "It's all ruined, Papa, my day is all ruined!"

"Naaah!" he said, poking his head even closer to hers as she opened her door wider. "You go get yourself ready, I'll have Marian come over to help you, and by the time you run that last brush through your beautiful hair, I guarantee the sun will be showing and the day will be just what you hoped it would be."

Lizzy's didn't look convinced, but knew that despite the ruined reception, she was getting married on that day, and no rain would spoil that. She opened her bedroom door the rest of the way. She gave Jed a sheepish look, then wrapped her arms around him and held on tight. He lovingly returned the hug.

"Hey, how about this?" Jed proposed as he stepped back from their embrace. "Marian won't be here for a few minutes, and we have plenty of time before we even have to think about getting ready. How about we go out onto the front porch and enjoy the sounds of the rain? You know, it will be my last chance to have a quiet cup of coffee with my unmarried daughter. Plus, Johnny Russell has already left to help out the women's auxiliary at the church, so it's just us. What do ya say, Sweet Pea?"

Lizzy pondered the thought for a moment, her heart melting at the sound of her childhood nickname, and her magical grin finally returned as she agreed. She slipped back into her room to grab her robe while Jed went to prepare coffee.

They sat in their usual favorite chairs and held on to the steaming cups. Both stared straight ahead and watched the rain pour down. Lizzy thought of the day to come, while Jed thought of Marian. He wanted to tell Lizzy, but remembered his promise to Marian and decided against it. *This is her day, not ours.*

They both felt the closeness of sitting out on their porch, just the two of them. As they sat quietly, it became obvious that something needed to be said on their last day together.

"I, uh, I know your mother would be so happy for you if she were here, Lizzy," Jed said, breaking the ice. "She always dreamed of the day when her only daughter would be married. She pictured you in a long white satin gown with a train so long that your flower girls would have to carry it. I can still remember her telling me so vividly what she planned to do with your hair. In fact, she said that it was only proper for the mother of the bride to do her daughter's hair and put together the . . . um . . . the . . . well, I'm not too good with this stuff, but I think it's called new, old, bad and stolen, or something like that."

Lizzy nearly choked on her coffee as she burst out laughing. "Papa!" He looked surprised by her reaction to his attempt at describing what her mother had planned. "Papa, it's something old, something new, something borrowed, something blue." Her laughter was contagious, and after a few moments they were laughing uncontrollably.

"I'll be thinking of Momma all day, Papa. I, too, had looked forward to spending the day with her as she helped me get ready. Even as a little girl, I dreamt of this day." For a few minutes, they listened to the rain and reminisced about days past when Abigail was still alive.

"Papa, you know, she'll be with us all day today," Lizzy said. "She knows she can't miss out on the most important day of my life, so I know that she's going to be right there next to you, watching and smiling." Lizzy's face turned soft when she realized that her mother would be there, and she was comforted by the thought.

"Besides, I'm having Marian help me out just like Momma would have." Jed turned his head with a start, spilling coffee onto his lap.

"What?" she asked crisply. "Why the sudden surprise? You two are an item now, you know that, right, Papa?" She took a sip from her cup. "In fact, I wouldn't be surprised to find out that you have already proposed to her."

Jed gulped down the rest of his coffee and said, "I . . . uh . . . I need more coffee . . . can I get you some more, Lizzy?"

He took both cups, and when he returned Lizzy continued. "It's all right with me, Papa, and I kind of think it would be good for Johnny Russell to have a new mother figure around now that I'll be leaving."

"A . . . a new what?" Jed asked, startled again.

"Oh come on, Papa, you two are in love and it's just a matter of time." He stared at her in bewilderment as he wondered how on earth she could know so much. He even wondered for a second if Marian had told her, but he shook the idea off because Marian had been the one who told him that doing so would ruin the day for Lizzy.

"We do enjoy each other's company, but—" Jed began to say.

"But nothing, Papa, you two are going to be husband and wife, and like I said, it's just a matter of when." Lizzy turned her head so Jed couldn't see her.

"You know, Papa?" Lizzy said, a thought brewing inside her head. "If, and I'm saying it's a big if, you had already proposed, then we could turn this day into a double wedding—Martin and me and Marian and you! Boy, wouldn't that have been a grand scene, huh, Papa?"

Jed completely choked on that comment and began coughing profusely as Lizzy laughed hysterically at her father's expense. She looked out at the rain and to the street beyond their front yard. She saw that Marian was approaching in her buggy.

"Well, look there, here she comes, Papa," Lizzy teased. "Now, Papa, while I start getting ready, you do what you need to do, and then when the time comes today, you can marry us, and then Pastor Albright can marry the two of you. Wouldn't that be great?"

Lizzy leaped from her chair and quickly left the porch. Jed could hear her laughter all the way up the stairs and behind the closed doors to her bedroom. He frowned in utter confusion and tried to calm himself down. He raised his arm and wiped his brow with his sleeve. He was visibly shaken. Marian noticed his anxiousness as soon as she approached the porch steps.

"What in the world?" she said. "You look like you just saw a ghost."

They both laughed after Jed told Marian the whole story. They agreed that the coincidence of the whole conversation was remarkable, but the idea was obviously out of the question. Once they had regained their composure, they turned to each other, raising their eyebrows and shrugging their shoulders as if both were saying the same thing. Their eyes returned to the yard. The rain had stopped and blue skies were overtaking the departing clouds, bringing on the bright sunshine that Jed had predicted.

They laughed when they heard Lizzy yell, "It's not raining anymore, *YIPPEE!!!* And for anyone who doesn't know already—I am getting married today!"

The whole ceremony went off without a hitch with Jed presiding. A surprise guest arrived to give the bride away, and no one was more delighted than Lizzy herself. Fez had arrived a few days before the wedding, but kept himself hidden until the moment when he came up behind Lizzy.

"Would you mind if a very old man escorted a very pretty young woman down the aisle?" The words startled Lizzy, but the voice was so familiar that when she turned around she was already falling into the outstretched arms of her Grandpa Fez.

He had traveled all the way from Independence to surprise his granddaughter. Though initially he had written to say that he wouldn't miss the ceremony, his most recent letter had indicated that due to his health, he would be unable to make it. In truth, regardless of his health, Fez wouldn't have let anything stop him from being there for his granddaughter.

As the two gallantly walked down the aisle arm in arm, Jed had to compose himself, as he was nearly overcome by emotion from the sight.

"And, uh, who, uh . . . who gives . . . who gives this, uh, this woman to be married?" said Jed, finally.

"Well!" Fez said with a loud baritone voice, "I am here to tell you that her father is happy as all get-out, so I'll say it for him, but also, I have a vested interest in her mother's side of this thing, and if she were able to be here, she would be the proudest one of all of us. So—I'm going to say that her father *and* her mother give this beautiful woman—uh, my granddaughter—to be wed today."

Fez bent down and kissed one of Lizzy's tear-soaked cheeks, then proceeded to sit in the front row on the bride's side, taking his proper place in the second seat to the left.

Jed did his best to preside over the ceremony as the preacher chosen to wed a loving couple in the name of God. Yet his bride being his daughter made the chore virtually impossible, and he faltered throughout. Lizzy's ceremony lasted twice as long as was customary, both from Jed's halting delivery and his need to bring out his handkerchief several times.

Until he finally said the words everyone had come to hear:

"And I would like to pronounce the marriage of Mr. and Mrs. Martin McKeever . . . uh . . . yes, Martin, you may kiss the bride."

After the couple had walked down the aisle and out the church's front doors, Jed stood while the guests filed out row by row. He kept his eyes focused on the white runner down the center aisle, and recalled just how much Lizzy had assumed the roles and responsibilities that would have been Abigail's during all those years. He thanked God that he was blessed with a loving relationship with his daughter. They were as close as he could have asked for, and he knew that she felt the same way.

He was happy for her, a bittersweet happiness from the knowledge that instead of taking care of Johnny Russell and him, she would now do all those things for herself, her husband, and their future family.

His sorrow was quickly replaced by pleasant thoughts of the next couple who would be using that same white runner. He was comfortable with the way that his relationship with Marian had progressed. He knew he still had to announce their engagement to his friends and relatives, but he had no reason to think that anything other than joy and well-wishes would result. He did want to talk with his father-in-law privately before any announcement was made. Jed was happy that Fez had agreed to his request to attend the wedding. The Higgins were the only others to whom Jed had sent a telegram, but they had to decline because of health issues.

After retrieving his third cup of punch, Jed joined Fez at a corner table in the large yard, which had been festively decorated for the event. After spending several minutes on small talk and reliving their favorite wedding moments, Jed pointed out Marian, then went into detail about how they had fallen in love, and their pending plans.

Fez didn't flinch a bit, stood up and gave his son-in-law a warm bear hug that took the air right out of Jed's lungs. "Geez, Fez, at your age, you still got that same ol' bear grip, you know?"

"Some things never change, Jed. But to tell you the truth, Son, why is it that you've waited so long to move on? Abigail would have understood years ago, and you know I surely would have."

"It just wasn't the time, Fez," Jed said, "plus it took this long for someone to find it in their heart to even want me, you know what I mean?!"

Hearing that last bit, they burst out laughing as they immediately remembered their dear old friend Jim Bridger.

"Yep, we've had a good life, you know that, Jed?" Fez said while trying to slow his laughter. "Even through all that you and your family have gone through, you've always remembered that the good Lord had you in His hands. You never forgot that important lesson, now did you, boy?"

As they shared a knowing glance, Marian arrived at their table. "Mind if I jump into this conversation, gentlemen?"

"Not at all, young lady," said Fez. "And I hear congratulations are in order."

"Well . . . ah, um, well yes . . . and uh . . . thank you," Marian said, bashfully glancing at Jed. He seemed distracted, but was simply trying to decide what color of red her face had instantly become.

"In fact!" Fez yelled out while slapping his pant leg, "I've got a wonderful idea!" Fez announced much louder than necessary, causing Jed and Marian to look at each other with guarded anticipation.

Fez pulled up a chair and gingerly climbed up onto it, which was no easy task for a man his age. He asked for a cup of punch, and with his usual loud baritone voice said, "May I have everyone's attention, if you please?"

It took another loud request, and then the sounds of jingling silverware on glasses caused everyone in the yard to look toward Fez, who continued to stand on the wooden chair and held his cup high in the air.

"As you all know, I am the grandfather of the most beautiful bride of the day," Fez said, and then continued after a few hoots and applauses subsided. "I would like to have the honor of proposing a toast to the young couple and to years of happiness and many, many great-grand-children for me."

The crowd erupted in cheers and laughter and agreement could be heard throughout the yard. Lizzy and Martin made their way to thank Fez, anticipating that he was finished with his toast.

When the couple was close enough, Fez yelled out again. "And also—if I could have your attention, please."

The crowd froze and once again turned to face Fez, but this time his announcement was accompanied by confusion and whispers among the assembled crowd.

"I would also like to propose a toast to the very next happy couple that will be walking down the aisle to join in holy matrimony." Fez turned his attention to Jed and Marian, both of whom were frantically shaking their heads for Fez to stop.

"After this many years, it gives me such great joy to announce to all of you, the future Mr. and Mrs. Monroe!"

Silence filled the air, jaws opened wide, and eyes bulged. After a few tense moments, Lizzy slowly approached Jed with tears in her eyes and reached out to embrace him.

She held on tight and whispered, "I knew it, Papa! You have made my day even more perfect than it already was."

Lizzy tearfully and reluctantly let go of her father. She slowly turned and approached Marian. The two women looked at each other for a cherished moment until Lizzy opened her arms wide and embraced her future stepmother with the warmest hug that Marian had ever received.

Lizzy stepped back and locked her arm into Jed's before locking her other arm into one of Marian's. Now in complete control, Lizzy turned Jed and Marian around to face the crowd, and with a wide grin and the happiest of tears, yelled out, "To my parents!"

Chapter Thirty-Seven

Going Home Changed

1866

An unlikely couple continued their trek through the Shenandoah Valley, one of the two seeking freedom and the other relief from guilt. The long haul was almost over, and Micah could feel the nearness of the final destination as if it were waving a flag and urging him to put one more foot in front of the other. The journey had started just under three years before, but only during the last few months had he finally gained the courage to make the trip back home.

He credited Agatha for giving him that courage. When Micah was close to full recovery, she was the one who brought him back from the depths of despair and loss. She not only helped him regain his health, but also opened his eyes to what kind of person he had become. With her help, he was able to get past the guilt and achieve a clear conscience. In his prior state, he couldn't imagine ever going home again; now, however, there was nothing he wanted more.

The irony about Micah's situation was that he entered the war to protect the institution of slavery, yet was rescued from that way of thinking by a woman who was an oppressed captive of slavery. She sat by his side, listened to him for weeks, and nurtured him back to health while reading passages and singing worship songs that she had learned as a child.

In 1863, when Micah discovered what had become of Daniel, he became obsessed with the notion that he had caused his brother's death. By all means, he was one of the officers in charge that fateful day. It was his duty to make sure the front lines remained behind that murderous rock wall on the Sunken Road. He also was the one most likely to have called out the order to fire the volley that sliced his brother into pieces on that treacherous killing field. The image haunted him and convinced him to leave the army to search for a reason to keep living.

* * * * *

Once they were on their own, Agatha and Micah traveled throughout the South, he acting as her master and she as his slave. They followed the path of the once glorious and proud Army of Northern Virginia. Though he had vowed never to fire another round at any man, he closely followed the ways of war while listening for the answer to his trauma, one he knew that only God could share with him.

Agatha, the light-brown-skinned Negro slave, knew that her time as a slave was only a few battles from being over. Her loyalty and allegiance were not to her former master—he died at Gettysburg, and the plantation where she grew up had disintegrated. The other slaves she had spent her life with had scattered to find their own ways in lives of uncertainty.

Not Agatha. She had her certainty, and it was to bring Micah to the salvation the good Lord could offer. God had spoken to her and told her to stay with Micah until he found what he was searching for. She believed her God would give him the forgiveness he so desperately yearned for, and that it was her calling from God to lead him there.

The two were like fated partners who had embarked on a long and uncertain voyage. She uncovered things about him that he had been denying his entire life, while he gave her a purpose for living that she had never had as a slave. It just so happened that their final destination was the home he had avoided and detested most of his life. But he no longer tasted the bitterness; he felt the pull and hoped that it was indeed the right thing to do.

The trek was mired by mixed emotions and changes in direction. Several times they had been on the verge of giving up. Agatha was determined to ensure that Micah was delivered from his prison of guilt about not just Daniel, but also how he had treated his family. Their journey was coming to an end at the same time as Agatha sensed that Micah was beginning to register all that she had been trying to teach him.

* * * * *

Two years removed from the plantation, they found themselves watching from afar as a large brick house was surrounded by soldiers from both sides of the battle line. Micah could feel tension in the air. He watched General Lee arrive on his horse, then moments later saw General Grant arrive.

The scene unfolding in front of them clearly told the story. Throughout their seemingly endless plight, they had witnessed battle after battle while they stayed quiet and always concealed. They had become accustomed to staying hidden while following the army, but as they watched, they realized that they needn't hide anymore.

Even so, Agatha gave a look of surprise when Micah made his way out into the open. She slowly left her perch and joined him in the open unplowed field. She wasn't sure what had him so interested, but thought she heard him whisper something. She shook her head slowly and tilted it toward him. The look he gave back was a mix of defeat and, it seemed . . . relief.

"It's over," was all Micah said.

Agatha hadn't yet registered how much her life had changed, but could see from Micah's face that one more chapter was closed for him. They had traveled from outside of Fredericksburg to Richmond, to Cold Harbor, then to Petersburg, and finally here to the small town of Appomattox Courthouse, Virginia.

* * * * *

From that moment at Appomattox until now, Micah and Agatha had only drifted. It had been several months, but it seemed like yesterday. He frequently thought of home and his family, but discarded it as something he never would be a part of again. He knew what kind of person he had been and how he had treated his family. *It's no wonder they would never want me back.* The thoughts permeated his mind day after day.

The endless wandering gave him time to think. Most of his thoughts, both new and old, were of the things he'd never told anyone before, but all of them he freely shared with Agatha. During the year following the end of the war, he told Agatha that he felt dead inside. On reflection, he told Agatha that the person who rushed out of his family house in Fredericksburg in the spring of 1861 was an arrogant, unlawful, bitter, and ungrateful person. He told Agatha that he was determined to rebuild his life, and asked her to help him.

Agatha had watched him closely and seen the growth in him over several years. He became less bitter and angry. The anger he brought with him to the hospital in 1862 had shed its overpowering skin one layer at a time. Her work was far from over, though. She wouldn't be satisfied until she knew that Micah's search for God was complete. Then and only then could she move on with her own life.

Several months after Lee had surrendered to Grant, Agatha and Micah crested a hill on the trail they were traversing. Below them, a wide valley was spread out and dotted with interspersed stands of enormous trees. They descended into the valley.

Near the bottom, they spotted a side trail that entered in the middle of a stand of trees. Looking for a place to rest, they turned onto the trail and walked through dense brush and trees that suddenly opened on a hidden clearing. In the center of the clearing was a small but well-maintained church.

They walked to the front door and knocked. The door opened immediately, and out stepped an enormous black man shouldering a rifle that appeared to be Union Army issue.

"State your business," said the man. His inquisition was not unfriendly but neither was it warm.

"We're just looking for some water and a place to rest," Micah replied.

"And the two of you just happened along the trail to our little church in the middle of nowhere?"

"We thought it would be cooler in the trees, that's all," added Agatha.

"Well, I'm still waiting. State your business."

"We've been traveling for several months on our way to Wheeling, and we just needed a place to rest," said Micah.

"And you, miss? Should I assume you are following this fine gentleman to Wheeling?"

"Sir, my name is Agatha. I was a slave on a plantation, and my *friend* Mistah Micah helped me escape. We's followed the Army of Northern Virginia waiting for the war to end. Now's I'd like to find my family if they's still out there somewhere."

"And where would that be, miss?"

"Somewhere up North. Baltimore, maybe."

Suddenly the man beamed a giant grin. "Well, why didn't you say so? C'mon in. My name is Reverend Cyrus B. Shackleford, but my friends just call me Mr. Shackleford."

"Reverend?" asked Micah.

"Well, I'm not exactly a reverend. But then again, this isn't exactly a church. It's what you'd call a waystation for the Underground Railroad. Despite what you may have heard, the Underground Railroad still helps those in need. And little lady, you're right to look for your family instead of staying around here. The war may be over, but that won't stop any vigilantes from stringing up a Negro man—or woman, for that matter. And Virginia not be the place you wanna be to avoid that sorta fate."

Agatha and Micah went inside, where Shackleford had one of his "congregation" get water for them. There were about 20 men and women in all, and all were working the logistics for those traveling through to points north.

When they had met a few more of the folks in the church and rested up a bit, Cyrus walked them out.

"Good luck to the two of you, and little lady, you do come by when you're ready to venture north, won't you, now?"

"I will. Thank you, Mr. Shackleford."

"Oh, please. Call me Cyrus."

Agatha blushed.

Cyrus had a last word for Micah. "Son, I see you be eyeing my iron. So I'll answer the question you're thinking. Yes, it's Union issue. And no, I didn't steal it—I fought in the Union Army and I earned this gun with every drop of blood I spilled in the name of freedom."

"Sir, I'm impressed—"

"And you, too. Call me Cyrus from now on. And you best be takin' good care of this lady."

"I will, Cyrus, I will. I owe her more than I can ever repay. She saved my life."

"Well, that's a story I'd like to hear sometime."

The two men shook hands, and Agatha and Micah continued on their way. Later that night, they made camp just up the hill from the little church in the clearing.

A few days later, the two nestled close to a campfire at the same campsite. They began a conversation that would be like no other they had spoken before.

"I do believe this here rabbit is a sign that good times are right around the corner, Agatha," Micah said over his shoulder as he turned the small animal over their open fire.

"My momma would say that anytime anything good happened, we should give our thanks to the Lord," Agatha replied. "She would always tell me, 'In Him is where we find our peace.'"

"Your momma taught you a lot of that kind of stuff, didn't she?" Micah replied

"She was my heart and soul, Mista Micah," Agatha said. "You've got to understand, we didn't have a choice. We had chains that kept us from knowing what peace was all about. Momma taught all of us that our real protection came from God. I couldn't have lived the way our people were forced to live if I didn't have that. I owe it all to my momma."

Micah and Agatha sat on a fallen oak, picked the meat off the bones of the rabbit, and talked. The woods around them were thick with brush and fallen leaves. The creek behind them flowed with fury across small boulders that were scattered throughout the area. It was unseasonably warm for the beginning of December, but it was a welcome treat from the many cold nights they had endured.

They had become quite familiar with each other. Agatha learned about all of Micah's traits and heard all about what he was like in his earlier years. Micah learned about Agatha's past and how she was selected to be a house slave instead of the unthinkable, a field slave like her two brothers. She had been taught to read and write by the lady of the house, although she still had trouble at times. If the colonel had ever found out, Agatha would have been sent into the fields to rot in the heat and humidity of Virginia's horrendous summers.

Micah had never met a slave who could read and write. All the slaves he had encountered during the war couldn't even sign their own names. At first, knowing that Agatha was a literate house slave helped Micah get over his initial prejudice. Now, three years later, he no longer saw her skin color, and he relished her company and their conversations.

"I envy you, Agatha," Micah said between bites of rabbit. "You've found that special kind of peace that I've been searching for my entire life. I frittered it away and lost any chance of that while I was growing up. I was more of a pest to my folks and turned my back on my family, the only people who truly wanted to give me their love."

Agatha stayed silent and let Micah's words sink in for a moment. She heard the wind whistling through the trees and watched as a flock of guinea hens slowly made its way across their camp. Micah looked at her, surprised at the quiet demeanor of his traveling partner.

Agatha slowly raised her head and turned her gaze toward Micah. Her expression was one of resolution. "You's always had that ability to have the kind a peace I'm talkin' bout, Mista Micah."

Micah's mouth half opened, but no words came out. His eyes transfixed on hers, and his emotions were like eggshells.

"How?" was all he said as his eyes began to fill with tears. "I don't know how, Agatha."

"Just ask, Mista Micah, just ask for it."

"Ask? Ask who, ask what? I don't understand," cracked Micah's voice as he threw the rest of the rabbit meat into the flames.

"Ask, Mister Micah," Agatha said just above a whisper. "You know who you should be askin'. You're ready to be acceptin' God, ain't you? I see it in yo eyes."

Micah could fight the emotions no longer. His tears seemed to cleanse him of the heaviness that had consumed him. Agatha moved closer, took him in her arms, and comforted him.

"I . . . I need what you have," Micah tried to say. "I want what you have, Agatha. I want the God that you have to take care of me and take away all of this pain."

"Just ask, Mista Micah."

Micah's head leaned back and he looked up. "God, I . . . uh . . . I . . . " He struggled with the words between his sobs. "God, please come into my life!" His eyes were focused upward, unaware of the tears of joy coming down Agatha's cheeks.

Silence filled the air. They sat close, their hands held tightly to each other, one for support and the other for security.

"My father!" Micah whispered after several moments of reverence. "This is what my father was trying to find."

Agatha let go of Micah's hands and adjusted her seat on the oak tree. "What do you mean, Mista Micah? Your father's a *pastor*. He *must* know the love of God, or else how could he do what he's been doing?"

"No, you don't understand," Micah said. "For years my father would venture off and explore this or join that, would go to this war or on that wagon trail. But now I realize what he was really trying to do."

Micah shook his head slowly. He was beginning to understand what his father had gone through his entire life. That revelation brought a combination of grief and a yearning to see his father. "Oh my God, Agatha, that man has been trying his entire life to feel what I'm feeling right now."

He turned to Agatha and grabbed her hands with conviction in his voice. "I don't think in his whole life he's ever had peace like this!"

"Agatha!" Micah began again, "look what he's had to overcome. After Momma died there was Willie, and then there was . . . ," he trailed off, remembering the circumstances of his next thought, ". . . then there was Daniel."

Micah lowered his head and in a muffled said, "Oh, my God, that poor, poor man!"

Everything was becoming clear to Micah, and he realized what he needed to do. He stood up and walked to the other side of the smoldering fire, then turned to look back at Agatha. He was on fire with a passion he had never felt before. His mind was clearer than ever, and his love for his family was energizing him to act.

"Agatha, my father may be a pastor, but when you have two sons die and another walk out of your life, who could blame you for going through the motions as a pastor for God? I'm not saying it's right, but I understand him more now. That man has tried his entire life to bring a sense of security to his family, and each time he's tried, he's been shoved down."

Agatha got up from the oak and joined Micah on the other side of the fire pit. She stood next to him and looked up at his tall frame, her own tears now flowing freely.

"Now you're seeing it the way the good Lord has wanted you to see it all along, Mista Micah. I can sees the change in ya eyes and in ya voice."

She began to walk away from Micah, but he grabbed her hand and turned her around. "I need to go to him, Agatha. I need to share with him what I just found. I need to let him know that I love him. That God loves him. I believe that it will change him just like it did me."

Agatha gently caressed Micah's face and said not a word, but her eyes spoke plenty. She knew that her job was done. Keeping her emotions as concealed as possible, she tried to speak.

"I need to go to him, Agatha," Micah whispered as his eyes focused on hers.

"I knows, Mista Micah," she whispered back as she put her other hand on his cheek. "I's known it all along. You was always meant to help out ya father, but you couldn't do it until you was ready to ask for God's help. You wasn't ready before, but you is now."

Micah's euphoria was contagious, and Agatha could feel the Spirit of the Lord. She knew all too well that this moment meant something else as well.

As Micah moved about the camp with newfound joy, she slipped away and walked toward the creek. The sound of the water was soothing to her, and she thought of her family, of her mother. Long since passed away, her mother had done for her what she was able to do for Micah, and in her silence by the creek she looked up—*thank you, Momma.*

Agatha was filled with a mixture of emotions. She was happy for Micah, and she was excited yet apprehensive about what could be in store for her. She had never been free before, and she didn't yet know the steps to take next. She pondered the idea of trying to locate what might be left of her family. She wasn't sure exactly where to start, but she was pretty sure that the "congregation" at the Underground Railroad waystation could get her pointed in the right direction. Surprisingly, although she was still quite apprehensive, she wasn't scared.

She believed in her God, and knew that He would guide her to where she needed to go. She also knew that her time with Micah was over. He had said he would find a place for her with his family, but she knew enough of the outside world to know that life for a single Negro woman in a West Virginia town would be far from ideal.

In the end, Agatha knew that Micah needed to move on and begin his new life with his family in Wheeling, and she needed to begin her new life as a free woman, and perhaps find her family. Now she just had to break it to Micah.

"It just seems odd," Micah said as she got back to the camp. In his sense of euphoria, he hadn't noticed that she'd gone to the creek. As he turned her direction, he saw her coming his way. "I say, it seems odd, I mean it just seems so natural for the two of us to be together. I mean, think about it, you nursed me back from the dead, you traveled with me through thick and thin, and here we are, still together."

"We did have some good times, didn't we?" she said as she carefully and subtly changed her speech to past tense when describing their time together. "But look at you now! I is so happy for you, Mista Micah. I know you're going to do great things no matters what you set your mind to."

Although the inevitable was about to happen, the thought that they might separate hadn't registered with Micah until that moment. He stopped and looked at Agatha with an endearing gaze, yet knew the words would come no matter what he did.

"It just won't be the same without you," Micah said. "Where will you go?"

"I'm going to see the folks we met at the church waystation a few days ago. I promise that when I gets to where God's taking me, I be reaching out to you. It's just easier that way, cause I knows where you'll be, and I definitely knows what you'll be doing, I can still see it in ya eyes. And I didn't miss that we've stayed at this camp for a while, with the 'church' just down the valley from here."

"Well, I wasn't sure of your plans, but I wanted to make sure you had an option if you decided not to come with me to Wheeling. I will *never* forget you, Agatha," Micah said emphatically.

They knew that come morning, both would be leaving in opposite directions, and the thought of it was unsettling yet exciting. They embraced, and neither wanted to be the first to let go. Agatha broke the silence by taking a small step back, and in her attempt to make the separation less awkward asked, "When do you think you'll be arriving in Wheeling?"

"My best guess would be sometime around Christmas."

Agatha only nodded, her emotions starting to erupt.

"Yea, I can even see myself making my surprise visit on Christmas Eve, just in time to open the presents and carve the turkey, right?"

"No, Mista Micah." Agatha swallowed hard to hold back her need to cry. "I think you gonna *be* the Christmas gift for your whole family the moment you show up."

"You know, Agatha," Micah began, "it's kind of funny in a way, but now it's gonna be my turn to help someone, and what better day to do it than on Christmas Eve, huh?"

Agatha stifled her desire to cry again and looked at him with pure joy. She couldn't speak; her voice was choked with tears of endearment.

"I owe my father so much, Agatha, and now God has given me the task of going to him and telling him just how I feel," Micah continued.

Micah moved closer to Agatha and put his hand gently on her cheek. "I owe you my life, Agatha, and I will always remember what you did for me."

She looked deeply into his eyes, leaned upward, and gave him a loving kiss on his cheek. Without saying a word, she lowered her head and lay down to sleep, anticipating the new morning.

Her tears now flowed freely down her cheeks, but a wide smile appeared on her face as she breathed in the crisp night air. She was so pleased for Micah, and for the very first time in her life, she too felt free. Now it was her time to find out what God had planned for her newfound life.

Chapter Thirty-Eight

A Nervous Town
1866

Martin walked up the steps of the Monroe house two by two and noticed Johnny Russell lounging on the front porch swing and sipping a bottle of root beer "Whatcha drinking there, Johnny Russell?" he asked his thirteen-year-old brother-in-law without giving him a chance to answer.

The idea of Lizzy as a married woman still hadn't sunk in for most people. She and Martin knew that in time everyone would be used to it, and then it would all start over again when Marian joined the family as the next Mrs. Monroe.

Jed and Marian's wedding plans had been postponed until the spring of 1867 to give Jed a chance to finish the inside of the church and prepare for his annual Christmas Eve service. The outside of the church had been completed for a while, but Jed still wanted to perform some minor interior fixes just to, in his words, "make it just the way my papa would have wanted it to be."

Martin scowled at Johnny Russell with jealousy at the thought of tasting a wonderful root beer, but turned his attention toward the front door. As he opened it and peered inside, he prepared himself for how to bring up the delicate topic that had been heavy on his mind.

"Jed, you in here?" Martin yelled out.

"Back in the office, Martin," replied Jed.

Martin navigated around the front room and found Jed sitting at his desk, deep in thought.

"How's the Christmas Eve sermon coming?" Martin asked.

"It's coming along fine, Martin," Jed replied. "In fact, just so you know, I've had the privilege of hearing from so many critics that I think the content will be the best piece of theological work the church has ever heard."

They both laughed as Martin poured himself a drink from the side cabinet and sat down on the dark leather sofa across from Jed's oak desk.

"Jed," Martin began, "I first want to thank you again for helping us out with the wedding. I still can't believe that your father-in-law made the long trip just so he could walk his granddaughter down the aisle."

Jed sat back in his chair, now curious as he observed how nervous his son-in-law appeared to be. Something was off, as indicated by the odd formality of Martin's demeanor. His suspicion deepened when Martin paused to refill his drink.

Jed glanced at the grandfather clock against the wall and noticed the time. "A bit early in the day to start enjoying a little libation, isn't it Martin?"

"It might be so, Jed, but I've been hearing some god-awful stories lately, and quite frankly it's got me a bit on edge. Besides, you know plain and simple that you have more water in your brandy than anything. I believe you just leave it here to appease the town mayor when he comes by and asks for a drink."

Jed laughed and nodded his agreement, but his grin faded quickly when he realized that Martin hadn't laughed at his own joke.

Jed moved his desk chair to the side to get a better barometer on the seriousness behind Martin's concerns. "What is it that's got you all riled up, Martin?"

"That blasted war has been over for close to a year and a half now, but it seems we are no safer now than when Lee and Grant were going after each other down South." Martin stopped to take another sip and asked if he could light up one of the new cigars he had received as a wedding present from his Uncle Joe.

"Marian and Lizzy are going to be here soon, and I don't want to hear from either one of them about the foul smell of cigars, if you know what I mean," Jed replied.

Jed chuckled, but mostly to himself, at the thought of that possible encounter and his use of Bridger's old phrase. "Now, Martin, what exactly has you upset?"

"I really think that the whole nation is in chaos right now, and we're living in a state that could very well be a prime target," Martin explained

"I'm not sure I understand," Jed replied. "You'll need to slow down a bit and start over, Martin. Why West Virginia?"

"Jed, first look around the country," Martin began. "Number one, we have a want-to-be killer in your old stomping grounds of Missouri who's trying to rob every bank and kill every Pinkerton man who walks. I hear his name's Jesse James. You know the name?"

Jed shrugged his shoulders.

"Number two, although President Johnson has declared the Civil War officially over, so far only Tennessee has been readmitted into the Union. I mean, think about it Jed. A year-plus later, and we only have one state returning so far?"

"Number three, we have a pudgy overweight president who has little power over anyone, including his overbearing wife. It's like every time he tries to do something, Congress wants to shut him down and throw him out of office. Don't you see it, Jed? What kind of a country can we live in if even our own president can't control his office?"

"Okay now, Martin," Jed said, putting up a hand to calm his young son-in-law down. He pulled open a desk drawer and pulled out a dusty bottle of Irish whisky.

"Full proof . . . no water," Jed said while assessing his son-in-law's level of concern. As he proceeded to pour himself and Martin a drink, he said, "I've always kept this standing by, just in case a situation comes up, you know—kind a like this one."

Martin, still worked up, took the drink and swallowed it in one gulp.

"And number four, Jed!" Martin blurted out, not listening to the attempt at humor made by his father-in-law. He took the liberty of pouring himself another drink as he sat back down to continue ranting, as Jed looked on.

"There is so much talk about us, Jed, the kind of talk that makes a man stay awake at night with one hand on a club and the other on his pistol."

Jed was dumbfounded, not really knowing what to do. Should he pour himself a drink or start laughing at the silliness of this whole conversation? "I'm sorry if I seem a bit naïve here, Martin, but what kind of talk or articles circulating about our family can be so damaging that they cause you this much stress? Did Johnny Russell knock down Mrs. Mahoney's white fence again, or did I insult someone *again* during last week's sermon?"

"Jed!" Martin stood up, knocking over his glass of whisky, in disbelief that his father-in-law did not get his meaning. "West Virginia, not the Monroe family—West Virginia!"

"West Virginia?"

"Yes, Jed!" Martin yelled in fear as he poured another drink with his shaking hands and sat back down.

Martin took a moment to regain his composure, wiped his brow with his handkerchief, and took a deep breath before continuing. "Okay, let me try to make sense of all of this for you. First of all, many in the South are still fuming from losing the war, right? And I mean fuming! Second, they don't look at us—I mean West Virginia—as a Northern state. Those in the South look at West Virginia as a Southern *traitor* state. Keep in mind, we *were* a part of Virginia, and when they seceded, we broke from them to join the Union. There have been numerous letters and articles, and lots of violent talk of revenge against anyone who was here during the war and followed the state against the South."

Jed sat back in his chair and contemplated this. He too had heard of anger regarding the statehood of West Virginia, but most Virginians knew that the western portion of the state had never seen eye to eye with the central state in most everything, so in his opinion it was not a surprise, and the breakup of Virginia was inevitable.

"The latest rumor is hotter than molasses, Jed, and to me, very reliable," Martin said, more calmly now. "I actually heard that a gang of guerrilla rebels has been going from town to town in West Virginia and destroying buildings. They're leaving burning crosses in the middle of streets. Granted, the latest news was from the eastern part of the state, but that was a few weeks back, and heaven knows where they might hit next. To be honest, Jed, I'm damn worried, and that comes from a man who ran a portion of the Underground Railroad for a year and a half."

The sounds of footsteps coming up the front porch steps caused the two men to stop their conversation. Marian and Lizzy entered the office, arms filled with boxes from their latest shopping excursion and seemingly oblivious to the heated discussion that had been taking place.

"Well, good day, gentlemen," Marian said, moving her glance from Martin to Jed. "I see from the empty glasses and the thumping finger of my soon-to-be husband that a serious conversation has been taking place. Would you rather us womenfolk move to another room so you two can continue, or are you going to oblige us with the content that has generated such concerned looks on both your countenances?"

The women set their daily purchases outside the office, next to the large grandfather clock that had been given to Jed by Fez years before. It had impeccable woodwork and craftsmanship, but its inability to keep time drove Jed crazy.

"Now if you would stop that finger from tapping long enough to bring my future stepdaughter and me up to speed, I would certainly be obliged," Marian said to Jed while giving Martin a stern look.

Jed recounted the previous conversation to Marian and Lizzy as the two ladies took seats on the sofa.

"I'm goin' down the street to play with Herman and Joe, if anyone's gonna look for me!" The loud shout from Johnny Russell startled them all as he jarred the front door open and slammed it behind him, not waiting for an approval from his father.

"I still can't believe I survived thirteen years with that boy!" Lizzy said with a laugh, but she was the only one laughing.

Martin took the liberty of pouring himself another drink, even over the raised eyebrows of his new wife. "I just don't get it!" he said, sitting back hard in his chair and spilling a portion of his drink on his vest. "We all have been living a life of killing or being killed. Why is it so difficult to gain a little bit of peace for a change? I mean, Jed, you always talk about your search for peace whenever you stand on that pulpit. Let me ask you—have you found that peace yet, through all the years of war and death?"

Lizzy shot an angry look at her husband, but Jed held up a hand. "No, it's alright Lizzy, I can answer Martin, and in fact I too question the concept of peace. In fact, that is partially the reason I speak about it in most of my sermons."

Lizzy's eyes showed the memory of her father's pain that only she knew. Marian moved to where Jed was sitting and sat next to him, putting her hand on his back to lend emotional support. The grandfather clock chimed four o'clock, and Jed looked at his pocket watch. He guffawed at the actual time of six o'clock, put his watch back in his pocket, and began speak.

"Yes, I admit I've been searching for that feeling and reassurance for as long as I can remember, even before you were born, Lizzy. I won't go into all the details of my journey, but you might be surprised that although I am the pastor of this town, I do still search for God's direction, and it often seems to elude me. On paper, I should be ashamed at my lack of faith, but each time I reach that point where serenity should surround me, I am swept away by another broken heart."

The room was still, and even though Martin had digested most of the carafe of whisky, he sat upright and alert to Jed's testimony. Lizzy held his hand and all eyes were on Jed's.

"Lizzy, over the years, your mother and I followed the scripture, and we knew those certain verses that speak of God's peace: Isaiah 26:3: 'Thou wilt keep him in perfect peace, whose mind is stayed on thee: because he trusteth in thee.' John 16:33: 'These things I have spoken unto you, that in me ye might have peace. In the world ye shall have tribulation: but be of good cheer; I have overcome the world.'"

Lizzy's eyes filled with tears at just the memory of her mother, and she wanted to reach out to her father and embrace him. If she could, she would take away all the hardships that he had endured.

Jed looked at Marian, and with a soft kindness in his voice said, "You have filled that big gap that I carried for so many years, and I want you to always remember it. You've been my blessed reminder that God has a plan for me. I am so thankful for all of your reading of scripture to me on those lonesome nights when I was searching for God and He was not there."

"I know you don't believe that, Jedidiah," Marian interrupted. "You know that God and the Holy Spirit will never leave or forsake you. You are the one who has always told me that you relish the times when you're alone and read Psalm 46:10: 'Be still, and know that I am God.' In all the time I've known and loved you, I believe that still is one of your favorite verses. Or is it Isaiah 30:15? 'In returning and rest shall ye be saved; in quietness and in confidence shall be your strength.' "

Jed's eyes were set on the ground and his right index finger had stopped thumping long before. He was in a calm sense of revelation as he said quietly, "It's always been me pushing God's presence away. He has always had his love for me to embrace, but I chose to use every single tribulation as an excuse to turn my back on His gift. It hasn't been Him turning His back on me."

Jed looked at Martin and said, "Martin, I can see that you're scared about what's going on in West Virginia. I also know that you think it's unfair for all of us not to be receiving the peace we've all waited for after so many years of war. I would say, son, that there will always be bank robbers or rebel guerrillas who will follow Satan's plan to destroy us. Son, we have to be strong and not give in to that master deceiver who wants us to believe that God's plan is out of our grasp."

The room became quiet, and Jed thought about what he had just told Martin. For a mere moment, Jed reflected and realized that what he had said was exactly what he'd not been doing his entire life.

Martin put his hand on top of Lizzy's and looked at her. While wiping the tears from her cheeks, he said, "You're right, Jed, I do feel a bit foolish coming in here with all that crazy talk of things that we really have no control over anyway, right?"

Jed glanced at Lizzy sitting in front of him, then to Marian beside him, before returning his attention to his son-in-law. "Nah, don't you fret none, it was just the two of us talking about a lot of 'what ifs'."

"Papa?" Lizzy's voice was soft, but her aching eyes caught Jed's attention. "What is it, then, that is keeping you from finding your true peace? You've said that you know it's there for you. You even tell others to accept it as the greatest gift God could give us. You seem to advise others, but you block it out for yourself, and I don't know why. Is it Mama? Is it Abel, Willie, or Daniel?"

Lizzy paused to find the courage to continue. "Papa, is it Johnny Russell, or is it . . . um . . . is it because of me?"

The room became painfully still, and Jed looked at Lizzy with an empty forlorn sadness in his eyes. The sight frightened her, because she didn't understand the cause. She wanted to run to her father and embrace him and take away the unknown pain that surrounded his entire being. It hurt her so to not know why her father was so sad and incomplete.

"No, my daughter, it's none of those things," Jed said softly as he motioned Lizzy to come closer. She moved to the floor in front of Jed, leaving her husband on the sofa behind her. "All that you spoke of broke my heart beyond belief, as you can imagine it would for any father. I've lost loved ones and friends, but it doesn't compare to the one thing that I did that I will never be able to forgive myself for, no matter how many times our precious God tells me that He has already forgiven me."

"I don't understand, Papa," Lizzy whispered, ignoring her stream of tears. "I've lived with you my entire life, and I have only known you as a kind and loving man, a caring husband, and a giving pastor. You've always been loving, nurturing, and gentle to all of your children, and each one of them would say the same if they could."

"Not Micah," Jed said softly with his head lowered.

Lizzy crooked her neck, not quite sure she had heard him right.

"I let Micah down," Jed continued. "He reached out to me so many times, and I never saw it."

"Papa, that's not so," Lizzy said defensively.

"Yes it is, sweetheart," Jed said as he tried to explain. "As far back as I can remember, it was always Willie and Daniel, Daniel and Willie, and when you came on board it was Willie and Daniel and their only little sister. Micah was lost in the mix, and I never saw it."

Lizzy looked at Marian for help, but Jed continued.

"He grew up hating me, and when he charged out that door in Fredericksburg, a big part of me died," Jed said. "If I had only . . ."

"Papa, you did all you could!" Lizzy exclaimed, seeing the despair in her father's eyes. "I was there, Papa. You did all you could. Micah wouldn't listen to anyone! I hate to admit it, Papa, but there were times when I hoped that he would just stay away for good. I prayed that maybe, just maybe, he'd realize what he'd become, who he'd hurt, and then, and only then, would I want him to come home again."

"I don't even know if he's still alive," Jed's voice cracked as it trailed off.

"I know it, Papa!" Lizzy said sternly. "I feel it in my heart."

Lizzy rose onto her knees and reached for her father's hands. "Micah may never come home again, Papa, but I have to believe he's alive. We all have to believe that, Papa—you must believe!"

Jed looked around at everyone in the room, sniffled, and forced a chuckle. "Look at us here. What started out as a simple talk between two men has turned into a babbling, rambling, fifty-year-old preacher spilling his sorrows and lost causes to his family. Go figure!"

"And that's exactly how it should be," Marian said defiantly. "You're letting out your pain and emotions to the very ones who love you the most."

"Yea, who'd have thought this would be the time and place to let it all out, huh?" Jed wiped his nose with his handkerchief and laughed.

"I'll tell you all something else. Even though it might sound strange, I feel like I've endured a lot over the years, but each time God kept me moving forward."

Jed turned and looked at Lizzy. "In fact, sweetie, I have to admit, that's why we moved so many times. I had to keep trying to find that place where God was going to show me a peaceful place to lay our heads. I've always known that the security I was searching for was inside me and it was from God. My issue with Micah has kept my heart blocked. I do hope and pray that someday my heart will heal again and I can fully trust in the Lord."

After a short pause, Jed looked at both Lizzy and Marian and said, "I just don't think I'll ever completely have peace of mind until the day I can hold my lost son in my arms and ask for his forgiveness."

"God has already forgiven you for anything you think you might have done, Jedidiah." Marian urged.

"God may have forgiven me, Marian, but I'll always need my son to forgive me as well. If that's not meant to be, then my days of searching for serenity will never end."

They were startled by the loud crash of the front door slamming into the grandfather clock. The heavy weights of the clock jarred into one another, creating the sound of bell towers.

Jed lurched out of his chair. "What in heaven's name?"

Johnny Russell entered in a gust toward the four adults. His chest visibly heaved as he tried to catch his breath. Panic and fear flashed across his face as he tried his hardest to form words.

"What is it, Johnny Russell?" Jed demanded. "Speak up, Son!"

"Papa!" he yelled frantically. "Papa, our church!"

"What about our church, Son?" Jed yelled back, and an eerie feeling began to consume him.

"Our church is on fire, Papa!" he screamed.

Jed was the first to bolt out the door. He ran through the yard and down the street toward his father's newly remodeled church. He was disbelieving, as his youngest son had a tendency to exaggerate.

He came to a sudden stop a few houses away from the church, with the others close behind. They stood in awestruck anguish. The bright flames had reached the roof line, and the entire church was engulfed in an infernal firestorm.

Jed was too shocked too cry and too stunned to be angry. He turned and looked at Lizzy and Martin. He quickly searched for Johnny Russell and found him nestled behind Marian. Realizing that his family was all with him and all safe, he fell to his knees as the moment began to sink in.

Lizzy's voice was barely audible through the draft of the fire, but it caused Jed to look her way. She was blocking a portion of the flames and Jed tried to see the words forming on her lips even though he could hardly hear her. He saw that her eyes were filled with tears, and panic surrounded her every move. He could barely read the words from her lips as the sound of the crackling, burning wood penetrated his senses.

"It's a cross, Papa!" she yelled and pointed, but her voice was still scarcely audible.

Jed thought he had read her lips correctly, but he didn't register their meaning. In his sense of desperation, as he tried to bring logic to it, he finally looked beyond Lizzy's outstretched arms. He gasped when he saw what she was pointing at. In front of his burning church lay a large burning cross.

And he fell to the ground and wept.

Chapter Thirty-Nine

Waiting for the Word

1866

It was a time of celebration and remembrance of the newborn baby Jesus. The long-awaited Christmas Eve service was just a few days away. By all accounts, the attack on Wheeling was a sign that the message of Christmas was not to be told. Lost souls of the old Quantrill Raiders had done their best to cast a dark light on what should have been the brightest illumination of the winter season. Five days before, the church had stood as a symbol of hope, praise, and peace. Three days later it smelled of burnt wood and spilled kerosene.

Jed and Marian walked across the remains of the church's foundation, which once had been solid and firm. They gingerly followed the path from where the pulpit stood to what had been the back wall of the newly painted sanctuary. Jed leaned over and picked up three charred books, tossing them into a wooden box. Marian watched him carefully as he viewed what was once a newly finished ceiling, but now only showed the morning's sky. He wiped his charcoaled hands off on his pants while glancing from side to side, trying to rationalize the meaning behind it all. She was prepared to watch him implode and fall into his world of lost hope and despair. She told herself that in this case, she wouldn't blame him. In fact, if this was the type of tribulation that he had been dealing with his entire life, it was no wonder that peace was continually evading his reach.

As they strolled through the debris in silence, Marian was pleasantly surprised that she didn't see what she was expecting. The look of despair and loss didn't come. She watched as Jed moved from one helper to the other, acknowledging them with a pat on the back and an encouraging word. His moves were deliberate and with purpose. Marian was perplexed but amazed at the scene taking place around her and within Jed. She needed to know what was going on in his head.

"I'm actually quite impressed, dear fiancé," Marian said as she guided Jed to a broken and charred pew to have a seat. "From the looks around here and from the stories you've told me, this is exactly the scenario that has followed you the past forty years."

"Yep," was all that Jed said as he nodded his appreciation and recognition to a passerby.

"But, Jedidiah?" Marian began. "You look as though the Christmas tree is decorated, gifts are all wrapped and you need to get home to enjoy the Christmas turkey feast!"

"Yep."

"Okay, Mister!" Marian said with a laugh and a fake scowl. "What's going on in that big beautiful head of yours?"

Jed shifted his body to face her. He glanced around the area of devastation. He took her hand into his and instead of the look of defeat he had the look of triumph in his eyes. "Look at all of this, Marian!"

"I am looking at it, Jedidiah!"

"No, I mean, really *look* at it. Look at the people, look at the perseverance, look at God working."

Jed stood up, unable to sit quiet anymore. "Marian, this town had been looking so forward to its Christmas Eve service, and God is telling me plain and simple that He wants it, too."

As Jed walked along, he reached out to hold Marian's hand. He stopped, turned, and looked into her eyes. "You know Jesus gave his best sermon on a mount with no roof and no walls, kind of like this place."

He looked at her with a mischievous yet confident grin. "God has told us so many times that all He wants is for us to love Him and ask for Him to live inside us. No raid, no fire, no symbol of defiance can match up with what God wants us to do."

Marian pulled at Jed's hand, encouraging him to sit. She could see the excitement in his eyes. She could hear it in his voice. There was no despair, but a conviction in him that she had never seen before.

"Marian," Jed continued, "I've been searching for my own peace—no, my own sense of peace—for years. But it doesn't come from a place or a situation. It's right here, Marian, right here in the midst of all of this desolation and waste. All of my life I've searched high and low to get through this same type of wretchedness and anguish. You've even tried to tell me again and again that we all will be persecuted and go through the trials of life. I should know that God has us go through these times to strengthen us for His glory, not our own sense of comfort."

Marian had never seen Jed like this, and her heart leaped for joy. All of her evenings of reading the Bible with him, listening to him as he searched for the version of peace he yearned for, was now becoming crystal clear for him. She had always known that he knew it. She had been amazed by how well he preached it on Sunday mornings, but his emotional connection had always been missing. She listened to him now and could hear that at long last he was making the connection. She could only pray that this was the missing link that could offer what he had been searching for.

Jed jumped up onto a large wooden box propped up next to what was left of the church's piano. He took one glance at Marian and with a mischievous look called out, "May I have your attention, please?"

The townsfolk and members of the church stopped what they were doing and gathered around Jed to see what their pastor had to say.

"First of all, I want to tell you all how grateful I am for all that you are doing out here," Jed began. "Although we were brutally attacked two days ago, we're definitely not defeated!"

Jed watched to see if he'd gotten their full attention before continuing. "Remember that the Bible says that if God is for us, who then shall be against us. Jesus told us in John 16:33 that 'I have told you these things, so that in me you may have peace. In this world you will have trouble.'"

Jed wiped his brow with the palm of his hand, and then focused back to the audience in front of him. "And as you can see all around us, we have just had our share of trouble, right?"

Jed waited until some of the laughter subsided. "Jesus also said in that same verse, 'But take heart! I have overcome the world.' Remember people, none of this means anything as long as we know that Jesus has won the ultimate victory and He has claimed our peace through Him no matter what kind of trouble we find ourselves in."

He could see joy still surrounded the people of Wheeling, and at that moment he knew what he needed to do. "I am here, right now, standing on what's left of this charred block of wood to remind you that in two days we *will* all be right back here in this very spot."

Jed could sense their confusion by his comment. "Each year, we look forward to the blessings of our annual Christmas Eve service. I'm telling you that God is right here with us now. He's still quite alive and He, for one, wouldn't be very happy if we just quit and walked away, right? No, my family, we *will* have our Christmas Eve service. Yes sir, no blazing fire, and definitely no act of this type of cowardly violence will stop God from sharing His message to His people. So . . ."

Jed trailed off and looked at what had become a crowd of over fifty. "So, whatcha think, can we put this place together in two days to hear what God has in store for us?"

The crowd erupted with cheers. Immediately, plans were drawn up by the townspeople to hastily shore together a makeshift church that would seat a hungry congregation in need of a spiritual meal. Marian reached out to hold Jed's hand and gave him a look of admiration and pride. He kissed her cheek and said, "I've got some writing to do, don't I?"

* * * * *

Jed awoke on Christmas Eve and stared up at the ceiling of his room. He had been preparing his sermon for two days while the town worked on fortifying what was going to be their church. The town was counting on him.

As he lay there, he realized how personal this sermon had become to him. It had taken him over fifty years to finally feel the sense of peace that God had always wanted to give him. He reflected on the many trials and tribulations he had gone through.

He glanced across the room and could see a tree through the window, that same ash tree his mother had loved to sit under. He got up and went to the window. He looked down at what had once been a beautiful bed of roses. He smiled at the thought of his mother's love for roses. He thought of Abigail, of Abel, of Willie and Daniel. All gone, but never forgotten. He thought of his father, of the lessons he had tried to teach him, and a warm feeling came over him. He saw images of his friends in Independence: Fez, Big Jim, and John Fremont. So many memories, yet so much had been missed by not having peace from God all along.

After reminiscing over his past, he dressed, walked outside and over to the church grounds. He could smell the charred ruins and looked serenely at what was left. It was benevolently quiet; all the workers had done their best with what remained of their church. He stopped just prior to the opening flap of where the front door once stood and looked up as if to pray. The revelation hit him hard. He felt the overflowing joy of God's presence and knew at that moment that he was going to make some last-minute changes to the sermon he had prepared.

Jed walked down the center of the church. He looked from side to side at the blackened pews as he made his way to the front and sat down in the first row. He peered at the pulpit standing firmly in front of him. Despite the gloomy surroundings, God's spirit filled him and was invigorated by the evening's event. Yet one thing still troubled him. *If only Micah were here.*

As he scanned the remnants of what had been a church, he battled his conscience, thinking it ironic that he had been scarred just as much as the building in which he sat. He got up from the front pew and turned to inspect the setting that in just a few hours would be filled with people.

The makeshift church was made up of broken beams held upright with tethered rope. The dirty worn out canvas tarp was holding up well as a temporary roof. The splintered slats of charred wood were propped up on fragments of ruined bookcases and acted as the church's pews. The ash had been swept from the floor, but the smell of stale smoke mixed in with burnt wood permeated the room. Wood torches replaced the broken glass lanterns that were destroyed in the fire. Jed surveyed the area and was pleased with the outcome. As he was about to leave, he returned one last time to look at the empty shell of a church. *This is going to be perfect; now I just need a perfect sermon to go with it.*

* * * * *

After locking himself away for a couple of hours and writing and rewriting feverishly, Jed had completely revised his sermon. It was unlike any he had ever written or given before. He was anxious because he honestly wasn't sure if people would like it. What he did know, however, was that his message would be impactful.

The evening rolled in and the crowds kept coming. The starting time was pushed back by a half an hour to make time to seat everyone who was filing in. More wooden planks were needed to make it possible for everyone to have a seat.

Jed looked from behind a dirty curtain to the left of the pulpit. Marian stood by his side and held his hand gently. He saw Lizzy and Martin in the front row with Johnny Russell sitting next to his sister. Jed thought for a moment on how those two had been inseparable for years. A sense of pride overwhelmed him as he silently thanked God for his two children. He thought how she was a grown woman now, married to a fine young man. Johnny Russell had just turned thirteen and was looking more and more like Jed every day. Homer and Helen Plunkett were in the row behind his children and sitting with them was Sheriff Hancock. Martin's parents sat across the middle aisle along with the members of the Wheeling Women's Society.

"There are so many people," Jed said softly.

Marian nudged Jed lovingly. "It's going to be perfect, Jedidiah. It's exactly what this town needs."

"No, Marian," Jed said, "it's exactly what I need right now. There's so much I want to say to all of them. So much I want to say to my children. I just don't know if I'll be able to pull it off. I hate to say it, Marian, but, uh, I don't think I've ever been so nervous."

Jed turned his head slightly to peek at her expression. "I know it's silly. Heck, I'm a pastor; this is what I do, right? I just don't know how to explain it. I'm just downright scared."

Marian turned Jed's head so she could look in his eyes. She held his hands firmly in hers and said, "I know you're going to be great, my darling. God has placed you in this moment for a purpose. Like you said, it's not just those people who need this, so do you and I know you're going to do great!"

Jed's eyes widened with apprehension as the true meaning of the evening came to him. He was going out there not just to give a sermon, but to share his testimony, and it was God who was going to lead him. As he took his first step toward the splintered pulpit, he turned to Marian and slowly shook his head as if something was missing.

"If only Micah . . ."

"Shh now, Jedidiah." Marian put her fingers up to his lips. "He's here in spirit and you need to believe that. Now you go and you give that sermon of a lifetime. You do it for God and you do it for you."

Jed nodded, wiped the tears from his cheek and gave her a long warm embrace. As he turned to go through the curtain he leaned back one last time and whispered. "Keep praying, alright?"

The distance to the pulpit was but a few feet, but it seemed like it took forever for Jed to make it there. He glanced out over the crowd and could barely see all the faces. The glow from the torches made it difficult to see more than halfway back. He could see that the crowd extended far past the end of the makeshift church. What he did notice, though, was that all eyes in the crowd were on him.

Yes, keep praying . . .

Chapter Forty

Peace in Wheeling

1866

"Proverbs 3:5 says, 'Trust in the Lord with all thine heart; and lean not unto thine own understanding.' Isaiah 40:31 tells us, 'But they that wait upon the Lord shall renew their strength; they shall mount up with wings as eagles; they shall run, and not be weary; and they shall walk, and not faint.' In Second Corinthians 12:9 through 12:10, Paul wrote that Jesus said, 'My grace is sufficient for thee: for my strength is made perfect in weakness.' Then Paul tells us, 'Most gladly therefore will I rather glory in my infirmities, that the power of Christ may rest upon me. Therefore I take pleasure in infirmities, in reproaches, in necessities, in persecutions, in distresses for Christ's sake: for when I am weak, then am I strong.'"

Jed looked up from his notes and stepped to his left. He fanned the room to gauge the attention in the room. He looked to Lizzy, who smiled and gave him a subtle nod.

"Peace, hope, and tranquility," Jed began again as he made his way back to the pulpit. "All of you have been a part of some kind of torment. Look around you and see the latest episode. So what is it that keeps you struggling onward? Oh, it would be so easy to pull the curtain down around us and call it quits. By all measure, we are weak, very weak. We remain humbled day in and day out, and what you see here is far from the last persecution you will experience. No, you will face the trials and tribulations of this world time and time again. But remember, as you struggle through and you want to pull down that curtain—Christ Jesus by his own blood has conquered this world, and there is nothing, and I mean nothing, that can take that away as long as we all believe."

Jed paused and looked to a dark spot on the floor that was just within his view from the lectern. For a mere second, he flashed back to his childhood, that moment when he hid under the porch. He reflected on just how far he had come. He looked at his notes, turned them over, and walked away from the lectern.

"I can remember all the times when I faced trials. I am the son of a preacher, and I was the youngest member of a missionary expedition, and I faced trials at a very young age.

"Maybe that doesn't ring true for some of you—what *trials* could *I* have possibly faced? But trust me that there were many. And there's this, too—as I look back now, I tell you, I failed at first, and I never stopped failing. When I faced a trial, I fled; or I hid my head under a rock and waited it out until the debris had settled so that I could begin again. I would move, join a cause, fight a war, explore some idea of grandeur, anything that kept me from having to deal with the fallout I had created."

Not only was Jed no longer reading from his notes—he had tossed out his original sermon entirely and was now preaching purely from memories and adrenaline. "I look out upon this group of fine people, and I see folks who neither ran nor hid when faced with this trial. No, from the moment word got out that there was a raid on our church, you all came out and helped. You were there the next day, and the next, to rebuild and persevere. You, my friends, were much stronger than I ever was. I learned so much as I witnessed your ability to look past the trial to see God's hand leading your way. It's God's power that is displayed in weak people, and that should always give us courage. Though we recognize our limitations, as I was able to do eventually, we must not congratulate ourselves and rest. The enemy will be knocking at our door again soon, and we need to always rely on God and the promises that He has made to us. In Him we are strong, and in Him we will find peace."

There was a crashing sound, and the entire congregation turned toward the front doors of the church. Jed strained his eyes, but could see nothing in the darkness. He looked at Lizzy, but she shrugged her shoulders in response. Jed walked back to the center of the platform, trying to remain focused on the message he wanted to deliver. The congregation, seemingly having satisfied its curiosity, returned its attention to Jed.

"I've learned a lot from all of you during the past few days, and I want to express my sincere gratitude. You showed me that in spite of our struggles, we are not alone. Jesus will not abandon us to our struggles. If we remember that the ultimate victory has already been won, we can claim the peace of Christ in the most troublesome times."

Jed heard another sound from back, this time coming from a far corner. *I guess that's where the restless are sitting.* He chuckled at a memory of Micah as a youngster, always hiding in some corner.

"My family, here tonight, is fully aware of my lifelong search for what many claim is an easy prize . . . peace. There are so many stories I could tell you about my search for that supposedly simple word. Each time I grabbed for it, I found that I had been misled. You see, I've lost so much over the years, but so have many others. I've been led astray, but then again, I'm not alone in that, am I? So what is it that makes my story any different?"

Jed contemplated sharing some of his personal stories, but risked losing the interest of his audience. He remembered what Marian told him just before he walked out: "This is just as much for you as it is for them."

"Some of you knew my folks. When they were murdered, I gave up—on life and on God. Somehow, I moved on. I was a selfish young man and only wanted what the world could give me. I wanted personal satisfaction, from the thrills of wilderness trails to the prestige of being a soldier."

Jed's eyes closed as he remembered Abel, but he kept speaking. "In fact, I left my wife so that I could find out who I was on a battlefield. Yet when I returned, I found that not only had I left my wife so that I could play soldier, but also I had left her while she was pregnant. The dreadful end of that story is that while I was gone, *finding myself*, my wife somehow lived through the death of our child and had to deal with the fallout all alone."

Jed could hear gasps from the audience, but he had no choice now but to let it all out. "She never blamed me, though. No, she was too gentle and kind to ever hold anything against me. Yes, to my surprise and despite my guilt-filled heart, she stayed by my side, even as I *continued* searching for something I couldn't find."

"That story aside, I was blessed with five wonderful children, two of whom are here in the front row."

He stepped from the platform, moving closer to his children so that he could speak directly to them. "Lizzy, you have always been my rock. I made you take on such responsibility at such a young age, but you never said a disparaging word, and you always offered to help more, even as you sacrificed your own childhood so that I didn't come apart. You were my rock—with your mother gone, I'm not sure how I would have survived without you."

He scanned the crowd. "You see, folks, I lost my wife, and Lizzy assumed the role of caring for me and for her baby brother." He looked Lizzy in the eyes once again, as a tear streamed down one of her cheeks. "I will forever be in your debt, Sweet Pea."

Jed turned his head slightly and looked intently into the eyes of Johnny Russell. "You are my youngest, Johnny Russell, and the reason I keep going. You're my future, Son, and my next generation. I have so much to be thankful for in you, and yet so much to regret."

At that last, Johnny Russell frowned and fidgeted uncomfortably. "I never spent enough time with you, Son, never took the time to just hear you and see you grow up. Now look at you—I couldn't be more proud, Son, couldn't be more proud."

Jed turned and stepped back onto the platform. Again there was a commotion in the back. He looked, but still it was too dark. *I hope this half-burned building isn't going to fall down on us.*

"I was blessed with a beautiful family, and I took it all for granted. I lost my wife and I . . . I lost two sons. I remember asking God how He could possibly want me to go through the trial of holding my wife, then one son and another in my arms as each breathed their last breath. Yes, I was angry at God, and I waited for a long time before I was ready to open my heart again to listen to Him. But when I finally did, I heard Him loud and clear."

The wind blew sharply against a canvas side, knocking down a wooden plank with a loud crash. "Yep, just like that, He spoke to me." The crowd laughed, allowing Jed to regain his composure before continuing.

"This is Christmas Eve, folks, and we are here to celebrate the birth of our Lord Jesus Christ. He was born, lived about thirty years, died, and rose again. In His blood we are saved, and we no longer have anything to fear, not fires and not attacks. We must trust in Him, and in Him we will receive the peace we long for."

Jed looked out and noticed some movement in the back, but then it was gone. He turned his notes over, took a quick look at them, and then in a single motion he sent them aloft and into the fire blazing in an oversized iron bowl nearby. When he looked back at the audience, he saw that all them, Lizzy and Marian included, were taken aback. He jumped down from the platform, and as he landed he began quickly pacing down the middle aisle.

"I often think to myself that I don't deserve any of the kindness that all of you have given me. I definitely never have felt that I deserve the love of our Jesus Christ. I thought I had put together a wonderful sermon for this special evening, but as it turns out, I just need to talk with you all. As you all may have noticed, I'm way off my script here, but I think I have a message to share, one that's more personal than a few fancy words on a page. You see, I'm just a man. I'm no different than any of you. You all have the same types of stories that I do. Some people realize where their true peace is from the start—others, like me, well, it takes them some time."

Lizzy stood, walked to Jed, and wrapped her arms around him tightly. Johnny Russell joined them, and the three stood as the packed crowd watched in silence, wondering what would come next.

Marian came out from behind the side platform canvas, walked up the aisle, and put her arms around the three. Even in the heat of the moment, Jed was driven on by the spirit he felt inside himself, and looked up as he addressed the packed room.

"This, my dear friends, is what I've been given by our most loving and caring God."

As Jed's family took their seats, he continued softly. "I found my peace. God knew the timetable and the trials that I would have to endure. You see, my dear friends, He wants us all to trust Him, be still, be quiet and let Him lead us."

"Christmas Eve is a time to celebrate, and it is also a time to be obedient to our Lord," Jed said as he made his way back onto the platform. "He has asked us to trust, have faith, love, and pray. In fact, He even gave us instructions on how to pray, and I think it is most fitting on this, the eve of His birth, to take His lead and follow with the prayer He first taught the disciples."

Jed pondered the words, then spoke with clarity and purpose. "Our Father which art in heaven, hallowed be thy name. Thy kingdom come. Thy will be done in earth, as it is in heaven. Give us this day our daily bread."

Jed's voice trailed off as he faced the room. "When I say these words, I think about how mighty and great our Lord really is. I thank Him for everything that is and that will be, if it be His will and not ours."

Jed reflected on his life's challenges and said, "That was one of my biggest trials. I wanted it to be *my* will, not *His* will. I wanted to get on the trail, I wanted to fight a war, I wanted to find gold, I, I, I . . ."

Jed couldn't continue, and after wiping his brow with a handkerchief, looked back at the room. It was all becoming clear to him, even more so than when he and Marian had walked through the debris of the church two days earlier.

"*I* had to provide, *I* had to raise a family, *I* had to find work, and *I* had to change my father's direction for me *again*—it was *I, I, I . . .*"

He looked at Lizzy and saw that she was crying, and it broke his heart. He wanted to go to her, but he continued. "Give us this day our daily bread. Yes, but do we rely on Him to provide for us in a way that is unconditional?"

Jed thought of his Christmas Eve sermon and took a moment to chuckle a bit. *Not exactly the way you planned it, huh?* "We are here to celebrate Christmas Eve, and what better way to do it than to give Him thanks for everything that He has given us and will always give us. We all have so much, and granted, our building was destroyed, but it's just that—a building. Our God is in all of us, so He surely lives on, and we are stronger because of the faith and perseverance all of you have shown."

"And forgive us our debts, as we forgive our debtors," Jed said as the words trailed off again. *Forgive us, as we forgive our debtors.* He stopped and stared at the ground. He looked at Lizzy, at Johnny Russell, and then at Marian. Tears filled his eyes. His throat closed in on him. *Micah . . .*

Jed raised his voice with everything he had, and pushed through. "Forgiveness!" His voice cracked. He slowly shook his head, swallowed hard, and tried to clear his throat before continuing. "I told you that my wife and two of my sons died. What I didn't tell you is that I also lost a third son, who I pray is still alive."

Jed looked at Lizzy and felt her pain. He continued to address the church, but his eyes were glued to hers. "I lost two sons in my arms, but I lost my third son because I was too stubborn and hardheaded. I turned my back on him."

Jed looked at the congregation again, at the people he'd come to love. His heart yearned for their understanding. "Jesus speaks here of forgiveness, and I tell you, my church family, that I don't know if I will ever see my son again."

He lowered his head before continuing. The room was still and silent other than sniffles from the crowd. "I would give anything to ask him, just once, if he had it in him to forgive *me*."

Jed cleared his throat and attempted to stand straight. "We know that we are all forgiven for our sins through our Christ Jesus, but we are also commanded by Him to forgive. I can only hope and pray that someday I too can be forgiven for turning away from my son."

Jed tried to compose himself to finish his sermon. It hadn't turned out as he had planned, but he could feel the energy of the crowd and knew that it was important that he continue. As he made his way to the lectern, he felt God's presence, and knew that God was in charge of the evening, not him.

Lizzy and Johnny Russell once again walked onto the platform in support of their father. They took Jed's arms in theirs as Marian looked on in tears. Jed motioned to her, and to Martin. Jed figured the best way to finish his Christmas Eve sermon was as a family.

"I know this wasn't exactly the Christmas Eve sermon you all had planned on, but it was, in my humble opinion, what God had planned. I know each of us can find the peace we are searching for, and I know that you need not search any longer, because it's all right inside you, in the name of Christ Jesus. Each of you in this room can receive His peace and His salvation by just asking for it, and take it from me, don't wait too long."

As Jed's family surrounded him on the platform, the congregation began standing one at a time, applauding as they rose. Jed slipped from his family's embrace and looked out to the congregation with humility as the applause grew, nodding his acknowledgment.

As the applause subsided, still surprised to receive such warm recognition, he looked at his family and raised an eyebrow. He wanted nothing more than to hold his children and enjoy God's gift of family. *How can it get any better?* he thought.

Lizzy heard it first. She looked puzzled. Then she heard it again. A noise from the back.

"Papa!" she cried out.

The sound was faint at first and barely audible. Marian moved closer to Jed, and Lizzy looked at Martin to see if he'd heard it as well. The sound continued to grow.

"I want *your* forgiveness!" the voice echoed.

The commanding voice caused the room to grow still. Jed thought it might be a member of his congregation who desperately needed a Christmas Eve prayer. Jed slowly but deliberately moved forward, slipping away from his family, and walked a few steps up the middle aisle to find out who was in need of his help.

"I want *your* forgiveness!" the voice bellowed again. Church members moved aside to let the man pass as he headed down the aisle.

Jed blinked several times to clear his vision. The light was dim, and the evening's torches were almost out. He squinted as he tried to see the man who was coming toward him.

"I want *your* forgiveness—you don't need mine!" The voice was crystal clear, and Jed found its familiarity perplexing. *Not mine?* Jed tried desperately to understand. As his eyes fixated on the shadowy figure coming toward him, his finger began to twitch frantically. Lizzy gasped loudly as she registered what was happening, unable to hold back her cry.

"Papa, I want *your* forgiveness!" Micah cried.

Jed dropped to his knees and began to weep uncontrollably. He spread his outstretched hands as far as they'd go, and with one sweeping motion swallowed up his son as Micah fell into his arms.

Jed's peace had finally come . . . and at last, his finger twitched no more.

With his hands tightly clasped around Micah's arms, Jed stood and addressed his congregation to finish the Lord's Prayer.

". . . and lead us not into temptation, but deliver us from evil." He turned and faced Micah. "For thine is the kingdom, and the power, and the glory, for ever."

"And ever! Amen!"

Author's Note on Historical Elements

As one would expect from a work of historical fiction, this book contains a fair number of historical characters, locales, and the like.

Even with the requisite desire for accuracy and respect (or disdain) for historical characters, some artistic liberties were taken in the name of expediency and a logical story line. Historical characters appear when and where they *could have* during their lives, and critical events they experience in the book are the same as those they experienced in real life (Louis Carpenter being killed at an antislavery rally in Kansas, for example). The mannerisms of and syntax used by these characters were written to be consistent with what is known about these characters' personalities and voices while on this mortal coil.

Readers may note occasional time shifts in the occurrence of certain events. That is, the relation of historical events to the season of the year or a character's age may be slightly off. Though rare, those shifts were sometimes needed in order to synchronize Jed's story with particular seasons, events, or locations. Such changes are irrelevant to the overall story, though historians no doubt would argue that these dates are indeed quite relevant. Similarly, locations and events as portrayed reflect the resources and technology of the period. There may be cases, however, when a character is eating mutton but the import of mutton to the area was a few months or years behind. To such artistic license, as it were, we say, "Bon appetit!"

Finally, words and phrases in the book generally reflect those of the period. Readers may run across an occasional odd word here or there (e.g., *all right*, *yea*, and *yins*) substituting for the words more commonly used today (respectively *ok*, *yeah*, and *y'all* in the prior example). Sometimes a phrase that seems to be of the time did not actually come into use until years or decades later (*she's the spittin' image*, for example), but accuracy was sacrificed because the accurate usage was so offputting or unfamiliar (*she's the spit of*). It's also entirely possible, given the limited avenues for long-distance communication at the time, and considering that Webster did not publish *An American Dictionary of the English Language* until 1828, that some words already in common usage were delayed in being recognized as such.

We understand that some readers may disagree with certain choices, and apologize in advance for any feathers that become ruffled.

CPSIA information can be obtained at www.ICGtesting.com
Printed in the USA
LVOW11*2149150216

475259LV00004B/20/P

9 780996 967952